More praise for
THE SILENT WOMAN

"The vibrant scenes of teeming city streets and river-ways clogged with tall-masted ships could never be contained on a flat stage backdrop. And the lusty players who fret and strut in such grand theatrical style are too vital to let a curtain fall on them."
—*The New York Times Book Review*

"Fascinating... Marston crams his story with myriad plots and subplots, as well as vivid historical detail."
—*Kirkus Reviews*

"Marston has penned another robust historical mystery featuring Nicholas Bracewell.... [He] continues to deliver an entertaining and artfully engineered balance of ribald comedy, suspenseful action, and tender intrigue."
—*Booklist*

"Sparkling with humor, dramatic twists and deft turns of phrase, the sixth adventure of Marston's Elizabethan acting troupe exhibits all the aplomb and panache that mark its lead player, Lawrence Firethorn."
—*Publishers Weekly*

Also by Edward Marston
Published by Fawcett Books:

In the Nicholas Bracewell series:
THE QUEEN'S HEAD
THE MERRY DEVILS
THE TRIP TO JERUSALEM
THE NINE GIANTS
THE MAD COURTESAN
THE SILENT WOMAN

In the Domesday Book series:
THE WOLVES OF SAVERNAKE

THE SILENT WOMAN

Edward Marston

FAWCETT CREST • NEW YORK

A Fawcett Crest Book
Published by Ballantine Books
Copyright © 1994 by Edward Marston

Library of Congress Catalog Card Number: 94-52

ISBN 0-449-22375-2

This edition published by arrangement with St. Martin's Press

Manufactured in the United States of America

First Ballantine Books Edition: December 1995

10 9 8 7 6 5 4 3 2 1

To
my own
silent woman
without whom
my life
would have been
unbearably
quiet

*"How often have forced contracts been made
to add land to land, not love to love?
And to unite house to house, not hearts to hearts?
Which hath been the occasion that men have turned
monsters and women devils."*

—THOMAS HEYWOOD
A Curtaine Lecture

Chapter One

A WIND FROM HEAVEN BLEW UPON THE FIRE OF hell and spread damnation. The spectators who were packed into the yard of the Queen's Head in Gracechurch Street thought at first that it was all part of the entertainment, some new and carefully rehearsed piece of action that had been woven into the fabric of the play for their benefit. It made them laugh even more. But they soon learned that their mirth was completely misplaced and that they were caught up in a real crisis. Riotous comedy became stark tragedy. Catastrophe threatened.

What they were watching on that sunlit afternoon was *The Devil's Ride Through London*, a staple drama from the repertoire of Westfield's Men, one of the leading theatrical troupes in the capital. The plot was simple. Deciding to visit the city in order to terrify its inhabitants, the Devil—as played with manic hilarity by Barnaby Gill, the company's resident clown—found it impossible to make any impact because the pain, misery and wickedness he encountered on earth was far worse than anything he could offer in hell. The man who most embodied the evils of London, and around whom the play revolved with giddy speed, was Sir Henry Whoremonger. Traitor, coward, liar, thief, drunkard, gamester and lecher supreme, he kept the seven deadly sins

1

spinning through the air with the skill of a master juggler. The role of Sir Henry drew yet another masterly performance from Lawrence Firethorn, the actor-manager and unrivalled star of Westfield's Men, enabling him to amuse, shock, instruct and excite the audience by turns and whip them into an uproar with the crack of a line whenever he chose. Firethorn made villainy attractive and won the hearts and minds of all who watched. It was no wonder the Prince of Darkness concluded that Sir Henry Whoremonger was by far the greater devil.

Instead of frightening the citizens with dire warnings of what lay ahead, His Satanic Majesty was so shaken by the horrors of everyday life in London that he fled back to the nether regions as far as his cloven feet would take him. Crouched over a brazier at the rear of the stage, he warmed his hands at the flickering coals and mused on the folly of his visitation.

> *The sulphurous stench of my own estate*
> *Is perfume compared to Billingsgate.*
> *My vilest tortures are petty sores*
> *On putrefying, pox-ridden Eastcheap whores.*
> *Our howls of anguish are happy sighs*
> *When heard alongside Bedlam's cries.*
> *My foulest poison can never compete*
> *With Marwood's ale in Gracechurch Street.*
> *In the stews of Southwark they have worse fare*
> *Than those who toil here in the Devil's lair.*

The first gust of wind brought the brazier to life and flames leapt up to lick at Barnaby Gill's red-gloved hands. He pretended that he had deliberately stoked up the fire and he danced around it with comic despair.

> *Mortals, behold! You have all witnessed how*
> *London is the truer Purgatory now.*
> *Henceforth I'll lease out cold and timid hell*
> *And dwell instead in fiery Clerkenwell.*

Clothed from head to foot in a blood red costume, the Devil flung back his flowing red cloak and adopted a pose of utter defeat. He did not hold it for long. As soon as his garment passed over the top of the brazier, a phantom wind blew so hard on its coals that it became a roaring inferno. The cloak was ignited, the Devil became a being of dazzling light and Barnaby Gill charged around the stage in wild agitation as he tried to rid himself of his burning apparel. His plight earned him no sympathy from the audience. They rocked with laughter and cheered with delight. This act of spontaneous combustion was the funniest thing they had ever seen, and they marvelled at Gill's expertise. When the hapless clown blundered against the backcloth that hung from gallery above the stage, however, all humour was instantly extinguished. The painted flames of hell were now horrendously real. The playgoers were not, in fact, seeing a remarkable feat by an accomplished comedian. A human being was, literally, on fire in front of them.

Panic descended. Men yelled, women screamed, horses neighed and kicked in their stables. All ceremony was abandoned. The hundreds of patrons jammed shoulder to shoulder in the yard itself fought madly to get to the nearest exit. Gallants and their ladies, who had paid an extra penny or two to sit in the galleries, knocked over their benches in their desperation as yellow sparks flew up at them and offered to turn their fine clothes into balls of fire. Nicholas Bracewell was the first person to burst onto the stage. Having controlled the performance from behind the scenes, the book holder now thrust himself purposefully into the action, darting out with a wooden bucket of water and hurling it over Barnaby Gill's cloak before tearing the garment from him. Nicholas burned his fingers slightly, but he undoubtedly saved his colleague's life. Still shrieking with fear, the Devil went sprinting off into the tiring-house to make his escape. Nicholas took stock of the situation, but it was beyond his resourcefulness. The fire had gained a purchase on the backcloth and was eating its way hungrily upwards. A wall of flame confronted the hysterical onlookers.

Pandemonium now set in. The whole inn seemed to be

ablaze. Wherever people ran, they were engulfed by smoke. The acrid smell filled their noses, the crackling flames attacked their ears, the fear of a hideous death crazed their minds. They were as frantic and helpless as the animals now bucking wildly in their stalls. Preferring to live in poverty than to die rich, pickpockets in the crowd took no advantage of the chaos and used both hands to claw a passage out of the yard. *The Devil's Ride Through London* had turned the Queen's Head into a veritable hell. Survival was all that mattered. Self-interest was deafening.

Nicholas Bracewell wasted no time. He knew that the real danger lay in the overhanging thatch on the topmost gallery. Dried by the sun and crumbling with age, it would go up like tinder, if set alight, and the entire establishment would be destroyed along with several of the adjoining buildings. It was vital to contain the fire as quickly as possible and to stop its upward climb. Nicholas pulled out his dagger and raced to the rear of the stage to hack at the rope that held the backcloth aloft. Cut free from its moorings, it was blown up into the air for a second before coming down like a huge hand of doom to clutch at the fleeing multitude with scorching fingers. This was no longer a merry romp. It was the Last Judgement.

The book holder grabbed another bucket of water from the tiring-house and rushed back onstage to douse the burning backcloth. He then jumped bravely into the flames and tried to stamp them out. Others now followed his example and brought fresh supplies of water. Thomas Skillen, the ancient stagekeeper, emptied his bucket over the brazier then yelled at his assistants to throw their water over the backcloth. While these lowly members of the company hurried off to refill their buckets from the waiting barrels, the actors themselves came out to fight the common enemy. Fire was a great social leveller. Position and dignity were forgotten in the swirling calamity. Westfield's Men were not just helping to save their patrons. They wanted to preserve their theatre and their livelihood.

Lawrence Firethorn came hurtling back onstage with a sodden blanket in his hands. Deprived of his curtain call and of what he saw as the due reward for his towering performance as Sir Henry Whoremonger, he yelled with fury and beat vengefully at the flames. Edmund Hoode was anguished by the sudden termination of one of his best plays, and he came out with a bucket of water dangling from each hand. Barnaby Gill had recovered his composure enough to reappear with a fire shovel and smack away at the smouldering timbers. The burly figure of Owen Elias emerged from the mouth of hell that was the tiring-house and heaved out one of the large water barrels. Nicholas leapt across to help him, and the two of them strained to tip it over. The flaming backcloth became a hissing river of smoke that all but obliterated the innyard. Commotion now reached fever pitch.

And there in the middle of it all, adding to the clamour and hindering the rescue operation, dancing on his toes and flailing his arms like a windmill in a gale, was Alexander Marwood, the embattled landlord of the Queen's Head, a man whose whole life had been a continuous rehearsal for this one final moment of truth. The prophet of disaster had lived to see his prophecy fulfilled and he announced it with almost gleeful terror.

'God is punishing me!' he wailed.

'Help with the buckets,' urged Nicholas.

'This play was sinful!' continued Marwood, leaping around the stage and colliding with each member of the company in turn. 'We are being called to account!'

'Stamp out those rushes!'

But the landlord was too absorbed in his personal conflagration. Flaming guilt shot through his body. Smoking remorse filled his mind. He was being roasted to death like a Protestant martyr at the stake. Searing perspiration burst out of every pore. Yet deep in the great black horror of his nightmare was one tiny consolation. His prediction had been correct. Alexander Marwood had always believed that his association with Westfield's Men would one day end in ruin. Armageddon had finally come to Gracechurch Street. There was a fleeting satisfaction in being a messenger of doom who had delivered his missive to the correct address.

Lawrence Firethorn cannoned into the landlord.

'Out of my way!' he boomed.

'Look what you did to my inn!' screeched Marwood.

'It may yet be saved.'

'You are to blame, Master Firethorn. You and your devilish play. You and your gibes about my ale. You and your crew of madmen. I tell you, sir—'

But Firethorn had heard enough and decided that a bucket of water over the landlord would do far more good than over the fire. He discharged his load with angry precision then ran away to refill his bucket. Drenched to the skin, Marwood went off into an even wilder set of imprecations, but nobody had time or inclination to listen. The short, thin, spindly creature was utterly alone amid the heaving sea of bodies, delivering his soliloquy to a deaf audience and grabbing at his remaining tufts of hair like a demented gardener uprooting weeds. Alexander Marwood was burning with indignation while soaking wet.

Then the miracle happened. The wind that had created the fire and comprehensively wrecked the performance now repented, vanishing as swiftly as it had come and sending in its place a gentle shower of rain. Embers lost their fierce glow. Flames climbed with less force and conviction. Smoke slowly began to clear. There was still much to do, but the fear of total devastation was past. Those struggling to subdue the fire swarmed across the stage and up into the galleries with increased vigour. They sensed victory.

Nicholas Bracewell was everywhere, giving orders to one group while leading others by example, directing the efforts of his fellows to the crucial areas and ensuring that the flames did not reach any adjacent properties. The risk of fire was a constant threat to theatre companies, and careless pipe smokers could cause appalling damage with their discarded ash. Nicholas knew only too well what an uncontrolled blaze could do, and he therefore took thorough precautions before every performance. An abundant supply of water was kept in all parts in the building and dozens of buckets were at hand. He even gave the company's hired men some basic training in how to cope with an emergency.

6

That training had been nullified by the size and suddenness of the fire, but it now began to show through. People started to work together instead of at random. Water continuously hit its target instead of being wasted by prodigal hands. Method replaced instinct. Confidence grew. They were winning.

'Look to my thatch!'

Everyone heard Alexander Marwood this time. He pointed a skeletal finger up at the topmost gallery and hopped about with renewed trepidation. Burning splinters of wood had been blown up to lodge in the thatch, and it was now starting to smoke and crackle. Nicholas needed only one glance. Instant response was their only hope. Running to the side of the stage, he shinned up the timber support and hauled himself over the balustrade of the first gallery. The others all stopped to watch and exhort him on as he went up his charred route like a sailor going up the rigging. The thatch was now seething with crimson rage and threatening to explode. As soon as Nicholas reached it, therefore, he hacked out its glowing centre and a cascade of burning reeds scattered those below. Feet balancing on the balustrade, he then stretched right up to fling the upper half of his body down onto the still-burning thatch.

It was an act of such folly and bravery that it drew applause from the onlookers, but their apprehension was not stilled. High above them, glimpsed through the curling smoke of fifty dying fires, a man was risking his life to save the roof of the inn. His feet rested precariously on blackened timber, his chest was pressed down hard on smouldering thatch and his dagger was sunk deep into the reeds to give him some support. Eyes closed tight, muscles taut, he retched violently and felt the hot sweat course down his face. Only a buff jerkin and the power of his broad chest separated him from a hideous death. Nicholas Bracewell's courage now began to look like a perverse act of suicide.

Yet somehow it worked. The rain intensified, the smoke thinned and his agony gradually subsided. Denied any license, the fire was being choked out of existence inch by

7

painful inch. The vast parallelogram of thatch that topped the building had been rescued. Buckets now reached the upper gallery and waves of water surged up at Nicholas. The danger was over and he dared to relax. He was not, after all, being broiled to death on the roof of the Queen's Head. Cheers from below told him that he was the hero of the hour. It had cost him his jerkin and gained him several more minor burns, but they were a small price to pay. Effectively, he had just rendered the greatest possible service to Westfield's Men. He had saved their theatre from certain annihilation.

Ten minutes later, the last glimmering remnants of the fire had been put out, and Nicholas stood in the middle of the yard, panting from his exertions and offering up a silent prayer of thanks. There were bruises and burns galore among his fellows, and a few broken bones among the fleeing patrons, but nobody had died and none of the horses had been injured. God had been truly merciful. Nicholas could now receive the congratulations of the others. Lawrence Firethorn was the first to wrap him in a warm and affectionate embrace.

'Nick, dear heart! We are ever in your debt!'

'You are our Deliverer,' added Edmund Hoode.

'I will never act with a brazier again,' said Barnaby Gill testily. 'My performance was ruined.'

Firethorn bristled. 'The fate of the company is more important than the quality of your performance. It was your idiocy that is to blame, Barnaby. Thanks to you, our theatre was almost razed to the ground. Thanks to Nicholas, we still have a future at the Queen's Head.'

'Not for some time,' said Nicholas with a sigh.

The smoke how now cleared enough for him to appraise the extent of the damage. It was far less than it might have been and was largely confined to the tiring-house and to the galleries directly above, but substantial rebuilding would still be necessary. Main beams had burned through or been severely weakened. Floors had collapsed. Nicholas could see that it would be several weeks—if not months—before the Queen's Head was able to host a theatre company once more.

Alexander Marwood set an even longer time limit on their return. When the fire was eventually brought under control, he did not know whether to be happy that his inn survived or feel hurt because his prophecy did not, and so he opted for a relieved misery by way of compromise. He hated plays, he loathed players and he was revolted by the sight of the debris all around him. This was his reward for the lunacy of permitting irresponsible actors to hire his property. He twitched his way across to Lawrence Firethorn and issued his death sentence.

'Westfield's Men will never play here again!'

'But we have an agreement,' said Firethorn.

'It has been revoked.'

'Silence, you gibbering nonentity!'

'That is my final word, sir.'

'And so it shall be!' snarled Firethorn, pulling out his dagger and raising it to strike. 'Die, you venomous little toad! Perish, you vermin!'

'Hold!' shouted Nicholas, interposing himself between the two men and easing Marwood away. 'Do not be too hasty here,' he said in soothing tones. 'This has been highly unfortunate and we regret it as much as you, but the Queen's Head still stands. It can be restored to its former glory. And we have been spared to continue our work.'

'Not in my inn, Master Bracewell.'

Firethorn's dagger glinted. 'Remember our contract.'

'It was the bane of my life.'

'A contract is a contract.'

'No, Master Firethorn!' The landlord was adamant. 'You were entitled to stage your plays in my yard not to burn down my premises. Behold your accursed work, sir!' Marwood made a histrionic gesture with his arm that was worthy of the actor-manager himself. 'The Devil has no need to ride through London when Westfield's Men may do his work for him. Talk not to me of our contract. It has gone up in smoke!'

* * *

London was a rapidly expanding community that had long since pushed out beyond the high city walls that had defined and defended it since Roman times. Suburbs thickened both north and south of the Thames to make the capital ten times larger than Norwich, its nearest English rival. In size and importance, it was the equal of any city in Europe with a bustle and energy that were beyond compare. The sounds and smells of London spread for miles in every direction. It was much more than a geographical phenomenon. Whether serving as a home, market, port or seat of government, the city was wholly and triumphantly alive.

There was no better place to observe the variety and vitality of the place than at Ludgate, one of the mighty portals that pierced the wall and allowed citizens and visitors alike to stream in and out beneath the raised portcullis. The gate had recently been rebuilt and the decorative statues of Queen Elizabeth, King Lud and his two sons now looked down from renovated perches upon the scene of activity below. Carts, coaches and drays rumbled into the city. The clack of hooves was never ending. Children played recklessly amid the traffic. Dogs sniffed and fought and yelped. Beggars lurked to solicit newcomers or to importune those taking their leave. Friends met to converse. A knot of spectators gathered to watch a malefactor being whipped by a beadle. Darker punishments were being endured by those who were incarcerated in Ludgate prison and who thrust their imploring arms through barred windows in search of food and drink. Birds flapped and swooped.

The man who sat astride his horse just outside the gate observed it all with a shrewd eye. His build and bearing suggested a yeoman but his doublet and hose were closer to those worn by a city gentleman. There was fur trim around his hat. He was of medium height and his craggy face bore the imprint of at least thirty eventful years. His raven black beard was well barbered enough to hint at vanity and he stroked it with ruminative care. The faint air of a countryman seemed to linger only to be dispelled by the knowing sophistication of a Londoner.

He had been there since dawn when the market traders

streamed into the city with their produce to set up their stalls. Nobody who passed through Ludgate during a long morning escaped his scrutiny, and the man hardly moved from his position of vantage, except to dismount from time to time in order to stretch his legs. Even when he relieved himself against a wall in a sheltered corner, he did not relax his surveillance. As noon was proclaimed by a jangling choir of bells, he was back in the saddle, raking the latest batch of arrivals with a stern gaze, then clicking his tongue in irritation when he did not find the face he so earnestly sought.

Could he have been mistaken? It was impossible to think that his vigilance had been at fault, but the sharpest eyes were useless if trained on the wrong location. Supposing his quarry had come along Holborn in order to enter the city through Newgate? Supposing he had struck even farther north and passed beneath the crenellations of Aldersgate or even Cripplegate? He discounted these alternatives almost as soon as he considered them. Someone who had ridden so far already would not needlessly add to the length of his journey. Most travellers approaching from the south-west would come by way of Westminster to Charing Cross then continue along the Strand until it merged into Fleet Street. That made Ludgate the only logical point of access.

So where was he? Had some accident detained or diverted him? The man's information came from a reliable source and it had placed his quarry at Colnbrook on the previous night. Could it take so long to cover a distance of fifteen miles? Someone who was so eager to reach London would surely not be delayed. Unless he had some forewarning of what lay ahead. Was his absence due to a timely premonition? Did he sense what awaited him in the shadow of Ludgate? Had fear sent him by a more anonymous route into the city?

The anxious sentry was still trying to assimilate this new possibility when his long wait came to an end. Another bevy of travellers, some twenty or so, came trotting towards him. They were hot and dusty from a long ride but their discomfort was forgotten in the excitement of their arrival.

11

For most of them, it was clear, this was a first and over-whelming visit to the capital. These were provincial gapers. Eyes that had bulged at the myriad wonders of Westminster now widened in awe as the cathedral of St Paul's rose up above the wall ahead of them like a mountain. The experience was at once exhilarating and intimidating.

He spotted his prey at once. The youth was in the middle of the cavalcade, using his companions as a protective ring, transfixed by what he saw and riding along in a kind of reverential daze. Short, plump and pale, he had plain features that were centered on a snub nose. His skin was soft, his face clean-shaven, his eyebrows thick and unsightly. He wore buff jerkin and hose with a cap pulled down over his close-cropped hair. The man put him around seventeen and knew that this was his designated target. Everyone else in the company was much older and the youth fitted in every detail the description he had been sent.

As the leaders went in through Ludgate, the man turned his own horse to join the rear of the group. There were fresh cries of astonishment as the travellers came face-to-face with the true heart of the city, with its mad jumble of houses, inns, churches and civic buildings, and with the happy turmoil of its streets. Voices lost in the din, they picked their way through the seething mass of bodies that converged on St Paul's churchyard. By the time they reached Watling Street, they started to disperse to their destinations, some heading up towards Cheapside, others cutting down towards the river, a few turning off into Cordwainer Street to make a first purchase from the shoemakers.

The youth stayed with the rump of the party as it bore due east into Candlewick Street. Riding alongside him was a big, well-dressed man of middle years on a chestnut mare. Unlike the others, he was evidently a seasoned traveller who had only joined the company for the safety it offered. Patently at ease in London, he showed an avuncular concern for the youth and pointed out each new item of interest. As further members of the group peeled away, only a handful were left to turn at last into Gracechurch Street.

12

Still trailing at a discreet distance, the man with the black beard watched the youth and his obliging friend swing into the yard of the Queen's Head. Though the fire on the previous day had closed part of the building down, the taproom was as busy and noisy as ever.

'Come, lad. A drop of ale will revive you.'

'No, sir. I will not tarry.'

'A dusty ride leaves a dry throat. Swill away the taste of the journey before you go your way.'

'There is no need, sir.'

'I'll not be denied. You'll share a pint with me in the name of friendship. It is the least you can do.'

'Indeed it is,' conceded the youth. 'I thank you for your help and I will drink to you but I may not stay long.' He glanced nervously around the taproom. 'I must be about my business.'

They were seated on stools beside a low wooden table. The youth was distinctly uncomfortable but his companion was very much at home in such surroundings. A waved hand brought a serving wench over and two tankards of ale were soon set in front of them. Pewter struck pewter in a toast then the man quaffed half of his pint in one thirsty gulp. The youth merely sipped at his drink. Having left his horse with an ostler, their shadow now stole into the taproom and sidled up so that he was within earshot. He took something from the pouch at his belt, waited for the youth to speak again then moved quickly in with an ingratiating smile.

'I know that voice!' he said with a soft West Country burr. 'It has a Tiverton ring to it, I'll be bound!'

'Not Tiverton, sir,' said the youth. 'But from that part of the country, it is true.'

'Well met, lad!' The black beard came close to the young face as the man clapped him on the shoulder. 'Devon is a sweeter place than London. What brings you here?'

An embarrassed stutter 'An . . . an errand, sir.'

The youth was quite unable to cope with this sudden ac-

13

quaintance thrust upon him and his travelling companion rose to come to his defence but his help was superfluous.

'Welcome, young friend!' said the newcomer, backing away with a farewell grin. 'Enjoy your stay here.'

As he moved swiftly away they lost sight of him among the shifting patterns of humanity beneath the low beams. Both had resented the intrusion and were glad that they were now alone again. Neither had noticed that something was slipped deftly into the boy's ale as his fellow-Devonian leaned across to him. The older man now raised his tankard once more.

'Drink up, lad!' he insisted.

'Very well, sir.'

The youth supped more deeply this time. To please his kind friend, he even pretended to enjoy the bitter taste. The man finished his own ale and licked his lips while beaming across at his companion. There was no better way to mark the end of a long journey than to celebrate good fellowship in a hostelry. He chuckled happily. It never occurred to him that he had just become an accomplice in a murder.

Chapter Two

THE MEETING WAS HELD AT LAWRENCE FIRETHORN'S house in Shoreditch because it was imperative to keep well clear of the fulminating landlord at the Queen's Head. On that point, at least, there was general agreement. On a more pressing issue, however, there was deep dissension, and it came from a most unlikely person.

'No, no, no!' said Edmund Hoode firmly. 'I will not.'

'Leave off these jests,' cooed his host.

'I speak in earnest, Lawrence. I will not quit London.'

'Stay here and we starve,' said Barnaby Gill with utter distaste for the notion. 'Westfield's Men must tour. I quiver at the thought of wasting my God-given genius on the heathen swine of the provinces, but there is no help for it. Actors who lose a theatre must seek elsewhere for another.'

'Edmund will join us in that quest,' said Firethorn with assurance. 'He would never desert us in our hour of need. Betrayal is foreign to his nature. He would sooner die than see his company struggle off into the wilderness. The name of Hoode is a seal of loyalty and comradeship.'

'You'll not persuade me, Lawrence,' said Hoode.

'I merely remind you of your reputation and honour.'

'They are needed here at home.'

'Home is where the company is,' chanted Gill with a petulant flick of his hand. 'It is your duty to come.'

'Duty and obligation,' reinforced Firethorn.

'I do not give a fig for either.'

'Edmund!'

'Pray excuse me, gentlemen. I am wanted elsewhere.'

'Stay!'

Firethorn barked a command that would have stopped a cavalry charge in its tracks then he placed his ample frame in the doorway to block his friend's departure. Hoode met his steely gaze with equanimity. They stood there for some minutes, locked in a trial of brute strength. Firethorn went through his full repertoire of glaring, eyebrow raising, lip curling and teeth grinding, but all to no avail. Barnaby Gill threw in an occasional flaring of the nostril and stamping of the foot but even this additional parade of displeasure failed to bring the miscreant to his senses.

The three men were all sharers with the company, ranked players who were listed in the royal patent for Westfield's Men and who were thus among the privileged few in the profession to be accorded legal recognition. Being sharers entitled them to first choice of the major parts in all plays that were performed as well as a portion of any profits made by the company. There were a number of other sharers but policy was effectively controlled by this trio. To be more exact, it was devised by Lawrence Firethorn and then placed before his two colleagues for their comment and approval. Barnaby Gill, conceited and temperamental, always challenged Firethorn's authority as a matter of course, and the house in Shoreditch had frequently echoed with the sound of their acrimonious exchanges. Edmund Hoode's accustomed role was that of peacemaker and he had reconciled the squabbling rivals more times than he chose to recall, yet here was this same gentle, inoffensive man, this moon-faced romantic, this poet and dreamer, this voice of calm and moderation, this apostle of friendship, daring to abandon his fellows at a time of acute crisis. It was unthinkable.

Firethorn shattered the tense silence with a bellow.

16

'Obey me, man! Or, by this hand, I'll tie you to a hurdle and drag you along with us.'

Hoode was unmoved by the threat. 'I will not go.'

'You will.'

'Take another in my place.'

'God's tits, Edmund! You *must* come!'

He attacked the renegade with a burst of expletives that turned the air blue and dislodged clouds of dust from the overhead beams. Hoode winced but he did not weaken. It was time for Barnaby Gill to take over and to replace apoplectic bluster with cool reasoning. Edmund Hoode was the resident actor-playwright, the creative source of the company, the only true begetter of that gallery of characters immortalised on the stage by the sheer flair of Firethorn and Gill. The way to appeal to him was through his work.

'We will perform your new play, Edmund,' he said.

'It is not yet finished.'

'Use the time out of London to complete it.' Gill took his arm and guided him across the parlour to the bow window. '*The Merchant of Calais* will be your masterpiece. We may try it out on tour and polish it until it dazzles like the sun. Anything penned by Edmund Hoode commands attention but this play will lift you high above your peers.' Personal interest intruded. 'Is my part written yet? Does it have true passion? Are there songs for me? And I must have a dance.' He squeezed Hoode's arm as he offered further flattery. '*The Merchant of Calais* will take the stage by storm. Does that prospect not entice you?'

'No,' said the playwright angrily. 'I do not wish to take the stage by storm in front of farting country bumpkins in some draughty village hall. Is that the only carrot you can dangle, Barnaby?' He turned to face his colleague and brushed away his hand. '*The Merchant of Calais* was to have been performed at The Rose in Bankside before the cream of London. I'll not let it be played in a barn to please the vulgar taste of rustics with a piece of straw in their mouths. Find some other argument. This one falters.'

'Mine will not,' said Firethorn, seizing the initiative once more and striding across the room to confront him. 'You

17

have no choice but to travel with us, Edmund. Loyalty demands it. Friendship compels it. Legal process enforces it.'

'I am deaf to all entreaty.'

'Hell and damnation! You are a sharer!'

'Then I will share in the joys of London.'

'You are contracted to serve us.'

'I do that best by resting from the company.'

'You have no choice, man!'

'My decision is final.'

'This wrings my heart,' said Gill, striking a pose.

'It rots my innards!' howled Firethorn. 'No more evasion. We are sworn fellows in a sacred brotherhood. Deny us and you deny God himself. Look me in the face, Edmund.' His voice took on an eerie stillness. 'Now hear me plain. Cease this nonsense and pledge yourself to this tour. Or never call me friend again.'

The warning had the power of a blow and Hoode recoiled from it. His eyes moistened, his cheeks colored and his Adam's apple grew restless. His resolve had finally cracked and he was visibly squirming in pain as he wrestled with his dilemma. Westfield's Men were his family. To foresake them now would be an act of malign cruelty, but as contrition began to flood through him and make his lower lips tremble, an even louder prompting filled his ears. Edmund Hoode could simply not leave London. With a supreme effort of will, he mastered all his misgivings then made a swift but dignified exit. The ultimate plea had failed.

Torn between rage and sadness, Firethorn gesticulated impotently, shocked that the most reliable member of his company should dare to reject him. Hoode's behaviour was quite baffling until Barnaby Gill snorted with contempt and provided the explanation.

'This is woman's work, Lawrence,' he sneered.

'Edmund? Never!'

'The fool is in love.'

'He is *always* in love, Barnaby. Suffering is the badge of his existence. There is no surer way to wallow in anguish than to scatter the seed of your affections on stony ground,

18

and he does that every time. Edmund Hoode is a martyr to
unrequited love. When he dies, they will make him the patron saint of pining hearts.'

'He is not pining now.'

'How say you?'

'Some woman has at last returned his love and be-
witched his legs. They will not stir from London lest he
lose her. Our amorous poet is being led by the pizzle.'

'Can this be so?'

'Have you seen him so *happy* before? It is unnatural!'

Firethorn was astonished. 'What simpleton of her sex
would choose Edmund as her swain? He would sooner
stroke her body with his verses than lay lascivious hands
upon her. I will not believe it. Westfield's Men are in dire
need of him. Who is stupid enough to put the charms of a
woman before the fate of his fellows?'

'*You* are, Lawrence, to name but one.'

'What!'

'Have you so soon forgotten Beatrice Capaldi?'

'Hold your serpent's tongue!'

'Then there was Mistress Par—'

'Enough!' roared Firethorn, glancing around with apprehension in case his wife should hear them from the kitchen.
'*I* am not on trial here. It is Edmund Hoode who stands accused of corruption.'

'He caught the disease from you,' said Gill with a vin-
dictive leer. 'The infection is called the Itching Codpiece. It
is compounded of naked folly and throbbing inflammation.'

'Your own codpiece has itched enough when it caught
the scent of a male varlet,' retorted Firethorn vehemently.
'At least—thanks be to heaven!—Edmund does not suffer
from *your* contagion. He would never sell his soul for pout-
ing lips and a pair of boyish buttocks.'

'Enough! I'll not endure this!'

Barnaby Gill stamped his foot so hard this time that it
jarred his body and made his teeth rattle. He and Firethorn
knew how to rub salt in each other's wounds then add vin-
egar for full measure. They smarted together for a long
time before common sense finally deprived them of their

weapons and imposed a truce. Another brawl between them would not bring their errant poet back into the fold. Joint action had to be taken and swiftly. They shook hands on it.

'We must find out who this woman is, Barnaby.'

'Then pluck him from between her lusty thighs.'

Firethorn grinned. 'That will be my office . . .'

Nicholas Bracewell removed another garment from its hook and folded it carefully before placing it in the basket. Hugh Wegges, the tireman, a conscientious soul with responsibility for making, altering and taking care of the costumes worn by the company, identified each one as it was packed away by the book holder, and he ticked it off on the list before him.

'Item, one scarlet cloak faced with green velvet and silver lace,' he intoned. 'Item, one woman's gown of cloth of gold. Item, one black velvet pea with gold lace and blue satin sleeves. Item, Charlemagne's cloak with fur. Item, a hermit's grey gown. Item, one white satin doublet. Item, one pair of embroidered paned hose scaled with black taffeta . . .'

Nicholas was about to fold the next garment when he noticed the scorch marks and set it aside. The antic coat had been used during *The Devil's Ride Through London* and was one of many casualties. All the costumes worn by actors who fought the blaze were damaged, and many of those hanging in the tirehouse had perished when the flames penetrated to that area. What fire had not destroyed, smoke had blackened. The foul smell still lingered in the material. It was the day after the tragedy and Nicholas had slipped unseen into the Queen's Head with Hugh Wegges to salvage what they could from the tiring-house and add it to the larger stock of costumes, which was kept in a private room at the inn. It was important to make a proper inventory before the whole collection was moved to safer lodgings in the attic of Firethorn's house. The list that the tireman would present to his employer would help to determine the plays that could be performed on tour.

'*The Devil* will ride no more,' said Wegges feelingly.

'Not unless the whole cast goes naked for penance. The costumes are ruined, and I've no time to make new ones.' A resigned note sounded. 'Master Firethorn will not have room for me when the company moves on. I am like that antic coat you hold there—burned out of my occupation.'

'We shall return to London ere long,' said Nicholas.

'When we have no theatre?'

'Our landlord may relent.'

'And it may rain sovereigns!' came the sarcastic reply. 'Those of us set aside may never work with a company again.'

'Take heart, Hugh. Bear up.'

But Nicholas did not feel as optimistic as he sounded. In order to tour, Westfield's Men would have to reduce the size of the party to its bare essentials. The sharers would go along with the apprentices, but many of the hired men would be discarded. A tireman and his assistant were luxuries that could not be afforded when the troupe took to the road. Nicholas would be given the unhappy job of telling several actors, musicians and other members of the company that their services were no longer required. For men like Thomas Skillen, stagekeeper with Westfield's Men since its creation, the parting could be final because he might conceivably have died before they returned. The defects of age, which debarred him from the multiple rigours of a long tour, were only kept at bay by the daily exercise of his functions behind the scenes. Without chores to do and underlings to berate, the venerable figure would soon go into decline.

It all served to increase the sense of guilt that Nicholas felt about the fire itself. Though he could not have foreseen the freak gust of wind that turned the glowing coals into a lethal inferno, it had been his idea to place the lighted brazier onstage in the final scene, and none of the praise that was afterwards heaped upon him for his bravery could hide the fact that he was somehow obscurely responsible for the disaster. Since he had inadvertently brought about the loss of the company's venue, he vowed that he would restore it to them when the renovations were complete. That would entail more delicate restoration, the careful rebuilding of a relationship with the irascible landlord, and such work could not be rushed. In the short term, therefore, everything must be done to appease Alexander Marwood and all trace of his despised tenants removed from the premises.

When Nicholas and Hugh Wegges finished, they loaded their baskets on to a waiting cart to make a stealthy exit, but their secret visit to the inn did not go unnoticed.

'Master Bracewell!'

'Good day, sir,' said Nicholas, throwing the words over his shoulder and eager to leave. 'We must hurry.'

'But I have news for you.'

The amiable voice made him turn and he saw a welcome face approaching. It belonged to Leonard, a huge, waddling barrel of a man with a beard still flecked with the foam of his last draught of ale. They were good friends, who had been drawn together while imprisoned in the Counter, and it was Nicholas who had secured Leonard's employment at the Queen's Head. The erstwhile brewer's drayman had much to thank him for and did so on a regular basis with touching sincerity.

'I did not know you were here,' said Leonard.

'It is but a brief visit,' explained Nicholas, 'and we would keep all knowledge of it from a certain landlord.'

'He shall hear nothing from me.'

'Thank you, Leonard.'

'I have shielded your good name once already today.'

'How so?'

'By speaking to the youth.'

'What youth?'

'The one inquiring after Master Nicholas Bracewell. He came into the taproom this very hour, worn out by travel and by the weight of the message he bore.'

'Message?'

'It was for you, sir, and needed instant delivery.'

'What did you tell this youth?'

'Well,' said Leonard, putting his hands on his broad hips to relate his tale, 'my first task was to drag him away from Master Marwood, for when the young man spoke of you, my employer began to curse you and your company with such an uncivil tongue that you might have ravished his wife and run off with his daughter, Rose.' Leonard chortled then he grew serious. 'I took the youth aside and assured him of your worth, then—seeing his honesty—I gave him the address of your lodging in Bankside. I hope I did right, master.'

'You did, Leonard. You say there was a message?'

'I judged it to be important because it had come on such a long journey. It was his way of speaking, you see.'

'Way of speaking?'

'The youth. His voice was just like yours.'

Leonard tried to mimic his friend's West Country accent, but his unskilled tongue mangled the consonants and tripped over the vowels. He shrugged an apology but he had made his point. Someone from North Devon had come in search of his friend. Nicholas sensed trouble. He thanked Leonard for his news, told Hugh Wegges to drive the cart and its cargo out to Shoreditch then took his leave of them both. He went out into Gracechurch Street and headed towards the river, dodging his way along the crowded thoroughfare and wondering what bad tidings were now pursuing him from the home that he had decisively turned his back on so many years ago.

Anne Hendrik was alarmed when her servant brought the youth into her. The boy was bent almost double as he clutched at his midriff and yet he would not hear of any relief for his distress. His one concern was to deliver a message to her lodger. When Anne suggested that she might take charge of the missive until Nicholas returned, the youth explained that he had no letter to hand over. His was a verbal message, but he went off into such a fit of coughing that Anne doubted if he would be in a condition to utter it. She and her servant guided the visitor up to Nicholas's chamber and made him rest on the bed. The servant was then dispatched to fetch a surgeon to the Bankside house. Anne was a compassionate woman who hated to see anyone in such pain, but when she tried to nurse the stricken

23

messenger, she was once more waved away. Desperately ill as he clearly was, the youth still refused to be touched and begged to be left alone until Nicholas Bracewell came home.

Bankside was notorious for its haunts of pleasure and vice, but Anne Hendrik represented one of the pockets of respectability in the area. The English widow of a Dutch hatmaker, she had inherited his house, his thriving little business in the adjacent premises and his positive attitude towards life. Instead of mourning his demise, therefore, she took over the management of the business and worked hard to improve its fortunes. She also took in a lodger—largely to provide a modicum of male company—but the relationship between them had developed well beyond the accepted one. In Nicholas Bracewell, she found an upright, caring and sensitive man, and he saw in her a handsome, intelligent and remarkable woman. They were kindred spirits and occasional lovers.

Nicholas had been enormously helpful to her and his solid presence had been a convenient refuge from the unwanted attentions of other admirers. Anne had never felt more in need of him than now. A sick youth was babbling his name as if he were some kind of saviour. She wanted Nicholas there to take control of the situation, to give succour to the ailing visitor and to calm the unsettling thoughts that were beginning to flit through her own mind. Even in their most intimate moments, Nicholas never talked about his life in his native Devon. It was a closed book to Anne. This youth had staggered in to open the pages of that book and she was not at all sure that she would enjoy reading them.

There was a dull thud from upstairs that made her jump then start towards the stairs. At the same time, however, the latch was lifted and Nicholas Bracewell came hurrying in. Anne had an impulse to fling herself gratefully into his arms but she was somehow held back. The expression of mingled anxiety and remorse was one she had never seen on his countenance before. He was both lover and stranger now.

'Did anyone call here for me?' he said.

'A young man. He is still here and failing fast.'

'Where is he?'

'In your chamber. I have sent for the surgeon.'

'What has the youth said?'

'He will speak to none but you, Nick.'

She stood aside as he dashed up the staircase then she hurried after him, but they were far too late. When they went into the bedchamber, the youthful caller lay twisted on the floor at an unnatural angle, the face pallid and contorted with agony. Nicholas felt for signs of life but there were none. He caught a whiff of something from the lips and bent low to inhale the sour odour more carefully.

'Poison!' he whispered.

'May God have mercy on his soul!'

He stood to comfort her. 'Come away, Anne.'

'Leave me be.'

'You should not dwell on such a sight.'

'It is my house, Nick.'

'This is villainous work.'

'But the issue of it lies dead under my roof.'

'There is nothing you may do here. Turn away.'

'No!'

Wanting his embrace, she yet held up her palms to keep him away. Intuition overcame need. Anne Hendrik knew at that precise moment in time that a trusting relationship that had flowered over some years had changed irrevocably. He was no longer the man she thought she knew. Nicholas Bracewell inhabited another world and part of it lay sprawled out on the floor of the bedchamber like some dreadful accusation. He saw her consternation but could find no words of apology or explanation. Instead, he bent down again to make a closer examination of the corpse.

A rush of sympathy brought tears to Anne's eyes.

'Poor wretch! What a hideous way to die!'

'Someone will pay dearly for this,' he murmured.

'He came all that way to see you.'

'No, Anne.'

'And this is his reward.'

'Look more closely.'

'Can anyone deserve such a miserable death?'

'There is something you have missed.'

'He was but a youth on the threshold of life.'

'I fear not,' he said, rising to his feet once more and speaking with quiet outrage. 'This is no youth, Anne. The killer is more callous than we imagined. He has poisoned a young woman.'

Edmund Hoode was racked with doubt and tortured with regret. The surge of power that had enabled him to defy his colleagues and walk out of the house in Shoreditch had now spent itself. He was left feeling weak and helpless. As he ambled through the streets of Bishopsgate Ward, his heart was pounding and his feet encased in boots of lead. The impossible had happened. In a rare burst of single-minded action, a modest and highly unselfish man had behaved with brutal selfishness. Edmund Hoode put his own needs and desires before those of the company he had served so faithfully for so long. A series of interlinked betrayals—of Lawrence Firethorn, Barnaby Gill and other sharers—was exacerbated by the wilful negation of his own creative role. In spurning Westfield's Men, he was helping to suffocate his own career as a playwright.

Dejection turned an already bloodless face into a white mask of sorrow. Hoode was a traitor. He felt like a convicted felon in Newgate prison, who, given the choice between the summary horror of hanging and the languid misery of being pressed to death, opted for the latter because it permitted his heirs still to inherit his estate. Great weights were indeed loaded onto him, but they were not all made of steel and stone. One of them was Nicholas Bracewell, his closest friend in the company, stunned by Hoode's treachery and pressing down hard in the way he had done on the burning roof of the Queen's Head. Firethorn was there, too, along with Gill, the one stamping unceremoniously on him and the other dancing one of the famous jigs that adorned so many of Hoode's plays. Both left deep footprints on his wayward heart. As for his own last will and testament, what did he have to bequeath except his work for Westfield's Men? As an author and an actor, he existed only in performance. Piracy was rife in the theatre. Those same plays of his—staged with unvarying distinction by the company—were guarded by the book holder with his life. Could Edmund Hoode really put his private urges before the public good? Could he hold Westfield's Men to ransom?

The weight of guilt and indecision was so excruciating that it brought him to a halt. If he went on, he lost the respect of his dearest friends: if he turned back, he missed his one real opportunity for true happiness. He had walked aimlessly for a long time but his feet had known their duty for they had brought him to the very place where the first glimpse of Elysium had been vouchsafed to him. He was in her street, standing opposite her house and looking up at her chamber window. An invisible hand must have guided him there to resuscitate his drooping spirits. No sooner did he realise where he was than the sweet face of his beloved rose up before him. A hundred friends would not separate him from her. A thousand theatre companies could not induce him to leave London so long as she graced it with her angelic presence. A million spectators could not deflect him.

She was called Mistress Jane Diamond and her beauty sparkled as preciously as her name. Edmund Hoode was entranced from the moment he set bulbous eyes on her. Poised, graceful and vivacious, she was brimming with a delightful wit. Jane Diamond was a veritable queen among women, and the fact that she was already encumbered with a king—her husband was a dull but prosperous vintner— did not diminish his readiness to pay court to her. Hoode's romantic involvements always verged on calamity and he had characterised them, in a moment of savage introspection, as examples of the unlovable in pursuit of the unattainable. Jane Diamond was different. Not only did she encourage his interest, she actually returned his affection. She admired his plays, she doted on the verses he sent her

27

and she loved his many sterling qualities. It was only a matter of time before consummation followed.

As he remembered that, he realised why he had walked insensibly in the direction of her house. Jane Diamond had agreed to be the jewel in his bed when time would serve, and she had promised to signal the fateful night by putting a lighted candle in her bedchamber on the same afternoon. For the past fortnight, Hoode had found reason to go back and forth to her house ten times a day but the darkness of his desire was not illumined with the flickering flame of hope. Until—did his eyes deceive him?—this moment. Even as he looked up at the casement, a slim figure appeared in it and set a tallow candle on the ledge. There was a pause, a tiny explosion of light and then a shimmering invitation that warmed his whole being. On the previous day, a spark of fire had ruined his play and destroyed part of their theatre, but this new flame was benign and joyful. It told him that an undeserving husband would be away for the night and that a gorgeous wife would be his.

Every trace of recrimination left him and he now felt as light as air. Westfield's Men could no longer impinge on his consciousness. The assignation had been made and that was all that mattered. London was paradise.

Events moved swiftly in the house at Bankside. The surgeon arrived to find the girl beyond his help and to confirm the likely cause of her death. There was nothing about her person to indicate her identity, and whatever momentous news she carried had expired with her. Constables were summoned and the body was taken off to a slab in the morgue. Nicholas Bracewell, Anne Hendrik, the servant and the surgeon all made sworn statements to the coroner but there was no question of any rigorous pursuit of the killer by the forces of law and order. The coroner's rolls contained countless murders by person or persons unknown, and it was possible to investigate only a tiny fraction of them. Priority was based firmly on the importance of the victim. Resources would never stretch to a full inquiry into the fate of a nameless girl from a distant county.

Innocents were always at risk in a crime-infested city where a ragged army of predators waited to pounce on the unwise and the unwary. There was hardly a day when some battered corpse was not discovered in some dark corner or lugged out of the stews or dragged from the river. This hapless young woman, decided the coroner with a world-weary sigh and threadbare sympathy, was just one more fatality to enter in his records with her death unexplained and unavenged.

Nicholas Bracewell craved retribution. Since he could expect none from official quarters, he would have to find a means to deal it out himself. The girl had been poisoned, but she still had a small amount of money about her person and her clothing was of value. Theft had not been the motive. The murderer had even left her horse untouched, so he was not one of the cunning priggers of prancers who roamed the capital to steal horses wherever opportunity appeared. It was with the animal that Nicholas would start his search. He was convinced that the girl had been struck down in order to stop her passing on some news of vital import to him. Reluctant even to consider the idea of returning home, he yet knew that the only way to find out who she was and what tidings she bore was to go back once more to Devon. If that mystery were unravelled, he would have a clearer idea of why the young messenger was murdered and by whose fell hand.

Anne Hendrik had been on edge since the unheralded visitor first tottered across her threshold, and nothing that had occurred since had relieved her disquiet or eased the growing tension between her and Nicholas. Indeed, she was so upset that she pointedly ignored her lodger and asked the surgeon to escort her and her servant back to her house. When the man went off with the two women, Nicholas gave the coroner a fuller account of the circumstances and of his own involvement in the case. He made application for custody of the victim's horse so that he could take it back to its rightful owner in Devon and explain what had befallen its rider. The girl would have anxious parents or a concerned employer with the right to know of her misfortune.

After close questioning of his witness, the coroner judged him to be a man of good reputation and sound character. Nicholas gave stern undertakings and signed a document that bound him to his stated purpose on the penalty of arrest. He then took charge of the horse and mounted it at once to ride straight back to the Queen's Head. When he trotted into the yard, he questioned all the ostlers to see if any of them remembered having seen the roan before. They handled too many horses in the course of a day to be sure, but one of them vaguely recalled stabling the animal along with another around noon. A young man had dismounted from the roan. His companion had been much bigger, older and in the attire of a merchant.

Nicholas took this ambiguous description off to the cellar to see if Leonard could correct or add to it. The affable giant was in the process of lifting a barrel of ale onto his shoulder when his friend came down the stone steps, and he put it back down again in order to give a proper greeting. Leonard was only too eager to help but he could contribute no significant new details about the victim's companion. What he was certain about was the fact that the older man had more or less forced the boy—as he still thought him—to finish his pint of ale.

'And the tankard was emptied?' said Nicholas.

'I stood over him while he supped the last drops. Not that it gave him any pleasure.' Leonard scratched his beard. 'Lord knows why. It was our best ale yet he drank it down as slow as if were hot pitch.'

'In some sorts, it was.'

'Why, master?'

'I believe that tankard was poisoned.'

Nicholas explained and the massive visage before him first lit up with surprise—"A girl? Drinking in a tavern in the guise of a man?"—then crumpled with sorrow and bewilderment. Aware of how important even the tiniest shred of evidence was, Leonard now began to cudgel his brain unmercifully but it could yield little more than had already been disclosed. Girl and travelling companion had been alone together, he could vouch for that. A third person might have tampered with the ale but the balance of probability pointed to the older man as the culprit. No other visitor to the Queen's Head that day had been struck down by poison, so the fault could not be laid at Alexander Marwood's door.

'Who served them with their ale?'

'One of the wenches.'

'Find her out and bring her to me directly.'

'Could you not go into the taproom yourself, master?'

'I could,' said Nicholas, 'but I do not want to make the landlord any more choleric. Bridges must be mended before Master Marwood and I can speak cordially again. The less he sees of Westfield's Men at the moment, the better. I would be most grateful if you could do my errand.'

'I'll about it straight.'

'Thank you, Leonard.'

It was five minutes before he came back and the serving wench he brought with him was not at all willing to come. Fearing that she was being lured into the cellar for some nefarious purpose, she chided and protested at every step. The sight of Nicholas reassured her slightly and her smudged button of a face even smiled when he slipped a few coins into her hand. She brushed back her lank hair so that she could study him properly. Nicholas asked her about the two travellers who came in at noon and she was able to give a reasonable description of both but she had heard nothing that passed between them and saw nobody else joining them at their table. What she did notice was how ill at ease the younger patron had been in the tavern.

'You'd have thought it his first visit to a taproom.'

'First and last,' muttered Nicholas to himself.

With nothing more to be gleaned at the inn, he thanked them for their help and collected his horse. He was soon making his way along the ever-populous Gracechurch Street until it became Bishopsgate Street. When he came to the gate itself and rode out beneath the heads of the traitors who had been set on spikes there, he was able to coax a

31

steady canter out of the roan, and the journey to Shoreditch was over fairly quickly. Reaching his employer's house, he tethered his mount and ducked under the eaves. Lawrence Firethorn answered the door himself and whisked his book holder straight into the parlour.

'You come most promptly upon your hour!'

'It is needful.'

'We must have urgent conference, Nick.'

'That is why I am here.'

'Sit down, man, sit down,' said Firethorn, ushering him to a chair and pushing him into it. 'Take your ease while you yet may for there is little hope of rest ahead of us.'

'I must speak with you on that subject.'

'Only when you have first listened.'

Firethorn punched his guest playfully on the shoulder and stood back to appraise him with a fond smile. A theatrical career was a precarious one at the best of times and few sustained it with any consistency over a long period of time. Lawrence Firethorn was one of those exceptions, a durable talent that never seemed to fade, an actor of infinite variety and bravado. Admirers spoke of his superb voice, gesture and movement while others were swept away by his commanding presence. Supreme when he was on stage, he knew full well how much he owed to the controlling figure of his book holder behind the arras. With Nicholas Bracewell at his back, he could lead his company to triumph after triumph.

'Ah, Nick!' he sighed. 'What would I do without you!'

'I fear that you may have to find out.'

'Our theatre may burn down, our landlord may oust us and London may drive us on to the open road but I am not in the least troubled. As long as I have you, I have hope.'

'With regard to the tour—'

'It is all arranged,' interrupted Firethorn, moving around the room. 'Barnaby and I have laboured long and hard today to stitch it all together like tidy seamsters. Our esteemed patron, Lord Westfield, has shown his usual concern and offered money and guidance to send us on our way.' He gave a ripe chuckle. 'The money, alas, will never appear because our dear patron is more adept at borrowing than loaning, but the advice came in abundance. It has determined our itinerary and given us promise of certain welcome along the way.' He snatched up a sheet of parchment from the table and handed it to Nicholas. 'This is our company. Small it may be in number but it is large enough in talent to present a wide repertoire of plays. See that each man is informed of our purpose. We will set forth tomorrow.'

'You will do so without me, I fear, Master Firethorn.'

His host gulped. 'What is that you say?'

'I beg leave to be excused.'

'Excused!' repeated Firethorn. 'Excused! Nick Bracewell being excused from Westfield's Men! It is like excusing London Bridge from spanning the Thames. God's death, man, you are our very foundation! Excuse you and we plummet straight down into a swamp of oblivion.'

'The choice is forced upon me,' explained Nicholas.

'There *is* no choice. You are ours.'

'My decision will hold.'

'I override it. You leave with us on the morrow.'

'It may not be.'

Firethorn extended his arms. 'We *rely* on you, dear heart!'

'I will rejoin the company as soon as I may. You have my word on that. Thus it stands with me . . .'

He recounted his story as succinctly as he could and Firethorn's manner changed at once. Obsessed as he was with himself and with his company, the actor–manager could yet feel pangs of sympathy. The murder of a defenceless girl had laid a deep responsibility on Nicholas Bracewell and nothing would prevent him from discharging it. He was being forced to return to a home he left and a family he had renounced.

'There is no other way,' he said in conclusion. 'Early tomorrow, I will set off for Barnstaple.'

A derisive snort. 'Barnstaple?'

'Barnstaple.'

Nicholas sat back and waited for the tempest to break.

33

Few men dared to oppose the will of the actor-manager and fewer still survived with their self-esteem intact. When Firethorn was truly roused, his voice could blow with the force of a gale and his invective was scalding rain. As he looked into his employer's eyes, Nicholas saw the hurricane begin with sudden fury and then evaporate harmlessly to be replaced by a merry twinkle. Instead of unleashing the whirlwind of his passion, Lawrence Firethorn actually smiled. The smile broadened into a grin, the grin enlisted the support of a chortle, the chortle soon developed into a full-throated laugh and then uncontrollable mirth sent his body into a series of convulsions. He had to sit down beside his friend to regain his breath.

'Barnstaple?' he asked again.

'There is some jest here?'

'No, Nick,' said Firethorn, arm around his shoulders. 'It is not the laughter of mockery but the happiness of relief. Barnstaple, indeed! Heaven provides better than we ourselves. You shall go. Your needs will be answered.'

'Then why this celebration?'

'Because you will serve us on the way.'

'How?'

'We will alter our itinerary,' explained the other. 'We had thought to go south and make Maidstone our first port of call. Then on to Canterbury and other towns in Kent, but they can wait. Canterbury has pilgrims enough.' He lowered his voice to a whisper to put his proposition. 'Westfield's Men will bend a lot towards your purpose if you bend a little towards ours. Is this not a fair bargain?'

'Tell me more that I may judge aright.'

'Our patron's brother lives in Bath.'

'That is well in the direction of Barnstaple.'

'Hear me out, Nick. This will be our route.' He used a finger to draw a map in the air. 'We make straight for Oxford and play before town and gown. From there we travel down to Marlborough, where they have always given us a cheerful welcome in their Guildhall. Then on to Bristol, where a bigger audience and a longer stay beckon.'

'And Bath?'

34

'A pretty enough little town but we will perform at the home of Sir Roger Hordley, younger brother of our patron. We need you to pilot us through Oxford, Marlborough and Bristol, but we can set up in the hall of Hordley Manor ourselves.' He nudged his companion. 'Have you caught my meaning?'

'I make for Barnstaple by slower means.'

'You combine our necessity with your mission.'

Nicholas pondered. 'It puts days on my intent.'

'We make a sacrifice, so must you.'

'Bristol is a city that I love.'

'Take us there and we will wish you God speed as we send you off to Barnstaple. Discharge your duties at home then you may catch up with Westfield's Men at your leisure.' Firethorn pulled him close. 'Both of us are satisfied in this. Tell me now, does not this offer please you?'

'It tempts me greatly.'

'Then you will accept the commission?'

Nicholas gave an affirmative nod and Firethorn replied with a hug of gratitude. The actor-manager furnished him with all the necessary details then walked him back out to his horse. The sight of the roan jolted them and brought the murder victim back to the forefront of their minds. A young woman had gone to extraordinary lengths to bring a message all the way from Barnstaple to London, and her fortitude had cost her a high price. Her murder was already having severe repercussions on the life of Nicholas Bracewell. As he recalled the image of her tormented body on the floor of his bedchamber, his determination to track down the killer was reinforced. The Devil had indeed ridden through London that day to seize his prey. A girl who had never been inside a tavern before would never do so again.

Like a true actor, Lawrence Firethorn drew the shroud of a quotation across the anonymous corpse.

*My foulest poison can never compete
With Marwood's ale in Gracechurch Street.*

Chapter Three

A HARROWING AFTERNOON SHADED INTO A LONG evening then turned imperceptibly into a restive night. Anne Hendrik was sorely perplexed. The home that she prized so much, and within whose walls she felt so secure, had been invaded. A dying girl, who refused to divulge her message, had splintered the ordered calm of her life in Bankside and the assumptions on which it was based. Anne had been taught just how much she loved Nicholas Bracewell but just how little she knew of him. What she had always admired as restraint and discretion she now saw as secretiveness. He had been hiding something from her all this while and it had now emerged into the light of day like a long-buried mole to threaten the whole future of their friendship. Pleasant memories have no need of suppression. Only murkier secrets have to be concealed.

Anne paced anxiously up and down, at once longing for his return and praying that he would not come back. Her heart wanted Nicholas to sweep into the house and smother all her hostile thoughts beneath a pillow of explanation, but her head knew that he could never do that. His behaviour had been an open admission of guilt. What dread secret had he tried to outrun when he left his home in Barnstaple?

36

What fearful consignment was the girl carrying to him? Who had sent the grim message and why was it transported in such a strange manner? She speculated on the possibilities and found none that brought comfort. As the night wore on, her nerves became even more frayed, and she was thoroughly jangled by the time she heard him arrive back and stable the horse. Anne quickly took a seat and tried to muster her composure. When Nicholas let himself into the house, he moved with a wary fatigue. Clearly, he did not expect his usual hospitable welcome.

'You are late,' she said crisply.

'There was much to do, Anne.'

'It draws toward midnight.'

'You should have retired to your bed.'

'I feared that you might join me there.'

She blurted it out before she could stop herself and the force of the rebuff made him flinch. A mutual code of conduct was immediately ruptured. Whenever Nicholas and Anne had serious disagreements—and they arose often between two strong-willed personalities—they always resolved them as soon as possible in each other's arms. That source of reconciliation had been summarily closed off to him.

'We leave for Oxford in the morning.'

She stiffened. 'I had thought you would ride post haste to Barnstaple,' she said sharply. 'Someone has sent for you. Do not let *me* detain you here.'

'Anne—'

'More important business calls you away.'

'Do but hear me—'

'I listened to that girl instead. Her silence was all too eloquent. It spoke of another Nicholas Bracewell, of a man with whom I have never been acquainted, of a hunted creature who has been using my house as a hiding place.'

'That is not so!' he insisted.

'Then why have you lied to me?'

'I have always told you the truth.'

'No, Nick,' she said, rising to confront him, 'you have told me only enough to content me and held back the rest.

37

The face that you wear in London is only a mask and I took it for the real man. It is a cruel deception. Who *are* you!'

'I am yours, my love.'

He reached out for her but her eyes flashed so angrily that he retracted his arms at once. Her rejection of him was doubly painful. Westfield's Men were due to leave London the next day on a lengthy tour. On the eve of previous departures, Nicholas invariably took a fond farewell in the comfort of her bed but this custom was also being breached.

'You do me wrong,' he said softly.

'Then I repay you in kind, Nick.'

'The situation is not as it may seem.'

'Enlighten me.'

An awkward pause. 'I may not do that.'

'Because you do not care enough about me.'

'I care too much, Anne, and would not wish to hurt.'

'Is that your ruse, sir?' she said tartly. 'You beguile me freely until your past begins to overtake you, then you pretend it was all done in order to protect my feelings. I have been misled here. I have been abused. Why?'

'I do not know the bottom of it myself.'

'Go back to the beginning,' she suggested. 'Why did you flee from Devon?'

'I have told you before, Anne,' he argued. 'I sought adventure. I did what thousands of young men do when they hear the call of the sea. Drake was leaving on his voyage around the world and it was too great a temptation for my questing spirit. I left Plymouth in the *Pelican*. When we sailed back into the same harbour three years later, our ship had been renamed *The Golden Hind*.'

'That was not the only change you suffered,' she said levelly. 'It was Nicholas Bracewell, the son of a Barnstaple merchant, who set sail. He came back to be the book holder with a theatre company in London.'

He nodded soulfully. 'You are right, Anne. The voyage wrought many alterations. I saw and endured things I do not care even to think upon now. Anybody would have been changed by such an experience.'

'Why did you never go back home?'

'I chose to remain here.'

'Who is now sending for you from Barnstaple?'

'I do not know.'

'Is it a man or a woman?' His hesitation was all the proof that she required. 'Even so! It is a woman and one who still has much power over you that you race to obey, even though her call has brought murder in its wake.' Anne was now glowing with indignation. 'And this is the man I have allowed to share my house and—God pardon me!—my bed! Well, ride out of London tomorrow but do not expect to lay your head here when you return.'

'Anne, wait!' he implored as she turned on her heel. 'We must not part like this. You judge me too harshly.'

'Then where is your denial?' she said, rounding on him once more. 'Tell me all and put my mind at rest.'

'That is beyond my power,' he admitted sadly, 'but I will not have you believe that all that has passed between us has been a pretence on my part. It is not so! Some of the happiest moments of my life have been with you. And if you wish to know the true reason I prefer to stay in London rather than return to Barnstaple, then it stands before me.'

His plea was so heartfelt and genuine that her anger cooled for a second and she saw once more the man to whom she had ineluctably been drawn. Nicholas Bracewell was indeed a loving friend to whom she had willingly yielded herself. He had many sterling qualities but contemplation of them only served to embitter her again. As a result of an undelivered message from Devon, she lost an honest man and gained a duplicitous one. While enjoying her favours, he always had an invisible lover lying beside him. Anne Hendrik had merely shared him.

Nicholas resumed softly. 'What has happened between us under this roof has been very dear to me, Anne, and I treasure those memories. I did not dissemble. You saw me for the man I really was.' He offered a tentative hand. 'I would not be exiled from you for all the world.'

'Then I will put you to the test,' she said, ignoring the outstretched palm. 'Remain here.'

'How so?'

'When the company leaves tomorrow, stay with me.'

'But I am bound to Westfield's Men.'

'A second ago you were bound to me.'

'I have given my word to Master Firethorn.'

'You gave it just as easily to me even now.'

'He and I came to composition.'

'We have done that, too, often enough.'

'I travel with the company as far as Bristol and then strike on alone to Barnstaple to . . . to . . .'

'Go on, go on,' she said. 'State your true purpose.'

'To settle my affairs.'

'While I sit here like patient Griseld to await my lord's return. Is that your hope?'

'Anne,' he soothed, 'please hear me out. Imagination plays tricks on you. Be steadfast as before. Do but trust me until I return and I will—'

'No!' she snapped. 'This house is barred to you from this day forth. I ask you to account for yourself and you cannot. I ask you to stay in London and you will not. There is only one thing for it.' Her tone was icily dismissive. 'Go to her, Nick.'

'Who?'

'That creature who lies with you in my bed.'

'You talk in riddles.'

'The silent woman. Run back to her.'

Nicholas felt a stab of pain that made him reel. At a time when he desperately needed Anne's love and support, it was being withdrawn completely from him. He stood rooted to the floor as she mounted the stairs, and he suffered another spasm when he heard the door of her bed-chamber slam behind her with an air of finality. It was minutes before he found the will to creep furtively up to his own room, to gather up his belongings, to take one last valedictory glance around and then to slip out into the black wilderness of a life without her.

* * *

Midnight approached rapidly and Edmund Hoode quivered with anticipatory joy. It was the appointed hour when he and his beloved would come together at last and drown the weeks of enforced separation in the turbulent water of passion. He felt truly elated for the first time in years. At this stage in most of his romantic attachments, he would be suffering the cumulative humiliations that afflict those who are perennially unlucky in love and who are singled out by fate as objects of scorn and mockery. Jane Diamond had redeemed his earlier miseries. In encouraging his advances, she had given him a confidence he would not have believed possible, and in succumbing to his desires—nay, replicating them with her own frank yearnings—she had lent a touch of arrogance to his manner. He was a new man.

Hoode deserved her. He had earned his good fortune by the sustained fervour of his devotions. Letters, verses and gifts had been showered upon his mistress. Every time she watched him perform at the Queen's Head, he wrote additional lines for himself in a code that only she could comprehend. Every time they saw each other in public, she replied with secret gestures that were meaningless to anyone but him. Jane Diamond was not simply a vision of loveliness with a disposition to match. She was the finest creation of Edmund Hoode, poet and playwright, the character he had delineated for himself in his robuster fantasies, as near to perfection as a human being could be and with one quality that outshone all the others. She was his.

He lurked in a doorway opposite her house and listened for the midnight bell. Only one minute now kept them apart and he used it to reflect on his newly acquired strength of mind. That very afternoon, Lawrence Firethorn and Barnaby Gill had launched a two-pronged attack on it, but his defences held. In the evening, it was the turn of Nicholas Bracewell to remind him of his commitments to Westfield's Men, but not even his friend's promptings could turn him aside. Hoode refused to struggle his way around the provinces. London could offer him a far more exciting tour for he sought no other stage on which to perform than the pillowed scaffold of Jane Diamond's bed.

The bell chimed, the lighted candle appeared and Hoode went skipping across the dusty street to tap lightly on the door. It was inched open by a whispering maidservant.

'Is that you, sir?'

'It is.'

'My mistress awaits you.'

'You serve us well.'

He dropped two coins into her waiting palm then the door swung back to admit him before creaking back into position again. She turned a key in the lock. By the light of her taper, he could just make out the thick iron bolts. Before he could ask why she did not bolt the door, she led him off towards the stairs. Once the ascent began, all thought of security left him. He was inside her house and inside her heart. The sweetest penetration of all now awaited him. He would be able to drink his fill from the finest wine in the vintner's cellar.

They reached the landing and made their way along the undulating oak boards of a corridor. Pausing at a door, the maidservant knocked then indicated that he should enter. She herself curtseyed and withdrew towards the stairs. Edmund Hoode took a deep breath. The door was the gate to heaven and he stroked it with reverence before pushing it gently open to reveal her bedchamber.

'Come in, Edmund,' she called.

'I am here, my love.'

He stepped into the room and closed the door behind him then inhaled the bewitching perfume of her presence. He had painted this scene in his mind a hundred times but reality beggared his invention. She looked and sounded far lovelier than he had dared to imagine and the bedchamber was a most appropriate setting for her. In the subtle and calculating light of a dozen small candles, she reclined on the bed amid a flurry of white pillows. Her face was a flower, her hair a waterfall of brown silk. She wore a long satin nightgown with a drawstring at the neck, and the contours of her body were at once displayed and concealed. Jane Diamond was the answer to a much over-used prayer, and she lay ready for him on the altar of Venus.

He took a faltering step towards her.

'I have missed you cruelly, Jane.'

'Come closer that you may tell me how much.'

'I thought this moment would never come.'

'Patience and constancy have their due reward.'

'No man is more patient than I,' he declared, moving nearer to her. 'And as for constancy, the Tower of London will crumble sooner than my devotion to you.'

'I know it well, Edmund.'

Now he had come into the circle of light, she was able to inspect him more closely and she was pleased with her examination. Edmund Hoode looked immaculate. He wore a blue velvet doublet with green satin sleeves, and embroidered paned hose scaled with yellow damask. The lawn ruff at his neck held up the big, white, willing plate of a face. When he saw her look up at his blue velvet hat with its trembling ostrich feather, he doffed it at once and gave an apologetic bow. She crooked a finger to bring him to her, took his hat and put it aside, then raised her lips for him.

The first tremulous kiss dissolved all inhibition and he took her in his arms with unrestrained ardour. They had waited a long time for this supreme moment and both intended to savour it to the full. Jane was soon plucking at the fastenings on his doublet while he used his teeth to pull at the drawstring on her nightgown. This was no sordid act of adultery. The purity of their love lifted them on to a more ethereal plain. Their senses were immeasurably heightened. Their lips found a rich honey with each kiss, their hands found warmer flesh with each caress. The aroma of pleasure made them almost giddy and this was their undoing for they did not hear the knock of the real world on the door of their fantasy. Only when the maidservant burst into the room did they come down from their clouds of bliss.

'Make haste, mistress!' cried the intruder. 'The master has returned.'

'That cannot be!' cried Jane in alarm.

'He's here below. I wonder you did not hear him open the door, it creaks so loud.' The maidservant hissed at

Edmund Hoode. 'Fly, sir! He will surely kill you if he finds you in his bed.'

The maidservant rushed out again and the lovers leapt up. Jane pulled down her nightgown and sped on tiptoe into the corridor in time to hear the heavy tread of boots upon the stairs. She waited long enough to see her husband's hat and cloak come out of the gloom then she darted back into the bedchamber and closed the door. Two bolts were slid into place and she flung her back against it for extra fortification.

'Run, Edmund!' she advised 'Run!'

'I try!' wailed the stricken wooer, attempting to gather up his clothing from the floor. Valour flickered. 'Should I not stay to defend you, my love?'

'He will murder us both if he sees you. Go!'

A thunderous banging on the door convinced Hoode that a speedy exit was his only hope of salvation. Opening the window, he hurled his clothing out then dived madly after it without any concessions to self-respect. A forgotten ruff trailed down disconsolately after him then the window was closed tight. The interrupted swain grabbed his apparel and sprinted off through the streets as if a pack of hounds were on his tail. Jane Diamond might have turned London into an enchanted garden but her husband had just made a tour with Westfield's Men seem infinitely more appealing. He did not stop running until he reached the comparative safety of his lodging and even there he barricaded himself in.

The lady herself was covered in distress but spared the ultimate horror of being interrogated by her husband. In response to his pounding, she told him that she was already in bed and that he was disturbing her slumbers. Accepting her word, he mumbled an apology and trudged off to spend the night in another chamber. Jane Diamond was so relieved by her narrow escape that she flung herself down and buried her head among the pillows. She was still rehearsing the excuse she would use next morning when she eventually fell asleep.

The real beneficiary of the night's work was the maidservant. In addition to gratitude from her mistress and money from Edmund Hoode, she was given a much more generous payment by Lawrence Firethorn. In the cloak and hat provided by the maidservant, any man could have looked like a returning husband who is only glimpsed once on a dark staircase, but the portrayal had been given real authenticity by a master of his craft. The absent spouse had cause to be eternally thankful to Lawrence Firethorn. Not only had the finest actor of the day deigned to impersonate him, he had also saved him by a hair's breadth from certain cuckoldry.

Firethorn collected his horse and rode off towards Shoreditch in a mood of self-congratulation. Once he had found out the address of Hoode's inamorata, he had won over the maidservant with a combination of charm and bribery, and been informed of the tryst. It had been simple to set up his performance and to achieve the desired response. A much-needed member of the company had been forcibly returned to its bosom and a wandering wife had been frightened into fidelity for at least a fortnight. Firethorn could now play the returning husband at home and while away his last night there in connubial delights. His wife, Margery, was made of sterner stuff than Jane Diamond. When she took her man into her bed, nothing and nobody would be allowed to interrupt her until she had wrung the last ounce of pleasure out of him. Firethorn's heels jabbed the horse into a gallop.

Catastrophe had been averted at the Queen's Head but the fire there had still been sufficiently destructive to merit a ballad on the subject. It was being sung in the taproom by a dishevelled old pedlar with a once-melodious voice that was thickened by drink and cracked by age. Leonard was among the crowd who listened to the ballad.

> *'The fearful fire began below*
> *A wonder strange and true*
> *And to the tiring-house did go*
> *Where loitered Westfield's crew*
> *It burned down both beam and snag*

And did not spare the silken flag.
Oh sorrow pitiful sorrow yet all this is true!

'Out run the ladies, out run the lords
And there was great ado
Some lost their hats and some their swords
Then out runs Firethorn too
The Queen's Head, sirs, was blazing away
Till our brave book holder had his say
Oh courage wonderful courage yet all this is true!'

Five verses were allotted to a description of how Nicholas Bracewell had helped to prevent the fire from spreading across the roof. The pedlar had not witnessed the event but he had picked up enough details from those who had to be able to compose his ballad with confidence. Using the licence of his trade, he embellished the facts wildly but nobody complained except Alexander Marwood. The landlord sang a woeful descant until he was cowed into silence by the reproach of the final verse.

'Be warned now you stage strutters all
Lest you again be catched
And such a burning do befall
As to them whose house is thatched
Forbear your whoring breeding biles
And lay up that expense for tiles
Oh sorrow pitiful sorrow and yet all this is true.'

Leonard clapped his huge palms together to lead the applause then lumbered forward to buy one of the copies of the ballad. Though he could not read, he stared at it in utter fascination and let out a rumbling laugh.

'I'll give this to Master Bracewell himself,' he said proudly. 'It will send him on his way in good humour.'

'Where does he travel?' asked a neighbour.

'With Westfield's Men, sir. Our yard is so damaged that they have no theatre and needs must make shift. They are forced to go on tour.' Leonard enjoyed being the holder of privileged information from his friend. 'The company makes for Oxford and Marlborough, I hear, but they will lose their book holder at Bristol.'

'Why so?'

'Because he must go on to Barnstaple.'

The other man blenched. 'Barnstaple?' he exclaimed, his West Country accent breaking through his London vowels.

'He has been called back home. And your voice tells me that you may be from those parts yourself.' The gravity of his news made Leonard speak in a respectful whisper. 'We have had strange portents. A message was sent to him but the messenger was poisoned here in this taproom.'

'How then was it delivered?' asked the man.

'The murder was message enough for Master Bracewell. He knows that he is needed in Barnstaple and he will be there when time and Westfield's Men allow him.'

The listener stroked his raven black beard and cursed himself for not killing his victim more promptly with the thrust of a dagger. The poison had only done its worst after the messenger had reached the intended recipient. Hired for his ruthless proficiency, the man had for once failed, and dangerous loose ends now trailed from his botched work. Those loose ends would have to be severed before he could collect his reward. He turned back to Leonard, who was still perusing the ballad with a childlike delight.

'When do Westfield's Men leave London?' said the man.

'At noon, sir.'

'From the Queen's Head?'

'No,' said Leonard, 'they would not show themselves here while our landlord still burns so brightly about their fire. I'll be taking this ballad to the Bel Savage Inn on Ludgate Hill. That is where they set forth upon their adventure.'

'What manner of man is this Nicholas Bracewell?'

'A hero, sir.' He waved the ballad. 'Here's warranty.'

'How would you pick him out from his fellows?'

' 'Tis no great art,' said Leonard. 'He is a proper man in every aspect with fair hair and a beard of like description. And though he lives among players who are practised at

47

catching the eye, he is the tallest and the best of them.' He beamed with nostalgia. 'Master Bracewell is my friend. I know him by his kindness and good fellowship.'

His companion thanked him and drifted away. He had heard enough to identify his target. Preparations had to be made. There must be no margin of error this time.

Nicholas Bracewell was the first to arrive at Ludgate Hill. Having spent the night at a friend's lodging in Southwark, he was up early to make the last arrangements for the departure of Westfield's Men. Taking a company out on the open highway was always a hazardous enterprise and it obliged them to travel armed and ready to repel attacks from one of the many bands of robbers, outlaws and masterless men who roved the countryside. The quality of their venues would fluctuate drastically, and their audiences would be neither as large nor as well tuned to their work as those in London. Bad weather would only hinder a performance at the Queen's Head. It could cause the company far more inconvenience if it struck them suddenly on some lonely road, soaking their costumes and sapping their morale. Nicholas Bracewell knew that wet, unhappy actors are far more inclined to friction than those who are dry and content.

'Good morrow, Nick!'

'Welcome!'

'A plague on this damnable tour!'

'Yes, Owen,' said Nicholas. 'and yet it is the one tour that is not forced upon us by the plague. London is having a healthy summer and there is no cause to close the theatres and throw us out of our occupation. Fires drives us away.'

'And it may keep us there in perpetuity.'

'The Queen's Head will be restored when we return.'

'But will that miserable maggot of a landlord allow us near the place? Diu! It gives me the sweating sickness just to look upon Marwood, yet for all that, I'd sooner endure his woebegone hospitality than drag my talent the length and breadth of England.'

Nicholas smiled. 'What about Wales?'

'That is different. I would gladly lead Westfield's Men across the border to the land of my ancestors.'

Owen Elias was an exuberant Welshman, who was becoming one of the mainstays of the company. Dark and manic, he was a gifted actor whose career had been held back by a quickness of temper and a fatal readiness to acquaint people with his true opinion of them. Wearied by his lack of progress, Elias had defected to his company's arch-rivals, Banbury's Men, and he was only brought back by the promise of promotion to the rank of sharer. Now that he had a real stake in Westfield's Men, his forthrightness was slightly diminished, but he still enjoyed a rancorous dispute when he felt—as he did without fail—that he had right on his side. Nicholas Bracewell was very fond of the Welshman and knew that his talent was strong enough to bear the extra weight that a tour placed upon it. A sturdy, fearless character of middle height, Owen Elias was also an extremely useful man to have at your side in a brawl or a swordfight.

'How now, gentlemen!'

'Hail, sirs!'

'I am glad to see your worships so well.'

'God save you all!'

'A thousand welcomes.'

'Farewell, dear London!'

'Owen, you rogue!'

'Nick, dear heart!'

Greetings assailed them as the company arrived, singly or in pairs, many with tearful wives or sweethearts clinging to their arms and a few, like Lawrence Firethorn, with their entire family. It would be a poignant leave-taking. The Bel Savage was an apposite location. Standing outside Ludgate itself, it was a big, sprawling, cavernous building that had been in existence for over a hundred and forty years and which occupied its site with half-timbered familiarity. Savage's Inn, as it had initially been called, was also known as the Bell on the Hoop, and the names had made common cause to give the property a clear title. Long before the first custom-built theatre in London was opened in 1576, the Bel

Savage had been staging plays in its courtyard, and it was in this evocative arena that Westfield's Men now met. Countless prizefights, fencing displays and other entertainments had been held there as well, but the actors saw it solely as part of their heritage. When they gazed up at the three levels of galleries that jutted out at them on every side, they saw cheering spectators and heard the ghost of some dear departed speech. It was only when they glanced across at their leader that they realised the ghost had come back to life because Lawrence Firethorn was declaiming one of the soliloquies he had spoken when he played Hector at that same venue in his younger days.

Nicholas Bracewell had chosen the meeting place as the closest alternative to the Queen's Head, but he might have been less ready to nominate it if he had known that it overlooked the very spot where the messenger from Devon had first been marked out by her killer. The yard continued to fill and servingmen brought out ale to whet the appetite of the travellers. All but one of the company had now appeared, and Nicholas was touched to see how many of its discarded members had also made the effort to get there in order to wave off their fellows. Thomas Skillen stood nearby, alternately chiding and hugging George Dart, the smallest and youngest of his assistant stagekeepers, clipping his ear as he warned him to discharge his duties correctly and enfolding him in his old arms lest it be the last time they might ever meet. It was a moving sight and it epitomised the true spirit of theatre. Tradition was handing over the torch to innovation.

George Dart would have quailed to hear that such a construction was being placed on his separation from a loved but feared mentor. The hired man occupied the most menial station in the company and it obliged him to be the butt and scapegoat with depressing regularity, yet at least he was still employed. A tour would double the already heavy work load that was thrust upon him and condemn him to play a string of minor parts in the plays, but even these guarantees of additional pain and humiliation were preferable to being cast out with Thomas Skillen and the others.

It was the scurrying legs of George Dart that Nicholas Bracewell used on the previous evening to notify the chosen company of the time and place of departure. The tiny stagekeeper had been given good news to spread while Nicholas reserved for himself the more onerous and saddening task of telling the rest of his fellows that they had been set aside. Knowing their haunts and their habits, he had spent long hours in tracking them down to pass on the bad tidings as gently as he could. It now struck him as a harsh irony that a man enjoined to oust so many others had then himself been ejected from a cherished home.

Emotions were running high in the yard and sobbing was breaking out among the women. When Nicholas saw husbands reassure their wives and lovers embrace their mistresses, his sense of desolation grew. The only person he wanted to see at that moment in time was not there. At the start of any previous tour, Anne Hendrik had always sent him on his way with love and best wishes, but there would be no farewell kiss this time. It emphasized the anomaly of his position. Nicholas was in limbo. He was making a journey between past lives, between a woman who had turned him out and a family he had disowned. It was a dispiriting itinerary because it left him without a final destination.

Someone else took note of his condition and intervened.

'Come here, Nicholas!'

'Gladly, mistress.'

'Where is your good lady?'

'Detained elsewhere, I fear.'

'Then I shall give you her due of kisses as well.'

Margery Firethorn fell on him with unashamed affection and planted her lips firmly on his. A handsome woman with a vivacity that tilted towards excess, she had always been fond of the book holder and sensed his dismay at Anne Hendrik's absence. Relationships within the theatrical world explored all the extremes of human behaviour, and Margery had learned to accommodate the caprices and eccentricities of her husband's colleagues. Nicholas Bracewell was the most stable man in the company in every way. If he had parted from a lover, it would not have been done lightly.

'Write to her, Nick,' she purred in his ear.

'What do you say?'

'Absence can soften even the hardest heart.'

She gave him another kiss then went across to snatch her children away from the arms of Lawrence Firethorn so that she could take a wifely leave of him. Like everything that the actor did, it was a performance in itself and he might have been playing a scene from a tragedy of love. Margery was an ideal soul mate, matching him in passion and tenderness, yet able to summon up reserves of fury that made even his tirades seem mild by comparison. Whether she was caressing or quarrelling with her husband, she was a most formidable woman. Husband and wife now reached down to lift up the children again into communal embrace. When it was over, the actor-manager leapt into his saddle, pulled out his rapier and held it high as he delivered a short speech to give inspiration to his company.

It was time to leave. Nicholas rode up beside him.

'We must tarry, master. Edmund is not yet here.'

'He was amongst the first to appear.'

'I do not see him.'

'That is because he does not wish to be seen.'

'He is hidden in the waggon?'

'Our poet has found another disguise. Mark this.'

Firethorn nudged his friend and indicated the crooked figure of an old parson who sat on a horse near the gateway. He was completely detached from the others and seemed to be deep in solemn contemplation. Firethorn brought him out of it with a clarion call.

'Edmund!' he cautioned, 'there's one Master Matthew Diamond here to seek a word with you.'

The parson came alive, the horse neighed and the pair of them went cantering out into the street. Westfield's Men took their cue and rolled out after him. The tour had begun.

Waving his hat in farewell, Lawrence Firethorn led his company away on his bay stallion, a prancing animal with a mettle commensurate with that of its rider. Barnaby Gill rode beside him on a striking grey mare, dressed in his finery and revelling in the opportunity to parade it through the streets. True to prediction, no money was forthcoming from their patron, but Lord Westfield did lend a bevy of horses from his stables so that most of the sharers could make the journey in the saddle. One who did not was Owen Elias, self-appointed driver of the wagon that carried the company's costumes, properties and scenic devices. The two mighty animals between the shafts were also pulling along the four apprentices and a couple of hired men. George Dart and two other unfortunates trotted at the wagon's tail with the weary resignation of convicted criminals being dragged to the place of execution. Only when the procession left London and needed to pick up speed would they be allowed to ride aloft with the others.

Nicholas Bracewell brought up the rear on the roan that he had inherited from the dead girl. This not only enabled him to make sure that the pedestrian members of the company did not straggle, it also gave him the opportunity for a last, long, hopeful gaze around the yard as he left it but there was still no sign of her. Leonard trotted beside him and thrust the ballad into his hand.

'You are famous, Master Bracewell.'

'That is not how your employer would speak of me.'

'Forget his hot words,' said Leonard. 'I will work on him in your absence and change his mind completely.'

'Thank you, my friend.'

'Come back to us one day.'

'We will, Leonard.'

'God be with you!'

Leonard had more to say but no breath with which to say it. He staggered to a halt and let his smile and his wave convey his message. Clustered around him were the other well-wishers, calling out their farewells and their encouragement. When the waggon and its cargo were swallowed up in the seething morass of people in the Bailey, a sudden grief descended on the watching group. Touring had its hardships but it was preferable to being left behind. As the company now headed west along Holborn, it left unemployed men and weeping women in its wake. Set apart from the former by virtue of his occupation, Leonard sided instead with the latter and copious tears trickled down his face. Westfield's Men made the Queen's Head an exciting place to work. It would seem dull and lifeless without them.

One observer was impervious to the general melancholy. The man with the trim attire and the well-barbered black beard was pleased with what he had witnessed. He had singled out Nicholas Bracewell at once and studied him intently. All that he needed to know was the route the company had taken out of the city and that was now clear. They had followed the line of the city wall as far as Newgate then swung left to take the Uxbridge Road. There was no hurry to follow them. He could judge their pace and how far it was likely to take them by nightfall. His pursuit needed to be stealthy. Their progress would be remarked by all whom they passed on the way, so it would be easy to pick up their trail by inquiry. Westfield's Men were a memorable spectacle.

He estimated that their first day on the road would take them into the Chilterns. Beaconsfield was probably too close a destination and Stokenchurch too far, so they would find some intermediate spot to spend the night. That was when he would strike. He carried dagger, rapier and club, but it was the knotted cord in his capcase that elected itself as the murder weapon. Putting his foot in the stirrup, he hauled himself up into the saddle and patted the leather bag, which held the cord. It would lie quietly in there like a snake in its lair until it was allowed out to strike with its deadly fangs. Nicholas Bracewell was evidently a strong and alert man who would need to be taken unawares. He was a far worthier target than the innocent girl whose life he had so casually snuffed out. She had been no match for him but Nicholas was a quarry he could be proud to hunt.

He would enjoy killing him.

Chapter Four

MORNING BROUGHT NO RELIEF FROM A NIGHT OF suffering. Anne Hendrik awoke from a troubled sleep to find that Nicholas Bracewell had left. His bed had not been used and his room had been stripped of all his possessions. As she stood alone in the small, bare, forlorn chamber, she was hit by an onrush of guilt that made her sway and reach out for support. She had been too quick to condemn him, too slow to give him the benefit of the doubt. Years of trust and understanding had been vitiated in one burst of anger, and he had been forced to sneak away from her house in the middle of the night like an outcast. It was a severe punishment for a crime that might not even exist.

What had Nicholas actually done? Twenty-four hours earlier she had thought him the best of men and could call up a thousand examples of his goodness and reliability. Then a young traveller staggered into the house in search of her lodger and all was lost. Evidently, the messenger was bringing a call for help, and it had sent Nicholas off to Devon, albeit by a winding route in the company of Westfield's Men. Anne Hendrik's first thought was that a woman was certainly involved. Shorn of her male attire and laid out on a stone slab, the girl had the look of a maidservant whose short hair and thickset features allowed her to conceal her sex. Her borrowed clothing had quality and her horse good breeding, so she had clearly worked in a prosperous household. No man would dispatch such an unprotected creature on such a difficult errand. Anne therefore assumed that she was sent by her mistress to summon the aid of Nicholas Bracewell, who was possibly her former lover, even her husband. But was this necessarily the case?

Nicholas did not deny the existence of a silent woman in his past but there did not have to be any romantic implications. Could the woman not just as easily be his mother, or sister or a relation? And was there not—now that she paused to reflect upon it—another reason for his refusal to offer her a full explanation? Nicholas was shielding Anne. The message that the girl brought had already cost one life. He did not wish to put hers in jeopardy as well. As long as Anne Hendrik was kept in ignorance, she was safe. That was why he could not take her completely into his confidence. He had begged for her trust and she had held it back. Anne's blind jealousy had clouded her judgement and blunted her finer feelings. She had lost him forever.

Yet even as she swung once more towards him, there were considerations that drew her back into pained disapproval. Nicholas Bracewell had rejected her appeal. Given a stark choice between staying with her and going to Barnstaple, he selected the latter. Anne was hit by the realisation that, even if Devon had not been an option, he would still have left with Westfield's Men. They were the true centre of his life. She was merely a pleasant appendage to a real existence that took place elsewhere. It was a doomed relationship. Margery Firethorn had once told her that to marry an actor was to hurl oneself head first into a whirlpool of uncertainty. Sharing her bed with a man of the theatre had left Anne Hendrik in the same helpless predicament. The most sensible thing she could do was to put him from her mind and concentrate on her work.

'You do not need to do this, mistress.'

'What is that, Preben?'

'I have been making hats for over thirty years and I am

56

too old to learn new ways. Please do not stand over me like that.' The Dutchman smiled respectfully up at her. 'You are in my light.'

'I am in your way,' she said with a shrug, 'but you are too kind to put it like that.' Anne glanced around the room where her four employees and the apprentice were bent over the respective hats that they were working on. 'Are there no more deliveries to be made this morning?'

'None.'

'What of our accounts?'

'They are all in order and up-to-date.'

'There must be something I can do, Preben.'

'No, mistress.'

'Perhaps I could help to—'

'Let hatmakers make their hats,' he suggested quietly. 'That is why you pay us. If you seek employment, go out and find new orders to keep our trade healthy.'

'That is good advice.'

'When Jacob was alive, he led by example and we toiled to keep up with his nimble fingers. His memory lives on to guide us. We will not skimp or slack because we are left alone in our workplace. Jacob Hendrik watches over us.'

Anne sighed and accepted the wisdom of his comments.

Preben van Loew was a tall, spare, wizened man in his fifties with skills that had been chased out of his native Holland and that had settled in London. Dressed severely in black, he was modest and unassuming and always wore a dark skull cap on his domelike head. Anne owed him a tremendous amount because he had kept the business going when Jacob Hendrik, his closest friend, had died, and he had instructed her in all the subtleties of his craft when she decided to take over the reins herself. Her talents lay in managing the others, finding commissions, dealing with their many customers and helping to design new styles of headgear. Until that morning, she also knew when to leave her staff alone to get on with their work. Now she was simply using them to occupy her mind, and her presence was disruptive.

With a gesture of apology, she moved to the door. Preben

van Loew spoke without looking up from his task of snipping through some material with his scissors.

'I had hoped to see Master Bracewell this morning.'

'Nicholas?'

'He is leaving with Westfield's Men.'

'I know.'

'He usually calls,' said Preben with mild censure. 'Whenever he has to go away for any length of time, he usually calls in here to bid us farewell.'

'Nicholas was in a hurry,' she explained.

'He has always had time for friends in the past.'

Anne Hendrik needed a moment to control her features. 'Times have changed,' she said, then went sadly out.

Buckinghamshire was painted in its most vivid colours at this time of year and its variegated richness was refreshing to those whose palates had been jaded by city life and whose nostrils had been clogged by its prevailing stench. Westfield's Men spent the first stage of their journey marvelling at the beauties of nature and inhaling clean country air. It helped them to forget their sorrows. The county was split in half by the Chilterns, which ran across it from east to west to lend a rolling charm. In earlier centuries, the hills had been entirely covered with magnificent beech trees, but they had been thinned out at the order of successive abbots of St Albans, who had owned much of the Chilterns, in order to help the Welsh drovers who were bringing their animals to sell in London. The beechwoods were ideal cover for thieves who stole cattle, sheep, pigs and geese with relative impunity until their places of ambush and refuge were felled by the axe.

Meadow and pasture now predominated, much of it set aside for the feeding and fattening of livestock from Wales before the last part of its trek to the capital. The clay soil responded to the plough and much corn was grown in addition to the grass and hay for the drovers' animals. Sheep seemed to be grazing everywhere and the rumble of their waggon could make a whole flock go careering around a field as if their tails were on fire. What was amusing to the passing company of actors, however, held a more serious meaning for others. Because of the profits to be gained from offering keep, many landowners converted from arable farming to sheep grazing. The subsequent enclosures brought grave hardship to small farmers, tenants and labourers, and Buckinghamshire was one of several midland counties that suffered periodic rioting against the new dispensation. A tranquil scene held rebellion in its sub-soil.

Lawrence Firethorn led his troupe at a steady pace and they only paused once, at an inn near Uxbridge, to take refreshment and to rest the horses after the first fifteen miles. Anxious to make as much headway as daylight and discretion would allow, the company then pressed on to Beaconsfield before making a final spurt of five miles to bring them to High Wycombe. Firethorn was satisfied. They were over halfway to Oxford and they were offered cordial hospitality at the Fighting Cocks, a fine, big, rambling inn with good food and strong ale in plenty, and rooms enough to accommodate them and three more such companies. For that night at least, they would all sleep in fresh linen.

Nicholas Bracewell took charge of the stabling of the horses and the unloading of the waggon. Everything was carried into the hostelry and put under lock and key. The item that Nicholas guarded most carefully was the chest in which he kept the company's stock of plays. Since most of them only existed in a single copy, the chest contained the very lifeblood of Westfield's Men. It was stowed beneath his bed in the chamber that the book holder was to share with Edmund Hoode, a particularly suitable venue since the chest held the entire dramatic output of the playwright.

Hoode had now exchanged his clerical garb for doublet and hose, but his sombre mood retained its hold on him. He stared down at the chest with doleful eyes.

'Such small accomplishment in so many years!' he said. 'That chest contains my whole misguided life, Nick.'

'Your plays have brought delight to thousands.'

'And misery to their author.'

'Edmund—'

'Bury that box in the ground,' he said. 'It will give but short work to the spade. Those are the useless relics of an idle brain and they should be covered with unforgiving earth.' He heaved a sigh and wrote an epitaph. 'Here lies Edmund Hoode, a poor scribe, who took his own life with quill and parchment, and left no memory of his passing. Pity him for the emptiness of his existence and despise him for the failure of his ambition. Amen.'

Nicholas put a consolatory arm around his shoulders. Yet another of his friend's love affairs had miscarried and yet another set of lacerations had been inflicted on a soul that was already striped with anguish. In view of his own broken relationship, the book holder now had a closer affinity with the wounded playwright.

'Let's go below for supper,' he said. 'A full stomach will remind you of your sterling worth, then you may tell me what has happened.'

'The words would choke me, Nick!'

'You need some Canary wine to ease their passage. Come, sir. Let's join the others.'

After locking the door, they went down to a taproom that was already bubbling with merriment. Westfield's Men had taken over the largest tables and were tucking into their meal with relish. Fatigue was soon washed away with ale. The landlord was a fund of jollity, the other guests warmed to the lively newcomers and there was a general atmosphere of camaraderie. It was all a far cry from the charred wreck of the Queen's Head and the ever-lamenting Alexander Marwood. Mine host of the Fighting Cocks clearly liked actors.

His affection was shared by some of the other guests.

'You are players from London, I hear,' said one.

'Westfield's Men,' announced Lawrence Firethorn with pride. 'No company has finer credentials.'

'Your fame runs before you, sir.'

'It is no more than we deserve.'

The man stood up from his chair to cross over to them. His grey hair framed a long, clean-shaven face that shone with affability, and his bearing indicated a gentleman. He

wore fine clothes and there was further evidence of his
prosperity in the rings that adorned both hands. He was in
excellent humour.

'Westfield's Men,' he said with a chuckle. 'Are you not
led by a titan of the stage called Lawrence Firedrake?'

'*Thorn!*' corrected the other, irritably. 'Firethorn, sir. If
you saw him act, you would never mistake his sharp thorn
for the quack of a drake. Lawrence Fire-*thorn!*'

'Pardon me, sir,' said the man. 'No offence was intended,
I assure you.' He glanced around. 'And is this same Master
Firethorn with you at this time?'

The actor-manager rose to his feet and drew himself to
his full height, hands on hips, feet splayed and barrel chest
inflated. Inches shorter than the older man, he yet seemed
incomparably taller as he imposed his presence upon the
taproom. An arrogant smile slit his beard apart.

'Lawrence Firethorn stands before you now, sir!'

'Then we are truly honoured,' said the man with a mixture of delight and humility. 'My name is Samuel Grace
and I travel to London with my daughter, Judith.' He turned
to indicate the attractive young woman who sat at his table.
'She has never seen a company of actors perform and I
would remedy that defect. I beg you, Master Firethorn, let's
have a play here and now.'

Other guests seized on the idea and added their pleas.
The landlord was in favour of anything that kept his guests
happy and the girl herself, pale, withdrawn and demure,
looked up with trembling interest. Firethorn knew better
than to comply before any terms had been offered. He held
up his hands to quieten the noise then spoke with mock
weariness.

'We thank you all for the compliment of your request,'
he said, resting a hand on the table, 'but we have travelled
well above twenty miles this day. You call for a play that
would last two hours and drain us to the very dregs. Our
reputation rests on giving of our best and we will not offer
your indulgence any less.'

'Come, come, we must have *something!*' insisted Samuel
Grace. He appealed to the other guests. 'Is that not so?'

'Yes,' agreed a voice from another corner. 'Give us a scene or two, Master Firethorn. Speeches to stir our hearts and songs to delight us.'

'Well-said, friend,' thanked Grace, resuming the task of persuasion. 'Amuse us with a dance at least. I never saw a play yet that did not end in a fine galliard or a merry jig. My daughter, Judith—God bless the child!—loves the dance. Westfield's Men surely have enough sprightly legs among them to carry it off. Entertain us, Master Firethorn,' he instructed, putting a hand into the purse at his belt, 'and you will be five pounds the richer for it.'

'I will add half as much again,' said the man in the corner, 'if you will put on your costumes and treat this assembly to the wonder of your art.'

Firethorn closed with the offer at once. Seven and a half pounds was considerably more than they would be given at other venues where they might stage a full play, and there was a possibility, if they gave enough pleasure, that the company could coax more money out of other purses. It was a good omen for their tour. Firethorn had a brief consultation with his book holder then he withdrew with his company to acquaint them with the nature of their impromptu performance and to don the appropriate costumes.

Nicholas, meanwhile, aided by George Dart and the other hired men, cleared tables and chairs to create an acting area at the far end of the taproom. Candles and lanterns were set with strategic care to shed light on the arena, and the guests adjusted their seating accordingly. Samuel Grace and his daughter occupied a prime position in the front row. The other sponsor of the entertainment—a rather stout, florid man in his twenties—placed his chair so that he could both view the stage and feast his gaze on the maiden modesty of Judith Grace. He licked his lips in a manner that suggested he had really parted with his money in order to be able to view her reactions to the performance. Judith Grace was to be his night's entertainment.

The stage was set, there was a fanfare of trumpets and Owen Elias entered in a black cloak to declaim a Prologue. He cut such a dashing figure and attacked the lines with such vigour that he drew a burst of applause. Lawrence Firethorn then swept in as Charlemagne, leading four armed soldiers and yet somehow managing to convince the onlookers that he led a mighty host. He addressed his troops before battle to instil a sense of mission into them then he led the army off with a cry of such piercing volume that it shattered a bottle of Venetian glass that stood on a table for ornament. Martial prowess was followed by rustic comedy as Barnaby Gill took over to play a scene with Edmund Hoode from *Cupid's Folly*. The whole room was soon awash with laughter, and Gill compounded their glee by concluding with one of the hilarious jigs that were his hallmark.

It was left to Richard Honeydew to restore order and raise the tone. Dressed as a French princess, he sat on a stool, stroking his long auburn hair and singing plaintive love songs to the accompaniment of the lute. He was the youngest and most talented of the four apprentices and his piping treble had a most affecting timbre. The audience was enchanted and Judith Grace was so struck with it all that she almost swooned. Her father steadied her with his arm.

'It is only a boy who sings, Judith, no real princess.'

'I will never believe that is a boy.'

'She is a lad, I tell you. Cunning in his skills.'

'It is a girl, father. As I am a girl—so is she.'

Her ogling admirer leaned across to make contact.

'Your father speaks true,' he said in an oily whisper. 'Our princess is a mere apprentice with a pretty voice. Girls are not allowed to appear upon the stage. Boys must take their parts and they do it with rare skill.'

'Thank you, sir,' said Judith, then she joined in the clapping as Richard Honeydew ended his contribution and curtseyed. 'This boy is a girlish miracle.'

Watching from the side, Nicholas Bracewell had also been touched by the apprentice's solo performance but for another reason. Edmund Hoode had written the lyrics of the songs but they had been set to music by Peter Digby, the brilliant if erratic leader of their consort, yet another to be discarded through the exigencies of the tour. Digby had been replaced by a hired man who, as an actor-musician, could offer double value, indeed, would have a range of functions that his former director could never fulfil. The substitute was now leaving the stage with his lute but the next day would find him harnessing the dray horses, loading the waggon, setting up a stage when they got to Oxford, sweeping and strewing it with fresh rushes, then conning his lines so that he could play half-a-dozen different roles in a play he had never seen before. An actor's life was a rehearsal for the madhouse.

As Richard Honeydew and his accompaniest left, Nicholas whisked all furniture from the stage so that the six dancers who now entered could cavort at will. Moving with formal grace, they went through a whole range of courtly dances, and the flagstones of the Fighting Cocks became a marble floor at a royal palace. Farce now surged gloriously onto the stage as Barnaby Gill, Owen Elias and Edmund Hoode played three gullible bumpkins who, rousing themselves from a drunken stupor, mistake an old friar for Saint Peter and imagine that they had died and been sent to heaven. In the robes of his order, Lawrence Firethorn was a jolly churchman who took advantage of the men's stupidity to catechise them about their sins and see if they were fit to be admitted through the gates of what was, in fact, the very ale house where they had first become hopelessly inebriated.

Firethorn was so well versed in the part that he was able to touch off explosions of mirth and give himself the pleasure of gazing upon Judith Grace until the uproar began to fade. He noted that the portly man near the front of the audience had made her the object of his attention as well, but her father was too busy leading the laughter to observe this. Firethorn's rising lust had the excuse it needed. He would not be pursuing the girl for his own gratification but in order to rescue her from the clutches of a leering stranger. His holy friar vibrated with irreligious intent.

The audience was now treated to music in a lighter vein as two other apprentices—Martin Yeo and John Tallis—sang duets with a fuller musical accompaniment. Wigs, gowns and makeup transformed them into winsome young ladies, though the lantern jaw of John Tallis had an unfeminine solidity to it. When they left the stage, the climax of the entertainment was reached in an extract from *Vincentio's Revenge*, a full-blooded tragedy that was synonymous with the name of Westfield's Men. Lawrence Firethorn, supreme as ever in the title role, had chosen to play the scene in which Vincentio declared his love for the beauteous Cariola, unaware that she was already dying from poison that had been administered in her wine. Richard Honeydew was a superb foil for him as the ill-starred heroine. Here were the two ends of the acting profession—veteran and apprentice—meeting in the middle to produce ten minutes of memorable theatre.

The audience was enthralled, but Firethorn's interest lay in one particular spectator. His wooing of Cariola was an elaborate courtship of Judith Grace, and the girl eventually seemed to realise this. Surprise gave way to alarm but he soon turned that into burning curiosity. He could feel her gaze following him like a beam of light and when he finally allowed himself to meet her eyes over the fallen body of Cariola, he saw that the conquest had been made. Firethorn and Richard Honeydew took several bows before they were allowed to leave then they returned with the full company to take a final toll of applause.

Samuel Grace was positively hopping with joy. He pressed the five pounds into Firethorn's hand and thanked him for bringing the magic of theatre into his daughter's life. The actor-manager was given the opportunity to kiss her hand and inhale her fragrance. It was enough. The caress that she gave his fingers and the secret glance that she shot him were sureties of mutual pleasure and he vowed to bring even more magic into her life in the privacy of her bedchamber. Firethorn had a competitor. The plump man first paid up his share of the cost then tried to engage her in conversation, but Judith Grace turned away with head downcast and hands in her lap. Other guests came up to make smaller contributions for the entertainment and ten pounds in all went into the communal purse of Westfield's Men.

As the guests dispersed to their beds, Firethorn treated the company to a last drink. One by one, they, too, began to slip away, conscious that they would be off again soon after dawn and hoping to snatch some sleep before first light scratched at the shutters. Lawrence Firethorn produced a monster yawn and pretended to drag himself up the staircase in order to fall upon his bed. The performance did not fool Edmund Hoode for a second.

'The old cat is mousing again!' he said bitterly. 'How does he do it, Nick? *Why* does he do it?'

'Because he is Lawrence Firethorn.'

'Well, let him go his way! I do not envy him. I forswear all women. They will never ensnare me again.'

'How so?'

They were among the last to linger in the taproom and sat companionably at a table. Nicholas Bracewell was in no mood to hear about a fractured romance, because the scene from *Vincentio's Revenge* had reminded him irresistibly of his own loss. As the poisoned Cariola died in twitching agony, he saw the murdered girl from Devon stretched out on the floor of his chamber in Bankside. It was not only the young messenger who was beyond his reach. Anne Hendrik was gone as well. The killer had poisoned their friendship. Notwithstanding the twinges that it might bring him, however, Nicholas agreed to listen to Edmund Hoode's tale of woe for two reasons. It was his duty as a friend to offer sympathy and it would advantage the whole company if he could help to dig their playwright out of his pit of despair and restore him to his rightful position. The chest that held his other plays also housed his foul papers of *The Merchant of Calais*, last of the three new dramas he was commissioned to write that year. If Hoode were allowed to rid his mind of its latest torment, he might find the impetus to reach once more for his pen.

With this hope in mind, Nicholas turned to him.

'Who is she, Edmund?' he asked. 'Tell me all . . .'

* * *

When Lawrence Firethorn adjourned to his bedchamber, he put the money into his capcase then turned his thoughts to Mistress Judith Grace. Young and untutored, she was desirous of experience and ready to place her education in the hands of a master. Her brief taste of theatre had opened up both mind and heart in a most bewitching way. It would be churlish of Firethorn to deny her the crowning act of pleasure. In the nakedness of their embrace, he would also be her knight in shining armour, jousting with the unwanted attentions of his adversary and knocking the rude fellow from his saddle. Altruism would be truly served.

Twopence in the palm of one of the chamberlains had bought him the location of her bedchamber, and he gave her plenty of time to detach herself from her father and make her preparations. Meanwhile, he addressed himself to his moustache and beard, peering by candlelight into his mirror in order to twist the one and curl the other to the required degree of excellence. When fingers and comb had done their work, he left the room, locked the door then crept along the dark corridor with the noiseless tread of a seasoned lecher. Lawrence Firethorn was equally surefooted, whether performing at the centre of the stage or going about some backstairs work.

He felt his way to her chamber, tapped lightly on the door and waited. There was no answer. He knocked more loudly but still elicited no reply. Trying the latch, he was pleased to find the door unbolted and was inside the room at once. A lone candle was flickering beside the bed like a gentle invitation. Judith Grace had covered her modesty with white linen and was a timid protuberance between the sheets. He simply had to take his place beside her and wear down her token resistance. Before he could bolt the door behind him, there was another tap, accompanied by a hoarse whisper and the raising of the latch. Lawrence Firethorn leapt back into the shadows as a hefty profile came into view. The newcomer shut the door behind him then gazed at the bed.

'Judith!' he called softly. 'I have come.'

'Then you may depart again,' growled Firethorn, stepping out to confront the man who had tried to force himself upon the girl earlier. 'Away, you rogue!'

'I say the same to you, sir!'

'Will you quarrel with *me*?'

'I'll quarrel with anyone who stands between me and my prize. You intrude, Master Firethorn. I am here by right.'

'You are a walking insult to womanhood!'

'I was chosen.'

'A blind hag with a withered arm would not choose you.'

'Nor you, sir!'

'She swooned at my feet.'

'She preferred my wooing.'

'She squeezed my palm.'

'She gave me her handkerchief.'

'Stay further, and I'll strike you!' hissed Firethorn then he blinked as he actually heard what the man had just told him. 'Handkerchief?'

'What clearer signal could be given?'

'Handkerchief!'

'I have it here.'

Even in the gloom, Firethorn could see that it was hers and catch her perfume upon it. This fat and unprepossessing creature did actually have a reason for being in her bedchamber. The actor spun round to accuse Judith Grace but he was talking to some large pillows. Each man had thought himself a favoured lover when both of them were mere gulls. It was Firethorn who reacted most quickly to the situation.

'We are abused, sir,' he said.

'But why?'

'Return to your chamber.'

'My chamber?'

'They mean to rob us.'

'Heaven forfend!'

They went out, groping their way in opposite directions to their rooms. Firethorn found his unlocked and ran across to his capcase. The night's takings had vanished along with the rest of the money he carried. While he had been sliding off to deflower a virgin, she and her accomplice had robbed him and his company of over fifteen pounds. Vengeance sent molten lava coursing through his veins and he reached for his rapier. The clatter of hooves on the cobbles below took him quickly to the window where moonlight gave him a glimpse of two figures riding out of the yard before they merged conspiratorially with the darkness. Firethorn slashed the air wildly with his sword in a futile display of rage. What hurt him most was not that the thieves had escaped with his money, that of his supposed rival and, presumably, with additional valuables lifted from other unsuspecting guests. Real mortification came from the affront to his professional pride.

Lawrence Firethorn had been out-acted.

'Women are all devils, Nick,' said Edmund Hoode with glazed horror. 'They flaunt their beauty to drag us down to hell.'

'That is not the case here,' observed Nicholas.

'It is. She held me in thrall.'

'The fault may lie with you rather than her, Edmund.'

'Indeed, it does! I confess it. That is the hideous truth of it. I put my head willingly upon the block of disgrace. I am mine own executioner.'

Nicholas disagreed but he was too tactful to explain why. From what he had heard, he was fairly certain that the axe had been held by a familiar headsman. The unexpected return of an irate husband had the ring of stage management to him, and he guessed at once who had usurped his role. To tell Edmund Hoode that he had been duped by a colleague as well as being deprived of his carnal rewards would be to sew perpetual enmity between playwright and actor-manager. Nicholas was forced to conceal what he would never condone.

His distraught companion detected a pattern.

'Disaster is triple-tongued,' he groaned. 'This is the third time that it has blown its blast in my ears.'

'You have had ill luck, Edmund, that is all.'

'I have been punished for meddling with devils.'

'You do the lady a disservice.'

'Look back, Nick. You were there on both occasions.'

'Where?'

'At the scene of my calamities.' Hoode counted them off on his fingers. 'One, my play *The Merry Devils*. Remember what afflictions *that* brought in its wake, and how I suffered vile torments. Two, my other venture into hell, *The Devil's Ride Through London*. I paid for that rash mockery as well. Our theatre was all but burned to the ground. Three, Mistress Jane Diamond. The vintner was not her true husband. She was contracted to Satan himself and set me up to suffer the worst pangs of all. I have been well paid for my folly.'

'It is not so, Edmund.'

'Where is your proof?'

'Let me follow your numbers.' Nicholas held up his finger. 'One, *The Merry Devils* was not your play but a work jointly written by you and Ralph Willoughby. He it was who had the kinship with the Devil and who paid for it with his life. You at least survived. Two—'

But Nicholas got no further with his argument. Lawrence Firethorn came hurtling down the stairs with his sword in his hand and his teeth bared. The book holder abandoned one injured party and rushed to the assistance of a more recent one. Firethorn was berserk.

'What ails you, sir?' said Nicholas.

'Betrayal! Perfidy! Wickedness.'

Hoode actually laughed. 'She turned him down,' he said.

'The villains have robbed me!' yelled Firethorn. 'They took all the money that we strove to earn tonight.'

'How?' asked Nicholas.

'They got into my chamber while I remained here below. It was only when I checked the contents of my capcase that I discovered the theft.'

'Hold there, Lawrence,' said Hoode sceptically. 'Our takings went into your purse and stayed there until you went upstairs. They could not steal money that was not yet placed in your chamber.'

'Do you call me a liar!'

Firethorn bludgeoned him into silence with a burst of vi-

tuperation then gave an edited version of events. He could
never admit that he had been lured away from his room by
the wiles of a pretty face, though Nicholas was already certain that that was what had happened. Hearing of the flight
of the putative father and daughter, he pressed for detail.

'Has anyone else been robbed?'

'That fellow who paid us for our entertainment.'

'Master Fat-Guts?' said Hoode.

'They emptied his pockets as well.'

'How do you know?' wondered Nicholas.

'I met the man on the landing.'

'Did he *tell* you that he had been fleeced?'

'Forget about him, Nick,' said Firethorn. 'Our own
money is gone. That is our only concern.'

'I fear not.'

'Why?'

'There is deep villainy here. Call the landlord.'

'He cannot chase those two rogues.'

'They may be three in number,' said Nicholas.

Hauled from his bed, the landlord was alarmed at the
news and identified the obese guest as one William Pocock.
Nicholas asked to be taken to the man's bedchamber, and
all four of them went tramping up the staircase. The book
holder's fears were realised. When he saw that Pocock's
room was empty, he guessed that the man had gone off to
join his two partners. Evidently, all three had worked clev-
erly together.

Lawrence Firethorn was completely abashed. Cheated by
a young woman, he had also been led astray by another
ruse, for Pocock's role in the enterprise had been to detain
him long enough in Judith Grace's bedchamber for his confederates to gain entry to the actor's own room. Firethorn
was too busy nursing his bruised dignity to spy any poetic
justice in it all, but Nicholas saw it at once. Having caused
havoc in a bedchamber for Edmund Hoode, the culprit had
now experienced shame and panic of the same order. It was
not a thought over which the book holder lingered. In the
vague hope that Pocock might not yet have left the premises, he ordered the others to search the establishment and

went racing off downstairs to the taproom. He grabbed one of the lanterns and hastened out into the yard.

The place was deserted. Apart from the whistle of a slight breeze and the occasional movement of horses in the stables, there was no noise. To make a swift departure, Samuel Grace and his daughter—and Nicholas doubted very much if that was their true relationship—must have had their mounts saddled and ready. Pocock would likewise have an animal in waiting that could be ridden instantly away. Nicholas therefore headed for the stables, using the lantern to throw its meagre light a few paces ahead of him. He reached the door of the first stable block, lifted the wooden bar that held it in place, drew it open and went in. Hooves shifted in straw and there was a stray whinny from the far end of the stables. All the horses were tethered to their mangers. Wooden pails of water stood beside them.

Nicholas checked each beast but none was saddled. If Pocock had a horse in readiness, it must be on the other side of the yard. The book holder turned to walk back down the rows of horses when he had a mild shock. The door, which he had left open, had now been shut, and the faint square of light that he would have aimed for had disappeared. If the wind had been responsible, the door would have creaked on its hinges and banged. Some human agency was involved. The animals confirmed it because they became restive and inquisitive. One neigh set off a few more, a bucket was kicked over and the rustling of straw was constant. The lantern was an inadequate guide but it made Nicholas an obvious target, so he quickly doused the flame and put the object aside. He slipped a hand around to the back of his belt to remove his dagger from its scabbard.

Danger was an old enemy and Nicholas was not afraid of it. Anyone who walked home through the fetid streets and lanes of Bankside every evening developed a sixth sense for an impending threat. Who was in the stable and why was his presence so menacing? It was surely not Pocock, whose sole interest must be in immediate flight. Slovenly and overweight, the man was ill-equipped to take on the powerful Nicholas in any kind of fight. And what motive could he possibly have? The book holder carried no money. He was up against a more practised adversary, one who could close a squeaking wooden door without making a murmur, one who could lie patiently in wait for his quarry to come within range. Was he armed with sword, dagger or club? Or could he rely on the strength of his muscles to subdue Nicholas?

Amid the breathing of the animals and the motion of their feet, Nicholas strained his ears to listen for sounds of the man's whereabouts. The clink of harness made him swing around but it had been made by the toss of a horse's head against a dangling bridle. A startled neigh made him face in the opposite direction but he could make nothing out in the thick gloom. It was the rat that betrayed him. It came out of the straw with such rustling urgency that Nicholas found himself jabbing his dagger in that direction. Something hard and numbing crashed down on his hand to knock the weapon from his grasp then the man was upon him from behind, tightening a knotted cord around his neck and trying to put his knee into the small of Nicholas's back to get leverage. The cord had sharp teeth and seemed to be eating right through his throat. It was being held by a man who had used this instrument of death before.

Nicholas responded at once, using both elbows to pump backwards into the man's ribs then slipping one of his hands under the rope when there was a fleeting relief in tension. He began to twist and turn so violently that the man had to adjust his footing all the time and there was a slight loss of venom in the rope's bite, but Nicholas could still not dislodge him and his own strength was waning. His cheeks reddened, his eyes bulged, his veins stood out, his mouth went dry and the pounding in his head became more insistent. He felt as if a dozen sword points were simultaneously pushing their way through his neck in order to meet in the middle.

Summoning up all of his energy, he dipped down low then launched himself backwards, knocking the man into the side of a loose box with such force that his grip on the cord was lost. Nicholas tore it from his neck, threw it away and tried to meet his attacker face-to-face, but the flank of a horse came round at him to buffet him away. The man had had enough. Seeing the chance of escape, he scrambled to his feet and got in a glancing punch to Nicholas's face before he scuttled off down the stables and out through the door. It banged madly this time and Nicholas lurched towards it, but the strangulation had squeezed much of the power from his limbs and he could offer no swift pursuit. The attacker was, in any case, already in the saddle and spurring his horse away from the inn. By the time Nicholas staggered out into the yard to rub at the stinging red weal on his neck and stare around with blurred eyes, his adversary was hundreds of yards away.

When the mist cleared sufficiently from his mind for him to be able to think properly, Nicholas realised why the attempt on his life had been made. Simply because she bore a message to him, the life had been mercilessly crushed out of a harmless girl. Now that he was heading for home, Nicholas had become a potential murder victim. Someone was going to great lengths to stop him from reaching Barnstaple and he was lucky to be able to continue the journey. He would now do so with greater vigilance and increased determination because one thing was certain. The man who gained the advantage over him in the stables was undoubtedly proficient in his trade. He would strike again.

The three confederates met up again at an abandoned hovel near Stokenchurch. By the light of a candle, they counted out their booty and divided it into four equal parts. The older man handed one share to the girl and another to the erstwhile William Pocock. As their leader, he claimed the other half of the money and stuffed it into a capcase that was already bulging. They compared notes over the night's escapades and chuckled for a long time at the embarrassment they had inflicted on Westfield's Men.

'Firethorn was the biggest gull of them all,' said the older man. He put a sly arm around the girl's slim waist. 'To think he could bed my wife with a wave of his arms and couple of ranting speeches. He got his just deserts. No, you are all mine, are you not, Judith Grace?'

'Yes, Father,' she said with a sensual giggle.

'Kiss me.'

The other man nibbled on a stolen leg of ham while the two of them enjoyed a long embrace with guzzling kisses. The young woman eventually threw a compliment across at their corpulent associate.

'Ned served us well,' she said.

'So you did, Ned,' agreed her husband.

'Shall we work that ruse again?' asked Ned.

'No,' said the older man. 'We must find new ways to pluck the chicken each time or its feathers will stick. And we must give mine host of the Fighting Cocks a long rest before we use his inn as our lure again. We'll ride to the other side of Oxford before we choose our next cony. That will mean a change of apparel for Ellen and me.'

'I am Ellen again, am I?' complained his wife. 'I so enjoyed being Mistress Judith Grace. Virginity becomes me.'

'And I was happy as William Pocock,' said Ned.

The older man was emphatic. 'New places, new garb, new names. It is the one sure way to elude capture. If they search for a Samuel Grace, his beautiful daughter and a fat gentleman with his breeches on fire for her, they will not look at two old Oxford scholars and their servant.'

They ate, drank, discussed their plans further then lay out their bedding for the last few hours before dawn. As the three of them settled down, the old man came to a decision that made him cackle afresh.

'We'll hit them again.'

'Who?' asked Ned.

'Westfield's Men.'

'Think of the danger,' warned Ellen.

'They would tear us apart if they knew,' said Ned.

'That is the attraction,' explained their leader. 'It is a battle of wits here. Lawrence Firethorn is the prince of his profession and I of mine. We are well matched. He can play fifty parts at a moment's notice but he could not dissemble as well as I can.'

'Do you think he knows who you are?' said Ellen.

'He will, my sweet.'

She was proud of her husband. 'The landlord will tell him when he sees the truth. There is only one man who could lay such a bold plot for a whole company of players—and that is the famous Israel Gunby.'

'The infamous and wanted Israel Gunby,' said Ned.

'The *great* Israel Gunby,' she added.

Ellen snuggled up to her husband and they lay entwined. Though they shared a mean hovel in the Chilterns instead of a comfortable bed at the Fighting Cocks, she did not mind. This was where she wanted to be. They were rich, happy and free. The open road was their kingdom and they could feed off travellers whenever and wherever they liked. Westfield's Men had been given a generous amount of money by them and then robbed of far more. It lent a sense of style to the whole enterprise. She kissed her husband again then clung to his lean body like a squirrel holding on to the bark of the tree. Israel Gunby was the most notorious highwaymen of them all, and she loved him for it. Life with him was continuous excitement. Only one question now remained.

When would they need to kill their accomplice?

Chapter Five

LAWRENCE FIRETHORN'S WRATH DID NOT ABATE DUR-
ing the night. He awoke at cock-crow, caught sight
of his defiled capcase and lusted for blood. George
Dart was the first to feel the impact of his employer's ire.
Hauled from his bed and beaten soundly, Dart was ordered
to get the rest of the company up before doing a dozen
other chores, which would deprive him of all hope of
breakfast. As fresh targets came down into the taproom at
the Fighting Cocks, the actor-manager aimed abuse and accusation at them. Barnaby Gill was roundly mocked,
Edmund Hoode was berated, Owen Elias was threatened,
Richard Honeydew was criticised for his performance as
Cariola on the previous night, John Tallis was treated to a
withering analysis of his character defects and other members of the company came off far worse. In his general an-
imosity, Firethorn even had stern words for Nicholas
Bracewell. It was disconcerting.

Westfield's Men were even more disturbed when they
heard about the loss of their money. The success of their
first night on the road had been illusory. They now saw
only rank failure and it was less than reassuring to be told
that they had been the latest prey of a daring criminal. Everyone had heard of the man who outwitted them.

'Israel Gunby!'

'The master thief of the highway.'

'The most pernicious villain alive.'

'He would rob you of the clothes you stand up in.'

' 'Tis a wonder we were not murdered in our beds.'

'Israel Gunby is a monster.'

'A sorcerer.'

'A fiend of hell.'

'They say that Gunby once stole fifty sheep from a Warwickshire farmer then sold them back to the poor fool at market for three times the price.'

'Another time, he robbed a small party of travellers in a wood near Saffron Walden and rode off with their belongings. Not knowing that the rogue had placed an accomplice among them, they fell to boasting how clever they had been in giving the highwaymen the dross in their purses while holding back their real valuables, which they kept hidden about their persons. When Gunby robbed them again but two miles down the road, he was able to take everything he missed the first time.'

'I heard that he took their horses and boots as well.'

'Israel Gunby would steal *anything*!'

'The hair off your head.'

'Off your arse.'

'And your balls.'

'He'd rob Christ of his cross on the road to Calvary.'

'Add one more tale,' said Gill wickedly. 'Of how Israel Gunby dangled his whore in front of a great actor until his pizzle was giving off steam. She invited this idiot to share her bed for the night and while he was gone, she and Gunby broke into his chamber and took everything they could lay their thieving hands on. The great actor then—'

'No more!' decreed the great actor with stentorian force. 'I do not wish to hear the name of Israel Gunby ever again—unless it be linked with the date of his execution. I would ride halfway across England to see that foul rogue hanged by the neck. Until then, gentlemen, until then, Israel me no Israels and—if you value your lives—Gunby me no Gunbies.'

Lawrence Firethorn enforced his edict by glaring in turn at each man then he gave the signal to leave. He was keen to get away from the scene of his disgrace as soon as he could. With their leader at the head of the column, they set off from the Fighting Cocks on the road to Oxford, hoping that it might offer a fairer return for their labours. The exhilaration of the previous day had been replaced by a nagging pessimism. It was almost as if they had packed Alexander Marwood into the waggon with the rest of the luggage.

Nicholas Bracewell was glad to leave the inn but not before he had questioned the landlord and his ostlers. None of them could shed any light on the mystery attacker in the stables. After Westfield's Men arrived, no other traveller sought a bed for the night at the same hostelry. This meant that the man was either already there when they reached the Fighting Cocks or he had come along later and bided his time in the darkness until his chance came. Nicholas settled for the latter explanation. The would-be killer could not have been certain that they would choose that particular inn as their resting place. It was much more likely that he had trailed them from London, watched through a window and waited for the moment to pounce. Nicholas soon came round to the view that he was jumped on by the same man who had poisoned the girl. That gave him two scores to settle. He was riding the same horse that had carried the girl to her death, and he was determined it would not lose another passenger until it reached home in Barnstaple. Nicholas was therefore extremely wary as they moved along, scanning the horizon on all sides of them and exercising caution whenever the road took them beneath overhanging trees.

It was an hour before he accepted that he was safe in the bosom of the company. The man would not strike at him there. Nicholas was still a long way from Devon and there would be ample opportunities for a surprise attack on him during the journey. Lawrence Firethorn and the others were still inwardly cursing Israel Gunby and his two associates, but at least they had been visible rogues. The man who tried to strangle Nicholas had been a phantom, a creature of the night who was a natural predator. Nicholas knew his strength and could guess at his height from the feel of his body. A beard had brushed his head in the struggle. Beyond that, he had no information whatsoever about the man except that he brought a remorseless commitment to his work. He was not a person to abandon a task he had been set. The only way that Nicholas Bracewell could save his own life was by taking that of his assassin first.

'Not arsenic, I think, for that bears no taste in acid form. And we have evidence that the deceased found the ale very bitter to the tongue.' His sigh had a distant admiration in it. 'The means of death was very cunning. The girl had never drunk ale before and would not recognise its taste. She must have thought it was always as sharp as that.'

'So what was put into her ale?'

'I could not say unless they held a post mortem and even then we might not be certain. There are so many poisons that will serve the purpose and she was given a lethal dose of one, no doubting that. She must have been strong and healthy to hold out against it for so long.'

Anne Hendrik was still brooding on the death of her visitor and its sad consequences. That morning, in search of elucidation, she called on the surgeon who had been summoned to her house when the girl's condition had given alarm. He was a small, fussy, self-important man in his fifties with a grey beard that curled up like a miniature wave and bushy eyebrows of similar hue. He treated Anne with the polite pomposity of someone in possession of an arcane knowledge that can never be shared with those of lesser intelligence.

She tried to probe the mystery of his calling.

'Can you tell me nothing else about her?' she said.

'I examined her for barely two minutes.'

'Nicholas thought he smelled sulphur on her lips.'

'Master Bracewell is no physician,' he retorted with a supercilious smile. 'Do not rely on *his* nostrils to give us a diagnosis here.'

'He mentioned hemlock and juice of aconite . . .'

Sarcasm emerged. 'Then you should apply to *him* for counsel and not to me. Clearly, he can teach us all in these matters. I had not thought some minion of the theatre would one day instruct me in my profession.'

'He simply offered an opinion.'

'Do not foist his ignorance upon me.'

'Nicholas has seen victims of poison before.'

'I see them every week of my life, Mistress Hendrik,' said the outraged surgeon. 'Husbands poisoned by wives and wives by husbands. Brothers killing each other off with ratsbane to collect an inheritance. Enemies trying to win an argument with monkshood or belladonna. I have watched arsenic do its silent mischief a hundred times, and I could name you a dozen other potions that scald a stomach and rot the life out of a human being.' He looked aggrieved. 'And will you tell me that Master Nicholas Bracewell is a worthier man than I to discuss these matters?'

'Of course not, of course not . . .'

Anne had to spend two minutes calming him down and a further three apologising before she could get anything like guidance out of him. Surgeons were jealous of the high regard in which doctors and physicians were held, and it made them acutely conscious of occupying a more lowly station in the world of medicine. This member of the fraternity was especially prone to stand on his dignity. Only when his ruffled feathers had been smoothed did he consent to offer his informed opinion.

'I look for three things in a corpse,' he said briskly.

'What are they, sir?'

'Colour, position, odour. They are my spies.' He plucked at his beard. 'Her complexion told me much and her grotesque position indicated the agony of her death. The odour was faint but I could detect the aroma of poison.'

'What did it contain?' she pressed.

'Who knows, mistress? Some deadly concoction of water hemlock, sweet flag, cinquefoil and monkshood, perhaps. I could not be sure. White mercury, even.' He flicked a hand as he made a concession. 'And there might—I put it no higher than that—there might have been the tiniest whiff of sulphur. Red and yellow sulphur, mixed together with the right ingredients, could leave that tortured look upon her face.'

'How would it have been administered?'

'In the form of a powder or a potion.' He put the tips of his fingers together as he pondered. 'It must have been a potion,' he decided. 'Powder would not have dissolved fast enough in the ale. It would have stayed on the surface too long. My guess is that the guilty man carried the poison in a little earthenware pot that was closely corked. A second was all he would need to empty his vile liquid into the girl's drink.' He signalled the end of the conversation by opening the door for her to leave. 'That is all I may tell you, mistress. I bid you good day.'

'One last question . . .'

'I have other patients to visit and they still live.'

'Where would such a poison be bought?'

'Not from any honest apothecary.'

'It was obtained from *somewhere* in London.'

'Apply to Master Bracewell,' he said waspishly. 'He is the fount of all human wisdom on this subject. Good-bye.'

Anne Hendrik found herself back out in the street with only half an answer, but she had learned enough to encourage her to continue her line of inquiry. She went straight off to seek an interview with the coroner who had taken statements from them when the unnatural death was reported. It was a typically busy morning for him and she had a long wait before he could spare her a few minutes of his time. When she identified herself, he opened his ledger to look up the details of the case in question. The coroner was a distinguished figure in his robes of office but a lifelong proximity to death had left its marks upon him. Slow and deliberate, he had a real compassion for the people whose corpses flowed before him as unceasingly as the Thames. Anne Hendrik's request was both puzzling and surprising.

'A post mortem?' he said.

'To establish the cause of death.'

'We have already done that.'

'Can you name the poison that killed her?'

'No,' he confessed. 'Nor can I show you the dagger that murdered this man or the sword that cut down that one. Death scrawls its signature across this city every hour of the day. We cannot have a post mortem each time in order to decipher its handwriting.'

'If it is a question of money . . .'

'I do not have men enough for the task.'

'This girl died in my house. I am involved.'

'Then you should have attended her funeral, mistress.'

Anne gaped. 'Funeral?'

'The girl was buried earlier this morning.'

'Where? How? By whose authority?'

'Master Bracewell gave order for it.'

'But he did not know the young woman.'

The coroner gave a wan smile. 'He cared enough to pay for a proper burial. The poor creature was not just tossed into a hole in the ground with nobody to mourn her, like so many unknown persons. Master Bracewell is a true Christian and considerate to a fault. Because he could not be present himself, he arranged for a friend to take his place and pray for her soul.'

'A friend? Do you know the name?'

'He did not give it, mistress.'

'Was it a man or a woman?'

'A man.'

'A member of the company who was left behind?'

'All I remember is the name of an inn.'

'The Queen's Head in Gracechurch Street?'

'Yes, that was it. This friend worked there.'

Anne Hendrik had an answer. It was not the one she either expected or wanted but it pointed her in a direction that might yield a fuller reply. An upsurge of emotion warmed her. The body may have been buried but Anne's love for Nicholas Bracewell had come back emphatically to life. He had shown kindness and concern for the murdered girl. In paying for her funeral—he earned only eight shillings a week from Westfield's Men—he was making a real financial sacrifice. There was another factor that weighed heavily with Anne. The coroner spoke of Nicholas with the respect he would only accord to a gentleman. The surgeon made slighting remarks about Nicholas and dismissed him out of hand, but the coroner, an older and more perceptive judge of character, took the book holder at his true value. That pleased her.

She asked where the funeral had taken place, thanked the coroner profusely for his help then went off to pay her last respects to the dead girl.

Bright sunshine and beautiful landscapes were completely wasted on Westfield's Men. Lawrence Firethorn was forcing such a pace upon them and spreading such an atmosphere of gloom that they had no chance to enjoy any of the pleasures of travel. Actors were contentious individuals at the best of times and they now began to bicker in earnest. Nicholas Bracewell expended much of his energy intervening in quarrels with good-humoured firmness and trying to lift the company out of its Marwoodian mood of triumphant unhappiness. It was a very long and punishing journey to Oxford.

Barnaby Gill was at the forefront of the cavalcade and the carping. He heaped ridicule on Firethorn for being tricked so easily out of the money they had won with their extempore performance at the Fighting Cocks, and he insisted that he should take charge of any income in future, since he would never be enticed away from it by a devious woman. The actor-manager endured the vicious criticism for as long as he could then launched a counter-attack. Both men lapsed back into a sullen restraint. It was another five miles before Gill felt able to speak again.

'The Queen has visited Oxford on two occasions,' he said knowledgeably. 'The first time was long ago and the second but last year.'

'What care I for Her Majesty's perambulations?' said Firethorn grumpily. 'They have no bearing on us.'

'But they do, Lawrence. Oxford is a university town and it was university theatre that they thrust upon her. True players were passed over for callow undergraduates.' He pulled his horse in close to that of his colleague. 'Will you hear more of this?'

'Do I have any choice?' moaned the other.

'Let me begin . . .'

Barnaby Gill was not just an outstanding actor with comic flair, he was also the self-appointed archivist of Westfield's Men and of the wider world of theatre. His mind was an encyclopaedia of plays and players, and he could call up with astonishing clarity every performance in which he had ever appeared. Other companies were not ignored and he could list the entire repertoires of troupes such as the Queen's Men, Worcester's Men, Pembroke's Men, the Chamberlain's Men, Strange's Men, now amalgamated with Admiral's Men, having already merged with Leicester's Men on the death of the latter's patron in Armada year, and—since they were the major thorn in the flesh of his own company—he knew every detail of the work of Banbury's Men. For other reasons, Gill also kept abreast of the activity of the boy players attached to the choir schools of St Paul's and the Chapel Royal at Windsor, as well as at such schools as Merchant Taylors'. If a play had been staged during his extensive lifetime, he knew when, where and by whom.

'Our dear Queen,' he said with reverential familiarity, 'first visited Oxford in the year of our lord 1566 and lodged at Christ Church. It was there she witnessed a performance of *Palamon and Arcyte*.'

'I have played in such a piece,' boasted Firethorn.

'That was by another hand, Lawrence. It is an old tale and told by many a playwright. At Oxford, it was the work of Richard Edwardes that the Queen witnessed in Christ Church Hall.' He rolled his eyes. 'Unhappily, that is not all Her Majesty saw on that fateful night.'

'What else, Barnaby?'

'Tragedy, misfortune, chaos!'

'You must have been a member of the cast.'

'I was not *in* the play!' returned Gill, 'Nor yet of an age when drama had claimed me for its own. To return to my story about the Queen . . . Her courtiers occupied balconies that had been built onto a wall and she herself sat in a canopied chair on a platform with scenic decoration around it. Now we come to the disaster—'

'Enter Barnaby Gill!'

'Enter a large crowd from university and town. They came in with such force that they breached a wall protecting a staircase and brought it down upon them. Three persons were killed and five injured. The Queen was mightily upset.'

'Had she hoped for more slaughter than that?'

'She sent her own surgeons to attend to the injured.'

'What of *Palamon*?'

'It was well played, by all accounts, and made the Queen laugh heartily. She was very pleased with the author and gave him thanks for his pains.'

'Actors create plays,' boomed Firethorn, 'not authors!'

'Give a poet his due.'

'Keep the scribbling rascals in their place.'

'This Richard Edwardes had left the university to become Master of the Children of the Chapel, but he returned to present the first part of his play. The Queen was also favoured with the second part of *Palamon* days later, when no mishap occurred.' He wagged an admonitory finger. 'You have heard a cautionary tale, Lawrence.'

'I marked its warning.'

'What is it, then?'

'Do not invite the Queen to our plays.'

'Beware of wild behaviour. Control our spectators.'

'My performance will keep them in strict order.'

'Yes, they will fall asleep together.'

'I can captivate any audience.'

Gill sniggered. 'As you did at the Fighting Cocks, named after you and your fat rival.'

Firethorn turned to strike him but the mocking clown had already pulled on the reins of his horse and sent it trotting to the rear of the party. While the actor-manager fumed alone, his colleague struck up a conversation with the apprentices, who lolled on the waggon. Richard Honeydew had an inquiring mind and a natural respect for his elders.

'Have you been to Oxford before, Master Gill?' he said.

'I have been everywhere, Dicky.'

'What manner of place is it?'

'A comely town, set in lovely countryside, and bounded by a wall. It has fine colleges, large churches and excellent hostelries. Let us hope it will be kind to Westfield's Men.'

'They say that Cambridge is prettier.'

'What do you know of prettiness?' asked Gill with a twinkle in his eye. A shrewd glance from Owen Elias in the driver's seat made the horseman amend his tone. 'Cambridge? No, boy. It does not hold a candle to Oxford. If you have a mind to listen, I'll tell you why ...'

Nicholas Bracewell was close enough to overhear the exchange between the two of them but he was not worried. Owen Elias was protection enough for the apprentices. Gill's proclivities were well known and largely tolerated in the company, but there was an unwritten rule that its own boys would remain untouched. Whenever damson lips or an alabaster cheek or a graceful neck made Barnaby Gill forget this rule for a second, Nicholas was usually on hand to remind him of it. The older boys knew enough to take care of themselves when the comedian was around, but Richard Honeydew still had the unsuspecting innocence of a cherub. Nicholas would ensure that it was not taken rudely away from him.

'That is the curious thing, Nick,' said Edmund Hoode.

'Curious?'

'My sonnets, my verse, my inspiration.'

'What of them?'

'Stale.'

'How so?'

'Because she loved me.'

'You make no sense, Edmund.'

'Success was my very failure!'

Hoode was riding beside Nicholas and drifting off into a reverie from time to time. He emerged from the latest one with an insight that profoundly altered his attitude to his poetry. When he fell madly and inappropriately in love with some goddess, he was moved to pour out his feelings in honeyed sonnets and sublime verse. Indeed, the more unapproachable his beloved, the sweeter his lyrical vein. Only out of true suffering did his art achieve purity. Jane Diamond had mesmerized him at first then responded to his wooing with becoming eagerness. Hoode wrote poem after poem for her, hoping to construct a staircase of words so that he could ascend to her chamber and take the reward of a lover. When he recalled those verses now—line by embarrassing line—he saw that they were flat, mawkish and totally unworthy of their object. His staircase of words had led him down into a creative cellar. The divine Jane Diamond may have sharpened his self-esteem but she had blunted his talent beyond recognition.

The lovelorn author showed the first sign of recovery.

'Her husband was a guardian angel in disguise,' he said buoyantly. 'In pulling me from the arms of his wife, he gave me back my invention. I am Edmund Hoode once more.'

'We are glad to see you returned.'

'If her husband were here, I would thank him.'

Nicholas looked ahead at Lawrence Firethorn but said nothing. The angel in disguise had been a ruthless actor-manager reclaiming a wayward playwright for a tour, but that was a truth that must not be allowed to rock the fragile vessel of Edmund Hoode's fantasy. He was home again with his fellows and that was paramount. Nicholas prodded him about his recent tardiness.

'How stands *The Merchant of Calais*?' he asked.

'Indifferently.'

'It was promised for the start of the month.'

'I'll begin work on it again tomorrow.'

'Why not today?'

'Why not, indeed?' decided Hoode, shedding his torpor as if it were a cloak. 'You will help me, Nick. What man better? You come from merchant stock in Devon and you have been to Calais many a time. Tell me about merchants of the Staple.'

It was a disagreeable topic for Nicholas—especially in present circumstances—and he chose his words with care.

Before he could frame them into sentences, however, he was interrupted by the now soulful Edmund Hoode. Melancholy was returning.

'Teach me the way, Nick. I'll be an apt pupil.'

'What is my subject to be?'

'Happiness in love.'

'Find another tutor.'

'You are the example that I choose,' said Hoode. 'Since we have been friends, I have loved and lost a score at least of beautiful ladies who snatched my heart from my body and roasted it slowly before my eyes. And you? But one woman in all that time.'

Nicholas was evasive. 'My case is different.'

'That is why I pattern myself on you.'

'Continue on your own course, Edmund.'

'To further torture? You and Anne fill me with envy.'

'Appearances can deceive.'

'No, Nick,' said his friend, 'you two are made of the same mettle. I never saw a more contented couple—unless it be Lawrence and Margery when tearing small pieces out of each other! Mistress Anne Hendrik is a remarkable woman.'

'She is, Edmund,' confessed the other freely.

'In your place, I would marry her and retire from this infernal profession. What else does a man *need*?'

It was a question that Nicholas had been compelled to address in the last couple of days. Losing Anne from his life had left a hollowness that was indescribable. Marriage had never been a serious option before, but it suddenly had an appeal he would not have believed possible. The theatre brought many joys but it was a precarious and abrasive living. With Anne beside him as his wife, he would find a more suitable and worthwhile employment. Given a chance of lasting happiness, why indeed did he stay with Westfield's Men?

One look around the company gave him his answer and rubbed the tempting picture of Anne Bracewell out of his mind. Let her remain as the widow of a Dutchman. His place was here among his fellows, sharing their depriva-

tions and revelling in their moments of glory. There was a
play to complete and he must not let personal considerations hinder that. He smiled at Hoode and talked of someone he had not dared to think about for several years.

'My father was a merchant of the Staple,' he said.

Oxford was infinitely smaller than London yet it came to
assume a size and importance to the refugees from the capital that was out of all proportion to its true dimensions. It
was their coveted destination, a haven of rest after an ex-
hausting journey, a place to eat, drink and wench, to act on
a stage in front of a proper audience, to feel once again the
unique thrill of performance, to forget the horrors of the
fire at the Queen's Head and the hideous cost of their brief
stay at the Fighting Cocks. The whole tone of the tour
would be set at Oxford, and they were eager to get there in
order to lift their spirits and regain their sense of identity.

Each man and boy in the company had his own vision of
what the town would deliver. Lawrence Firethorn wanted to
make its ancient walls shake in wonder at the brilliance of
his art and reverberate with applause for a whole week. He
also hoped that Oxford would harbour his persecutor, Israel
Gunby, counterfeit father and cunning thief, so that Firethorn could hunt him down, dismember him with his bare
hands then slice his miserable body into a hundred strips
before feeding him to the stray dogs. Owen Elias had a
humbler ambition. Though anything but an academic, he
wanted to look at Jesus College, which had been founded
over twenty years ago by a fellow Welshman, Dr Hugh
Price, to instil a Celtic note into the voice of the university.
Standing in the middle of the quadrangle, Elias would then
declaim his favourite soliloquy, which he had translated
into his native language for the occasion. Richard Honeydew, afloat on high expectation, saw a place that was
dedicated to beauty and truth. John Tallis, with more immediate needs, thought only of Oxford food, Martin Yeo was
drooling at the prospect of a surreptitious swig of Oxford
ale and Stephen Judd, the oldest of the apprentices, now
contending with a rising interest in the female sex he was

paid to imitate, was dreaming of compliant young women with a sense of adventure. George Dart saw Oxford as a soft bed in which he could sleep out eternity.

Alone of the company, Edmund Hoode viewed the town as a noble seat of learning with an international reputation. He himself had been well taught at Westminster School by no less a tutor than Camden, but his formal education had stopped short of university and left him with the feeling that he had missed out on a vital stage of his intellectual and spiritual development. Most of his rival playwrights hailed from Oxford or Cambridge, while others had prospered at the alternative university of the Inns of Court in London. Though he read avidly and learned quickly, there were still huge chasms in his knowledge and he was therefore planning—literally—to rub shoulders with the collegiate buildings in the hope that some of their learning would stick to him. Westfield's Men were there to perform a play but he was repairing the deficiencies in his education.

Nicholas Bracewell experienced trepidation. Oxford took him nearer to a life he had relinquished and farther away from a woman he loved. It also held the possibility of a second attack from the man who had tried to kill him. There was safety in numbers, but he could not expect the company to form a cordon around him throughout their entire stay in the town. When Nicholas was alone, unguarded or asleep, he would be an inviting target for a man who could wait in the dark with catlike patience before leaping on his prey. Having failed with his knotted cord, he would next time choose a swifter means of dispatching his victim. Nicholas had to be ready for the flash of cold steel. He had a problem. In the hurly-burly of setting up the stage, marshalling the company and controlling the performance, he would be constantly distracted. Other eyes were needed to watch his back. He acquainted Edmund Hoode and Owen Elias with his plight and swore both to secrecy. When the former was not trailing his doublet against collegiate stone and the latter was not bouncing his Welsh cadences off the quadrangle at Jesus, they would be welcome sentries for a beleaguered friend.

Barnaby Gill was the real surprise. Renowned for his impish humour onstage, he was equally renowned for his morose behaviour off it, yet he was so excited when they came within sight of the town that he rode up and down the column to cheer on his colleagues and assure them that Oxford would redeem the miseries they had so far encountered. He was offering the leadership that Firethorn normally provided. His ebullience was due in part to the choice of a cherished play for the Oxford audience and in part to the fact that he knew of a tavern where he could get the sort of congenial company for the night that was difficult to find outside his London haunts. In addition to all this, Oxford gave him the opportunity to display his theatrical lore.

He drew his horse in beside Lawrence Firethorn again.

'When the Queen came here last year—'

'Spare me, Barnaby!'

'She saw two comedies presented by university actors in Latin. They were meanly performed yet Her Majesty listened graciously throughout. She enjoyed them enough to invite the actors to stage their work at Court, but as their repertoire was imprisoned in the cage of a dead language, they did not oblige. The Court is too stupid to understand Latin.'

'Is this another cautionary tale?' said Firethorn.

'I simply enlighten you about academic drama.'

'It is a contradiction in terms. Too much learning silts up the drama, and too much drama destroys the supremacy of the mind.' Jealousy rippled. 'Besides, what can prattling, pox-faced, pigeon-chested students know about the art of acting? We have no competition here.'

'That is my point, Lawrence.'

'They will have seen no talent of my magnitude.'

'Except when *I* last played here.'

'Stand aside and let true greatness take the stage.'

'I couple my first warning with another. Look for envy and suspicion from the scholars. We will meet opposition here. They hate strolling players and treat them as no more than vagabonds.'

'Lawrence Firethorn will mend their ways.'

'Ignore the gown and entertain the town.'

'I want every man, woman and puking student there!'

'The undergraduates will be on holiday.'

'Fetch them back! Or they will miss an event as rare and memorable as an eclipse of the sun.'

'Memorable, I grant you,' said Gill, 'but hardly rare. I eclipse your sun every time I pass in front of you onstage.'

They fell into a companionable argument until the town in the distance took on size and definition. An anticipatory buzz ran through the troupe. Relief was finally at hand. Wood and water gave Oxford a superb setting. Meadow, cow and hill added to its picturesque charm. Some towns were an imposition on the landscape, an ugly mass of houses, inns and civic buildings hurled by an undiscriminating hand onto the countryside to subdue the souls of those who lived there and offend the gaze of those who passed by. Oxford, by contrast, seemed to grow out of the earth like a stately mushroom, enhancing the quality of its environment while drawing immense value from it in return. Town and country sang in harmony and this impressed visitors from a capital city whose thrusting boundaries more often than not produced loud discord at its outer limits.

It was late afternoon and the sun had dipped low enough to brush the towers and steeples with a glancing brilliance. As they approached Pettypont, the fortified stone bridge over the River Cherwell, they marvelled at the Norman ingenuity that had constructed the crossing point. Christ Church Meadows stretched out expansively on their left but it was the looming tower of Magdalen College on their right that commanded attention. Directly ahead was the town wall with a cluster of buildings peering over at them with friendly condescension. Eastgate was a yawning portal that beckoned them on and gave Lawrence Firethorn a cue for a speech.

'Enter, my friends!' he exclaimed. 'Where sieges have failed, we will conquer. Where university actors have bored in Latin, we will delight with the Queen's English. Where religion has burned men at the stake, we will be kinder par-

93

sons to our flock. Where learning flourishes, we will teach unparalleled lessons. Where drama is respected, we will give it new and awesome significance.' His rhetoric took him through the gate and into High Street. 'On, on, my lads! Buttress your backs and hold up your chins. Let the people of Oxford know we are here among them. Westfield's Men arrive in triumph. We are no skulking players or roaming vagabonds. The finest actors in the world have come to this town and we must make it feel truly grateful. Smile, smile! Wave, wave! Make friends with all and sundry. Brighten their squalid existences. We wage a war of happiness!'

The brave words resuscitated the travellers and carried them up High Street in a mood of elation. The low buildings of St Edmund's Hall were on their right, followed by the ancient Gothic front of Queen's College. Almost directly opposite was the University College, reputedly the oldest foundation, and the heads which measured its imposing facade now switched back to the other side of the street to view the quieter majesty of All Souls. That pleasure was soon superseded by another as the imperious Parish Church of St Mary rose up to dwarf all the surrounding buildings and to spear the sky with perpendicular accuracy. Brasenose came next with Oriel College off to the left, fronted by a green that was speckled with trees. Beyond this open space and the scattered buildings around Peckwater's Inn was the largest college of them all, Christ Church, first called Cardinal College when it was begun in 1525 by Cardinal Wolsey and now reaching out with easy magnificence even beyond the scope of its founder's grandiose plans. Though still unfinished, it had an air of completeness, and permanence, an architectural landmark against which all future collegiate building would take direction.

Barnaby Gill relished his role as the official guide.

'Merton College is to the left, next to Corpus Christi, which stands by that woodyard. Back on this side, you can see Lincoln, then Exeter with Jesus College facing them across Turl Street.' He flapped a wrist. 'I can never tell whether Oxford is a town in which a university has taken root, or a university around which a town has somehow grown up, for the two are so closely entwined that it is impossible to see where the one begins and the other ends.'

It was a problem that did not afflict those who dwelt in Oxford, where the distinction between town and gown was so marked that the two halves were set irreconcilably against each other. The simmering hostility occasionally spilled over into violence and even into full-scale riot, but there was no sign of either now. A depressing uniformity had settled on the town and made the shuffling scholars merge peacefully with their counterparts among the townspeople. Nicholas Bracewell noted the same look on every face they passed. Players had often visited Oxford but the appearance of a celebrated London troupe should have elicited more than the dull curiosity it was now provoking. Lawrence Firethorn rode at the head of the company as if leading an invading army, but even his martial presence did not arouse interest. Nicholas leaned across to Edmund Hoode.

'Something is amiss,' he said.

'Other players are here before us.'

'The truth may be harsher yet than that, Edmund.'

'Why do the people turn away from us?'

'I fear there is only one explanation.'

Westfield's Men swung right into the Cornmarket then rode on down to the Cross Inn before turning gratefully into its courtyard. The journey had been a lifetime of discomfort but it was happily forgotten now. Oxford hospitality would solve all their problems.

The landlord of the Cross Inn robbed them of that illusion. Short, stout and hobbling on aged legs, he came out to give them a half-hearted greeting.

'You are welcome, gentlemen, but you may not play here.'

'We will act in the Town Hall,' announced Firethorn.

'Neither there, nor here, nor at the King's Head nor at any place within the Oxford, I fear.'

'What are you telling us, landlord?'

'Sad news, sir. The plague is amongst us once more.'

'Plague!'

The word devastated the whole company. They had come all that way to be denied the pleasure of performance and its much-needed reward. It was utterly demoralising. Plague, which had so often driven them out of London, had now shifted its ground to Oxford out of sheer spite and made their presence redundant. Disease festered in summer months and spread most easily at public gatherings. Plays, games and other communal entertainments were banned. The lodging of strangers was limited, and pigs and refuse were cleared from the streets. The haunted faces they had seen on their progress to the inn belonged to survivors. Westfield's Men had no purchase on the minds of such creatures. People who feared that they might be struck down with the plague on the morrow did not seek amusement on their way to the grave.

The landlord tried to offer some consolation.

'Fear not, sirs!' he called out. 'Our mayor will not be ungenerous. You may be given money not to play.'

'Not to play!' Lawrence Firethorn shuddered at the insult and bayed his reply. 'I am being paid not to play! And will you pay the river not to flow and the stars not to shine? Will you give money to the grass to stop it growing? How much have you offered the rain not to fall and the moon not to rise? Ha!' He smote his chest with lordly arrogance. 'I am a force of nature and will not be stopped by some maltworm of a mayor. Oxford does not have enough gold in its coffers to buy off Lawrence Firethorn.'

'We have the plague, sir,' repeated the landlord.

'A plague on your plague! And a pox on your welcome.' He swung round in the saddle. 'Nicholas!'

'Yes, master.'

'Go to this meddling mayor. Inform him who I am.'

'Yes, master.'

'And if he dares to offer us money to withdraw,' said Firethorn vehemently, 'curse him for his villainy and throw it back in his scurvy face.'

Nicholas Bracewell accepted a commission he knew that he could not fulfil because it was pointless to try to reason with the actor-manager when his blood was up. Plague was too strong an opponent and it had wrestled them to the ground once more. Whenever the company was on tour, Nicholas was accustomed to meeting civic dignitaries in order to get the required licence for performance. Westfield's Men were usually offered handsome terms to stage their plays but not this time. As Nicholas went off, he resigned himself to the inevitable, yet he was able to snatch one crumb of comfort. A plague town was far too dangerous a place to linger. Even an assassin would keep well clear of the contagion. Nicholas could afford to relax. Inside Oxford, he was safe.

Paternoster Row was famous for its literary associations, and many printers, stationers and booksellers had their premises there. Yet it was here that they found the apothecary's shop that they sought. After hours of combing the back streets and lanes of Cordwainer Ward, they widened their search and eventually came to the busy thoroughfare that ran along the northern side of St Paul's Cathedral. Merchants, silkmen and lacemen also lived in the area, which was justly celebrated as well for the number and quality of its taverns. For these and other reasons, Paternoster Row was never quiet or empty and Anne Hendrik was grateful for the reassuring presence of Leonard as she made her way through the crowd in his wake. They were an incongruous couple. His shambling bulk reduced her trim elegance to almost childlike stature. Unused to the company of a lady, Leonard fell back on a kind of heavy-handed gallantry that only made his awkwardness the more poignant.

When Anne called on him at the Queen's Head, he had been more than helpful, telling her all he could remember about his meeting with the doomed traveller from Devon. She could see why Nicholas had chosen this friend to represent him at the funeral. Leonard might be slow witted, but he was a kind man and completely trustworthy. With touching candor, he told her how he had wept at the graveside and wished that he could do something to avenge the girl's death. Anne gave him that opportunity. It was pleasant to be with a person who had such an uncritical affection for Nicholas Bracewell, and Leonard's powerful frame was a guarantee of her safety in the bustling streets.

They visited several shops without success but Anne was systematic. None of the apothecaries was able to help her but each one gave her a degree of assistance, albeit with reluctance in some cases, talking to her about the constituent elements of poisons and sending her on to another possible source of inquiry. The process had taken them into Paternoster Row and they called at the address they had been given. It was a small but well-stocked shop, and the man behind the counter had a neatness of garb and politeness of manner that set him apart from the grubby appearance and surly attitude of some of his fellows. The apothecary had brown hair, a pointed beard and the remains of an almost startling handsomeness. His faint accent joined with his exaggerated courtesy towards Anne to betray his nationality.

'What may I get for madame?' he said. 'Perfumes from Arabia? Spices from the East? My stock is at your disposal.'

'Does it include poison?' she asked.

'Poison?'

'Do you carry these items?'

Ann Hendrik gave him the list of possible ingredients, which she had first devised with the aid of the surgeon. At each shop, her list was amended or enlarged in line with the advice of respective apothecaries. From the general pool of expertise, she had fished up a final inventory. Philippe Lavalle studied it with interest and surprise. He was a French Huguenot who fled from his native country over twenty years ago to escape persecution. It had been a great struggle to establish himself at first but now, under the name of Philip Lovel, he was a respected member of his profession. Poverty was his chief customer. People who could not afford to send for a doctor or a physician would come to him. He could diagnose diseases, prescribe cures for many of them and bleed a patient where necessary. Anne Hendrik was not typical of his customers at all and he had assumed she was there to purchase some of the perfumes and spices that he kept in the earthenware pots that were arranged so tidily on his shelves.

'You *want* this poison, madame?' he said cautiously.

'I want to know if you have sold such ingredients.'

'But, yes. Everything here is in my shop.'

'And has anyone bought from you recently?'

'Why do you wish to know?'

'Please, sir,' she said, 'it is of great importance.'

'I do not discuss my business with strangers.'

'Help the lady,' grunted Leonard in an absurd attempt to sound menacing. 'She is with me.'

Philip Lovel threw him a scornful glance and ignored him for the rest of the conversation. Loathe to part easily with information about his customers, he yet sensed a hope of material reward. The man was plainly an oaf. Even in the aromatic atmosphere of his shop, Lovel could smell the beer on his visitor. Evidently, he was a drayman or tapster. The woman, on the other hand, was attractive, smartly dressed and well spoken. Money would not be the problem it was for the majority of his customers. Only a strong motive would bring her on such a strange errand, and he was intrigued to know what it was. He returned her list and gave an elaborate shrug.

'I may have sold these items, I may have not.'

'If you had, how much would they have cost?' she said.

'You wish to buy them yourself?'

'I am ready to give you twice as much money if you can describe the customer.'

He was tempted. 'Well . . .'

'*Three* times as much,' she decided, producing a purse to back up her offer. 'That poison killed a young girl.'

'He told me it was to get rid of some rats.'

'Then you *did* sell these ingredients?'

'Four days ago.'

'On the eve of her arrival in London.'

'It was an expensive purchase.'

'How expensive?'

Lovel stated his price and Anne put the money onto the counter. Before the apothecary could scoop up the coins, they were covered by the giant hand of Leonard. The reward had to be earned before it was paid over.

'I sold him the three powders on your list,' he said, 'and some white mercury. Then there was a quantity of opium in a double bladder. When I added a secret potion of my own invention—it is not known outside this shop—he had the means to kill fifty rats. That was his declared purpose and I took him for the gentleman he seemed.'

'Gentleman!' sneered Leonard. 'He was a murderer.'

'Tell us all you can remember,' said Anne.

Philip Lovel could remember a great deal because the customer had been as unlikely a visitor to his shop as Anne Hendrick herself and he drew his portrait with care. They were shown his height, his bearing, his features, his apparel. The apothecary even made a stab at the timbre of his voice. Convinced that she was seeing the poisoner come to life before her eyes, Anne committed every detail to her retentive mind. When Lovel had finished, she lifted Leonard's hand up to release the money then added the same amount again. The information she had just bought was invaluable.

Leonard was slower to react. It was only when they stepped out into Paternoster Row and began the long walk back that his brain assembled all the facts into one coherent picture. He stopped dead and slapped his thigh.

'I know him!'

'Who?'

'I've met the man. Even as he was described.'

'Where?'

'At the Queen's Head,' he recalled. 'He was there when the ballad was sung about the fire. It turned Nicholas into the hero. I know it by heart, mistress. I'll sing you a verse or two, if you wish.'

'The man, Leonard. You say you know him?'

'Not by name but it must have been him.'

'Why?'

'He asked about Nicholas going off to Barnstaple.' He took off his cap to scratch his head. 'And I do believe the fellow was there at the Bel Savage Inn to watch the company leave. Yes, I saw him there, I swear it.'

It took Anne a long time to extract the full details from him and she grew increasingly fearful as she listened. The man had secured his poison at the shop in Paternoster Row and prepared it in a form that could easily be slipped into a drink. In killing the girl, he was trying to stop her reaching Nicholas Bracewell, but that part of his plan had miscarried. Since the book holder was now making for the town from which the girl was sent, he himself could become a potential target for the murderer. Why else did the man take such an interest in his departure from London?

Nicholas Bracewell was in danger. Anne had to warn him.

'I must ask a favour of you, Leonard.'

'It is granted.'

'Take me to Shoreditch.'

Chapter Six

THE MAYOR OF OXFORD GAVE NICHOLAS BRACEWELL the expected response. Local government was effectively suspended and plague ruled the town. There was no possibility of Westfield's Men acting there, and since they were a body of strangers above a certain number, no inn would be able to give them hospitality for the night. Both as Thespians and as travellers, they were being ejected. The mayor was full of apologies but—he used the phrase repeatedly—his hands were tied. Nevertheless, he was able to use them both to gesticulate helplessly and to offer some measure of compensation to the disappointed troupe. He bestowed two pounds on the book holder and assured him that the company would be accorded a very different welcome on their next visit. Nicholas thanked him for his generosity and promised him that they would depart as soon as they had had time to rest the horses and take some refreshment.

When he left the Town Hall, he slipped the money into his purse and decided to leave it there until they had put Oxford many miles behind them. Lawrence Firethorn might be disdainful, but his company needed all the money that it could get and from whatever source. Nicholas decided to give his employer more time to cool down before he returned with the bad tidings and he took a stroll in the direction of the castle. It gave him an opportunity to reflect on the vagaries of life with a dramatic company. Robbed at High Wycombe, they had now been ousted from Oxford. The actors would begin to believe that their tour was damned. Inasmuch as it cut a day off his journey home, Nicholas was an incidental beneficiary of the plague, but that gave him no pleasure. Westfield's Men needed a performance at Oxford to steady their nerves. After riding into the town as one of the leading troupes in London, they would be slinking away like unlicenced strolling players. The loss of their venue at the Queen's Head had cast them out into the wilderness.

Nicholas paused to gaze up at the five great towers of Oxford Castle, one of the first stone-built fortresses to be constructed in England by the Normans. Steeped in history and surrounded by a moat, it was a formidable garrison in a town whose geographical position gave it immense strategic importance. Oxford Castle had a proud solidity but it was not enough to withstand an assault by a deadly enemy. As Nicholas watched, a horse and cart came out through the arched gateway with an all too familiar cargo. At the sight and smell of the shrouded figures, he turned quickly away and headed back towards the inn. The plague was insidious.

There were plenty of people in the streets, going about their business, but they did so without any real purpose or alacrity. An air of listlessness hung over the town as neighbours conversed with one another to find out who the latest victims were and to speculate on who would be struck down next. Like inhabitants of a flooded valley, they were waiting helplessly for the plague to wash over them and hoping that they would not be among the drowned. Their fatalism was saddening but it aroused Nicholas's pity. Westfield's Men had only lost a performance. Some of the people lurching along the streets had lost family members and friends.

That thought brought Nicholas to an abrupt halt. The crisis that they found at Oxford had obscured the memory of what happened before they reached the town. Without quite knowing how, he had spoken to Edmund Hoode about his own family in Devon and talked at length about his father. It was a conversation that would have been inconceivable only a few days ago when he was still suppressing all mention of his life before his voyage with Drake. His accent placed him firmly in the West Country but he acknowledged no family ties there, until the recent summons from Barnstaple. Yet he discussed his childhood for the best part of an hour with Hoode and trespassed freely on forbidden territory. Nicholas could not believe that he had confided so much personal detail to his friend, and he was amazed that he had been able to confront the spectre of his father without the customary pain and revulsion.

Robert Bracewell was a name he kept locked away in the darkest corner of his mind. He had not even spoken it to Anne Hendrik. On the ride to Oxford, his father had been set free at last. What was more remarkable was that, in talking about someone he despised and disowned, Nicholas actually came to feel vague pains of sympathy for him and even tried to excuse his faults. Robert Bracewell was a hostage to fortune. Ill luck had dogged him. Shortly after he became a merchant of the Staple, the last English foothold in France was lost and British merchants were promptly expelled. Queen Mary died saying that the name "Calais" was engraved on her heart, but it was tattooed on the soul of Robert Bracewell. More setbacks stemmed from that first dreadful shock, and Nicholas recalled the locust years when his father trembled on the verge of bankruptcy. It took enormous strength of will to rebuild his reputation and his company. Any man should surely be admired for that.

Nicholas's sympathy dried up instantly. Strength of will could destroy as well as create. The driving energy that enabled Robert Bracewell to win back his status in the mercantile community had another side to it, and his elder son had been one of its prime victims. Though he divulged much to his friend, Nicholas had concealed far more and he knew why. The deep shame of being a member of that family was still there, and it made the name he bore feel like a species of plague. Nicholas was frankly appalled at the prospect of going back to the town that held so many bleak associations for him but it was a sacred commitment that had to be honoured. He concentrated his mind on more immediate difficulties and lengthened his stride.

Westfield's Men had taken themselves into the inn for a restorative meal, but Lawrence Firethorn was waiting to accost his book holder in the courtyard. The actor-manager's belligerence masked his niggling despair.

'Where the devil have you been, Nick!' he demanded. 'I sent you an hour ago at least.'

'The mayor was engaged when I arrived.'

'Engaged!'

'I was forced to wait.'

'Engaged!' howled Firethorn. 'If the wretch had kept *me* waiting, I'd have engaged him with sword and dagger, then hanged him from the church steeple with his chain of office. What did the arrant knave tell you?'

'The plague has closed this town to us.'

'God's mercy! We are the *cure* for this contagion. Does he not see that? We bring joy into a cavern of misery. We bring life to a dying people. We bring hope.'

'The mayor appreciates that,' said Nicholas, 'but the ordnance holds. No plays, no games, no public gatherings of any sort. He sends his abject apologies but we must be out of Oxford before the sun goes down.'

'Out of Oxford!'

'We are strangers in the town and carry a threat.'

'I'll carry a threat to the viperous villain!' said the other. 'He'll have a plague of naked steel about his ears. Does he tell Lawrence Firethorn not to act? Will he order my company to leave his town?' He strutted around in a display of defiance then adopted his most regal pose. 'I am a king of the stage and he will not force me to abdicate.'

'It is no personal rebuff for you,' reasoned Nicholas. 'Plague deaths rise every day. If they continue at this rate then the churches will have to be closed. The market has already been shut down. These are the sensible precautions that any town must take when disease takes a hold.'

Firethorn accepted the truth of this. He still ranted away for a few minutes but the venom had been drained out of his bluster. Oxford was a lost cause. They had to move on. When Firethorn's bluster subsided, he raised an eyebrow.

'Were you offered any compensation?' he said.

'You told me not to accept it, master.'

'Indeed, indeed,' reaffirmed Firethorn. 'Fling it back at him, I said, and I hope that is what you did.'

'I declined the money.'

'Good.' The other eyebrow lifted. 'How much was it?'

'Two pounds.'

Firethorn's sigh of remorse was like a protracted hiss of steam. Thanks to his pride, they were creeping away from the town without a penny. Anger relieved him but it was an expensive item. Firethorn knew that the rest of the company would suffer as a result. He gave Nicholas a task that he had no heart to perform himself.

'Tell the others,' he said. 'We leave within the hour.'

'I'll about it straight.'

'Oh, and Nick . . .'

'Yes?'

'Say nothing of that two pounds.'

The house in Shoreditch was of middling size with a neat garden at its rear and a tiny orchard. A half-timbered structure like its neighbours, its second storey was fronted with plastered wattle work that was showing signs of age. Both storeys projected at least a foot above the floor below and they had settled into a comfortable position like two fishwives leaning their arms contentedly on a wall for a lifelong exchange of gossip. The roof was fairly sound, but it would soon need the attention of a thatcher. Whatever the defects of its exterior, the house was kept in an excellent state of repair on the inside. Margery Firethorn saw to that. She was a meticulous housewife who made sure that every floor was swept, every window was cleaned and every cobweb brushed away on a daily basis. She shared the abode with her husband, their children and servants, the four apprentices and the occasional hired man with nowhere else to lay his head. Margery loved her role as mother of an extended family and she offered all those who stayed beneath her roof the rather caustic brand of affection that she had developed through marriage to Lawrence Firethorn. The house seemed empty now and the rooms silent. She missed the happy turbulence of life with Westfield's Men and she was therefore delighted when she had two unexpected visitors to brighten up her day.

'And what happened then?' she said, all agog.

'We visited an apothecary in Paternoster Row,' said Anne Hendrik. 'It was there that we found guidance at last.'

'I know the man,' chimed in Leonard.

'What man?' said Margery.

'Him. The poisoner. That beard, that earring, that smell.'

'What is the fellow blabbering about, Anne?'

'Let me explain.'

Anne took over the narrative and Margery listened with a burgeoning apprehension. When she heard all the facts, she agreed that Nicholas Bracewell could well be in serious danger, and even if his own life were not threatened, he would value all the information that had been gleaned about the girl's killer. Leonard's contribution was the monotonous repetition of the story of his meeting with the man at the Queen's Head. Each time he mentioned this, he beamed vacuously, as if expecting a round of applause. Margery's tolerance soon frayed at the edges and she took the well-meaning giant into the kitchen, assigning one of the servants to look after him until he was needed again. She then went back into the parlour and sat in an upright chair beside Anne. Margery could now probe without hindrance.

'What will you do, Anne?' she asked.

'Send a message to Nicholas.'

'Why send it when you can take it yourself?'

Anne blinked. 'Me?'

'When a man's life is at risk, you do not count the personal cost or inconvenience. Look at me. I once rode all the way to York to reach Lawrence.'

'Was he in danger?'

107

'Yes!' said Margery with a laugh. 'From two madwomen he picked up on his way. One was a pilgrim and the other as near to a punk as decency would allow. If I had not mounted a horse and ridden north, Lawrence would have had the pair of them in the same bed, saying prayers with the one while he and the other recited a more sinful creed together. I had a sore rump from the journey but I saved my marriage.'

'My case is not the same,' said Anne defensively. 'You had reason to go. Lawrence was your husband.'

'He is my man. Is not Nicholas yours?'

Anne snatched back the words that almost sprang from her mouth and gestured with fluttering hands. Margery's shrewd gaze caught every nuance of her reaction. During her farewell to Nicholas at the Bel Savage Inn, she was alerted to the possibility of a rift between the two of them, and Anne's bruised silence now confirmed it. Anne lowered her head and played with the sleeve of her dress. Margery leaned forward with an understanding smile.

'You fell out over this poor girl,' she said quietly.

'Yes.'

'Did Nicholas not explain everything to you?'

'No, Margery.' Anne bit her lip then looked up at the other woman again. 'That is what vexed me so. Something calls him back to Devon yet I am kept ignorant of it.'

'Nick may have good reason for that.'

'He has never lied to me before.'

Margery cackled. 'Is that all the problem here? A few lies and deceptions? Forget them. Honesty is a virtue but it needs to be spiced with at least a hint of vice. I could never bear to live with a man who was so open that I knew everything about him. By my troth, I would die of boredom within a fortnight! Lawrence always garnishes the truth with a rich sauce of lies and I would have it no other way.' She became wistful. 'Secrecy makes a man interesting. That is why we all love dear Nicholas Bracewell—for his mystery.'

Anne's eyes filmed over and she struggled to keep the tears from flowing. In another mood, she would have taken

Margery's jocular advice in her stride but her estrangement from Nicholas made the words cut deep. His refusal to talk about his earlier life had indeed enhanced his appeal for her. Anne solved the problem of the hidden years in his life by inventing her own fantasy existence for him at that time. She knew him so well, she felt, that she could translate him back into the past and fill in the missing details of his childhood and adolescence by instinct. Her version was now shown to be highly romanticised and plainly inaccurate. She shared her life with one Nicholas Bracewell but there had been another quite different man living under the same name in Devon all those years ago.

Margery could see her visitor's ambivalent feelings.

'Go to him,' she urged.

'He may not wish to see me, Margery.'

'Pish! That's of no account. Do *you* wish to see him?'

'He must be warned!'

'Then take the warning with you.'

'No,' said Anne. 'This is not work for me. I still have too much to think about here before I see him again.' Sudden fear made her catch her breath. '*If* I see him again.'

'You will certainly do that,' Margery assured her. 'He is more than able to take care of himself. But we must get word to him and without delay.'

'That is why I came to you. We parted in anger so I have no knowledge of his whereabouts. Help me, Margery. What is their itinerary? Where are Westfield's Men now?'

'They should have arrived at Oxford this afternoon.'

'Oxford!' Anne grew hopeful. 'With a change of horses, a man might ride that distance in a day.'

Margery was doubtful. 'If he sets off in the morning, he will not find them there.'

'Will they not stay overnight and perform tomorrow?'

'Oxford will not allow it.'

'Why not?'

'There are rumors of plague in the town.'

'Plague!'

'I went to market today,' explained Margery. 'Some of
109

the traders who came in from Aylesbury caught wind of it. If the disease has a grip, it will send the company packing.'

'In which direction?'

'Marlborough.' Margery needed a moment to think it through, then she made up her mind. 'They will choose an inn to the south of Oxford and rest for the night. My guess is that Lawrence will have them in the saddle at first light and riding into Marlborough as soon as may be.'

'I'll reach him there,' decided Anne, then she glanced towards the kitchen as an idea formed. 'Leonard will carry it. A faithful friend will readily do such a service.'

'Take pity on a dumb animal.'

'Animal?'

'Yes,' said Margery. 'Leonard would never walk there on those tree trunks they felled to make his legs. It would take him a month or more. He would need a horse—and what animal is strong enough to bear such a weight and gallop at speed?' She pushed Leonard aside with a palm. 'Forget him. He is no swift messenger. Besides, we need one friend at the Queen's Head to speak up for Westfield's Men. Leonard must melt the icy heart of its landlord.'

'So who will take the letter?'

'A courier. It will be my charge to find the man.'

'I'll go home and write the letter at once.'

'We have ink and parchment here, Anne,' said the other woman. 'But a letter will not suffice.'

'How else can I warn him?' asked Anne. 'He must be made aware of what we learned at the apothecary's shop. I will pen a description of the man we believe did the foul deed.'

'Marry, there's a better way than that.'

'Show it me.'

Margery studied her. 'That is a fine hat you wear.'

'Why are we talking of my hat?'

'Who made it, Anne?'

'Preben van Loew.'

'At whose behest?'

'My own.'

'But from what design?'

110

'I drew a likeness for him to follow.' Margery grinned at her and Anne realised what was being suggested. 'No, no. I am no artist.'

'A hand that can fashion something as delicate as that hat can pick out the features of a man's face.'

'I have only the apothecary's description.'

'And Leonard to guide your fingers. He has *seen* the man, I do believe. He vouched for it three thousand times.'

The women shared a laugh then Margery called for her servant to fetch writing materials. Leonard was thrilled to be brought back into action again and to be given a major role in creating the likeness of the man with the raven black beard. Anne worked slowly but carefully with the quill, using the apothecary's description as her starting point then adding or amending as directed by Leonard. When the paper was a mass of squiggles, she took a fresh piece of parchment and worked to produce a clearer portrait. The face of a ruthless killer soon glowered up at them.

Leonard jumped about with lumpen excitement.

'That is him!' he congratulated. 'That is him!'

Oxford had murder enough of its own. With the plague now scything its way through the population and killing them in droves, there was no need for the man to enter the town in search of an individual victim. He might himself be infected before he could even reach Nicholas Bracewell and that would be a double catastrophe. The plague was an assassin that liked to torture its prey unmercifully before it finally released them to the grave. He preferred a waiting game, and his patience reaped its reward that evening. From his place of vantage on a wooded slope, he watched Westfield's Men leave the town and head south-west past the ruins of Osney Abbey, set among the island meadows beyond the castle. Plundered of its stone for the building of Christ Church, the abbey had a shattered grandeur that could still arrest attention and it did hold the distinction of being—for a few years after its dissolution as a monastery in 1539—Oxford's first cathedral. Its religious affiliations seemed to make Lawrence Firethorn even more irate and he pulled his horse in a semi-circle so that he could deliver a blistering rebuke to the town that had just evicted them.

The man on the slope was over two hundred yards away and concealed among the trees, but he heard the tirade as clearly as if he were standing beside the actor-manager. 'Oxford, adieu!' snarled Firethorn. 'The Devil take you! We quit your foul streets for fresher pastures. What is your famous university but a set of mangy, maggot-filled colleges set up by Roman Catholic prelates! Keep your bishops and your great fat cardinal. God has sent down a plague on your popery! We are true Protestants and refuse to ply our trade in this grisly Vatican.' He widened his attack to include the other university town. 'Scholarship rots the mind! It breeds Puritans in Cambridge and Papists in Oxford. Show me a student and you show me a lesser breed of man. If you begged us, Westfield's Men would not play before you.' A waved fist accompanied his final taunt. 'You do not turn *us* out: we spurn *you*! There is a world elsewhere.'

The words shot across the grass like a fusillade and scattered the wildlife before rebounding harmlessly off the town walls. Oxford was the target of much criticism for its vestigial Roman Catholicism, but it was in no position to defend itself against this latest theological attack. All its attention was fixed on a virulent plague that killed Christians of all denominations with random savagery. Lawrence Firethorn had merely exercised his lungs. He did nothing to revive a disconsolate company and they trundled away like outcasts.

When the man with the raven black beard saw the road they chose, he knew where he could catch up with them. Close pursuit was unnecessary and he was anxious not to be seen by Nicholas Bracewell. The scuffle in the stables at the Fighting Cock had taught him to respect his adversary. It was vital to retain the advantage of surprise if he wanted to succeed against such a powerful man. Forewarned and forearmed, Nicholas was now a very troublesome opponent. He would have to be stabbed in the back.

While the man stayed in his hiding place, the company

112

rolled unhappily away from Oxford. The haven of rest had been a hell of disquiet that had moved them on as fast as it could. What guarantee did they have that Marlborough would not do the same to them and manufacture some entirely new and even more jolting setback? Their tour was fast becoming a kind of penance. Lawrence Firethorn led them in search of an inn where they could spend the night, somewhere close enough to Oxford to spare them and their horses further weariness yet far enough away to be totally free from its pestilential air.

When an old shepherd stumbled out onto the road ahead of them, Firethorn called to him for advice.

'We seek shelter, friend,' he said.

'So do I, sir,' replied the shepherd, 'for I've been up since dawn chasing stray sheep.'

'Which is the nearest inn?'

'That could be the Bull and Butcher, sir.'

'How far is that?'

'Two mile or more,' said the shepherd, 'but the Dog and Bear may be closer. Then again, it may not. Let me think.'

The old man's ruddy face was largely obscured by a wispy grey beard and a battered hat, and he had a habit of clearing his throat and spitting absentmindedly onto the ground. His shoulders were hunched and his legs bent by the weight of the paunch he carried beneath the torn smock. He leaned on his crook as he deliberated, mumbling to himself in the local dialect while he weighed up the competing merits and locations of the two hostelries. Firethorn soon tired of the countryman's irritating slowness.

'Which one, man?' he pressed. 'Bull or Dog?'

'Bull, sir. Yes, I'd say Bull.'

'Thank you.'

'It'll put you on the way to Reading in the morning.'

'But we travel to Marlborough.'

'Then you need the Dog.'

'Saints preserve us! Make up your mind!'

'Dog and Bear, sir.'

'Are you sure?'

'Turn right when the road forks. The Dog is a goodly inn and you will soon reach it.'

'Thank the Lord for that!'

'If you want my advice—'

'Go your way,' said Firethorn, cutting him off. 'You have confused us enough already. We will find our Dog and you may search for your sheep.'

'That will I, sir.'

The old shepherd tugged deferentially at the brim of his hat then lumbered away across a field. Firethorn raised a hand and signalled the company forward. They followed the winding track in a careworn mood and longed for the comforts they had left behind in London. Hired men who considered themselves blessed to be taken on the tour now felt that a curse had been laid upon them. It had only subjected them to robbery and plague so far. What further trials awaited them?

If was half an hour before they turned into the courtyard of the Dog and Bear. Though much smaller than the Fighting Cocks, it gave them a ready welcome and marked the end of a most dispiriting day's travel. The inn sign, which swung in the light breeze, showed a bear chained to a stake, striking out with its claws at the dog who was baiting it. The violent image made Lawrence Firethorn growl in kinship. He himself was a great bear who had been chained to the stake of a cruel fate. While the animal on the sign had only one dog to contend with, the actor had a whole pack. With a surge of anger, he resolved to tear the stake from the ground and beat his enemies off with it. Westfield's Men had suffered enough. Firethorn would assert himself against misfortune and lead his company on to the glory they so richly deserved and the payment they so badly needed.

Nicholas Bracewell judged his moment well. As he and his employer dismounted, ostlers came forward to take charge of their horses. The book holder took Firethorn aside for a moment. Dipping a hand into his purse, Nicholas brought out the coins that he had been given in Oxford. He held them on his palm and affected a mock surprise.

'See here,' he said. 'That stubborn mayor would not be

denied his generosity. He must have thrust the money into my purse when I was looking elsewhere.'

'How much?'

'Two pounds.'

'We will not take it.'

'Then let me hurl it away into the trough.'

'No!' said Firethorn, grabbing his wrist as he made to discard the coins. 'Let us not be too rash here. There is a sense in which Westfield's Men *earned* that money. We entered that verminous town with the best of intentions. It was not our fault that the plague was giving its performance there.'

'Take it as a small reward, then,' offered Nicholas.

'I will not,' decided Firethorn, folding his arms with disdain. 'Our company cannot be bought off with Danegeld. Hurl it into the water and show our contempt!' Once again, he clutched at Nicholas's wrist to stop him. 'Wait!'

'Why not sleep on the matter?'

'That is good advice, Nick.'

'Take the money and get the feel of it.'

'Then decide in the morning, eh?'

'When you come to pay the reckoning.'

Lawrence Firethorn thought of his empty capcase and snatched the two pounds from his friend. Nicholas knew him so well and adapted so quickly to his caprices. Money that the actor-manager had repudiated in Oxford was legal tender now they were well clear of the town. Thanks to Nicholas, it was the first income they had managed to keep. Coins had never jingled so sweetly in Firethorn's hands. He dropped them into his own purse then gave his book holder a hug of gratitude. The actor had enjoyed his exhibition of pique but it was heartening to know that there was still one practical man in the company. Firethorn sounded a haughty note.

'I will merely keep it until morning,' he said.

Nicholas smiled. 'Of course.'

The old shepherd who directed them to Dog and Bear did not have to search long for his sheep. He found them browsing on the lush grass near the edge of a copse. Walking into the trees, he came to a clearing where two figures reclined on the ground. The fleshy young man was fast asleep but the girl jumped lightly to her feet and ran to embrace the newcomer. Israel Gunby tore off his false beard so that he could kiss his wife without impediment, then he shed both his hat and his threadbare smock. Ellen was inquisitive.

'Did you speak with them?' she said.

'I sent them to the Dog and Bear.'

'Were you not afraid they would recognise you?'

'I am the Lawrence Firethorn of the highway.'

'They did not suspect you?'

'No, my love,' said Gunby, lapsing back into the accent he had used as the old shepherd. 'I was born in these parts so the dialect is second nature. I could have talked for three whole days and not a man amongst them would have been any the wiser.'

'Do we strike at the Dog and Bear?'

'They have nothing left to steal.'

'What, then?'

'We meet them again at Marlborough.'

'When do they play there?'

'Tomorrow, if all goes well.'

'What parts shall *we* take?'

'I will assign them when I have worked it out.' He glanced across at their supine accomplice. 'That belly of Ned's is not so easy to hide. I can get rid of *my* paunch like this.' He pulled out the heavy padding that was stuffed inside his belt and flung it away. 'We cannot alter Ned's shape in that way.'

Ellen eased him away a few yards to whisper in his ear.

'There *is* a way we could hide that swelling stomach.'

'How?'

'Bury it six feet in the ground.'

Israel Gunby smirked. 'That will come, my dear.'

'When?'

'When he has served his purpose. Ned will be useful in

Marlborough, for three people may work much more craftily than two. We'll keep him alive till then.'

'And afterwards?'

'We'll cut the fat-gutted rascal down to size!'

Israel Gunby drew his dagger from his belt and hurled it with a flick of the wrist. It sunk into the ground only inches from the head of their associate and brought him instantly awake. Ned gabbled his apologies for falling asleep and scrambled to his feet. The stench of strong ale still hung around him.

'You drank too freely,' reprimanded Israel Gunby.

'That was my part,' said the other. 'I was to keep them merry in the taproom while you and Ellen sneaked into their chambers. We got away from the Bull and Butcher with all but a few pence short of twenty pounds.'

The haul had been far more than that, but they had given him a lower figure so that he could be cheated out of his portion. In the guise of a farmer, Ned had been the decoy at an inn once again and shown as much outrage as the rest of them when the theft was discovered. By the time the other travellers sobered up enough to give chase, Ned himself had vanished into the woods to join his confederates.

'We must ride on,' said Gunby, pulling on his doublet. 'I have had enough of being an old shepherd. It is a stinking occupation and it offends my nose.'

The bleating of sheep jogged his memory and he gathered up the smock and the hat before reclaiming his dagger. Strolling back through the trees, he came to a spot where an old man was trussed up half-naked on the ground. A dozen snuffling ewes were clustered around their shepherd with timid curiosity and they fled as soon as Gunby appeared. Smock and hat were dropped to the ground once more but the knife flashed in the hand. The old man let out a squeal of fear and closed his eyes against the pain, but the blade drew no blood from his ancient carcass. It sliced instead through his bonds and left him free to rub his tender wrists and ankles.

Israel Gunby kicked the man's smock across to him.

'Thank you, kind father,' he said. 'For my part, I would

117

rather be tied up for a week than wear that reeking garment for an hour, but it was needful.' He dropped a small purse into the man's lap. 'There's for your pains. I am a thief and a villain and all that men say I am. But you may tell them one thing more, my friend.'

'What is that, sir?' gibbered the other.

'Israel Gunby does not rob the poor.'

Nicholas Bracewell was in a quandary. Wanting to be alone with his thoughts, he yet needed the company of his fellows to ensure safety. The inn was comfortable, its hospitality was cordial and there was no whiff of danger within its walls but those qualities had obtained at the Fighting Cocks and he had nevertheless found himself fighting for his life against a vicious assailant. It was best to take no chances. On the ride from Oxford, he constantly scoured the landscape for signs of pursuit, but none came. That did not induce him to lower his guard. Nicholas had been unaware of being trailed from London yet that was almost certainly what had occurred. Shadows moved according to the disposition of the sun. They could walk briskly before you or steal silently after you. In the darkness, you never even knew that they were there.

After supper in the taproom, Edmund Hoode retired to his chamber to work on the new play. Nicholas was both pleased and nervous, delighted that his friend had recaptured his creative urge but fearful lest he use too much of the background material that the book holder had given him. *The Merchant of Calais* was set fifty years earlier, at a time when the French port was still an English possession. Hoode was attracted by the notion of a tiny segment of British soil perched on the edge of a large and hostile country. It allowed him to explore a number of favourite themes. What troubled Nicholas was the fear that his own father might now be introduced into the play. Hoode had been so intrigued by what he was told that he had been asking for further details ever since. Always ready to help the playwright, Nicholas did not, however, want to read *The Merchant of Calais* and find that Robert Bracewell was its

118

central character. The sight of his father being brought to life onstage by Lawrence Firethorn would be too painful for the renegade son to bear.

'What ails you, Nick?' said a concerned voice.

'Nothing, Owen.'

'You have been in a dream all evening.'

'I am weary, that is all.'

'Retire to your chamber.'

'Not yet. I will stay here a little while longer.'

Owen Elias was in a jovial mood now that he had supped well and shaken the unpleasant memories of their visit to Oxford from his mind. Actors were easily crushed by any form of rejection but they had a resilience that bordered on the phenomenal. Nicholas had seen it many times before, but it still astonished him when men who had been squirming in a pit of despair one minute could then stride onto a stage with gusto and acquit themselves superbly in a comic role. Owen Elias was an archetype, thriving on deep conflict, shifting from melancholia to manic joy in a twinkling, suffering blows to his self-esteem that seemed like mortal wounds and then leaping nimbly out of his coffin with boundless vitality.

'Have no fear while you are with me, Nick.'

'Thanks, Owen.'

'I'll be a trusty bodyguard.'

'Sharp eyes. Give me sharp eyes.'

'They would cut through teak.'

Nicholas was glad he had taken the Welshman into his confidence. Elias had his faults and it was the book holder's unenviable task to point them out to him from time to time, but the actor's attributes heavily outweighed his defects. There was another reason why the Welshman was so eager to lend all the help he could to Nicholas. It was the book holder who had manouevred his promotion in the company. After languishing for so long in the ranks of the hired men, Owen Elias felt that his true worth was not appreciated and he succumbed to the blandishments of Banbury's Men. Only some deft stage management from Nicholas rescued him from the rival company and secured his position as a sharer with Westfield's Men. Elias was eternally grateful to his friend and would fight to the death on his behalf. Nicholas hoped that he could solve the problem himself, but if assistance was needed, the strength of the pugnacious Welshman would be more useful than the diffidence of a gentle soul like Edmund Hoode.

Drink exposed a vein of regret in Owen Elias.

'We can never outrun the past, Nick,' he said. 'Try as we may, it will always catch up with us sooner or later. Look at my case. Wales never releases its sons.'

'You managed to break free, Owen.'

'A trick of the light but no more. Listen to this voice of mine. I can sound like an Englishman when I choose but my tongue hates to play the traitor.' He emptied his tankard and wiped the back of his hand across his mouth. 'I carry my country on my back like a snail carrying its shell. Wales will always be my home—even though I left a wife and a child and an honest occupation to run away to London when the madness of the theatre seized me.'

'I did not know you were married, Owen.'

'It was a mistake that I try to keep buried.'

'And a child, you say?'

'He died soon after I left. He had always been a sickly boy and not long for this harsh world.' He toyed guiltily with his tankard. 'I sent what little money I could back to my wife but we lost touch after Rhodri died. She was a good woman, Nick, and deserved better than me.'

'Have you never been back home?'

'Never.'

'Do you not wonder what became of your wife?'

'All the time, but I content myself with the thought that life without a bad husband must be an improvement of sorts. She has a large family and will not want for anything.' His hands tightened around the tankard. 'They do not speak well of me. I would not be welcome.'

'You have always talked so fondly of your country.'

'Wales is in my blood,' said Elias with simple pride. 'I could never deny my birthright. But a wife is another matter. I did not just leave, Nick, she begged me to go.'

'I see.'

'We all have our cross to bear.'

Nicholas was touched that his friend should confide something so private in him, and it helped to explain a maudlin vein that sometimes came out in the Welshman. At the same time, he realised very clearly why Owen Elias touched on the subject of the unforgiven sins of the past. In showing his own wounds, he was offering a set of credentials to a kindred spirit. He was assuring Nicholas of sympathy and understanding if the latter chose to talk about the problems that were taking him back home. Men of the theatre were nomads, wandering from company to company, drifting from woman to woman, leaving their failures behind them in the ceaseless quest for a perfection they would never attain. Talent and status were transient assets. Lawrence Firethorn had no peer as an actor yet here he was, having abandoned his family in London, scurrying from town to town with a demoralised troupe in search of work and wages. Security and continuity were rare commodities in the acting world, and those who joined it had to accept that. Indeed, for many—Owen Elias among them—its recurring perils and sudden fluctuations were part of its attraction. Theatre was a game of chance. With its unquestioning camaraderie, it was also a good place to hide. Elias could recognise another fugitive.

'Why are you going to Barnstaple?' he asked.

'I may tell you when I return.'

'If you return.'

'Oh, I will come back,' said Nicholas firmly. 'There is nothing to keep me there any longer. My only concern is that I actually reach the town.'

'Nobody will stop you while I am around.'

'We cannot live in each other's laps.'

Owen chuckled. 'Barnaby Gill would die with envy!'

'Meanwhile, we have plays to present. Think on them.'

'Oh, I do, Nick. I am an actor. My vanity is quite monstrous. I strut and pose before the looking glass of my mind all the time.' He winked at the other. 'But I can still spare a thought for a friend in need.'

121

'Thank you, Owen.'

'Do not be afraid to call on me.'

Nicholas smiled his gratitude. Some of the others began to play cards at a nearby table and Owen excused himself to go and join them. The apprentices had already gone to their beds and a few of the sharers had also seen the virtue of an early night. Lawrence Firethorn sat with Barnaby Gill and discussed the choice of plays for Marlborough and Bristol. Two actor-musicians were busy drinking themselves into a stupor. Nicholas was content to be left alone on his oak settle and let his thoughts swing to and fro between London and Barnstaple, between the pain of a loss and the impending displeasure of a renewed acquaintance. An hour sped by. When he next looked up, most of his fellows had tottered off upstairs and the taproom was virtually empty. Nicholas was just about to haul himself off to his own bed-chamber when one of the ostlers came in through the main door. He peered around until his gaze settled on the book holder then he hurried across.

'Master Bracewell?' he said.

'Yes.'

'Nicholas Bracewell?'

'That is me.'

'Then I have a message for you, sir.'

'Who sent it?'

'A gentlemen. I am to tell you he wishes to see you.'

'Let him come on in.'

'He wants private conversation, sir. Outside.'

'In the dark?'

'There are lanterns burning by the stables.'

'What did the man look like?' asked Nicholas.

'A fine upstanding fellow.'

'Young or old? What does he wear? How does he speak?'

'I was only paid to deliver a message, sir,' said the ostler, turning to go. 'He waits for you by the stables.'

Nicholas had a dozen more questions but the ostler had scampered off before he could put them. The man who summoned him needed to be treated with utmost suspicion.

He must have kept watch on the taproom until it was almost cleared then sent in a messenger to fetch out the straggler. Nicholas had no immediate support beyond two actor-musicians on the verge of collapse and a diminutive servingman. Owen Elias had now gone off to bed and Edmund Hoode was deep in the throes of composition. Why should the man invite him to the stables? Nicholas started as it dawned on him. He was being issued with a challenge. Having failed to dispatch him in the stables of the Fighting Cocks, his adversary was inviting him to a second duel. It had to be single combat. If Nicholas walked out of the taproom with others at his back, the man would vanish into the night. Only if he went alone would the book holder stand a chance of meeting and killing his foe.

His sword lay beside him and he snatched it up. He took a few steps towards the front door then checked. What if the challenge was a ruse? The man might have set a trap with the aid of confederates. Nicholas pondered for a moment then came to the conclusion that he was up against a lone enemy. If there had been accomplices, he would not have survived the first assault at High Wycombe. The man was paying him a perverse compliment. Nicholas was being congratulated on his earlier success and given a return engagement on more equal terms. Except that a man who tries to strangle an opponent from behind will always have distorted ideas of equality.

Nicholas accepted the challenge but tempered boldness with caution. Instead of leaving by the front door, he moved quickly to the back of the taproom and slipped out into the narrow passageway with a stone-flagged floor. The door ahead of him gave access to some outbuildings and he could use those as cover while working his way around to the stables. Letting himself noiselessly out into the night, he kept his sword at the ready and crept furtively along. An owl hooted in the distance. A vixen answered with a high-pitched call. Clouds drifted across the moon. The lanterns threw only the patchiest light onto the courtyard.

As he came round the angle of a building, Nicholas could hear the faint jingle of metal as a horse chewed on its bit. The animal was saddled and ready at the edge of the stables. Nicholas could just make out its shape in the gloom. He was now satisfied that he was up against only one man. The horse made possible a hasty retreat after the task was done, but Nicholas intended to frustrate his opponent's plans. Bending low, he inched forward with his weapon guiding the way. He heard the sound behind him far too late. There was a thud, a loud grunt and a brief clash of steel. When Nicholas swung round, he was hit in the chest with such force by a solid shoulder that he dropped his sword to the ground and did a backward somersault. Two figures grappled violently above him but the fight was over before he could get to his feet to join in. There was a howl of pain and a clatter as something hit the cobbles beside Nicholas, then one of the figures went haring across the yard and vaulted into the saddle of the horse. For the second time, the assassin galloped safely away into the night.

Nicholas jumped up to turn solicitously to the wounded man. He had recognised Owen Elias's yell and feared serious injury to his friend. Still holding his own sword in one hand, the Welshman was bent double in pain. Nicholas put out a steadying arm around his shoulder.

'Are you hurt badly, Owen?' he said.

'The villain cut my hand, Nick. 'Tis only a scratch but it bleeds all over me and stings like the devil!'

'Let me help you back inside.'

'I can manage. Leave me be.'

Nicholas took a step back to appraise him. 'What on earth were you doing out here?'

'Trying to save your life.'

'I thought you had gone off to your bed.'

'That is what I wanted you to think,' said Owen. 'If that coward was going to strike again, he would only do it when you were alone. I hid in the passageway and heard the ostler's message delivered. The sender tricked you.'

'He did,' confessed Nicholas. 'He knew that I would try to sneak up on him from behind so he laid his ambush here. But for you, I'd be lying dead on the ground with a dagger between my shoulderblades. A thousand thanks.'

'Your bodyguard has sharp eyes and even sharper ears.'

'You suffered injury on my behalf. Come inside and I'll bind up that hand. You can have all the ale you wish to medicine your wound.' Nicholas retrieved his sword then picked up a smaller weapon. 'He left his dagger behind.'

Owen shouldered. 'I'll use it to cut off his stones.'

'It may hold a clue for us.'

'Where's that ale you spoke of, Nick? I need it.'

'And I'll question that ostler more closely.' He heard approaching feet. 'We have company, Owen.'

Roused by the commotion, the landlord and a couple of servingmen now came rushing out with lanterns. Edmund Hoode and other members of the company were in attendance. They saw the drawn rapiers.

'What dreadful broil was here?' said the landlord.

'It is all over now,' reassured Nicholas.

'Who started the affray?'

'We do not know the villain's name.'

'But what brought you out here, Nick?' said Hoode in alarm. 'And what was that unearthly cry we heard?'

'That was me,' said Owen Elias with a brave smile. 'I was bleeding quietly to death.'

The Welshman was clearly in intense pain. He swayed with fatigue, made an effort to hold up his injured hand for inspection then fainted into the arms of Nicholas Bracewell.

Chapter Seven

DAYLIGHT BROUGHT NO RELIEF FOR WESTFIELD'S
Men. They awoke to find the inn washed by a
steady drizzle of rain. It would be a sodden journey to Marlborough. As they breakfasted on toasted bread
and ale, they were unhappy and mutinous. Life outside
London was a pilgrimage of pain. Owen Elias was still
weak from loss of blood because his injury was more serious than he had at first admitted. The dagger intended for
Nicholas Bracewell's back had instead sliced through the
sleeve of the actor's jerkin and left a deep gash down his
arm and hand. It was vital to stem the bleeding at once, and
Nicholas took on this duty himself. During his three years
at sea, he had witnessed some horrific injuries and some
hideous diseases. By swift and careful treatment, the ship's
doctor had saved many lives and returned countless broken
bones to full use. Nicholas had watched him clean and bind
up the most appalling wounds, and he followed the same
principles with Owen Elias. The tight bandaging would protect the wound until they reached a town where a surgeon
could examine and re-dress the injury.

Another blow hit the company, albeit in retrospect. The
farmer who brought in the daily supply of milk to the inn
also carried the local gossip. He told of a shepherd who had

been stopped and stripped of his smock, hat and crook by no less a highwayman than Israel Gunby. The disguise had only been used for an hour before being returned to its owner with a purse of money. Lawrence Firethorn was livid. To be deceived by Israel Gunby once was a humiliation: to be gulled a second time was unendurable. While Firethorn took it as a personal affront, the rest of the company saw it as a general threat. Having swooped on them once, Israel Gunby and his vulturous partners were now circling them again before moving in to pick their bones clean.

Their morale was lower than ever as they set off in the drizzle. Swirling discontent found a spokesman in Barnaby Gill. He identified the culprit with a sneer.

'I blame our book holder for all this!'

'You are unjust,' said Firethorn. 'Nick Bracewell is the very backbone of this company. He puts Westfield's Men first in all that he does.'

'Then why is he travelling to Barnstaple?' said Gill.

'Because his family live there,' replied Edmund Hoode.

Gill was testy. 'We all have families. Lawrence has one back in London, you have parents in Kent, I have a mother and two sisters in Norwich, even that heathen Welshman must have some sort of kith and kin across the border.' He sat upright in his saddle with pursed indignation. 'When the company has need of us, however, we do not go running back home in the name of family obligation.'

'Nick is loyal,' asserted Firethorn. 'He agreed to guide us all the way to the West Country before taking his leave of us. I ask you, Barnaby—where would we be without Nick Bracewell at the helm?'

'At the Queen's Head in Gracechurch Street.'

'We were burned out, man.'

'Whose mind devised that brazier?' said Gill acidly. 'Whose hand kindled that flame? Our book holder's. *He* is the cause of all our misery and it is never-ending.'

'Nick was the hero of the fire,' said Hoode with a passionate defence of his friend. 'Do you not remember the danger he averted? Can you not recall his selfless courage? Have you not heard the ballad about the fire?'

'A ragged piece,' said Gill, 'and not to be trusted for one moment. The ballad does not mention *me* at all. And I was the first victim of the blaze.'

The three men were riding together at the head of the party as it bumped along a rutted road near Wantage. Other sharers were strung out behind them, and the waggon was now loaded to capacity. Since Owen Elias was disabled from driving the vehicle, Nicholas Bracewell had taken over the reins. Owen sat beside him and sang a Welsh air in a doleful baritone voice. The four apprentices were huddled together under a tarpaulin, and the hired men aboard found what shelter they could beneath cloaks and blankets. George Dart had been given the signal honour of riding the roan, and he brought up the rear with a pride that no amount of fine rain could dampen. Alone of Westfield's Men, he thought it the most beautiful day of the year.

'Consider it well,' said Gill, returning to his attack. 'Nicholas Bracewell has brought us ill luck at every turn. He got us thrown out of London and robbed at High Wycombe.'

'You cannot lay the robbery at his feet,' said Hoode.

'At his feet and at Lawrence's codpiece. They are the guilty parts of the anatomy here.' He raised his voice over Firethorn's protest. 'We are the actors and have work enough to do performing our roles in a makeshift entertainment. We rely on Nicholas to set up the stage and weigh the audience in the balance. He should have picked out Israel Gunby.'

'How?' asked Hoode.

'By instinct.'

'In a taproom full of other travellers?'

'Nicholas is our great voyager, is he not?' mocked Gill. 'He has sailed around the world and seen all sorts and conditions of men. That has given him a sixth sense about people. Lawrence has turned to him again and again.'

'Yes,' said Firethorn, 'because Nick has never let us

down. He can read the character of a man at a glance and see into his virtues and his defects.'

'He did not read Israel Gunby at a glance.'

'No more did you, Barnaby. Nor I, nor Edmund here.'

'Nicholas is there to *protect* us.'

'Even he has limitations.'

'This tour has revealed them,' continued Gill. 'He has served us well in the past, I grant you, but he is now the symbol of our misfortune. Without him, there would have been no Israel Gunby to abuse us, no plague in Oxford to vex us and no second visitation from Gunby to tantalise us.'

'Do not forget this drizzle,' said Hoode sarcastically. 'Without Nick, we would be basking in bright sunshine and filling our pockets with the money that grew on every bush that we passed. This is arrant nonsense, Barnaby!'

'And is that injury to Owen Elias arrant nonsense?'

'That is another matter,' muttered Firethorn.

'Another matter for which our revered book holder must be held responsible,' persisted Gill. 'He was attacked at the Dog and Bear last night. The gallant Welshman came to his rescue and almost lost an arm. Will you absolve Nicholas there as well?'

'I will,' replied Hoode fiercely. 'You cannot blame a man because he is set upon by some drunken reveller.'

'That drunken reveller was as sober as a pine needle.'

'Owen will recover,' said Firethorn, trying to deflect his colleague from a disagreeable topic. 'That is all that matters as far as Westfield's Men are concerned.'

'Until this villain strikes again.'

'What villain?'

'The one who is stalking Nicholas.'

'There is no such person,' said Hoode weakly.

'Leave off this talk,' added Firethorn uncomfortably.

'Tell me who caused that disturbance at the Fighting Cocks and I will,' challenged Gill. His companions traded an uneasy glance. 'I am not blind, gentlemen. Nicholas went out to the stables and came back dishevelled. A horse was heard galloping away from the inn. Who rode it?'

'Israel Gunby's fat accomplice,' said Hoode.

'He would not dare to measure his strength against our book holder. An impudent rascal he may have been, but he was no fighting man. I believe that Nicholas was set on by the same person who came back again last night and maimed Owen. Deny it, if you will.' He paused. 'Well?'

Lawrence Firethorn and Edmund Hoode maintained a shifty silence. They had both been told by Nicholas Bracewell why he had to go to Barnstaple, and danger was implicit in that journey. Barnaby Gill had worked out for himself what they already knew and he drew a conclusion that heightened their discomfort considerably.

'We are marked men,' said Gill. 'As long as we carry Nicholas Bracewell with us, we are all at risk. When and where will this rogue launch his next assault? Which of us will be wounded on that occasion?' He nudged Firethorn. 'Get rid of him, Lawrence. Put the safety of the company first and send him off to Barnstaple. Or this fellow who pursues him will murder us all, one by one!'

Marriage to an actor was always a hazardous undertaking and when that actor was Lawrence Firethorn, the relationship could never even approximate to conventional notions of holy matrimony. Solemn vows made before the altar could not bind a couple in perpetuity. In the interests of survival, they had to be continuously re-arranged to meet each new situation as it arose. Margery Firethorn was a potent woman with a single-minded commitment to getting her own way, but even she could not impose a rigid structure upon her connubial bliss. Her husband could be guided but never wholly controlled. It would be easier to stitch the Lord's Prayer onto a soap bubble than to fit Lawrence Firethorn into anything that resembled normal married life, and Margery's own tempestuous nature could never be contained within a wifely role. Their love had been tested many a time, and although it had acquired layers of cynicism on her side and a few startling blemishes on his, it had never been found wanting. They might wrangle and accuse but they were always working together and the sense of a common vision kept them immoveably in each other's arms and minds.

The common vision took her to the Queen's Head.

'They have started in earnest.'

'I see that, Leonard.'

'The carpenters will be here for a fortnight or more,' he said, 'then the plasterers and painters will come, too.'

'There's thatch to be replaced as well,' she noted, looking up at the part of the roof where Nicholas Bracewell had prostrated himself. 'You'll need fresh reeds up there to keep out the wind and rain.'

'It will all be done in time, mistress.'

They were in the courtyard of the inn amid the rasp of saws and the din of hammers. Carpentry was a deafening occupation. The problem with the work of restoration was that the Queen's Head had to look worse before it could look better. A section of the balconies had been cut away entirely to leave a yawning hole in the corner of the yard. Wooden scaffolding held up the remaining part of the structure. Where supports had burned through, props had been temporarily inserted to prevent any further subsidence. They would be replaced in time by the stout oak of ship's timbers that were finding a useful purpose in life now that their sailing days were over. The work was slow, hard and expensive but it conformed to a definite plan.

'Did you find the courier?' asked Leonard.

'He left the city at dawn,' said Margery. 'With God's speed, he should reach Marlborough some time tomorrow. We must pray that the warning is in time to be of use.'

'Did you tell Master Bracewell that I saw the man?'

'It has not been forgotten, Leonard.'

'Thank you, thank you.'

'That portrait was largely your work.'

'I am glad to be of service.'

Margery gave him a gracious smile. 'Do not let me detain you from your duties,' she said, gazing around the yard, 'for I must be about mine. Where is that whining innkeeper who pays your wages?'

'He is in the taproom. Do you wish to speak with him?'

131

'No, I wish to know that he is occupied so that I may place my argument where it will have more influence. It is too soon to reason with Alexander Marwood.'

'It is,' agreed Leonard. 'He has a fit of the ague every time the name Westfield's Men is heard. I will hold back my plea until he is more settled in his mind.'

'Tread with care.'

'I go on tiptoe.'

'Choose your moment to woo the wretch back to us.'

'I will. And you?'

'Leave me to work upon his wife.'

They bade their farewells and parted. Leonard went off to unload some more barrels from the dray while Margery took a first small step towards repairing the shattered relations between the Queen's Head and Westfield's Men. She had come at the express request of her husband. While the company was on the road, she and Lord Westfield were its representatives in London. The aristocrat would be brought into the scheme of things later on when the pontification of a patron might have more impact. At this stage, Margery Firethorn was a much more effective advocate for the exiled troupe. She could insinuate herself into places here no sane man would ever dare to venture.

Sybil Marwood was in the room at the rear of the inn, which was used as a parlour during the rare moments when she and her husband could actually pause for rest. She was a plump, severe and unlovely woman who was spending her middle years bitterly regretting the follies of her youth. What had once been pleasant features had now congealed into a mask of deep disappointment. Sybil Marwood had so much iron in her soul that a team of miners would be kept busy for a month trying to extract it and several picks would be broken in the process.

She gave Margery a gruff welcome and invited her in.

'We have met before,' reminded Margery.

'Yes,' came the tight-lipped reply.

'I gave you sound advice. On that occasion, too, I was able to show you the error of your ways and point out where true profit and advancement lay.'

'What do you want?' hissed Sybil.

'To speak with you, woman to woman.'

'Wife to wife, more like!'

'That, too.'

'I know your game, Mistress Firethorn,' said Sybil with a derisive sneer. 'My husband has broken with your husband and you seek to use me to join them together again.'

'That is quite false.'

'Why else would you deign to visit me?'

'To keep them apart.'

Sybil Marwood was taken aback. She had been extremely displeased to see her visitor and to be reminded of the man whose company had all but burned her home and workplace to the ground. Her immediate assumption was that Margery had come on behalf of Westfield's Men to sue for reinstatement at the Queen's Head. What other motive would bring her there? Sybil turned on the basilisk gaze she usually reserved for her husband but Margery did not wilt. Calm and poised, she waited for her cue to offer a full explanation. Her husband had taught her the importance of dressing for the occasion, so Margery had put on her smartest attire and her most spectacular hat. Shoes, gloves and all accessories combined to give a stunning effect. Sybil Marwood was in the presence of a lady, and it made her self-conscious about her own drab clothes and greasy mob cap. She became fractionally more respectful.

'Would you care to sit down, Mistress?' she said.

'I may not stay long,' said Margery, glancing at the dust on every surface in the room and vowing not to soil her dress by contact with it. 'I have too much to do.'

'You spoke of keeping them apart.'

'So I did.'

'For what purpose?'

'Westfield's Men must never return here.'

'Nor will they,' promised Sybil. 'My husband has sworn that they will never cross our threshold again and I will keep him to that decision.'

'I pray that you do, Mistress.'

'Why?'

'Because our good fortune collapses else.'

'Good fortune?'

Margery took a step towards her and lowered her voice to a confidential whisper. The basilisk glare had now been diluted to a look of open-eyed wonder.

'May I trust you never to repeat this?' said Margery.

'On my honour!'

'Most of all, you must not tell your husband.'

'Alexander is a fool. I tell him nothing.'

'A sound rule for any marriage.'

'What is this good fortune?'

'Westfield's Men have been approached.'

'By whom?'

'Another innkeeper. Hearing that their contract here had been torn up, he straightway stepped in to offer a home for the company. Is not this wonderful news?'

'Why, yes,' said Sybil, uncertainly, feeling the first itch of envy. 'Who is this innkeeper?'

'That is a secret I must keep locked in my bosom. But I tell you this, though his inn be smaller than yours, he looks to make a larger profit out of his new tenants.'

'Profit?' The word was a talisman.

'He cannot understand why the Queen's Head would let such a rich source of income go.'

'That rich source of income set fire to our premises!'

'It was the wind that did that, mistress,' said Margery. 'Westfield's Men saved your inn from complete destruction. That ballad says it all. Nicholas Bracewell and the others put their lives at risk for you and your husband. It is one of the reasons that persuaded this other interested party to step forward. He admires men of such quality.'

'Where is this hostelry?' said Sybil.

Margery clapped her hands in glee. 'That is a further boon,' she explained, 'It is outside the city walls and therefore free from the jurisdiction of the authorities. They hate the theatre and do all they can to suppress it. If Westfield's Men leave here, they leave behind interference and disapproval. Nothing will hinder them from now on.'

Sybil was mystified. 'So why do you come to me?'

'To ensure the safety of the new contract.'

'In what way?'

'The innkeeper is a possessive man. He wants the company to be solely his. My husband has assured him that the Queen's Head has repudiated its contract with the company. Is that not so?'

'It is, it is.'

'Then it must be *seen* to be so,' stressed Margery. 'If your husband were even to consider renewing that contract, I fear it will frighten our new landlord away. He is very jealous and prone to impulsive action. You know how men are when they set their minds on something.'

'Only too well!'

'May we count on your help here?'

'Indeed,' said Sybil. 'I will ensure that Alexander has no further contact with Westfield's Men. What did the actors do except fill our yard with people of the lower sort?'

'They filled your balconies with gallants and their ladies,' reminded Margery. 'And they also filled your pockets with money. How much beer and ale did you sell when a play brought the crowds to the Queen's Head?' She rammed home another argument. 'How much fame did the company bestow upon your inn? Why did so many visitors to London flock to Gracechurch Street for their entertainment instead of to Southwark or Shoreditch? Westfield's Men gave you a noble reputation.'

'That is true,' conceded the other then hardened. 'But it is a reputation for licentious behaviour. Actors are born lechers. Our daughter, Rose, barely escaped with her virginity twice a day when we harboured those lusty gentlemen.'

'Come, come,' said Margery roguishly, 'we were young ourselves at one time. Think back. Lusty gentlemen were not so unwelcome then.'

A distant gleam of pleasure lit up Sybil's face, but it was extinguished immediately as she spat out an accusation.

'One of the players kept sending Rose some verses.'

'A rhyming couplet will not get you with child.'

'My daughter cannot read.'

'Then she is safe from corruption.'

'We are glad to see the last of Westfield's Men.'

'Then you see the last of the profits they brought in.'

Sybil snorted. 'Where is the profit in a raging fire? How much money do we make from fighting apprentices?'

'Fire is an act of God,' said Margery, 'and every inn and dwelling in London lives in fear of it. As for affrays among apprentices, they are caused by your ale and not by any play. Besides, no performance by Westfield's Men has ever been stopped because of a riot. Drama imposes order on the unruly. It is only afterwards that the drunkards fight.'

'Not any more. We have Leonard to quell any brawls.'

'And who brought Leonard to the Queen's Head?'

Sybil paused. 'Master Bracewell.'

'It was only one of many favours he did you.'

Margery had sewed the seeds of self-interest and given them enough water to promote growth. She could now let Sybil Marwood loose on her long-suffering husband. The notion of handing over a lucrative contract to another landlord would at least make Alexander Marwood think again, and the fact that their rival had been plucked out of the air by Margery would never occur to them. An abode that thrived on marital discord had now been given fruitful source of conflict.

Pausing at the door, Margery threw in a last argument.

'You have another reason to thank Nicholas Bracewell.'

'How so?'

'A messenger, sent to him from Devon, took refreshment here at the Queen's Head and died before the message could be delivered.'

'Died? From what cause?'

'Poisoned ale.'

'Our drink is the purest in London.'

'That is what everyone believes,' said Margery. 'I am sure you would not have them think otherwise.'

'How could they?'

'By mischievous report. Nicholas Bracewell says that poison was put into the ale in the taproom by one of your patrons. Murder occurred under this very roof.'

'Murder!'

'The messenger died elsewhere, but the villainy took place not twenty yards from where we stand. It would not advantage you, if that story were to spread.'

'It must not!'

'Nicholas Bracewell is discreet on your behalf.'

'We are greatly indebted to him.'

Margery Firethorn was a prudent gardener. 'Such an event could be the ruination of you,' she said, irrigating the seeds once more with a final sprinkling. 'When the Queen's Head was the home of Westfield's Men it had renown and distinction. Who would wish to visit an establishment that was notorious for its poisonous ale?'

She could almost hear the first green shoots pushing up.

Berkshire was a beautiful county and the drizzle relented to enable them to see it at its best. Warm sunshine dried them off, lifted their heads and gladdened their hearts. The Vale of the White Horse was unusual in being set aside almost exclusively for corn production, and fields of gold danced and waved all around them. Seen from the top of a rolling waggon, the simplicity of country life had an appeal that was very beguiling, and more than one of the travellers mused about exchanging it for the vicissitudes of their own existence. Local inhabitants took an opposite view, looking up in wonder as the gaily attired troupe went past and imagining the joys of belonging to such an elite profession. Even jaded actors knew how to catch the eye of an audience.

Wantage supplied a surgeon for Owen Elias, and the wound was treated before being bound up again. Since the injury had been sustained because of him, Nicholas Bracewell paid the surgeon, who complimented him on the way that he himself had first attended to the patient. An inn at Hungerford gave the company excellent refreshment, and they set off for the final stage of their journey with their misgivings largely subdued. Even Barnaby Gill had lost his sourness. With the prospect of willing spectators ahead of them, Westfield's Men rallied even more. The waggon broke into song and Owen Elias's voice was now merry as well as melodious.

When they crossed the border into Wiltshire, the company gave an involuntary cheer. They did not have too far to go now. Richard Honeydew clambered into the driving seat beside Nicholas Bracewell and sought to improve his education.

'They say that Wiltshire is covered with forests.'

'That is only partly true,' said Nicholas, still at the reins. 'There are belts of woodland stretching right across the county, and when we reach Marlborough, we will be sitting on the edge of one of the finest forests in England.'

'What is it called?'

'Savernake.'

The boy's face ignited. 'Does it have wild animals?'

'Hundreds of them, Dick.'

'Bears and wolves?'

'They were killed off centuries ago when Savernake was a royal forest. You'll still find foxes, badgers, rabbits and hares, not to mention herds of deer. And there are game birds of all description.' Nicholas turned to smile at him. 'But most of the wild animals there run on two legs.'

'Two legs?'

'Poachers,' explained Owen Elias, who sat behind them. 'When we get there, Savernake will have another two-legged wild animal. I can snare a rabbit or catch a pheasant with the best of them. Put your trust in me, lads, and we'll have roast venison for a week.'

'And the law down upon our necks,' warned Nicholas.

'You told me it was only partly true,' the apprentice said to him. 'What else does this county have?'

'Great, windswept plains and downs. That is where the real wealth of Wiltshire lies, not in its woods and its ploughland. Do you know why, Dick?'

'No.'

'Sheep.'

'We have seen hundreds already.'

'Travel around the county and you will see thousands upon thousands.' Nicholas warmed to his theme. 'Wiltshire

138

is able to support an endless number of sheep on its thin soil. Their fleeces and flesh have made many people rich. Take but the case of William Stumpe.'

'Who?'

'William Stumpe of Malmesbury.'

The boy giggled. 'It is a funny name.'

'Nobody laughed at him when he was alive for he became the most prosperous man in the town. Shall I tell you how?'

'Please.' Richard Honeydew nodded his enthusiasm.

'William Stumpe was a clothier,' said Nicholas. 'He bought himself an abbey at the Dissolution.'

'Why?'

'A man must have somewhere to set his looms. He paid over fifteen hundred pound for Malmesbury Abbey, then granted to the town the nave of the abbey church so that it could serve the parish.'

'What did he do with the rest of the building?'

'He moved in his weavers,' said Nicholas. 'Within a few years, they were turning out three thousand cloths a year. It brought in a huge income. Stumpe was of humble parentage yet he rose to be member of parliament and high collector for North Wiltshire. Even that did not satisfy him. He had another project that was far more ambitious.'

'What was it?'

'Osney Abbey.'

'At Oxford?'

'We drove right past it, Dick.'

'Did this clothier want to buy that as well?'

'Yes,' said Nicholas, who knew the story by heart. 'He planned to have as many as two thousand workers employed at Osney. Two *thousand*—can you imagine the size of such an enterprise? The cost of such an operation?' He shrugged. 'We shall never know if the scheme at Osney Abbey would have worked because he did not proceed with it, but you have to admire the man's boldness. Two thousand.'

'What happened to William Stumpe?'

'He invested his money in land, Dick, and that made him

wealthier than ever. He lived to see his son knighted, and his three granddaughters have all married earls.' Nicholas flicked the reins to coax more speed out of the two horses then he underlined the moral of his story. 'Stumpe showed the value of hard work and a clear imagination. No matter where you begin in life, you can fight your way up.'

'How do you know so much about him?' said the boy.

'My father told me.'

The sentence slipped out so easily that it was a few moments before Nicholas understood its significance. He was jarred into silence. Without realising it, he had just told Richard Honeydew a story that his father had often used as an example for him when Nicholas was about the same age as the apprentice. It was a cruel reminder of a time when Robert Bracewell would instruct and entertain his son for hours on end with his tales of enterprising businessmen. Wiltshire had always been a principal producer and exporter of cloth and—though its wool could not match the quality of that from the Welsh Borders and the Cotswolds—fortunes could still be made in the trade. Most of the output was now sold in London through members of the Company of Merchant Adventurers, which had superseded the old Merchant Staplers. Others now followed where William Stumpe had led.

Nicholas Bracewell had happily imbibed such stories and uncritically accepted his father's interests and attitudes. That was no longer the case. Disillusion was total. It was almost obscene to dwell upon a time in his past when he and Robert Bracewell had actually been friends. Nicholas stole a glance at his young companion. Richard Honeydew's innocence and inquisitive streak reminded him of his own. Since he was very much an alternative father to the boy, he resolved that he would never betray his illusions in the way that his own had been shattered. The apprentice must be saved from that.

Richard Honeydew was unaware of his friend's turmoil.

'Is your father still alive?' he asked.

'Yes.'

'He will be pleased to see you when you get to Devon.'
Nicholas could not trust his tongue with any words.

Marlborough was an attractive town. Set on a hill above the meandering River Kennet, it commanded a superb view of the Savernake Forest to the south-east and of the rolling landscape in other directions. The High Street was a wide thoroughfare that swept all the way down from St Mary's Church at the top to the Church of Saints Peter and Paul at the bottom. Houses, shops, inns and other buildings stood side by side in a street to which religion gave such clear demarcation. There was a profusion of thatched roofs.

Westfield's Men liked what they saw and the excited interest of the townspeople was especially gratifying after the subdued response of Oxford. Lawrence Firethorn led them down the High Street and turned in through the gate of the White Hart. It was a large and well-appointed inn with a yard in the shape of a horseshoe as well as a garden with three arbours. Though Nicholas knew that performances by visiting troupes took place in the adjacent Guildhall, he nevertheless assessed the yard as a potential outdoor venue. Its shape made it easily adaptable, and seating could be placed in the galleries above to increase the size of the audience. The White Hart would be an ideal amphitheatre for the actors. Like the Queen's Head in Gracechurch Street.

Firethorn wasted no time with formalities. While the waggon was being unloaded, Nicholas was sent off to find the town officials and secure permission to stage a play. On such occasions, the book holder always carried the company's licence because this legitimated their work and set them apart from the haphazard groups of strolling players who roamed the country in search of audiences less concerned with high quality. The law branded such actors as outlaws. Only licenced companies bearing the name of a patron could have a legal claim to perform whenever they visited a new town or city. Since officials were always officious, Nicholas never went to them without his credentials.

'Westfield's Men! We are honoured!'

'Thank you, sir.'

'Lawrence Firethorn has graced our town before.'

'It holds warm memories for him.'

'And for us, my friend. And for us.'

The mayor was a short, bearded, misshapen man in his fifties with such a fondness for his chain of office that he wore it at all times and fingered it incessantly. Though delighted to see the company, he had to season good news with bad. A few cases of plague had broken out in Marlborough. It had not yet spread and—they were earnestly praying in both churches—it might never reach the epidemic proportions it had attained in Oxford, but it did exist and visitors ought to be made aware of the fact. The mayor said he would deeply regret it if Westfield's Men felt unable to perform in the light of this intelligence, but he would understand if they decided that there was too large a risk involved.

'We will stage our work,' said Nicholas firmly.

'Then Marlborough greets you with open arms.'

'Master Firethorn would not hear of running away.'

'Our Guildhall will be put at your disposal.'

Nicholas was empowered to make all arrangements and to exercise his judgement. Westfield's Men, they agreed, were to give two performances, one in the Guildhall that evening and another at the same venue the following afternoon. That would enable a large number of the people of Marlborough to enjoy their work and would put them on the road to Bristol by the early evening of the next day. The brief stay also reduced the chances of contracting the infection, which had already killed off three victims. For the first performance, attended by all the town luminaries, the mayor volunteered to pay twenty shillings out of the civic purse. This was a generous offer. If Nicholas had perused the chamberlain's accounts for the last decade, he would have seen that most visiting companies were paid considerably less, some as little as two shillings. Like Westfield's Men, those troupes had been able to supplement the civic payment by charging admission money or by holding a collection at the end of a play. At the performance on the following afternoon, Lawrence Firethorn would instruct the gatherers to do both.

Nicholas took his leave of the mayor and hurried back to the White Hart to report to Lawrence Firethorn. Early signs of plague did not deter the actor-manager at all.

'Give me an audience and I'll play in a leper colony.'

Barnaby Gill sniggered. 'It would sort well with the quality of your acting,' he said.

'Do you dare to insult my art!'

'I will tell you if I chance to see it.'

'Away, you prancing ninny!'

'Those who come to see Lawrence Firethorn will go away talking about Barnaby Gill.'

'Who was that blinking idiot, they will say!'

'Genius will always shine through.'

'Remember that when mine dazzles your eyes tonight.'

A mood of contentment pervaded the White Hart. When Lawrence Firethorn and Barnaby Gill were at each other's throats again, all was right with Westfield's Men.

Nicholas Bracewell took control. Two of the hired men were despatched to go around the town and advertise the evening's performance. One was to beat a drum, the other to blow a horn. They were assigned to deafen Marlborough into submission then entice them to the play by declaiming a few choice speeches from it. Nicholas himself repaired to the Guildhall with his assistants to take stock of its potential. It was a large, low room with thick rafters bending to accommodate the dip in the ceiling. The book holder chose the location of the stage at once, placing it at the far end where a door to an ante-room gave them a natural tiring-house. Chairs would be given pride of place in the front rows, benches would seat those of lesser station, and there would be ample standing room for anyone else. A charge of twopence for a seat and a penny to stand would bring in a fair amount of money.

The major decision concerned lighting. Performances at the Queen's Head were at the mercy of the open sky, and the company relied on its audience to make allowances for this. But there was still ribald laughter when scenes that were set in the deserts of Asia were played by actors shivering in a cold wind, or when characters complained about snow and ice while sweating in the afternoon sun. Action set at the dead of night would always be mocked by bright weather. The Guildhall altered the performing conditions and permitted some measure of control. Nicholas decided to make use of the natural light that would stream in through the windows during the first half of the play, and to supplement it in gradations with candles, torches and lanterns. For the final scene, tarred rope would be set alight in holders.

Lawrence Firethorn came in on an exploratory prowl.

'Is all well, Nick?'

'I foresee no problems.'

'This Guildhall has tested my mettle before.'

'Voices carry well.'

'Mine will reach to Stonehenge itself!' boomed the actor with an expansive gesture of his hand. 'Listen! Can you not hear those stones cracking and shaking at the sound of my thunder? I can out-shout Jove himself!'

'I believe it well, master.'

Nicholas turned to the hired men who waited nearby and gave his orders. They ran off to collect the makeshift stage and curtains that had been brought in the waggon. A rehearsal was imminent and there was no time to dawdle. The book holder was a patient man, but he could be stern with anyone caught slacking. Nicholas was determined that the initial performance of their tour would set a high standard. It would not only enthral the audience, it would also release the company's tensions and restore its self-confidence.

Left alone with him, Lawrence Firethorn took the opportunity of snatching a private word with Nicholas.

'We must talk of Owen's injury,' he said.

'It will not stop him performing tonight.'

'I am more concerned with how he came by it, Nick. The dagger in the darkness was intended for you, was it not?'

'I fear me that it was.'

'Do you know who the villain is?'

144

'Not yet,' admitted Nicholas. 'The ostler at the Dog and Bear caught no more than a glimpse of the man in the shadows, and simply gained some idea of his height and age. These I had already surmised.'

'There is no more clue to his identity?'

'Nothing but this.'

He produced the dagger, which had been dropped in the scuffle on the previous night. It was a handsome weapon, a slender-bladed poniard with a decorated hilt that was shaped to allow a firm grip. As Nicholas held it again, he felt its perfect balance and looked with apprehension at its gleaming point. Owen Elias had been supremely lucky. The dagger was not used to inflicting mere wounds when it could kill with a single thrust.

'That belongs to no common cutthroat,' said Firethorn as he examined the weapon. 'Nor was it made by any English craftsman. That is French workmanship. The man who owned that paid highly for the privilege.'

'He will be back to collect it.'

'Then let him collect it between his ribs, Nick.'

'I will be watchful.'

'We need you *alive*, dear heart!'

'He will not take me unawares.'

'Call on your friends. We are here to protect you.'

'I need to tempt him to attack once more.'

'Are you run mad?'

'It is the only way,' said Nicholas. 'While he is out there, I am under threat, and the company suffers because of it. This man would kill me to stop me reaching Barnstaple. He must have good reason for that. I need to find out what that reason is. He must be drawn out into the open.'

'With live bait on the hook! No, Nick, it is lunacy!'

'Bear with me I will catch him.'

'When you do, hand over the wretch to me,' said Firethorn, taking the dagger and slashing the air with it. 'I'll cut the truth out of his black heart.'

The man reached Marlborough an hour before Westfield's Men and he was standing in the High Street when they rode into town. News of the evening's performance was soon broadcast and the ripples of excitement spread quickly out to the surrounding areas. London companies rarely toured when they could be playing to larger audiences in the theatres of the capital. Marlborough appreciated its good fortune and took full advantage. Both performances were guaranteed a capacity audience. The man decided to be among the spectators that evening. A third attempt on Nicholas Bracewell's life in as many days was unwise. The book holder would be at his most alert and—as the man had discovered to his cost—he had vigilant friends at his side. The assassin could not kill his way through the entire company in order to reach Nicholas. There had to be another means of achieving this vital aim. Watching the play that evening, he hoped, might suggest another route to his grisly destination.

He took a room at an inn near the ruins of the castle at the bottom end of the town. The afternoon gave him an opportunity to catch up on some of the sleep he had been forced to surrender in his pursuit of his elusive prey. Early evening found him refreshed and eager to prepare himself for the visit to the Guildhall. He called for a looking glass and the girl who brought it arrived with a compliant giggle. She had been struck by his craggy charm and marked him out as a gentleman. There was a saturnine quality about him, but it only increased his appeal. As she stood beaming before him, she expected money but hoped for a kiss by way of reward. She got neither. Her willingness irritated the man so much that he snatched the looking glass from her and pushed her out. The only thing that brushed her lips was the door, which was slammed in her face.

Though the man had brought a change of apparel, he kept on his riding clothes. They were less ostentatious in a provincial market town where he needed to blend into the crowd. Beard and hair were a different matter, and he spent a long while in front of the mirror with a comb. He held a pearl earring up to one lobe and enjoyed its sparkle before putting it aside again. What he could wear without comment in London would attract too much attention in Wiltshire. He was still angry at the loss of his dagger, but it had a matching companion and he slipped this into the scabbard at the rear of his belt. After checking his appearance in the looking glass once more, he was ready to leave.

The Guildhall was filling rapidly when he got there and his twopence bought one of the last few unoccupied chairs. He chose one that was in the middle of a row halfway back from the stage so that he could lose himself in the very centre of the audience. To the right of him was an amiable farmer who had ridden five miles in order to enjoy the treat. On his left was a fleshy young man with less interest in theatrical entertainment. He complained bitterly to his attractive wife for making him bring her to the Guildhall. The man paid little interest in any of his neighbours. He wished that the farmer's breath was not so foul and that the squabbling couple—a miller and his wife, judging by the few words he did overhear—would settle down to watch the play. The assassin was there for a purpose that required his full concentration.

The Happy Malcontent answered all needs. It was a witty comedy about a London physician, Doctor Blackthought, who went through life dispensing criticism and disgust wherever he could. Nothing could please him. He railed against the world and its ways with caustic invective. Instead of curing his patients, the malcontented Doctor Blackthought only infected them with his own vexation. The problem became so acute that his wife and friends got together to devise a plan of rescue for him, but it was all to no avail. When they addressed the fundamental causes of his rancour—and actually managed to remove them by financial or other means—Blackthought was outraged because he no longer had a mainspring for his black thoughts. He was only truly happy in his disaffection. When they realised this, the others wreaked such a cruel revenge on him that lifelong discontent was assured. The doctor howled against a malevolent fate with undisguised delight.

It was a good choice of play. The spectators adored it, the actors played it superbly, and Barnaby Gill went through his full range of comic gestures and voices as the dissatisfied doctor. The medical theme had a particular relevance for a town that was troubled by early signs of plague, and laughter gave them enormous relief from their anxieties. Gallows humour had more depth. Even in the attenuated version forced on them by a smaller cast, *The Happy Malcontent* brought rich contentment. It was a stylish and well-constructed piece to set before Marlborough.

Lawrence Firethorn was in his element. Westfield's Men were holding yet another audience spellbound and his was the star performance. Barnaby Gill might have the title role but it was the effervescent Sir Lionel Fizzle who stole scene after scene. As the ebullient knight, Firethorn turned in a cameo performance that was mesmeric. It was he who made the malcontent really happy in his misery by cuckolding him. During the seduction scene with Richard Honeydew, the winsome but knowing wife, Firethorn had such a powerful effect on the female segments of the audience that they could be heard swooning. It put the actor-manager in high humour. When he came offstage at the end of the scene, he had a brief exchange with Nicholas Bracewell.

'Barnaby still thinks that this play is his!'

'It is going well,' said Nicholas, keeping one eye on the prompt copy. 'Master Gill is in good form.'

Firethorn grinned. 'He is an old horse who gallops round and round the stage in circles while I do tricks on his back like a performing monkey.' He nudged the book holder. 'Pick your part, that is the secret of acting. Barnaby does all the work, I get all the plaudits.'

Nicholas eased him aside to give a signal to a group of actors who were now due onstage. George Dart—playing his fifth part of the evening—was one of them, and he went about his work with bewildered resignation. The reduced size of the company placed many extra burdens on the book holder but it was the little assistant stagekeeper who suffered most. As well as erecting the stage, putting up the curtains and placing all the costumes and properties in the tiring-house, George Dart acted as one of the gatherers who took the admission money before racing backstage again to change the scenery during the performance, to play each of his five parts with identical lack of talent and to discharge his more familiar role as the whipping boy of Westfield's Men. Here was one malcontent with no time to be happy.

The Guildhall rejoiced. The mayor joined in the guffaws at Barnaby Gill while his wife fell quietly in love with Lawrence Firethorn. Those in the chairs applauded, those on the benches stamped their feet and those standing at the back did both simultaneously while yelling their approval. Some of the wit went over the heads of the audience but there was still more than enough to turn the event into a rollicking entertainment. Even the miller enjoyed it in the early stages. As the play neared its end, however, he seemed to lose interest very abruptly and dropped off to sleep. His head fell first on his wife's shoulder and then, when she shook him off, onto the neck of the man in front of him. While everyone else was convulsed with laughter, the fleshy young man was snoring.

His immediate neighbour ignored him at first. Though he was there for a more sinister reason, he nevertheless enjoyed the play. He was especially impressed with the performance of Barnaby Gill and could not take his eyes off the actor. During the final scene, the hall was in darkness and the stage lit by candles and by the glow from the tarred rope, which burned in its bowls to give off a noisome smell. The snoring miller fell gently against the man with the raven black beard, who instantly prodded him away. The jolt did not wake him nor did the thunderous appreciation that followed the end of the play. Lawrence Firethorn and Barnaby Gill competed for the position at the centre of the stage, each convinced that he was the crowning success of the evening.

The assassin watched Gill closely as the actor gave a deep bow and blew kisses to his public, but the man's attention was soon torn away. Snoring louder than ever, the miller fell against his neighbour yet again but his hand was not asleep. With practised stealth, it closed on the man's purse and felt the weight of its prize before pulling it gently away. The pickpocket was too slow. A grip of steel grabbed his wrist. His eyelids lifted in horror.

Lawrence Firethorn drained the applause to the last drop then took his company into the tiring-house to shower congratulations on them. The evening had been an unqualified triumph and all their setbacks had been submerged by five acts of frenzied comedy. Westfield's Men had performed well and put an appreciable amount of money into their depleted coffers. They could now change out of their costumes and repair to the White Hart for a well-earned supper. Since the Guildhall would be locked, everything could be left there overnight until the performance on the morrow.

Barnaby Gill's vanity needed even more stroking.

'Did you recognise my performance, Lawrence?'

Firethorn groaned. 'It was gruesomely familiar.'

'I based it on a model.'

'It was certainly based on no human being.'

'Alexander Marwood.'

'Do not soil your tongue with that poisonous name.'

'I was a discontented innkeeper to the life.'

'Leave the theatre and embrace your true profession.'

Edmund Hoode interposed himself between them and the banter soon died away. Firethorn was happy now that he had once more made Gill malcontent.

The spectators filed out of the hall with buzzing memories of the evening's entertainment. Some recalled the jokes, others the comic songs and one even tried to mimic the steps of Doctor Blackthought's manic jig. Nicholas Bracewell gave them a few minutes then ventured out. Only one person remained in the audience, slumped in his chair and quite impervious to the general departure. The book holder moved across to wake him before the actors saw the man. Sleep was adverse criticism. Firethorn and Gill would round on anyone who dared to slumber during one of their performances.

'Awake, sir,' said Nicholas. 'We are all done.'

The man did not move. Ruddy features were now white.

'The play is over, sir. You must leave.'

Nicholas looked closer and half-recognised him.

'Wake up, sir. You may not sleep here.'

The book holder shook him with some vigour but the man was well beyond waking. His head lolled sideways and he flopped down onto the floor. When Nicholas kneeled down beside him, he saw who the man was. A change of garb and cap had turned the erstwhile William Pocock into a Wiltshire miller. The man had been stabbed so expertly through the heart that death had been instantaneous. Blood had welled up beneath his doublet and left a huge red stain on the material, but none of the spectators had seen it in the half-dark of the Guildhall. In the midst of their hilarity, one of their number had been callously murdered.

Nicholas Bracewell not only recognized Israel Gunby's accomplice. The killer's handiwork bore a signature as well. Nicholas had seen it already on the arm of Owen Elias. He paid the tribute of a small prayer for the soul of the dead man then he felt a shiver of alarm.

The assassin had struck again.

Chapter Eight

BARNSTAPLE WAS THE LARGEST TOWN IN NORTH
Devon. Proud of its history and secure in soul, it
had been a borough and market centre since Saxon
times. Its corporation ruled primarily in the interests of its
merchant members, whose main wealth came from coastal
and foreign trade. There was silting in the River Taw but
the town that sat on it remained the leading port in the area.
The neighbouring Bideford was located on the deeper and
straighter River Torridge, while Appledore enjoyed deep-
water anchorage near the confluence of the two rivers,
yet neither of these—in spite of their greater natural
advantages—could compete with Barnstaple.

The house in Crock Street was one of the biggest in the
town, but it reflected the prosperity and status of its owner
in a most unassuming way. Built on a corner, its frontage
was comparatively narrow but its total depth ran to almost
a hundred and forty feet. Its ground floor consisted of two
blocks of building separated by a courtyard, the front block
containing a shop, a parlour and a small buttery while the
back block comprised the kitchen, larder, main buttery and
a small brewhouse. Behind the kitchen block was a Great
Court, on either side of which was the warehouse. Stables
with hayloft above completed the ground floor.

Nowithstanding its size, it did not in any way dominate but instead fitted quietly into its place and allowed other properties to nestle right up to it and draw from its strength. It rose to a height of four storeys. On the first floor was the hall or main living room of the dwelling, with a small countinghouse leading off it. The principal bedrooms were on the second floor, directly above the hall. The fore-chamber overlooked the street by means of handsome mul-lioned windows, which gave a curiously distorted view of nearby West Gate and the adjacent Chapel of St Nicholas. From the upper storey, the shape and development of the greater part of the town could be seen. Over the top of West Gate, it was also possible to glimpse the ships sailing past on the River Taw and to understand the very essence of Barnstaple.

The woman who sat alone in the fore-chamber showed no inclination to explore the various views that her house offered. Her eyes could only look inward. She sat motion-less in a chair with an open Bible lying unread in her lap. Mary Whetcombe wore the dark and seemly apparel of a grieving widow, but the death of her husband, recent as it was, had not scarred her pale beauty. If anything, it had been enhanced by tragedy. The small, heart-shaped face that was framed by the well-groomed dark hair was given a forlorn charm it had never possessed before. Even in her mourning dress, her shapely body retained its appeal. Mary Whetcombe carried thirty years and more with surprising lightness. She was a slim, elegant woman of middle height who had sustained many blows from fate, but they left al-most no marks upon her. Suffering was somehow contained within where its pain was more acute but its damage less visible.

There was a knock on the door and she came out of her reverie with a start. A flicker of hope stirred but it vanished immediately when the door opened and a maidservant con-ducted a tall, thin, balding man into the chamber. Arthur Calmady wore the black garb of his office and the pious look of a man with a mission in life. As the maidservant withdrew and closed the door behind her, the visitor gave a respectful bow then moved across to the mistress of the house.

'Good morning,' he said softly.

'Good morning,' she seemed to reply.

'Have you been studying the text I recommended?' he said, noting the Bible. 'I hope it has brought comfort and consolation to you, Mary.' He waited until she could manage a small nod of affirmation. 'Bereavement is a time when we come fit our minds to the loss of a loved one but we must do it in no spirit of despair. Matthew's death was God's will. It was not a meaningless accident, Mary, but part of a divine plan. Draw succour from that thought.'

'I will try,' she murmured.

Arthur Calmady was the vicar of the Parish Church of St Peter. Only an occasional visitor to the house when Matthew Whetcombe was alive, he had called on a daily basis since the merchant's untimely death, and he liked to think that his brand of unctuous concern was having a beneficial effect on the widow. He was a sharp-featured man with a mole in the hollow of one cheek. His intelligence was admired and his conscientiousness praised, but the more wayward Christians in the parish could have done without his strictures from the pulpit. They wanted a caring shepherd to tend his flock and not to round it up like a holy sheepdog. Unmarried and celibate all his life, he had the other worldly air of a hermit, but this was offset by the beady eyes and the moist lips. Arthur Calmady discharged all his duties with commendable zeal but he did take especial pleasure from visiting bereaved women in the privacy of a bedchamber.

'Shall I read to you, Mary?' he offered.

'No, thank you.'

'It may help to soothe your mind.'

'I am content.'

'May I sit with you for a while?'

'If you wish.'

'May I share your sorrow?'

Calmady lowered himself into the chair beside her and took one of her hands between his. Mary made no protest.

As the vicar began to chant a prayer, she was not even aware of his presence in the room. Her thoughts were miles away from Barnstaple. Ten minutes passed before he released her hand and rose to go. Calmady covered his departure with a glib apology for disturbing her and crossed to the door. Holding it open, he turned back to her.

'Is there any news, Mary?'

'None.'

'How long has it been now?'

'Too long.'

'We must watch and pray,' he advised. 'It is the only way to combat fear and anxiety. Prayers cure all ills.' He became more businesslike. 'When there is news, let me know at once. Send a servant to the vicarage. It is important.'

'I will.'

'Good-bye, Mary.'

Arthur Calmady withdrew like a wraith and closed the door soundlessly behind him. To a man of such exaggerated religiosity, the whole world was the house of God and he moved about it with the measured tread of a true believer. His stately figure descended the newel stair as if walking down the altar steps. When the maidservant let him out through the front door, the street was the nave of a cathedral. As soon as he had left, the child came out of her hiding place behind the court cupboard and ran upstairs to the fore-chamber. She entered without knocking and went across to stand in front of her mother. Lucy Whetcombe was a slight but wiry girl who could have been anything between ten and fifteen. Her body sided with the earlier age but the tight little face veered towards the later. What she had inherited of her mother's beauty was sullied by anxiety and dismay. The dark, sobre dress accentuated the fairer tone of her hair and the pale complexion.

She forced a smile and nodded inquiringly.

'No, Lucy,' said her mother, shaking her head.

The girl's eyes repeated the question more earnestly but it got the same sad response. As Mary Whetcombe talked, she opened her mouth expressively so that her daughter could read her lips, and she supplemented her speech with graphic gestures of her hands.

'We have no news of her,' she said. 'We do not know where she went or why. But she did not run away from you. She loves you, Lucy. We all love you. Susan will come back to you. They will find her. She belongs here with us.'

When the girl had deciphered the message, she tried to answer it with words of her own, but all she could produce were dull and senseless sounds. In sheer frustration, she beat her fists on her thighs and began to cry in silence. Mary Whetcombe reached out to enfold her child in her arms and to hug her tightly. Her own tears now flowed.

'We have each other,' she said. 'We have each other.'

But the girl did not even hear her.

Israel Gunby had spent so long living on his wits that he could adapt to each change of circumstance with the speed of light. Instead of wasting time on remorse over the death of an accomplice, he sought to turn it to good account.

'Ned was not long for this life,' he said blithely. 'That stranger saved me the trouble of sending his fat carcass on his way.'

'He was killed *next* to me,' complained Ellen, still shaken by the experience. 'It was all I could do not to scream out in horror.'

'That would have been the ruin of us, my love.'

'I held back for that reason.'

'The law would have come down on us,' warned Gunby. 'All would be lost in the cry of a woman. And for what? Ned Robinson! Our plump pickpocket.' A short laugh. 'They may catch us one day, Ellen, and hang the pair of us side by side, but I will not go to the gallows because of a fool like Ned Robinson. He deserved what he got.'

'It was terrifying, Israel!'

'You did well, my love.'

'I was frightened.'

Israel Gunby pulled her to him and stroked his wife's hair. They were lying in a bed at the Fox and Elm, a small inn some miles to the south-west of Marlborough. Events at the Guildhall on the previous night necessitated a rapid departure from the town. While Ned Robinson and Ellen had been working in harness at the play, Gunby had been sitting a mere hundred yards away in the taproom of the Rising Sun. By talking to the innkeeper, and guiding the conversation with a steady hand, he had learned how many guests were staying at the establishment, how heavy their capcases had been and in which direction they would be travelling next morning. While one crime was being committed, Israel Gunby liked to set up several more. Careful planning was the basis of his career. When plans went awry—as they did in the Guildhall—he would move swiftly to make his escape and cover his tracks.

There was ample compensation in this instance.

'How much did Ned take before he was caught?'

'Seven pounds and more.'

'Those fat fingers were dexterous.'

'They were,' said Ellen. 'He took the first few purses as we pushed through the crowd going in. One man carried five angels. Ned slipped them to me for safekeeping.'

'What did he take during the play?'

'The purses of the two men in front of him and the one who sat on my other side. Ned leaned across me as if fast asleep, and the money was his in a flash.' Ellen clicked her tongue. 'If he had settled for that, he would still now be alive to share the spoils. But he took one purse too many.'

'And the killer?'

'A well-favoured gentleman with a black beard.'

'But not from these parts, I dare wager,' said Gunby with a chuckle. 'These Wiltshire people are too trusting. They would not suspect a foist if you climbed inside their purse and threw their money out coin by coin.'

'He turned my blood to ice.'

'Ned Robinson?'

'The murderer.'

'Forget him, Ellen,' urged her husband. 'He got away in the crowd and will be in another county by now. Ned was unlucky but we gain profit from his misfortune.'

She brightened. 'You are right, Israel. We are still free and together. That is all that matters in the end. Yet it was such a shame about Ned.'

'Why?'

'It spoiled the play. I enjoyed it so much until then.'

'*The Happy Malcontent* was it called?'

'A merry piece. The whole town laughed so.'

'Westfield's Men served us in this business. They brought in the purses and Ned Robinson stole them. People who are full of mirth are easy prey.'

'Lawrence Firethorn is the greatest actor alive,' she said with frank admiration. Were I not married to *you*, I would be happy to share his bed. And half the women in Marlborough would say the same as me.'

'I think not, my love.'

'How so?'

'Because I have snatched delight from his arms yet again.' He began to cackle. 'Lawrence Firethorn will make no conquest in this town, Ellen. I give you my word on that.'

'I'll not stand for this, sir! You abuse my hospitality!'

'Hear me out.'

'I would rather *see* you out and say good riddance.'

'But we have a performance to give this afternoon.'

'Yes, Master Firethorn! You wish to usurp my role and do my office between the sheets.'

'That is not true, sir.'

'Then why did you send a letter to my wife?'

'I did not!'

'Why do you woo her with warm words?'

'I have never even met your good lady.'

'Why do you inflame her passion?'

'Nothing is further from my desires.'

'Take your lascivious wishes out of Marlborough!'

'You are misinformed here.'

'Hawk your pizzle to another town!'

The mayor worked himself up into such a rage that his beetroot cheeks were fit to burst. His eyes smouldered, his body twitched and his little hands clutched at his gold chain like a drowning man clinging for the rope that might save him. Lawrence Firethorn wanted to laugh at such absurd antics but the status of his visitor and the accompanying presence of a town constable enforced more control on him. The mayor and his wife had sat in the front row during the performance of *The Happy Malcontent* but the actor-manager had spared her no more than a cursory glance. The Guildhall had been packed with far more comely sights than that afforded by a pink-faced middle-aged woman with a breathy giggle. She was too starved a subject for Firethorn's lust.

They were in a private room at the White Hart. When the mayor came storming in to see him that morning, Firethorn had assumed that he bore the communal congratulations of the town. Instead of hearing his performance praised, the actor was being accused of trying to seduce the mayor's wife.

'Fornicator!' yelled the mayor.

'Lower your voice, sir.'

'Liar and adulterer!'

'I deny the charges!'

'Traitor!'

'Call your wife and she will proclaim my innocence.'

'Aghhhhh!'

The mayor let out a cry of anguish and twisted his chain so tightly around his neck that he was in danger of asphyxiating himself. Women were vile creatures and love was a two-edged sword. *The Happy Malcontent* brought tears in the wake of its laughter. The mayor's wife had been completely carried away by the force of the play and the sensual power of Lawrence Firethorn's performance. Roused to a pitch she had not achieved for many years, she fell on her husband with such fervour in the privacy of their fourposter that he had time to do no more than tear off his breeches and pull down his hose. Consummation was instant and what pleased him more than anything else was that this uncommon event had occurred while he was still wearing his chain of office. Mayoralty and manhood had coalesced in a night of madness. But it was all a wicked delusion. His wife's ardour had been excited by Lawrence Firethorn and it was he who was the true object of her new-found appetite.

'Where is this letter?' asked Firethorn.

'It is couched in filth and flattery.'

'Show it me, good sir.'

'What have you brought into my town!' wailed the mayor.

'A feast of theatre.'

'One man murdered, one woman about to be defiled!'

'Hold there and show me this false document.'

'We will drive Westfield's Men out!' The mayor took the letter from his belt and thrust it at Firethorn. 'Take your foul proposals back, sir! My wife's favours are not for you.'

Lawrence Firethorn read the missive, recoiled from the bluntness of its carnality and scrunched it up in an angry hand. He held it up inside his bunched fist.

'Hell and damnation! I'll not endure this!'

'Did you not write it, Master Firethorn?'

'Write it? No, sir. Send it? Never, sir. Wish it? Not in a thousand years, sir. This is a trick practised on us to set the one against the other. You have a dear and loving wife. Do not let some villain turn her into a whore.'

'How can I believe you?' stuttered the mayor. 'This letter carries your name upon it.'

'My name but written by another hand. Fetch me pen and ink and I will show you my true signature. Compare the two and you will see the falsehood here. Besides, sir,' he said with a consoling smile, 'what fornicator, liar or adulterer would be so foolish as to reveal himself to the husband of a woman he is trying to lead astray? If you entreated a lady to bestow her favours upon you, would the letter bear your name and title?'

The mayor was persuaded. Lawrence Firethorn and his wife were not, after all, secret lovers. He might yet enjoy again unbridled passion in his chain of office. Relief and remorse seized him, but before he could bury the wrongly ac-

cused actor beneath a mound of thanks and apologies, there
was a knock at the door and the landlord entered.

'The chamberlain is here, Master Firethorn,' he said.

'Let him wait.'

'He will not. Some letter has put him to choler.'

'Not another!' snarled Firethorn.

'The town clerk also attends with impatience.'

'Here's a third ordeal!'

'He curses your name on account of his wife.'

'God's blood!'

Lawrence Firethorn mastered the urge to take the first
letter and force it down the throat of the landlord. It was
important to separate message and messenger. The landlord
was not responsible for the news that he brought. Firethorn
was evidently the butt of some mischievous pen and he
needed to identify the correspondent without delay. Unfolding the paper, he studied the uncouth hand that had dared
to impersonate his own. Who could seek to embarrass him
in this way? He thought of a bewitching young woman at
the Fighting Cocks, of a dispute in her bedchamber with a
supposed rival and of a pillaged capcase. He thought of an
old shepherd on the road out of Oxford. He thought of the
biggest villain in Christendom and he named his man at
last.

'Israel Gunby!'

Nicholas Bracewell had a much happier morning than his
employer. The shining success of *The Happy Malcontent*
had been besmirched by the murder of one of its spectators,
and this had obliged him to give a sworn statement to the
magistrate about how he had found the dead body. Nicholas
disclosed that the victim was an accomplice of Israel
Gunby, but he made no mention of the likely killer.
Westfield's Men were absolved of all involvement in the
crime and he wished to distance it from them as much as
possible. The assassin was a personal problem for Nicholas
Bracewell and he was keen to deal with it himself. Nothing
could be gained by speculations to the local representatives
of law and order. After joining the company in the now-

muted celebrations at the White Hart, he went off to spend a watchful night in his bedchamber.

Morning brought comfort, pleasure and qualified delight. Comfort came from the fact that he had, for once, spent a night outside London without being the subject of an attack. Pleasure was assured by the news that Edmund Hoode was now so caught up with *The Merchant of Calais* that he was locked in his chamber and writing furiously. With his creative juices flowing freely once more, the playwright would soon complete the new play and add it to their repertoire. Nicholas still had qualms about his own contribution to the work, but common sense now told him that it could not be as central as he feared. Edmund Hoode had been working on the new drama for several weeks now and the main lines of plot and character had already been laid down. Nicholas had merely added depth and reality to the scenes of mercantile life. The merchant of Calais would not be Robert Bracewell.

Delight came soon after. While Lawrence Firethorn was grappling with a disagreeable letter, Nicholas was handed one that was as unexpected as it was welcome. The courier had ridden hard from London. A change of horses at intervals and an overnight stop at an inn had brought him to Marlborough by mid-morning. The whole town knew where the players were staying and he presented himself at the White Hart at once. Nicholas was moved. To send a letter so far and so fast was highly expensive, and it spoke volumes for Anne Hendrik's generosity and concern. He thanked the courier, gave him a few coins then sent him off into the taproom to spend them.

When he broke the seal and opened the letter, the mere sight of her signature revived him. The substance of the message made his love for her surge even more. Anne had gone to enormous trouble on his behalf and enlisted the aid of Leonard. She had not only discovered the exact poison that killed the girl from Devon, she had even acquired a rough description of the man thought to be the poisoner. Nicholas looked at the sketch with interest and gratitude. Anne had no great gift for portraiture, but she had caught enough of the man's features for Nicholas to be able to recognise him if they met. Her letter was not just a testimony of her desire to help. It put a powerful weapon into his hands. He was no longer up against an invisible assailant.

His delight, however, was not unrestrained. The missive contained nothing of an intimate nature. There was no hint of regret, no apology for her harsh treatment of him, no wish that he should ever return to the house in Bankside. Anne Hendrik would go to any lengths to help to save his life but she did not appear to want to share it. Nicholas settled for a modified solace. Contact with Anne was re-established. It was a positive foundation on which he could build.

A rehearsal was now due and Nicholas could spend no more time perusing her words and studying the portrait. He was needed in the Guildhall to supervise matters. Pushing the letter inside his jerkin, he collected the hired men from the taproom and took them with him. He had a spring in his step and a sense of having crossed an important boundary.

One silent woman had finally spoken.

Their fears proved groundless. Because a murder had occurred during their performance of *The Happy Malcontent* on the previous night, Westfield's Men braced themselves for a greatly reduced audience on the following afternoon. People could not be expected to sit comfortably in a hall where a man had so recently been stabbed. The tragedy was bound to have an adverse effect on the company. In the event, the opposite was the case. Since the murder victim was not a local man, his death lacked any resonance to frighten away the townspeople. Prompted by the glowing reports of the company's quality and by a ghoulish curiosity to view the very seat in which Ned Robinson had expired, spectators came in such large numbers that not all could be accommodated in the Guildhall. All doors in the auditorium were left open so that people could stand outside and yet peer in at the play, and there were clusters of eager patrons outside pressing their noses against each window.

Marlborough had been blessed with ample entertainment that year with musicians, jugglers, tumblers, bear-wards and swordplayers making it a port of call. Wrestlers had also visited the town more than once, and a few companies of strolling players had been allowed to display their wares. Westfield's Men were a distinct cut above all others. They offered genuine quality in place of more homespun show. Mayoral blessing was another factor. Reconciled with his wife, the contrite mayor could think of no better way to please her and to placate Lawrence Firethorn than by coming to the Guildhall in his regalia for the second time. He was back in the front row, playing with his chain and with his fantasies, and meditating on the joys of married life. The seal of civic approval was firmly stamped on the company.

'George!'

'Here, Master Bracewell.'

'The bench.'

'I have it with me.'

'You have the small bench,' said Nicholas tolerantly. 'This scene requires the larger one.'

'Are we in act four already?'

'Act three scene two.'

'That is the small bench.'

'Large.'

'I know *Vincentio's Revenge* by heart.'

'We are playing *Black Antonio*.'

George Dart's confusion was understandable. He was near exhaustion. Since the joyous moment when he had been able to cram a breakfast into his tiny frame, he had not stopped fetching and carrying. His legs hurt, his arms ached and his mind was a total blank. Though he had made three separate entries in the play—as guard, servant and chaplain—he had been given no lines to speak. The play felt like *Vincentio's Revenge* to him even if it turned out to be *Black Antonio*. Both were swirling tragedies of thwarted love and each was propelled by a mixture of jealousy, intrigue and violence.

164

George Dart could be forgiven for his mistake. He could rely on Nicholas Bracewell to cover it with his usual discretion.

Act five called for the small *and* the large bench. In the final harrowing scene, Lawrence Firethorn, supreme as ever in a title role written especially for him, kicked over the one bench and fell headlong across the other. It was a death so poignant and dramatic that it struck the audience dumb. Transfixed by the fate of noble Antonio, they completely overlooked the demise of Ned Robinson. A real murder in the Guildhall was a small event. The feigned death of Lawrence Firethorn would be talked about in hushed tones for weeks. It would be something for the mayor to discuss in bed with his wife before he removed his chain of office.

Solemn music played, Antonio was borne away and the play ended. The only sound that broke the taut silence was the muffled weeping of women. It was a bright afternoon but the most exquisite sense of loss lay across them like penumbra. Black Antonio exhumed himself and strode out onto the stage to collect his applause in armfuls. The company followed and the audience gave them unstinting acclaim. Even George Dart took his bow with pleasure. He was always gratified when a play was finally over and his slow torture was suspended.

'Master Bracewell . . .'

'Speak to me later, George.'

'There may be no time. We leave Marlborough now.'

'Can you only talk within the town limits?'

'We are alone now. Others will be on the waggon.'

'Is it so important, George?'

'I think it is.'

'Then stand aside, lad, but be swift.'

The Guildhall had now been cleared of all trace of Westfield's Men. The prompt copy of *Black Antonio* was safely locked away in Nicholas Bracewell's chest, and both benches—along with all the other properties—were stowed in the waggon. Marlborough belonged to their past. Bristol was their future. As the company gathered in the yard of the White Hart prior to departure, George Dart saw the chance of a private word with the book holder.

'Speak up, George,' said Nicholas. 'What ails you?'

'They say you go on to Barnstaple.'

'That is so.'

'Take me with you!' he begged.

'What?'

'Take me with you to Barnstaple!'

'Why?'

'So that I may follow *you*.'

'I attend to family business and it may not be shared.'

'You mishear me, sir,' said Dart, checking that they could not be overheard so that his secret would not excite the derision of the others. 'I wish to follow your example. Take me to Barnstaple and I will run away to sea.'

Nicholas was astounded. 'You are no sailor, George.'

'I could become one,' said the other defensively. 'I am no true mariner of the theatre. I run aground too often. If I stay with Westfield's Men, I may mistake this play for that one yet again. A ship is a ship. No sailor would confuse it with something else.' He voiced his despair. 'I am not made for this life.'

'But we *need* you in the company.'

'*You* may do so, Master Bracewell. All that the others need is something to bully and beat and shout at.'

'Are you so unhappy?'

'I want to run away to sea as you did.'

'It is no life for you, lad,' said Nicholas sadly. 'You have to be born to it. I grew up by the sea and served my apprenticeship as a merchant. It is in my blood.'

'Then why have you left it?'

'I have not, George. Theatre is a voyage of discovery. I sail beneath canvas with Lawrence Firethorn as my captain now.' Nicholas gave him a confiding smile. 'He may be more pirate than naval commander but he runs a tight ship and I serve him willingly.'

'I am but the cabin boy here,' said George Dart.

'Would you rather beg in the streets of London? That is what some of those left behind will do. Stay with us.'

'The sea calls me.'

Nicholas grew philosophical. 'No, George. What calls you is the idea of escape. You are not running *to* something but *away* from it. That was my error, too, and I hope to put it right at last. If you do not like something, work to change it until it suits you.'

'I did,' moaned Dart. 'I changed *Vincentio's Revenge* into *Black Antonio*—and where did that get me?' Others came towards them and he was forced to make a final plea. 'Take me to Barnstaple with you and save my miserable life!'

Nicholas shook his head. 'I must go alone.'

'Show me the sea.'

'There are ships enough in Bristol.'

'I want to stand where you first stood,' said Dart. 'I want to make the choice that you made. You had the courage to sail around the world. Let me find courage of my own.'

'That is not what took me away, George.'

'Then what was?'

Nicholas confronted the truth without equivocation.

'Cowardice.'

An estate in the country was the dream and ambition of every merchant. It was not merely a symbol of achievement, it was a place where they could escape from the dirt and bustle of the towns where they did their business and enjoy the more leisured existence of landed gentry. Gideon Livermore was a typical member of the mercantile community of Barnstaple. Rich and successful, he bought himself a substantial property a few miles from Bishops Tawton. He was still within a comfortable ride of the port that had made his fortune, but the twenty acres of parkland which surrounded his home gave him a reassuring bulwark against the cares of trade. Gideon Livermore loved everything about the country and he could never understand why Matthew Whetcombe—his partner in many enterprises—had preferred to spend most of his time in his town house in Crock Street. To a man like Livermore, the most attractive feature of Barnstaple was the road out of it.

The house was a long, low, rambling structure that had

been built over a hundred and fifty years earlier by a wealthy landowner. By lavishing enormous amounts of money and care upon it, Gideon Livermore had turned a manor into a mansion. Existing buildings had been refurbished, a new and resplendent wing had been added and the stable block had been greatly enlarged. Costly furnishings and ostentatious gold plate filled the interior. Livermore shared his home with his five children and ten servants, but there were still rooms to spare for any guests. He was an expansive man in every way and had always leaned towards excess.

He raised a goblet of Canary wine in a toast.

'To a successful endeavour!'

'I'll say Amen to that.'

The two men sipped then leaned back in their chairs. Gideon Livermore was a sleek, self-satisfied man of forty with heavy jowls and a bulging midriff. His face was pleasant in repose but his cheeks were deeply tinged by his fondness for wine and spirits. He wore a doublet of blue and green satin with matching breeches. A lawn ruff held up the clean-shaven double chin. His companion was slightly younger but much leaner and paler. Barnard Sweete wore the more subdued garb and deferential smile of a lawyer. His beard was trimmed to the last detail.

'Tell me all,' said Livermore. 'Have they decided yet?'

'They have.'

'With what result?'

'You are to be elected without delay.'

'I expected no less,' said his host airily, 'but the news is both good and bad. Good, because Gideon Livermore is a most deserving alderman and should have been admitted years ago. Bad, because public duties will take me away more often from here.' He held out his palms as if weighing the advantages and disadvantages, then came out strongly in favour of the former. 'I'll accept this honour graciously. Alderman Livermore has a ring that will echo in the ears of the whole town. I am made, Barnard.'

'You could look to be mayor one day.'

'Or receiver or sheriff or even member of parliament. All

are chosen from within the circle. There are but twenty-four aldermen and they serve for life.' He introduced a resentful note. 'I was kept out long enough.' He scowled with resentment. 'It is fitting that the man I replace is Matthew Whetcombe.'

'Not only on the chamber.'

'We shall see, we shall see.' His affability returned and he sipped more wine. 'Do you have news of her?'

'There is none to report, Gideon.'

'You must have some intelligence. Mary is human like the rest of us. The lady must eat, drink and occupy her day somehow. What does she *do* in the barn of a house in Crock Street?'

'She keeps to her bedchamber.'

'No visitors?'

'None save Mr Calmady. Our vicar waits upon her daily.'

'Her family? Her friends?'

'She has locked herself away from them.'

'Still in mourning?'

'Not for her husband. She has some deeper sorrow.'

Gideon Livermore smiled. 'There is remedy for that.'

'In time,' said the lawyer cautiously. He opened the satchel that lay beside him and extracted a sheet of parchment. 'You asked to see the funeral charges.'

'I did, Barnard,' he said. 'I wish to see *everything* that touches on Mary Whetcombe. The most tiny item of her household expenditure is of interest to me. How much did it cost to send Matthew to his Maker?'

'Here is the list, Gideon.'

The merchant took it from him and scrutinised it. With growing annoyance, he read some of the charges aloud.

'Item, twenty yards of black material for the mourning clothes, thirty-one pounds; item, the funeral at the Parish Church of St Peter, eighteen pounds; item, an elm chest to hold the body, two pounds and three shillings; item, one tombstone, two pounds, eight shillings; item, for engraving the tombstone, one pound, four shillings; item, for payment of the gravedigger, two shillings.' He threw his visitor a glance. 'The list is endless, Barnard. It carries on all the way down to the funeral dinner in the hall at Crock Street. That cost twenty-seven pounds, making a total in all—I can hardly credit this—of one hundred and nineteen pounds.' He waved the paper in the air. 'Matthew Whetcombe had an expensive hole in the ground. I paid for the best when my own dear wife passed away, but her funeral did not amount to anything like this figure.'

'Matthew Whetcombe was a power in Barnstaple.'

'So was Alice Livermore,' said the merchant proudly. 'A wife of mine commands the highest respect.'

'No question but that she does.'

'A hundred and nineteen pounds!'

'I am to pay it out of the estate.'

'Do so, Barnard. Obey her wishes.' He shook his head in disbelief. 'A hundred and nineteen pounds! It is a lot to pay for the funeral of a husband whom you hate.'

He studied the list again, lost in contemplation of its details and implications. Barnard Sweete tasted his wine and waited quietly. His host would not brook interruption. The lawyer had found that out before. The merchant class of Barnstaple was small, compact and closely interrelated by marriage. It was also riven by feuds and petty jealousies. Sweete made a handsome living by serving the mercantile community, but doing so compelled him to keep abreast of all developments—commercial or domestic—in the town. People trusted him. Known for his discretion, he was given access to intimate details of his client's affairs and his retentive mind discarded none of them. Knowledge was money, and Barnard Sweete knew things that could deliver huge rewards.

Gideon Livermore at last put the list aside.

'I must have her!' he said covetously.

'All things proceed in that direction.'

'There must be no let or hindrance.'

'You have the law on your side.'

'And a cunning lawyer to interpret it.' He gave a curt nod of gratitude. 'I am a generous man, Barnard.'

'I have always found it so.'

170

Livermore added a rider. 'When I am pleased,' he said. 'You will have no cause for complaint.'

'Good.' He flicked a bloodshot eye once more at the paper. 'One hundred and nineteen pounds! Matthew Whetcombe had all that spent on his funeral, yet it still could not buy him some honest tears from his wife. And what of the girl? Lucy Whetcombe could not even let out a cry of pain at her father's passing. Fate is cruel. Matthew created all that wealth yet he could only produce one child, and she is such a poor monument to his manhood. The girl can neither hear nor speak. With her father in his grave, Lucy Whetcombe cannot even call out for her share of his inheritance.'

'A strong voice is needed at such times,' said the lawyer pointedly. 'Silence can bring ruin.'

'I rely on it.'

Gideon Livermore stood up and took his goblet across to the table to refill it from the glass decanter he had bought on a visit to Venice. He stared into the liquid for a second then drank it off in one draught. Barnard Sweete was certain that he would now be offered more wine, and he emptied his own goblet in readiness. But the invitation never came. There was a knock on the door and a young man entered with some urgency. He stopped when he saw the lawyer but Gideon Livermore beckoned him on. The two of them stood aside and the newcomer whispered rapidly to his employer.

Sensing trouble, the lawyer rose to his feet and watched his host in trepidation. The merchant's rage needed no time to build. His geniality became a malign fury, and he reached out to grab the decanter before hurling it violently against the wall and sending shards of glass flying to every corner of the room. His clerk withdrew and closed the door behind him. Gideon Livermore turned to glower at his guest.

'He is coming to Barnstaple,' he rumbled.

'Who?'

'Nicholas Bracewell.'

'Heaven forfend!' exclaimed the lawyer.

171

'He is on his way here.'

'But that cannot be.'

'My information is always sound. I pay enough for it.'

'Nicholas Bracewell! Did the message then reach him?'

'The messenger did. Before she died.'

'How much does he know?'

'Enough to bring him to Barnstaple.' He punched a fist into the palm of his other hand. 'He must be stopped. We do not want a Bracewell meddling in our affairs, especially this member of the family. Bracewells are stubborn.' Perspiration now glistened on his upper lip. 'They have long memories.'

'Can he be prevented?' said Sweete.

'He must be.'

'How?'

'By the same means.'

'Lamparde?'

'He will know what to do.'

'Then why has he not already done it?' said the lawyer nervously. 'Why has Lamparde not honoured his contract? This alters the case completely. If Nicholas Bracewell were to come to as far as—'

'He will not!'

'But if he did . . .'

'He will *not!*' thundered the merchant. 'Lamparde will not let us down. He values his own life, so he will not cross Gideon Livermore.' His explosion of rage had reassured him. 'Nicholas Bracewell will not get anywhere near us. We do wrong to have such foolish fears. We are safe and beyond his reach. Let us forget about him and his family.'

'Yet he is still on his way, you say?'

'Yes.'

'Alone?'

'He travels with a theatre company.'

'Where is he now?'

'Close to death.'

Nicholas Bracewell rode with them to the edge of the town and waved them off. He still had business in Marlborough and could soon overtake them on the roan. It was a spirited animal and a full day in the stable had made it restless for exercise. Lawrence Firethorn led his troupe off on the road to Chippenham. Westfield's Men were still buoyed up by the success of their performance that afternoon, and they could look to repeat it in Bristol. Firethorn himself was torn between elation and disquiet. Though his company had twice distinguished themselves before an audience, he was worried by the interference of Israel Gunby. The incident at the Fighting Cocks in High Wycombe still rankled, all the more so because he had found no balm for that particular wound. He had spent three nights away from his wife now and found nobody to take her place in his bed. *Black Antonio* rarely failed to excite some female interest, and he had hoped to snatch a fond farewell in his chamber with some local maiden while the waggon was being loaded but it was not to be. The mayor had been thrilled with the second performance and would not stir from Firethorn's side until he had explained why at least a dozen times. Guilt rustled beneath his mayoral chain. He spent so much time apologising to Firethorn for even thinking that he would wish to ravish another man's wife that the other men's wives who had come to throw themselves upon the actor could not get anywhere near him. Israel Gunby had come between Lawrence Firethorn and the spoils of war. Retribution was needed.

'Why does he stay?' asked Barnaby Gill.

'Your visage offends his eye,' said Firethorn.

'What does Marlborough hold for Nicholas Bracewell?'

'Go back and ask him.'

'No,' said Gill, 'I will give thanks for this small mercy and put distance between the two of us. I said that he would bring more misery down upon us and he did.'

'Yes,' teased Firethorn, 'he persuaded me to stage *The Happy Malcontent* and we had two hours of *your* strutting and fretting.'

'I was supreme.'

'It escaped my notice.'

'But not that of the spectators.' Gill preened himself as

173

they rode along. 'They loved me. I could feel the ardour. My talents left them breathless. I was inspired.'

'Feed off your vanity, if you will. Caress your own sweet self. But do not accuse Nick.'

'He killed that man in the audience.'

'How? With a prompt book in his hands?'

'Consider but this, Lawrence. Three days on the road have brought three disasters. Robbery, plague, murder. That is our book holder's record. Robbery, plague, murder. 'Zounds! What *more* do you need?'

'Women!'

'When Nicholas is with us, misfortune strikes,' said Gill. 'He is like some Devil's mark upon us. Let him stay in Marlborough as long as he may. We need no more stabbing among the spectators.'

'Then you must retire, Barnaby,' said the other, 'for your performances are daggers in the back of any audience.'

Barnaby Gill sulked on horseback for another mile.

They were approaching a tiny hamlet when they saw him. He was propped up against a tree by the side of the road. Even from a distance, they could see his tattered rags and wretched condition. The twisted figure was one of the vast and ever-increasing number of vagrants who wandered the countryside in search of charity. Rogues and vagabonds were a recurring nuisance to Marlborough and the town beadle was paid twopence for each one that he whipped. This old man had crawled to one of the outlying hamlets to escape yet another beating and to throw himself on the mercy of passing travellers. When they got nearer, they saw the matted hair and clogged filth of a creature who spent his nights in the fields with other wild animals. One eye was closed, the other sparkled hopefully as they approached. A begging bowl came out from beneath his shredded coat. They caught his stench from twenty yards away.

Edmund Hoode put a compassionate hand into his purse.

'Poor fellow!' he said. 'Let's give him comfort.'

'No,' counselled Gill. 'Give to him and you will have to

give to every beggar we pass. There is not enough money in the whole kingdom to relieve all these scabs.'

'Show some pity, Barnaby.'

'Ignore the fellow and ride past.'

'Leave him to me,' said Firethorn.

He raised a hand and the company came to a halt. They looked down at the old man with frank disgust. He was in a most deplorable state and did not even have strength or sense to drag himself into the shade. There was a further cause for revulsion. The beggar seemed to have only one leg.

The bowl was shaken up at them.

'Alms, good people!' cried a quavering voice. 'Alms!'

'Why?' said Firethorn coldly.

'For the love of God!'

'Beggars are no more than highway robbers.'

'I seek charity, sir.'

'For what reason.'

'To live.'

'Men who wish to live must work.'

'I am too old and too weak, sir.'

'Are you so?'

'I lost a leg in the service of my country.'

'You were a soldier, then?' mocked Firethorn.

'A sailor, sir. I was young and lusty once. But a man without a leg grows old so quickly. Give me a penny, sir, to buy some bread. Give me twopence and you'll have my blessing hereafter. Please, good people! Help me!'

Edmund Hoode was about to throw a coin into the bowl but it was kicked from the man's hand by Lawrence Firethorn. Dismounting at once, the actor-manager drew his sword and held it at the man's neck. The whole company gasped at what they saw as an act of wanton cruelty.

'This is no beggar!' said Firethorn angrily. 'This is the same vile rascal who fleeced us in High Wycombe. The same mangy old shepherd who played with us on the road from Oxford. The same slanderous villain who wrote letters to blacken my reputation.' He flashed his rapier through the air and the beggar retreated into a bundle of fear. 'Here is no honest wretch, gentleman. A sailor, does he say! This dunghill has never served his country in his life. He does not fool Lawrence Firethorn. He will not hide his leg from *me* and swear he lost it in a battle on the waves. I will not be beguiled again!' He grabbed the man by his hair to hoist him up. 'Behold, sirs! This is Israel Gunby!'

There was a groan of horror. As the beggar was lifted from the ground, his deformity became all too apparent. The hideous stump made the company turn away. The man was not Israel Gunby in a new role designed to taunt them. He was a decaying remnant of the young sailor he had once been.

Lawrence Firethorn was overwhelmed with guilt. He put the man gently to the ground and set him against the tree once more. Grabbing the bowl, he dropped some coins into it before taking it around the entire company. Instead of being killed by the actor-manager, the beggar now had enough money to feed himself for a fortnight. He croaked his thanks. Westfield's Men rode away in a cloud of shame and remorse.

It took him an hour to find the inn. Nicholas Bracewell had reasoned correctly. Convinced that the man would have taken lodging for the night in Marlborough, he went around every hostelry in the town. The portrait that Anne Hendrik had sent him was shown to a dozen or more innkeepers before he found one who vaguely recognised it.

'It could be him,' said the man uncertainly.

'When did he arrive?' asked Nicholas.

'Yesterday morning before noon.'

'Did he stay the night?'

'He paid for a bed, sir. But when the chamberlain went up this morning, it had not been slept in. Nor was the man's horse in our stables. He must have stolen away.'

Nicholas pondered. The man who was trailing him must have intended to bide his time and stay the night before he attacked again. During the performance at the Guildhall, he had killed Israel Gunby's accomplice and been forced to quit the town at speed. Nicholas had no doubt which direction the man had taken. He was somewhere on the road ahead. His task was to stop the book holder from reaching Barnstaple and he would stick to it with tenacity.

'Nan may help you, sir,' said the landlord.

'Nan?'

'One of my serving wenches. She was taken with the man, which is no great thing, sir, for Nan has a soft spot for any upright gentleman.' He gave a sigh. 'I've warned her that it will be the ruin of her one day but the girl will not listen and she is popular with travellers.'

'May I speak with her?'

'I'll call her presently.'

The landlord went out of the taproom and reappeared a few minutes later with the girl. She wore the plain garb and apron of her calling but had teased down the shoulders of her dress to expose her neck and cleavage. When a man sent for her, she always came with a ready smile, and it broadened when she saw the tall, sturdy figure of Nicholas Bracewell. He showed her the drawing and she identified it at once. She was certain that the man had lodged there on the previous day and spoke with some asperity about him. The only false detail in the sketch was the earring. He had not worn it when he stayed there.

'Did he give a name?' said Nicholas.

'Yes, sir,' said the landlord, 'but I have forgot it. We have so many travellers through here each day that I cannot remember more than a handful of their names. But if it is important, I can ask my wife.'

'Please do.'

'Her memory is sounder than mine.'

'She would earn my deepest gratitude.'

Nicholas asked for permission to see the bedchamber where the man had stayed. While the landlord went off to find his wife, the girl conducted Nicholas up two flights of creaking stairs to a low passageway. She moved along it with the easy familiarity of someone who could—and had done so on many occasions—find her way along it in the dark. She came to a door and unlocked it.

'Here it is, sir,' she said.

'Thank you.'

'It is just as he left it.'

'Has the linen been changed?'

'There was no need. It was not slept in.'

Nicholas looked around the room. Nothing had been left behind, but there was the possibility that the visitor had lain down to rest. He may not have slept in the bed, but his head may have rested on its flat pillow. Anne Hendrik's letter had contained a verbal description of the man to support the rough portrait. Leonard had talked about the man's "smell," though he could be no more specific than that. Nicholas bent over the bed and sniffed. He inhaled the faintest whisper of a fragrance.

'He did smell sweet," said the girl. 'That's what I liked about him. Most travellers have foul breath and stink of sweat but not this one. It was a pretty smell and I would like some for myself. What was it, sir?'

Nicholas inhaled again. 'Oil of bergamot.'

In his two encounters with the man, he had not had time to notice any fragrance. The musty atmosphere in the stable at the Fighting Cocks would subdue any sweeter odour and the scuffle at the Dog and Bear was over in seconds. What Nicholas had missed, both Leonard and the serving wench had remarked. He thanked the girl and slipped her a few pence. She stole a giggling kiss as further reward then took him back downstairs. The landlord had still not returned and Nicholas stepped out into the yard while he was waiting. Fresh air hit him like a slap across the face and forced realisation upon him.

He was alone. Westfield's Men were miles ahead of him and he was unprotected. It brought him no fear. Instead, it gave him a sudden sense of freedom. He was somewhere near the middle of his journey between London and Barnstaple. Behind him lay the ruins of a love that had sustained him for some years now: ahead of him was nothing but danger and uncertainty. If he turned back, he might yet recover what he had lost in Bankside. Anne Hendrik still cared. She sent word to him that might help to save his life, but that life would not be threatened if he abandoned his purpose. What could he hope to achieve in Barnstaple? The town was a branding iron that had burned so many white hot messages into his mind. Why suffer that hissing pain once more?

It was not just a decision between a new home and an old one. Nicholas was standing at a spiritual crossroads. If he went back, he would be renouncing a way of life as well. Westfield's Men were his closest friends, but it was a highly unstable friendship. The loss of the Queen's Head had not just expelled them from Gracechurch Street, it might keep them out of London forever and condemn them to an almost permanent tour of the provinces. Lawrence Firethorn would never tolerate that and neither would Barnaby Gill. Other theatre companies would woo them back to the capital and Westfield's Men would collapse. Nicholas did not wish to be there when that happened. A clean break now would rescue him from a slow professional death with an ailing troupe.

Even if the company found a new base in London, he was not sure whether he wanted to share it with them. Theatre was still a flight from reality. Owen Elias had reminded him of that. Nicholas was hiding. If he stayed in London and forged a new love with Anne Hendrik, he would be able to leave his refuge and live a normal life: if he pressed on to Devon, he would be calling up the very ghosts that had sent him away. Lawrence Firethorn and the others put enormous reliance on him, but it was not reflected in his status. Nicholas was still only a hired man with the company, one of the floating population of theatre people who were taken on and dismissed according to the whims of the sharers. The book holder might have created a fairly constant position in the company but it gave him only a very fragile security. In essence, Nicholas Bracewell was no better off than the disillusioned George Dart.

Going forward meant certain anguish while going back offered possible release. He would be insane to drive himself on. A settled life with a woman he loved was the best that any man could hope for. Nicholas wanted to start out for home at once and begin afresh with Anne Hendrik. She was the decisive factor in his life and it was time to acknowledge it. His love was guiding him back to her. Visions of quiet contentment came before him but they soon evaporated in the chill air of truth. Anne Hendrik was no longer alone. She had another lodger at her house, a dead girl who had made the long journey from Barnstaple in search of Nicholas. Her shadow would lay across that bedchamber forever unless she was avenged. Returning to London meant considering only himself. When he remembered the girl and thought of the man who had poisoned her, he needed no signpost to point his way. He simply had to go on to the end of the journey.

Nicholas untethered his horse from the post and leapt into the saddle. He was ready to gallop after his fellows and reaffirm his kinship with them before going on to more personal commitments in Devon. Only after that would he have any chance of a reconciliation with Anne Hendrik.

'Stay, sir!' called the landlord.

'What?'

'I have spoken with my wife.'

'I had quite forgot.'

'Then your memory is like mine, sir,' said the man. 'I knew that I could count on her. Names stick in her mind like dried leaves to a hedgehog. She recalls his name.'

'The man with the black beard?'

'Even he, sir.'

'What was it?'

'A fine, mouth-filling name, sir. He told it to her.'

'So what did the fellow call himself?'

'Nicholas Bracewell.'

Chapter Nine

BANKSIDE WAS NOT A PART OF THE CITY THAT Margery Firethorn often visited. Her only reason in the past for coming to Southwark was to watch Westfield's Men perform at the Rose, one of only three custom-built theatres in London. Since the other two—the Theatre and the Curtain—were both in Shoreditch, she could walk to them from her home. With a servant for company and protection, she crossed the Thames by boat and made her way to the house of Anne Hendrik. The latter was surprised and slightly alarmed to see her. She took Margery into her parlour.

"Have you heard any tidings?" she asked.

'The courier returned to London this very afternoon.'

'Did he deliver my letter?'

'In person,' said Margery. 'Nick is alive and well.'

'Thank God!' Anne waved her visitor to a chair and sat opposite her. 'Where did the message reach him?'

'In Marlborough.'

'And he is well, you say?'

'Excellent well, and delighted to hear from you.'

'Haply, our fears were in vain,' said Anne. 'We send a warning that he does not need. The man in my drawing may not be stalking him, after all.'

181

'He is, Anne.'

'How can you be so sure?'

'The courier told me,' said Margery. 'He drank with the players before he set off on the return journey. They were anxious to learn all the latest news from London but they had some of their own.'

'What was it?'

'Someone is indeed following the company.'

'They have seen him?'

'Worse still, Anne. They have tasted his venom.'

'He has attacked?'

'Nick has twice been his target.'

'Heaven protect him!'

'It already has,' said Margery. 'The courier spoke with Owen Elias. Our noisy Welshman, it seems, saved Nick from a dagger in the back on the second occasion. He paid for his bravery, too. Owen's arm was sliced open from top to bottom.' She gave a chuckle. 'But it did not stop him from playing in Marlborough. Owen Elias is another Lawrence. Nothing short of death would prevent him from going onstage.'

'This villain will not easily be stopped.'

'Nick has good friends around him.'

'But he'll go on to Barnstaple alone.'

'Trust him, Anne. He is a shrewd fighter.'

'Yet still in danger.' Anne fought to control a rising concern. 'Was there . . . any reply to my letter?'

'He sends thanks and good wishes.'

'No more than that?'

'Nick is judicious,' said Margery. 'He wanted to send his love but he was not sure how it would be received. You pushed him on his way and there was nothing in your letter that called him back.' She watched the other woman closely. 'Do you wish for his return?'

'I do not want him murdered.'

'And if he should escape—would you have him back?'

'To lodge in my house?'

'In your house and in your heart.'

Anne Hendrik shrugged her confusion. She was still in

two minds about Nicholas Bracewell. Days and nights of brooding about him had yielded no firm decision. She feared for his life and, since he was so far away, that fear was greatly intensified. If he had still been in London, she could see and help him, but Nicholas was completely out of her reach now. It meant that the news from Marlborough was old news. He might have been alive the previous morning when the courier located him but he could now be lying in a ditch somewhere with his throat cut. The poisoner might even have resorted to poison again. Anne shuddered at the notion of such an agonising death for Nicholas.

Concern for his safety, however, was not the same as an urge to see him again. She still felt hurt by the cause and the nature of their estrangement. Given the choice, Nicholas rejected her and went off to Devon, and he did so without giving any real justification for his action. Years of love and trust between them had been vitiated. She respected his right not to talk about his past life, but Anne had certain rights herself. When events from that past came bursting in to disturb the peace of her home and the happiness of her existence, she deserved to be told the truth. Why was it so shameful for him to confess?

Margery saw her wrestling with the contradictions. Fond of Nicholas—and in his debt for a hundred favours—she tried her hand at stage management on his behalf.

'I called at the Queen's Head,' she said.

'Did you speak with the innkeeper's wife?'

'Sybil Marwood and I are of one mind where husbands are concerned. They need to be rescued from their mistakes.' She grinned broadly. 'I worked so craftily on her that she now looks more favourably on Westfield's Men and thinks that her squirming beetle of a husband has been too hasty to expel them from the inn. She will need more persuasion and I'll do it privily. Convince her and we convince him. Here is no Alexander the Great. This Alexander is great only in stupidity and fear of his wife.'

'Westfield's Men may yet return to the Queen's Head?'

'That "may" gives us long difficulties for a short word

but I'll strive to master them. We have hopes, Anne, let us aim no higher. All is not yet lost.'

'That is good news.'

'It would bring Nick back to London.'

'If he still lives . . .'

'He lives and breathes,' said Margery confidently, 'and he'll want to come back to Bankside. Will you see him?'

Anne was candid. 'I do not know.'

'Will you not at least hear the man out?'

'He had his chance to speak,' she snapped.

'Do I hear harshness?'

'I asked him to stay here with me, Margery.'

'Was that a fair demand.'

'I *needed* him.'

'I needed Lawrence but he still rode off with them. What pleasure is there for me with my husband away and his creditors banging on my door?' She gave a resigned smile. 'They love us, Anne, but they love the theatre even more. Each play is a separate mistress who can charm them into her bed. Accept that and you will learn to understand Nick. If you think you can tear him away from the theatre, then you are chasing moonbeams.'

'Westfield's Men are not my complaint.'

'Then who is?'

'The person who calls him to Barnstaple.'

'What person is that?'

'He will not say and that is the root of my anger.'

'Nick will give a full account when he returns.'

'I may not wish to listen.'

'Why?'

'Because the insult cannot be borne.'

'What insult?'

'The worst kind, Margery. He turned his back on me. When I most needed his reassurance, he walked away. He preferred someone else.' Bitterness tightened her mouth. 'That is why I do not want him back. He put *her* first.'

'Her?'

'The one who sent for him.'

'Who is that?'

'The silent woman.'

Lucy Whetcombe had the heightened awareness of a child who is deficient in other senses. Her eyes saw much more than those of other people, her hands could read everything they touched, her nose could catch the merest scent of any kindness or wickedness. Her silent world had its own peculiar sounds. The girl lived a simple and uncomplicated life, inhabiting the very fringe of parental love and keeping well away from the communal turmoil of Barnstaple. Self-conscious about her disability, Lucy Whetcombe spurned, and was spurned by, other children. Since loneliness was forced upon her, she made a virtue of it. Her father had been a man of great substance who was respected by all in the town. Visitors were always calling or dining at the house in Crock Street, but Lucy kept out of their way. She resented adults for pitying and patronising her. She resented her mother for other reasons. Susan was her only real friend, and Susan had now vanished. Each day deepened Lucy's distress. The girl sensed a terrible and irreplaceable loss.

'We have still heard nothing, Lucy,' said her mother.

Deft fingers translated the words for her daughter.

'They will keep searching until they find her.'

A dozen questions hung unasked on the girl's lips.

'Susan loves you. She would not go away for good and leave you alone. Susan will come back one day.' Mary wanted to get rid of her. 'Go and play with your dolls. They will remind you of Susan.'

Though she could not hear her mother's voice, Lucy could feel its lack of conviction. The hands, too, gave signals that had more hope than authority. Her mother did not know the whereabouts of her young servant and she was too preoccupied to care. Mary Whetcombe had always had a strange attitude to Susan, at once liking and resenting her, showing her favour only to withdraw it again, using the servant to look after Lucy and keep her daughter out of her way. Lucy despised her mother for the way she treated the girl's one true friend. Mary Whetcombe had finally stirred out of the fore-chamber and brought herself down to the hall, but the physical move was not accompanied by any emotional change. She was still bound up in a grief that her daughter could not understand. All that Lucy knew was that it excluded both her and Susan.

There was a tap on the door and a maidservant conducted Arthur Calmady into the hall. He looked disappointed that he was no longer to be received in the fore-chamber but soon recovered his composure. Calmady had been through his daily litany of questions before he even noticed the child.

'How are you today, Lucy?' he enquired.

Pretending not to understand, she shook her head.

'You look very pretty.'

She stared at him with concentrated distrust.

'Your mother and I are going to read the Bible,' said Calmady. 'Though you have no ears to hear, the sound of Holy Writ will echo in your heart.'

His clumsy gestures got nowhere near a translation.

When he picked up the Bible, the girl took her cue to leave. Dropping a curtsey, she ran to the door and let herself out. She then went into her father's countinghouse and edged slowly forward until she could peep out.

The two of them were still there. One stood in Crock Street itself while the other lounged against a wall around the corner. The men kept the house under casual but constant surveillance. They could see everyone who came and went. Lucy did not know why they were standing there, but it gave her an uneasy feeling. She was imprisoned in the house. Susan would know what to do in this situation but Susan was not there to guide her and to be her voice. The servant had disappeared one night and taken the fastest horse in the stables. Where had she gone and why did she not take Lucy with her? They had talked before of running away together. Lucy had found the way to talk to her friend.

Leaving the countinghouse, she ran along the covered gallery, which connected the hall with the rooms over the kitchen block. It was here that Susan slept. Lucy used a key to let herself into the cramped, airless chamber, which caught all the pungent smells of cooking from below. It was a bare and featureless room, but she had spent some of the happiest moments of her life there. Susan had learned to laugh in silence like her. Lucy locked the door behind her, got down on her knees and lifted the truckle bed with one hand. The other reached in to pull out something that was bound up tightly in an old piece of cloth. Lucy placed the cloth on the scuffed floorboards and slowly unrolled it.

The dolls were all jumbled together, clinging to one another with their tiny arms and turning their faces away from the sudden light. Lucy lifted them up one by one and laid them gently apart. They were all there. Her mother, her father, Lucy herself, Susan and the other members of the household. Fashioned out of old pegs or twigs, they were no more than a few inches high with miniature suits and dresses made out of scraps of material. Lucy picked up the vicar and sniggered at the sombre face that Susan had painted on him. Lucy had done the sewing and given the most colourful attire to Gideon Livermore. The lawyer's garb had been much easier to make. Susan's brush had dotted in the neat little beard of Barnard Sweete.

Lucy surveyed the collection with pride and affection. It had taken them a long time to make all the dolls. Her whole world now lay before her in microcosm but it contained two errors. Matthew Whetcombe was no longer part of it. His severe face with its disapproval of his only child could be wrapped away in the cloth. When they first began to make the dolls, Lucy kept them in her own bedchamber so that she could play with them there, but her father had discovered the unflattering likenesses of himself and his wife and broken them to pieces. Lucy and Susan had both been punished and forbidden to indulge in any more mockery of their elders. Matthew Whetcombe was enraged by their lack of respect and gratitude. He ignored both girls for weeks afterwards. They made the new dolls in secret and hid them from him.

With her father now in his winding sheet, Lucy used softer fingers to pick up Susan. She had fallen out of the collection as well. The girl kissed the strands of cat fur that served for her friend's hair, then pulled Susan to her breast. She used her free hand to arrange all the other dolls in a circle then stood in the middle of it. She was surrounded by enemies. One of them had died but the others were still constricting her freedom. A surge of rebellion made her want to escape, and she lifted Susan up to her ear to listen to her advice. The crude doll with its plain and grubby dress broke through a silence that nobody else could penetrate. Lucy heard the words and trembled with joy.

She now knew how to get out of the house.

Bristol gave them such a cordial welcome that they felt like prodigal sons returning home to the fatted calf. Westfield's Men had spent a restful night at Chippenham before rising early to continue their journey. By pressing their horses hard, they reached Bristol in the afternoon and were given instant proof of its bounty. Nicholas Bracewell went off to seek official permission for the company to stage their work in the city and came back with thirty shillings and the promise of at least three performances. As in Barnstaple, the government of the town was almost entirely in the hands of merchants, and they rejoiced at the thought of bringing their wives and friends to watch a London theatre company at work. The first performance—attended by the mayor and the entire corporation—was due to take place in the Guildhall in Broad Street on the following afternoon, and the thirty shillings that the treasurer had already paid would be enlarged by admission money charged at the doors.

Westfield's Men were delighted. There was no sign of plague in the city and no sense of being rushed on. In size and commercial importance, Bristol was second only to London among British seaports, and its bustling streets kindled fond reminiscences for the visitors of the clamour of the capital. Lawrence Firethorn liked the feel of the place and the magnitude of his potential audience. Bristol had a population of fifteen thousand people. While many were not playgoers, enough of them could be coaxed along to the

Guildhall on successive days to guarantee Westfield's Men a profitable stay. Three performances had been agreed, but Firethorn believed they could sustain enough interest to keep them there for a week.

The company lodged at the Jolly Sailor in St Nicholas Street on the west side of the city. Lawrence Firethorn seized playfully on the name.

'St Nicholas Street for our own St Nicholas,' he said.

'I am no saint,' said Nicholas Bracewell.

'Mistress Anne Hendrik can vouch for that!'

Nicholas winced slightly. 'This is a comfortable inn,' he said. 'That is the only reason I chose it.'

'Beshrew this modesty, Nick. You guided us here as you have guided us all along. We are but children in your hands and you have been a true patron saint to us.'

They were in the courtyard at the Jolly Sailor and the hired men were singing happily as they unloaded the waggon. Lawrence Firethorn turned to practicalities.

'When must you leave?' he asked.

'As soon as possible.'

'We need you mightily for tomorrow's performance.'

'I will hold the book for *Death and Darkness*,' said Nicholas, 'and I will instruct my deputy in his duties while I am away. Then I must leave for Barnstaple.'

'How long will we be without you?'

'I will not know until I reach the town.'

'Let us make sure that you *do* reach it,' said Firethorn grimly. 'Westfield's Men cannot afford to lose its book holder to that murderous villain with the black beard. Take care, Nick. We are half the company without you.'

Nicholas was oddly unsettled by the compliment. Having worked so hard over the years to make himself indispensable to the company, he now felt the weight of responsibility a little oppressive. Though he was not looking forward to the journey to Barnstaple, it would buy him an appealing release from his onerous duties. Nicholas still had to negotiate the major obstacle that stood between himself and his former home. The man who had used his name at a Marlborough inn had been mocking the book holder. He had stayed his hand at Chippenham but would almost certainly strike in Bristol. Nicholas had taken the precaution of showing Anne Hendrik's portrait of the man to his friends. Lawrence Firethorn, Edmund Hoode and Owen Elias would also know whom to guard against now. Four pairs of eyes could scour the streets of Bristol for danger.

The waggon was emptied and its cargo stowed securely away until it was required next day at the Guildhall. Work was over. Westfield's Men had a whole evening of pleasure in front of them. Firethorn watched them roll off into the inn.

'Cakes and ale, Nick. Cakes and ale.'

'They deserve some jollity.'

'And so do we, dear heart. What more could I want now than a plate of eels and a pint of sack to wash them down?' His voice darkened. 'One thing more to please my appetite.'

'What is that?'

'The head of Israel Gunby on a silver platter.'

Barnaby Gill was a vital element in the success of any performance by Westfield's Men, and he blended perfectly with the rest of the cast when he was onstage. As soon as he stepped off it, however, he felt completely detached from his colleagues and treated them with lordly disdain. Their world was not his. Bristol impressed this strongly upon him. With an evening of freedom at their disposal, the members of the company responded in ways that were all too predictable, and this gave Gill even further cause for remaining aloof.

Lawrence Firethorn drank heavily in the taproom and flirted with female guests and staff alike. A few of the sharers joined him but others had gone off to the stews in search of wilder women and noisier company. The hired men found the prices in the taproom a little too high for their leaner purses and they were dicing and drinking in a nearby alehouse. The apprentices watched their elders with patent envy and longed for the time when broken voices and manly bodies would help them to break out of the

dresses they wore onstage and entitle them to take their full
due of sinful pleasure. Richard Honeydew was the exception, and Gill missed his contemplation of the boy's naive
beauty, but the youngest of the four apprentices had left
with Edmund Hoode on a tour of the city. Nicholas
Bracewell was their guide because he had known Bristol in-
timately since his youth and had promised to show them all
the sights. There were some places in the city, however,
that even the book holder could never find, and it was to
one of these haunts that Barnaby Gill set off as the light began to fade over the port.

Bristol was a fine and ancient city with the mediaeval
pattern of its streets largely unchanged. It boasted a formidable castle, an abundance of churches and some civic
buildings that could startle both with their quantity and
quality. The whole city was enclosed within a high stone
wall, which was pierced by a number of gates, many of
them crowned by churches. Its position made it the guardian of the West Country, and it had been built to defend.
But the predominant feature of Bristol was its magnificent
natural harbour. Ships that came up the Severn Estuary
could sail up the supremely navigable River Avon into the
very heart of the city, and its mercantile life had always
been vigorous and profitable as a result. Wharves, warehouses and cellars were always piled high with goods from
coastal or foreign trade. Bristol felt in recent years that it
was suffering unfair competition from London, but its harbour was still kept busy and the inns, taverns and ordinaries
along the Shambles were always swarming with sailors.

It was in the direction of the harbour that Barnaby Gill
now strode, and the seagulls were soon crying and dipping
above him to teach him the way. Out of deference to the
more subdued fashions of the provinces, he had eschewed
his more elaborate apparel and chosen a doublet of scarlet
and black satin with slashed sleeves and a pair of matching
breeches. His red hat sported a white ostrich feather and his
buckled shoes had a bright sheen as they clacked over the
paving. An Orient pearl dangled from one earlobe.

There was prosperity and poverty in Bristol, and he saw

examples of both as he picked his way through the streets. The city burgesses had plenty of money but little idea of how to spend it on their apparel or on that of their wives. Gill groaned with contempt at some of the fashions he saw and he averted his gaze in disgust at some of the vagabonds and crones who crossed his path. Bristol had the same heady mixture of fortune and filth as London itself. Barnaby Gill spent so much time reflecting on the close juxtaposition of the two that he did not realise that he was being followed.

The Black Boy was in a narrow, fetid lane that ran down to the harbour. From the outside, it looked like any of the scores of other inns and taverns in the area. But its door was locked and admission was carefully controlled. Gill knocked boldly and a small grille opened before him. Dark eyes studied him closely for a second then heavy bolts were drawn back on the other side of the door. It swung ajar for him to enter then slammed behind him. He was in a large and ill-lit room that was cluttered with tables and chairs. Barnaby Gill looked around with the satisfaction of a weary traveller who has been a long time on a hostile road before reaching a favoured destination. The room was only half-full but its atmosphere was captivating. Well-dressed men lolled in the chairs or on the settles. Attractive young girls served them with drinks or reclined in their arms or even shared their pipes of tobacco. The thick fug of smoke was an added attraction for Gill. A big, beaming woman wobbled over to him and conducted him to a seat, calling for wine with a click of her fingers and offering Gill her own pipe. When he had inhaled his first lungful of tobacco, he blew it out through pursed lips and the woman planted a soft kiss on them.

Two of the youngest and prettiest serving girls now came to sit beside their new guest, and all three sipped Canary wine. Barnaby Gill was soon deep in conversation with the two of them, transferring his affections from one to the other with capricious joy and ordering another flagon of wine when the first was empty. This was his private universe and he so relaxed into it that he did not observe the man with the raven black beard who was allowed into the room by the doorkeeper. Barnaby Gill was in Elysium. Here was pleasure of an order undreamed of by any of his colleagues. They had only base appetites and conventional tastes. Gill lived on a higher plain. The woman who presided over the establishment shook with mirth, the girls replied with brittle laughter and the swirling smoke ignited desire. Barnaby Gill was a man at home among men. As the two boys giggled beside him in their taffeta dresses, he decided to choose the one who resembled Richard Honeydew.

'A word in your ear, kind sir.'

'With me?' said Gill, looking up.

'Are you not the man I take you to be?'

'And who is that, sir?'

'You may not wish me to name you before others.'

Lamparde waited half an hour before he moved across to speak to Gill. He drank freely, spent money liberally and enjoyed the company of one of the serving girls but his gaze never strayed far from the actor. When he sensed that Gill was ready to leave, he stepped across to interrupt him.

'Name me, by all means, if you may,' said Gill proudly. 'Fame is a cloak which I wear wherever I go. Who am I?'

'One of the best actors in the world, sir.'

'You know me well enough.'

'I have seen you play in London many a time.'

'My name?'

'Master Barnaby Gill. You have no peer.'

Lamparde knew how to flatter. He let the purring accent of his native Devon give the words a more honeyed charm, but it was his eyes that did most of the talking. They gleamed with such a powerful amalgam of admiration and challenge that Gill was hypnotised. Here was a man indeed, sturdy and well-favoured, educated in his tastes and worthy of note. His apparel was made by a London tailor and the earring was the twin of that worn by Gill himself. It was the beard that really enthralled the actor. Sleek and well trimmed, it lent a satanic quality to its owner that was irresistible. No boy could compare with a man like this.

Lamparde gave him a respectful nod of the head.

'I have hired a room here, sir. Will you wait upon me?'

'Gladly.'

'Let me conduct you to the place.'

'I follow willingly.'

'This privilege is overwhelming.'

'Lead on.'

The two boys who had worked so hard to entertain their guest were somewhat peeved, but a signal from their employer sent them off to blandish a newcomer. If the men wanted a private room in which to improve their acquaintance, they would pay a high price. Whatever guests chose, The Black Boy would profit accordingly.

Barnaby Gill was taken along a dark passageway with the utmost courtesy by his new-found friend. Both of them were denizens of such establishments and spoke its language. Plague had deprived Gill of his visit to a similar haunt in Oxford and there had been no equivalent in the dull and unenlightened Marlborough. Male brothels were highly illegal places, and both prostitutes and clients would face bestial punishments if they were caught, but this danger only served to intensify the pleasure involved. Gill's favourite haunt in London was a brothel in Hoxton, but its premises were relatively safe from official raids because it numbered among its clients such influential people as Sir Walter Raleigh and Francis Bacon. The fear that was missing there was ever-present here, and it sharpened the edge of his desire. Peril was his aphrodisiac.

They climbed a staircase and stopped outside a door. Lamparde unlocked it with the key that he had been given. He then stood back and gestured for his companion to enter.

'This way, Master Gill,' he invited.

'After you, kind sir.'

'You are my guest at this time.'

'Then I'll be ruled by me.'

'You are the actor. I am but a humble spectator.'

'That is as it should be.'

There was a touch of arrogance in Barnaby Gill's walk.

He went into the room as if making an entrance onstage. The door shut behind him. He was about to turn to face his new friend with a benign smile when the club struck him so hard across the back of the head that he was knocked forward onto the floor. Lamparde did not need to check the efficacy of the blow. He used cords to bind his victim hand and foot then gagged him with a piece of cloth.

Barnaby Gill had entered The Black Boy with a confident strut. He now left it over the shoulder of a murderer.

The Parish Church of St Peter was, appropriately, the tallest building in Barnstaple, and its massive tower, which was topped with a lead-covered broach-spire, reached much nearer to heaven than any other structure in the town. Set on open land between the High Street and Boutport Street, it had withstood centuries of attack by the elements and frequent squalls in the religious climate. Systematic rebuilding had been carried on throughout Elizabeth's reign, and it was paid for by the raising of a church rate. New slates were fixed on the roof, the ceiling over the communion table was repaired, the floor was re-tiled, the lead guttering was renewed and the whole building washed with seven bushels of lime. The churchyard was newly paved and given a new gate.

Another change that had occurred was the developing interest in private pews. Wealthy families who worshipped regularly in the church wanted more comfort during the long sermons of Arthur Calmady. They paid to have pews erected for their own use, thereby exhibiting their status in public while ensuring a privileged degree of privacy. The pews were known as sieges, and it was in the Whetcombe siege that a small figure in a black coat was now kneeling in prayer. When Matthew Whetcombe rented the pew, he did so to attest his position in the community and to hide away the deaf-mute child who was such a constant embarrassment to him. That same daughter was now praying, not for the soul of her dead father, but for the safe and speedy return of a household servant.

Lucy Whetcombe rose from her knees and looked

around. Her plan had worked. She and Susan had often played games of hide-and-seek in the labyrinthine interior of the house in Crock Street, and the girls knew every inch of it. That knowledge had helped her to escape. The two men outside the street could only watch who entered or left the building by the front or side doors. They could not see the entrance at the rear of the warehouse, still less the door to the granary, which stood above it. Lucy waited until the sky began to darken then made her move. Dressed in hat and coat, she made her way stealthily across the Great Court, into the warehouse and up the ladder into the granary. Grain was lifted up in sacks by means of a rope and pulley. Lucy used the device for her own purpose, shinnying swiftly down the rope before racing off towards the church. Those who caught a glimpse of the darting child did not recognise her and the two men on duty did not even know she was gone.

Now, however, it was time to go back. Lucy offered up a prayer that her means of escape had not been detected. She needed the rope to regain entry to the house. It was now dark outside and the curfew would soon be sounded. She crept towards the church door and lifted the iron latch before swinging the massive timber back on its hinges. After a final glance up at the main altar, she slipped out and closed the door behind her.

She was about to sprint off back home when she saw two figures a short distance away. They were engaged in an animated conversation. Lucy could only see them in stark profile but she recognised them immediately. Arthur Calmady seemed to be having a heated argument with Barnard Sweete. The vicar and the lawyer were both men of extraordinary self-possession, yet here they were in open dispute, waving their arms about like two customers haggling over the same purchase in the market. Lucy Whetcombe could not hear what they said but it involved the church in some way. At the height of the argument, Sweete pointed towards the building to emphasize a point and Calmady finally backed down. It was a subdued vicar who finally slunk away.

Lucy Whetcombe ran back to the house and climbed in through the door of the granary. Nobody saw her and she had not been missed from the house. When she got back to Susan's chamber, she let herself in and took the dolls out of their hiding place. Arthur Calmady was in one hand and Barnard Sweete in the other. She held them to examine them then banged them together in a fierce fight. The vicar's head eventually snapped off. The lawyer was the man to fear.

The flapping sound brought Nicholas Bracewell instantly awake. He sat up in his bed with a knife at the ready in his hand, but no attack came and the door remained locked. When the noise continued, he wondered if a bird had somehow got into the chamber and was flying around. Nicholas had chosen to sleep alone in one of the attic rooms. After the injury to Owen Elias, he did not wish to put the life of another friend at risk by sharing a bedchamber with him. It was dawn and a tiny filter of light was probing the shutters. Nicholas peered into the gloom and listened intently. What he could hear was no bird but it might be the softer beat of a bat's wings. The creature might somehow have gained entry through the cracks in the roof. Nicholas got out of bed and opened the shutters to throw more light into the room.

It was then that he saw it. The piece of parchment was trapped under his door. A stiff breeze was blowing in off the river and causing a draught in the attic of the Jolly Sailor. The parchment was vibrating like a wing. Nicholas picked it up and opened the door but there was no sign of any messenger. Unfolding the paper, he took it to the window and held it up to the light. He could just make out the words and they jerked him completely awake. The message was from his appointed assassin. It was written in a fine hand and its doggerel was a derisive sneer at the company.

> *Fair exchange is all I seek*
> *Bracewell Nick for Master Gill*
> *Merchants wise are never meek*
> *Strike a bargain or I kill*

Come at once or Westfield's Men
Will ne'er see Barnaby again.

Nicholas blenched. He was being offered the hardest bargain of all. If Barnaby Gill really were in the man's hands, then he would be murdered without scruple. The only way to release him was to confront the man. Care had been taken with the message. In case it went astray, it was in a code that only Nicholas could understand. The key line jumped out at him to give him the meeting place.

Merchants wise are never meek.

Wise Street lay in the network of lanes and alleys around the harbour. Meek Row joined it at the far end. It was an area full of warehouses and cellars. The cargo waiting there for collection was Barnaby Gill, but there was no proof that he was even still alive. Nicholas dressed quickly and wore sword and dagger. When he put on his buff jerkin, he concealed the poniard up his sleeve. Even with three weapons, he felt he was at a disadvantage. The man was several steps ahead of him all the time.

Nicholas first went down to check Barnaby Gill's chamber, but it was empty and the bed was unused. He really was being held hostage. It was a way of luring Nicholas out of the safety of the company. There was no point in taking anyone with him. Nicholas was quite sure he would be watched all the way to the harbour. If he left the Jolly Sailor with Owen Elias or Edmund Hoode, they would arrive to find Gill beyond rescue. The choice of target showed the man's keen intelligence. Having watched the performance of *The Happy Malcontent* at Marlborough, he had seen Barnaby Gill's crucial importance in the work of Westfield's Men. He had also picked out the loner in the company, the man who wandered off to enjoy his pleasures in private and who therefore made himself more vulnerable.

Leaving the inn, Nicholas made his way briskly towards the harbour. It was a dry day with a searching breeze. A number of people were already moving about the streets.

Traders were streaming in from the country to sell their wares at market. Eager housewives waited with baskets to get the earliest bargains. The whole city would soon be buzzing with the sound of trade. He hoped that his own transaction would somehow end in success.

Nicholas did not need to look again at Anne Hendrik's sketch of the man. It was fixed clearly in his mind. He had learned something else about his adversary now. He was a Devonian. Only a local man would have known that Nicholas Bracewell's apprenticeship as a merchant entailed a three-month stay in Bristol. Wise Street and Meek Row would be meaningless names to most of the inhabitants of the city. Someone who had worked in and around the port would know them, however, and the man had banked on that knowledge. The killer might even be from Barnstaple. It would explain why he had been selected to intercept the messenger to London.

He was close to the harbour now and his steps slowed involuntarily. From this point on, the utmost vigilance was needed. Having drawn him out of the inn, the man might well have laid an ambush. Nicholas jerked the poniard down inside his sleeve so that its handle could be flicked into his palm in a split second. He kept to the middle of each thoroughfare so that he could not be jumped on from any doorway or recess.

Wise Street eventually stood before him. Some of the warehouses were already opening and several people were arriving for work. Meek Row was at the far end. There was a building at the junction of the two, and Nicholas saw at once why it had been chosen. It was a small warehouse, but part of it had been gutted by fire and it had no roof. Doors and windows were boarded up but there were gaps between the timbers where a man could easily squeeze through. It was the ideal place to hold a hostage. Nobody would search for him amid the debris of a burned-out property, and the location gave the man holding him three possible exits. He could come out into Wise Street, into Meek Row or into the courtyard at the rear of the building then vanish into a veritable maze.

Nicholas walked around the warehouse twice before he ventured in. One of the timbers had been torn away from the door at the rear and this was his entrance. He came into the main body of the warehouse and scrunched his way over the charred remains of its stock. When he was in open space in the middle of the area, a voice rang out.

'Stay there!'

Nicholas halted. He had been right. The voice had a distant echo of Barnstaple. He was up against a fellow Devonian. He tried to work out where the man was hiding.

'Throw down your weapons!' ordered Lamparde.

'When I see Master Gill.'

'Throw down your weapons or I'll kill him now.'

'Prove to me that he is still alive.'

There was a long pause and Nicholas began to fear that the man had carried out his threat. A dragging sound then fixed his gaze on the door to the other part of the warehouse. Still bound and gagged, Barnaby Gill was being hauled unceremoniously through the debris. He looked across at Nicholas Bracewell with eyes that were bulging with fear and panic. Gill was alive but harrowed by his ordeal.

'Throw down your weapons!' repeated the man.

'How do I know you won't kill both of us?'

'This idiot is of no interest to me,' said Lamparde as he kicked the prone figure. 'And I keep a bargain.'

Nicholas Bracewell took the full measure of the man who had stalked him so relentlessly. After two murders and two attempts on his own life, he was finally face-to-face with him. Anne Hendrik's drawing had a flimsy accuracy but it caught nothing of the man's menace. The missing earring was now back in place and the beard was positively glistening.

The man drew a sword and held it to Gill's chest.

'You have one more chance to throw down your weapons.'

Gill writhed around on the ground but the sword was still aimed at his heart. He stared up at the man with whom he had entrusted his most intimate secret. Betrayal at such a moment and in such a place was totally unbearable.

Nicholas tossed his rapier and dagger to the ground.

'Step towards us!' ordered the man then stopped him again when he was well clear of his weapons. 'Take off your jerkin!' he said.

'Why?'

'Take it off so that I may see you have no concealed weapons.' His sword touched Gill's chest again. 'Now!'

Nicholas obeyed. He was now only ten yards away from them but twice that distance from his sword and dagger. There was no hope of reaching his rapier in time to tackle the man on equal terms. He took off the jerkin with great care, first removing his left arm then letting the garment drop down his back before peeling it down his other arm. Nicholas now held it over the wrist of his right hand to cover the poniard. Spreading his arms wide, he exposed his shirt and belt.

'Turn round!' said Lamparde. 'Turn slowly!'

Keeping his arms out, Nicholas rotated his body and took a firmer grip on the handle of the poniard. It was soon needed. With his prey now apparently at his mercy, Lamparde lunged forward to cut him down with his rapier, but Nicholas was ready for him. Swinging on his heel, he flung the jerkin around the end of the blade and deflected its viciousness. At the same time, he brought the poniard flashing up to slash at his assailant's doublet and open up the sleeve. Blood gushed out and Lamparde let out a cry of indignation. He pulled his sword free and lunged again but the swinging jerkin was this time thrown into his face. His own dagger once again drew blood, cutting across his sword hand and forcing him to drop the weapon.

Nicholas flung himself upon the man and knocked him to the ground, but Lamparde was a powerful man in any brawl. He grabbed the wrist which held the poniard and applied such brute strength that he turned the point of the weapon towards Nicholas's face. As they rolled and grappled on the ground, the book holder saw the poniard moving inexorably closer and aimed at his eye. To release the dagger from his grasp would be to yield his weapon but it had been turned against him with such force that he was finding it hard to resist. Pretending to fight against the downward pressure, he suddenly gave in to it and twisted his head sharply to the left, allowing the poniard to sink harmlessly into the ground and throwing his assailant off balance.

A well-placed knee and a roll of the shoulder sent Lamparde off him and Nicholas leaped to his feet with the dagger turned on him. Lamparde dived for his rapier but a heavy foot got first to the blade. The man was not finished yet. Scooping up a handful of blackened debris, he threw it in his adversary's face and gained a precious moment to get up and flee towards the doorway. Nicholas wiped the dust from his eyes than gathered up the rapier. When he got to Barnaby Gill, he used the latter to slice through the cord that held his hands then left him the weapon to cut through the rest of his bonds. He himself went through the door into the other part of the warehouse.

Fire damage had been less extensive here and many of the old beams still stood. Down one wall was a series of bays where the goods had been stacked. Boxes and huge piles of old sacks offered further hiding places. Nicholas was back on equal terms again. The man would certainly have a dagger and his prowess with the weapon had already been shown. As Nicholas crept along the wall of the warehouse, he knew that the first thrust would be decisive. One mistake would be fatal.

Lamparde was motionless. Incensed by his wounds, he was determined to kill Nicholas for sheer pleasure now. He tried hard to control his laboured breathing. All he had to do was to wait behind the thick wooden beam and his target would present itself. Through a chink in the timber, he could see Nicholas approaching. The advantage had swung his way again. To poison a girl had given him no real satisfaction and to stab a pickpocket during a play was a reflex act of revenge. This would be different. He would slowly cut the life out of Nicholas Bracewell.

Moving carefully in a crouched position, Nicholas looked

down and saw the spots of blood on the ground. The man was somewhere in front of him. He got closer and closer to the beam that concealed his enemy but did not sense the danger at first. It was only when he was almost level with the hiding place that something made him pause. He sniffed the air. Leonard had spoken about a smell and the serving wench in Marlborough has noticed it as well. Nicholas identified it again. Oil of bergamot. A sickly sweet fragrance for a man who set such great store by his appearance that he courted the looking glass every day. The aroma was quite unmistakable and it saved Nicholas's life.

He mimed a step forward past the beam then lurched straight back as the murderous dagger came out at him. His own weapon struck home this time, piercing the man's heart and sending him to the ground with a long wheeze of outrage and pain. Nicholas stood panting over him. Barnaby Gill came staggering up with the rapier in his hand and looked at the dead man with a squeal of relief.

'Did you see him!' he said. 'He all but killed me!'

'We are both safe now.'

'He took me hostage because of you.'

'Where did that happen?' asked Nicholas levelly. 'How did you allow a man like that anywhere near you?'

Barnaby Gill's anger was quickly replaced by shame and just as quickly superseded by gratitude. He burst into tears and clutched pathetically at Nicholas. Seeking pleasure, he had unwittingly surrendered himself to a killer who had used him to entice Nicholas to the warehouse. But for the book holder's bravery, both he and Gill would have been murdered.

'This will have to be reported,' said Nicholas.

'I'll vouch for you, Nick,' promised Gill. 'You killed in self-defence. No man can be arrested for that.'

'We may have further proof of this man's villainy.'

Nicholas bent to search the body and found a letter inside his doublet. It was an instruction to murder the messenger who was travelling from Devon and it gave details of the girl's appearance and likely time of arrival at the capital. The writer had been careful not to reveal his own identity but the recipient of the letter was one Adam Lamparde. It was a name that meant nothing to Nicholas and neither did the other that was in the document, but two vital parts of the mystery had finally been solved. Nicholas at last knew who had been trying to kill him and who had ridden all the way from Barnstaple to fetch him.

The murdered girl's name was Susan Deakin.

The Long Bridge in the town of Barnstaple was almost three hundred years old. Spanning the tidal River Taw, it had sixteen arches that were built high enough to admit the passage of small craft. The bridge was an architectural wonder whose impact had been dulled by familiarity, but there was still a momentary excitement—even for the most jaded and cynical—in sailing up the river and catching the first sight of the structure. On a sunny day, its reflection was caught so perfectly on the surface of the water that an approaching craft seemed to be offered a right of way through any one of sixteen huge oval openings. The value to pedestrian traffic was incalculable and the Long Bridge was an integral part of Barnstaple life.

Gideon Livermore stood at the quayside and gazed up at the bridge. He remembered being pushed from it as a small boy by his brother and discovering that he could indeed swim. He recalled his first disastrous attempts at rowing beneath one of the arches and of the damage he did to the boat when he collided with the uncompromising stone. The quay was the hub of Barnstaple. Ships, barges, wherries, smacks and fishing vessels bobbed at anchor. Cargoes were loaded or unloaded. Woollen felts, calico, linen, canvas, brass and pewter pots, shoes, soap, wine, ginger, cheese, salt, sugar and pepper were being sent to the Welsh coast while a ship from Milford Haven was delivering sheepskins, rabbit skins and leather along with barley, wheat, rye and a consignment of oysters. More exotic imports came from countries farther afield. Newfoundland, Guinea and Bermuda all traded regularly with Barnstaple. Maritime enterprise had even brought the Caribbean Islands within reach of the north Devon port.

Gideon Livermore had watched with fascination the changes and developments over the years. He now stood near the spot where local merchants sealed their bargains in the Jewish manner by putting a down payment on the Tome Stone before witnesses. Trust underpinned all mercantile activity. Barnard Sweete came hurrying over to greet him, but Livermore had no time for the courtesies. He had left his beloved mansion to ride into town and wanted good news by way of reward.

'Did you see her, Barnard?' he said.

'I spent an hour with her,' replied the lawyer.

'How did you find her?'

'Still distracted.'

'Does Mary understand the implications?'

'I have explained them to her more than once.'

Gideon Livermore sighed. '*Why* on earth did she marry Matthew Whetcombe?'

'She is asking that same question of herself,' said Sweete. 'Grief still sits on her but it is streaked with regret. Mary Whetcombe was not a happy wife and she has been forced to see that. I feel pity for her, Gideon.'

'So do I, Barnard. So do I.'

'She is still such a beautiful woman.'

'The whole world can see that, man!'

'Not if she hides herself away.'

'That will soon be changed.' Livermore massaged his chin with a flabby hand. 'Did you commend me to her?'

'I have done so every time we meet.'

'How did she respond to my name?'

Sweete was diplomatic. 'Favourably.'

'Has she consented to see me?'

'Not yet.'

'How much longer must I wait, Barnard?' said the other. 'I grow impatient. Use your lawyer's smooth tongue. Bend her to my wishes. Work, work, man!'

'The business cannot be rushed, Gideon.'

'Proceed apace.'

'She is still in mourning.'

'That is the best time.'

Gideon Livermore marched a few paces away to show his displeasure. Barnard Sweete went after him to offer apology and explanation. Mary Whetcombe was still in a delicate state of mind and could not be expected to consider such major decisions so soon after her husband's demise, but the lawyer promised to advance at a swifter pace from now on. He then came to news that he imparted with some reluctance.

'She had a visitor yesterday.'

'A visitor?'

'He called again this morning but she refused to see him. The man was sent packing in no uncertain manner.'

'Who was it?'

'She will admit nobody but myself and the vicar.'

Livermore turned on him. 'Who *was* it?'

'Robert Bracewell.'

'Robert Bracewell?' he growled.

'He was turned away twice and that smartly.'

'You allowed Robert Bracewell to call at the house?'

'He only came to pay his respects, Gideon.'

'Keep him away.'

'My men had orders simply to watch the house.'

'Keep him away!' roared Livermore. 'He is the last person I want bothering Mary Whetcombe at a time like this. Inform your men. Bracewell is to be warned off.'

'If you wish.'

'I *do* wish, Barnard.'

'He cannot do any harm now.'

'Heaven forbid, man! The mere sight of that creature would be enough.' He squeezed the lawyer's shoulder to instil his commands more forcefully. 'Robert Bracewell must not be allowed anywhere near her. He has done enough damage in this town as it is. That is one of the reasons I wish to take her completely away from Barnstaple. It is too full of cruel memories.'

Barnard Sweete nodded and the hand was removed. He tried to rub away the pain in his shoulder. Gideon Livermore was a strong man who liked to use that strength to hurt.

'What of the girl?' asked Livermore.

'Lucy is quite bewildered.'

'Did you talk with her?'

'I tried to but she ran away. I seem to frighten her.'

Livermore guffawed. 'With a face like that, you could fright any woman. Maybe it was the sight of your visage that struck her dumb, Barnard.' He saw the other's dismay and patted his arm. 'I tease, man. I do it but in fun.'

'Lucy is no problem to us. Mary Whetcombe is.'

'I must have her!'

'The possibility grows stronger every day, Gideon.'

'I must have her!'

Sweete was about to add a comment when he realised that his companion was not talking about Mary Whetcombe at all. With a merchant's instinct for the approach of a new sail on the horizon, Gideon Livermore had turned to look downriver. A stately vessel was approaching the harbour. Even at that distance, Livermore could pick it out. Its size and its position in the water were clues enough for him. He was looking at the ship that Matthew Whetcombe had named after his wife, a one-hundred-ton vessel that carried eighty men aboard and was the pride of Barnstaple. Few of the merchants owned their own ships. Even wealthy ones like Gideon Livermore only had shares in one. Matthew Whetcombe was the exception to the rule in this as in everything else, and it stirred great envy. After a career based largely on a quarter-share of a sixty-ton ship, Gideon Livermore coveted the vessel that was now riding towards them on the waves.

Mary Whetcombe might one day lie beside him as his wife, but a much deeper desire burned inside him. He wanted the *Mary* itself. That was the real marriage that he sought. The love affair between a merchant and a ship could only be sanctified in ownership.

'I must have her!' he repeated.

They broke away and walked back up towards the town. Livermore had documents to sign at the lawyer's chambers and business to conduct with associates. He led the way in through West Gate so that they could look up at the house where Mary Whetcombe kept her forlorn vigil, but it was not the lovely face of his future wife who gazed down on him. It was the hard and unexpressive countenance of Lucy.

Gideon Livermore turned away and hurried quickly past. 'Have you spoken with Mr Calmady?' he said curtly.

'We had a long discussion.'

'Is he of our mind?'

'He is now, Gideon.'

'You had resistance from this prating vicar?' said the other with irritation. 'What is the fool playing at?'

'He thinks himself a man of principle.'

'Why, so do I, and so do you, and so does every one of us. We are all men of principle but we must learn to bend them to necessity. Ha!' He slapped his side in annoyance. 'I'll brook no argument from a churchman who earns a mere thirty pounds a year.'

'Arthur Calmady does hold other benefices.'

'But they are far away, Barnard,' said the merchant. 'The law now stops a man from holding benefices within twenty-six miles of each other and it is right to do so. These nibbling ecclesiastics will eat up the whole church if they are allowed. They'd have a dozen parishes giving them money and never serve one of them honestly.'

'Our vicar is conscientious, let us grant him that.'

'Yes,' mocked the other, 'he is a man of principle. But I am old enough to remember other men of principle who took the cloth in Devon. One was so drunk on a Sunday that he could not say service. Another wore a sword and was a notable fornicator. One even brewed ale in the vicarage and sold it to friends like any common innkeeper.'

'Arthur Calmady is not guilty of those crimes,' argued the lawyer, 'but he can be obstinate. I think I have cured that obstinacy. With the vicar on our side, we are assured of success. It is only a matter of time.'

'That thought fills my every waking hour.'

'There is no cloud to threaten us.' He paused. 'Save one, perhaps.'

'And what is that?'

'Nicholas Bracewell.'

'That cloud has blown over, sir. There'll be no storm.'

'Can you be certain?'

'Lamparde knows his trade. I employ only the best.'

'Nicholas has his father's determination.'

'He is dead even as we speak.'

'You have heard?'

'I do not *need* to hear.'

'But if Lamparde should fail . . .'

'Have faith in him.'

'I am a lawyer,' said Sweete 'and we do not believe in faith. Facts are our currency. You have faith in Lamparde, but fact put Nicholas Bracewell on the road to Bristol. That is too close for comfort. If your man should fail . . .'

'Even that has been considered,' said Livermore, 'for I leave nothing to chance. If a miracle occurs and he escapes from Lamparde, he will never get within ten miles of here.'

'Why not?'

'I have placed six stout fellows on the road that he must take. They have orders to stop him in his tracks and bury the evidence where it falls.' He smiled complacently. 'You have my word on it. We are secure. There is no way that Nicholas Bracewell could possibly reach Barnstaple.'

Bristol harbour was as busy as ever that morning with ships docking while others cast off to set sail. Fishermen were landing their catch. Merchants were buying and selling. Craft of all sizes drew patterns of foam with their prows. Seagulls swooped around the sterns of the departing vessels as they headed for open sea. Westfield's Men were well represented. Lawrence Firethorn was there with a cheerful wave and some bellowed advice. Edmund Hoode mixed anxiety with his good wishes. Barnaby Gill mumbled his embarrassed thanks over and over again. Owen Elias found a song to suit the occasion. Richard Honeydew cried at the temporary loss of his friend and George Dart, at last confronted with reality of the sailor's life, noting the weather-beaten faces and sea-hardened eyes of the mariners on deck, hearing the vigour of their obscenities, watching the intense physical demands made on a crew, began to think that life in a theatre company might, after all, have its virtues.

The six of them set up a rousing cheer to send the ship on its way. With the horse securely tethered aboard, Nicholas Bracewell was setting sail for Barnstaple.

Chapter Ten

ISRAEL GUNBY NOTICED THE DIFFERENCE IMMEDIATELY. As he sat with the audience in the sumptuous Guildhall, he watched a performance of *The Happy Malcontent* and felt a niggling disappointment. The play was a delight, the actors skilled and the whole production well-crafted. Indeed, the people of Bristol who had come in such numbers to see Westfield's Men clearly adored the rich comic talents that were set before them. Laughter was virtually continuous and applause broke out spontaneously at regular intervals. Gunby, however, was still dissatisfied without quite knowing the cause of that dissatisfaction. On the previous afternoon, he had been one of the standees at the back of the hall when the Mayor and his Corporation had been stirred by the tragic wonder of *Death and Darkness*. The whole company had been superb on that occasion and Gunby had wept real tears when Count Orlando killed himself in a fit of grief so that he could lie in the vault beside the wife who had been cruelly cut down on their wedding day. Lawrence Firethorn had been so magnificent in the leading role that Gunby had almost felt a twinge of guilt at having robbed him of money and of carnal pleasure at High Wycombe.

A lesser brilliance radiated from *The Happy Malcontent*

and Ellen was able to identify one of the main reasons for this. She had enjoyed the play so much in Marlborough that she was eager to see it again in Bristol but the second performance was only a pale imitation of the first. Ellen was dowdily dressed as the wife of the fat old merchant beside her. She leaned across to her husband.

'Master Gill is unwell,' she decided.

'The whole company is ailing.'

'He has lost his voice, his power, his joy.'

'And his legs,' added Gunby. 'He danced better for us at the Fighting Cocks. Something has taken the spring from Barnaby's step.'

'Look,' said Ellen, pointing. 'I am right.'

The play ended to general acclamation and the company came out to take its bow. Barnaby Gill had rushed to the centre of the stage in Marlborough but he yielded that position to Lawrence Firethorn here and stood slightly behind him. Signs of strain were now all too apparent. Gill was so exhausted by the performance that he almost keeled over and Firethorn had to steady him before helping him off. The audience thought that Doctor Blackthought's stagger was a final humorous comment on the character and they clapped appreciatively. Israel Gunby and his wife were not misled.

'There is something else amiss,' he said ruminatively.

'Master Gill's indisposition affects them all.'

'No, Ellen. These are cunning actors. They could carry one man and hide his shortcomings but there was another hole in the fabric of their play.'

'It was much too slow.'

'Fast enough for the burgesses of Bristol.'

'Yet half the pace of Marlborough.'

'Who is to blame for that?'

Gunby realised. 'They have lost their book holder!'

The play had not only been weakened by a lacklustre actor onstage, it had been seriously hampered by the absence of a controlling hand off it. Entrances had been missed and changes of scenery had been slow. When Barnaby Gill fumbled his words and signalled for a prompt, it came so late and so loud that it seemed to be one more comic touch deliberately inserted to amuse the audience. Israel Gunby had enjoyed the performance which he had commissioned at the Fighting Cocks but it was not only the actors who caught his attention. Nicholas Bracewell had organised everything with laudable expertise. His invisible presence was the scaffolding which held the whole company up. Without him, Westfield's Men were distinctly rickety.

'Master Bracewell has gone,' said Gunby.

'Why?'

'That is his business, my love.'

'Apart from Master Firethorn, he was the handsomest man among them,' said Ellen. 'Were I to play that love scene we have just witnessed, I think I would just as soon be seduced by the book holder as by the actor. Master Bracewell was a marvellous proper man.'

'Yet he has left them.'

'His deputy is a poor substitute.'

'Westfield's Men will suffer.'

'We have seen that already.'

'They will suffer off stage as well as on, Ellen,' he said as an idea formed. 'Master Bracewell was their sentry. With him gone, their defences may more easily be breached. Do you follow me here?'

'I do, husband.'

'Their loss is our gain.'

'When do we strike?'

'Give them a day or so,' he advised. 'That will make them feel more secure and put more money into their coffers. *Death and Darkness* filled this Guildhall until it burst and *The Happy Malcontent*, as you see, has made the coins jingle. If we wait awhile, Firethorn's capcase will have twenty pounds and more in it.'

'How will we empty it?'

He gave his wife a sly smile and squeezed her arm. The other spectators had largely drifted away now and they were among the stragglers. Nobody sat in front of them so they had an uninterrupted view of the makeshift platform which Nicholas Bracewell had erected at the end of the hall

213

so that it would catch maximum light through the windows. The stage was still set for the last act of the play.

'You admired Lawrence Firethorn, I think,' he said.

'Every woman here did that.'

'And you said before, you would like to play that scene with him. Could you do it as well as Richard Honeydew?'

'Better.'

'The boy was excellent.'

'But he remained a boy. His voice and gestures were a clever copy of a young woman but he could not compare with a lady herself.' Ellen bunched her fists in envy as she looked at the stage. 'Had I been up there with Lawrence Firethorn, I would have overshadowed the young apprentice quite.'

'Women are not allowed to act upon the stage, my love.'

'That is a pity and a crime.'

'They may still perform in another theatre.'

'The bedchamber?'

'You'd oust this apprentice there!' said Gunby with feeling. 'I know that to be true! But could you carry it off with Firethorn himself?'

'No question but that I can.'

'He is a shrewd man and will not be easily fooled.'

'I have done it once and may do so again.'

'There will be danger, Ellen.'

'I do not give a fig for that,' she replied. 'Where danger lies, the best rewards are found. You taught me that. Lawrence Firethorn will never recognise me for a second.'

'Then let's about it!'

'I'll need some new apparel.'

'All things will be provided.'

'Then I'll show him how a real woman can act!'

Israel Gunby chuckled and put an arm around her. When they got up to walk towards the door of the hall, they saw the distraught figure of George Dart holding out a bowl to the last few spectators. They had already paid an admission fee but the performance had inspired them to part with a few additional coins. Gunby tossed an angel into the collection and Dart gabbled his gratitude. It was a chance to confirm the facts. The assistant stagekeeper was more harassed than ever. He did not connect the fat old merchant with Samuel Grace at the Fighting Cocks. Gunby used a local accent.

'Master Bracewell is not with you, I hear.'

'No, sir.'

'Has he left the company?'

'I fear me that he has!' wailed Dart.

'Where has he gone?'

'To Barnstaple.'

'A strange departure when he is needed here.'

'Even so, sir. He will return one day but it may not be for a week or more and we struggle without him.'

'That was my observation,' said Gunby. 'Westfield's Men have a fine reputation but it will not be enhanced by the bungling of your present book holder. We have seen many plays performed in this hall but few with such a lack of judgement behind the scenes.' He leaned in close. 'Tell me, young sir. What poor, fumbling idiot took over from Master Bracewell as the book holder today. Who was that fool?'

George Dart's hunted face answered the question.

'That fool stands before you,' he admitted.

Gunby threw another angel in the bowl and they left.

The *Gabriel* was a coastal trader that was owned by five Barnstaple merchants who each had an equal share. It had been to Carmarthen and Tenby before putting into Bristol and its cargo included tin, oats, barley and four thousand sheepskins. The *Gabriel* was a vessel of only fifteen tons and it was one of a number with overtly religious names. Nicholas Bracewell soon learned that there was nothing angelic about its embittered old captain.

'A turd in his teeth!' sneered the sailor.

'You know him, then?'

'Everyone in Barnstaple knew Matthew Whetcombe.'

'Knew?' echoed Nicholas. 'He has left the town?'

'No, sir. He is still there—God rot him!'

'Then your acquaintance must hold.'

'It does,' said the other. 'I may speak to the good merchant on my own terms now. Whenever I pass his grave, I can spit on it twice and lift a leg to fart on it three times. That's all the conversation he deserves.'

Nicholas had been fortunate enough to find a vessel that was sailing to Barnstaple. It was not the speediest way to reach the town but it would save him from a long and dangerous journey alone over extremely bad roads. It would also help him to elude any trap that was set for him near Barnstaple. Nicholas had killed off one threat but the man who had employed Lamparde could pay a dozen more to do the same service. It was important to find out as soon as possible who that paymaster was and he could not do that if he was ambushed before he even reached the town.

The *Gabriel* was a small and aging vessel but it was good to be under sail again and to feel the wind ripping at his hair and clothing. Nicholas stood in the prow and let the salt spray bathe his face. In the port books, the ship was listed with a flourish as *Le Gabryelle de Barnstaple* and its gnarled captain was proud of a name he constantly used without ever getting close to an intelligible pronunciation of it. The man was teak-hard and foul-mouthed but Nicholas was more than ready to share his company. Though hailing from Ilfracombe, the sailor had worked out of Barnstaple for the last decade and he knew all the leading merchants there. In the taverns along the wharf, he picked up all the local gossip and it was this which Nicholas now mined.

'When did Matthew Whetcombe die?'

'A month or two back, sir. Maybe more.'

'What was the cause of his death?'

'Plague, pox and sweating sickness.' He spat into the wind. 'At least, it would have been if I'd had *my* choice of his going. I'd have bound the villain in chains and used him as my anchor, so I would, excepting that I've too much respect for *Le Gabryelle de Barnstaple* to have him hanging from it.'

'You did not like the man, I see,' said Nicholas with cool understatement. 'What dealings did you have with him?'

'None, sir, and that's the rub!'

216

'You sought employment?'

'I deserved it!' ranted the sailor. 'There's no more experienced a seamen along the Devon coast than me. When he was looking for a new master of the *Mary*, he should have looked no further than me, but he scorned my claim, sir. He said I was too old! Old! Ha! I'm young enough to drop a turd on his coffin the next time I go past!'

The narrative broke down into a welter of expletives and Nicholas had time to assimilate the facts he had so far managed to glean. Matthew Whetcombe had been immensely wealthy but that wealth was based not so much on legitimate trade as on privateering. Nobody appreciated the hypocrisy that underlay that word more than Nicholas Bracewell because he had sailed under one of the most celebrated privateers in England. Letters of marque had given Francis Drake, and many others like him, a licence to indulge in piracy. In the five years since the Spanish Armada, privateering had been particularly rewarding and Matthew Whetcombe had been one of its beneficiaries.

In 1590 the *Mary* had sailed over the bar with a full crew and a fine array of cannon. After a raid on a foreign vessel off the coast of Guinea, she returned to harbour with a prize that kept the whole town in a state of excitement for a week. Four chests of gold were unloaded from its hold along with a basket of jewellery. The total value of the haul was almost fifteen thousand pounds, a fortune which elevated Matthew Whetcombe above the wealth of any of his contemporaries. Though he boasted that the money had been made in trade, it was the fruit of naked piracy. Letters of marque were no more than a legalised skull and crossbones.

To stop the captain's wild fulminations, Nicholas moved him to an allied subject. He gritted his teeth before asking the question but he had to learn the truth sooner or later.

'Have you heard tell of one Robert Bracewell?'

'I might have done some years ago.'

'Is he then dead as well?' said Nicholas in surprise.

'Oh, no, sir. Fallen on hard times, I think.' He removed his cap to scratch his head with cracked fingernails. 'My

217

mind is not what it used to be but I do recall the name. Let me think now. It will come.' Eventually it did and he replaced his cap to mark the event. 'Robert Bracewell, eh? Was not he a one of the merchants who exported kersey and baize to France?'

'That was him.'

'I have him now. His ship would bring back flax and hempen cloths from Rouen and St Malo.' The sailor nodded. ' 'Tis the same man but not with the same trade. He works only in a small way on the quayside.'

'He had two sons,' prompted Nicholas.

'That was part of his tragedy, sir. The younger fell out with him and went off to live in Exeter. He is a merchant there himself, I do believe, and is well clear of his father.'

'And the other son?'

'He broke his father's old heart.' The captain had more grasp on the tale now. 'This other lad went off to Plymouth to sail with Drake. He never returned. Gallant Sir Francis is a great seaman, no doubt of that, but he lost far too many men on his voyage. I'd keep a keener eye on my crew. If I'd taken the *Mary* around the world, I'd not have lost a single man. I should have been master of that ship.'

He chuntered on but Nicholas was not listening. He was still absorbing what he had just heard. Robert Bracewell had lied yet again. To explain the disappearance and continued absence of his son, he invented a death at sea for him in some distant part of the globe. It was his father's way of coping with the problem. He simply killed his elder son off.

The *Gabriel* made good speed along the coast and Nicholas was no idle passenger. When sail needed to be trimmed, he worked alongside the crew. When navigational skills were called for, he weighed in with friendly advice. The captain found him a tidy seaman and even let him take the wheel for a time. It was a costly treat. Though Nicholas enjoyed his moment at the helm, he had to listen to yet another barrage of moans from the captain. Sailors were like fishermen. The ship which got away from them was like the monster salmon which just escaped their clutches. This man could never have commanded a ship as large or as difficult to sail as the *Mary* but he would nurse his grievance for the rest of his days. The captain of *Le Gabryelle de Barnstaple* was lashed to the mast of his dreams.

Contrary winds obliged them to tack as they sailed past Ilfracombe but they found a kinder passage once they had come round the promontary and struck due south. Barnstaple Bay finally crept up on the horizon and Nicholas experienced the sudden joy of the sailor, catching a first glimpse of home after a long and tedious voyage. When he thought of what awaited him in the town, joy became apprehension. For one last time, he trespassed on the captain's prejudice.

'Did Matthew Whetcombe leave a family?' he said.

'Indeed, sir,' replied the other. 'A pretty wife and a slip of a daughter.'

'Only one child?'

'You may well ask, sir. I've six myself and few of the merchants in Barnstaple have less than three or four. But not Matthew Whetcombe.' He gave a rasping chuckle. 'The curse I put on him must have worked. The rogue could only bring one girl into the world and she was so half-made that he would never be seen with her in the street.'

'Half-made?'

'Deaf-and-dumb, sir.'

'Poor child!'

'Poor child, rich mother.'

'What's that?'

'The wife, sir. He named his ship after her.'

'I gathered that,' said Nicholas quietly. 'Mary. Her name is Mary Whetcombe. He was blessed in his wife.'

'Blessings now fall on her,' said the captain. 'She will have ship and houses and fortune and all. This is a rare woman. I'll wager that Mary Whetcombe is the richest widow in Devon. She'll have more suitors around her than flies around a cow's arse in summertime.' He gave Nicholas a confiding nudge. 'Are you looking to get married, sir?'

* * *

He timed his visit perfectly. Barnard Sweete was shown into the hall of the house in Crock Street fifteen minutes after Arthur Calmady. The vicar had unloaded his daily shipment of condolence and read to her from the Bible. Mary Whetcombe was in a receptive mood. She made no protest when the lawyer was shown in by the maidservant.

'I apologise for coming so early,' he said. 'I did not wish to intrude upon you and Mr Calmady.'

'We were almost done,' said the vicar solemnly. 'I will leave you alone with Mistress Whetcombe.'

'Stay!' said Sweete.

'You will wish to discuss business.'

'Your presence will advance it, Mr Calmady.'

'Then I obey.'

The vicar sat back in his chair with the readiness of a man who was not in any case going to stir from it. He had already been warned that he would have to remain but Mary Whetcombe was too numbed to realise this. Eye signals which passed between her two visitors went unnoticed by her. With the Church and the law shutting her in, she felt trapped.

Barnard Sweete cleared his throat and delivered the speech he had rehearsed in his chambers. His tone was smooth and plausible, his expression one of polite sadness.

'The question of your husband's last will and testament must be addressed,' he said. 'Matthew Whetcombe was a very wealthy man and that he wanted that wealth distributed to a number of different people. The nature of his illness and the unlooked for speed of his death left no time for long discussions about the inheritance of his estate. He penned no detailed instructions himself. What we have . . .' He coughed again as Mary's attention wavered. 'What we have is a nuncupative will. That is to say, a will which is declared orally by the testator and later written down. This is a perfectly legal form of procedure and not at all uncommon.'

A glance at the vicar brought his endorsement at once.

'Indeed, no,' he said. 'Nuncupative wills are accepted

practice. I myself have been a witness of some. The Church has many functions at the death-bed.'

'Thank you, Mr Calmady,' continued Sweete, opening his satchel to take out a sheaf of documents. 'Here is the last will and testament of Matthew Whetcombe of Barnstaple as witnessed by myself and other persons, Gideon Livermore among them.' He put slight emphasis on Livermore's name and looked up for a reaction but none came. 'I leave it with you for your perusal but its main clauses are as I have already indicated. You and your daughter, Lucy, are well-provided for and need have no financial worries but the bulk of the estate, together with the *Mary*, has been left to your late husband's close friend and former partner, Gideon Livermore.'

This time there was a reaction and it was one of such acute loathing that Barnard Sweete made a mental note to omit it from the full report he would need to make to Livermore of his visit. The merchant had been a frequent caller at the house while Matthew Whetcombe was alive and he made no secret of his admiration for Mary. It was not mutual. Mary Whetcombe shivered at the thought that Gideon Livermore would not only be able to visit the house in future, he would own it. With Lucy and her servants, she would have to move out and take up residence in their country house some five miles away from Barnstaple. It was a grim prospect. Hers had been an unhappy marriage but Matthew Whetcombe had given her both countenance and security. Both had now been stripped away by means of legal process.

'Let me clarify the procedure,' said Sweete, referring to a page in front of him. 'Matthew Whetcombe's nuncupative will was made on April 23rd. He died two days later. He was buried on May 1st. On the following day, as is customary, an inventory was made of all his worldly goods. I have a copy of it here, dated May 2nd, and duly witnessed by myself and others. That inventory will be exhibited here in Barnstaple in ten days time when the will is proved.'

'That is admirably clear,' said Arthur Calmady.

'Have you any questions?'

'None, sir,' said the vicar with lofty obsequiousness.

'I was speaking to Mistress Whetcombe.'

'My apologies, sir.'

'Do *you* have any questions?' mudged the lawyer.

The vicar tried to coax her. 'Mary . . .'

They waited for some time before deciding that Mary Whetcombe had nothing to say. Sweete tidied the documents he had brought and left them in a neat pile on the table. He was confident that she would do no more than glance at them. The inventory was plain enough but the will was so enmeshed in legal jargon that she would never be able to disentangle it to her advantage. Barnard Sweete thought it foolproof.

Muttering niceties, he rose to leave and the vicar got simultaneously to his feet. Both were backing away when she spoke in a voice of remarkable firmness.

'Matthew made a proper will.'

'And here it lies before you,' said Sweete easily.

'I talk of a written will, set down in his own fair hand and witnessed by others.' The men resumed their seats. 'The end was quick but the doctor had warned him about his heart. Matthew made a will then. Dr Lymette was a witness.'

'He was also a witness of the nuncupative will.'

'Can one cancel out the other?'

'That is its function.'

'Yes, yes,' agreed Calmady, singing the prescribed response. 'What we decide at one time may seem inappropriate at another. It is only when a man faces his Maker that he is able to make a true judgement.'

'The *last* will and testament,' noted Sweete. 'It does not matter how many came before. The last one only counts.'

'Where is the first one?' she asked.

'That is immaterial.'

'It is not to me, sir. Where is it?'

'A copy must have been lodged with you,' said Calmady innocently, turning to the lawyer. 'Do you have the document still in your possession?'

'We do not, Mr Calmady.'

'Why not?' asked Mary with a flash of spirit.

'Yes, why not?' said the vicar, changing his allegiance.

'Because, sir,' replied Sweete pointedly, 'we have many clients in Barnstaple and in the surrounding area. Hundreds of wills are deposited with us and some are altered or re-fined many times. If we retained every version of every in-valid will, we should have no room in our chambers for anything else. Does that satisfy you, Mr Calmady?'

The vicar was suitably cowed. 'Oh, yes. Yes, yes.'

'What of the copy?' wondered Mary.

'Copy?' said Sweete.

'Of the first will.'

'I have just told you that it was destroyed.'

'That was *your* copy, sir. I speak of Matthew's.' The two men shifted uneasily in their chairs. 'My husband had his faults—which husband does not—but he was meticulous in his affairs. The will may have been lodged with you but he would have retained a copy of it in case yours were mis-laid.'

'Wills are never mislaid by us.'

'Destroyed, then.'

'Is the copy not here in the house, Mary?' said Calmady.

'We have searched in vain.'

'Nothing was found among his papers when the inven-tory was done,' said Sweete. 'His own copy must therefore have been mislaid or destroyed.' He rode over her objection before she could voice it. 'In any case, the earlier will has neither value nor interest here. It is replaced by another. Though I may tell you now that the terms of the first are very largely replicated in the second.'

Mary was so hurt by this information that she did not question it. Barnard Sweete was a reputable lawyer. He had served her husband for years. Why should he lie to her? She glanced wearily across at the pile of documents and nodded her head. It was a sign of defeat.

The lawyer jumped smartly to his feet and gestured for the vicar to follow suit. They bade a farewell then stole across to the door but their departure was blocked a second time. After a loud tap, the maidservant entered and stood between them, not sure if she should wait till they had gone before she delivered the message. Mary had nothing to hide.

'Well, what is it?' she said.

'A gentleman waits below for you.'

'Did he give a name?'

'Nicholas Bracewell.'

As soon as he disembarked with the roan, Nicholas rode along the Strand and entered the town through West Gate. He did not pause to take stock of his birthplace or to allow any room for sentiment to intrude. He was there on urgent business and that took precedence over everything else. All he had to guide him was the name of a dead girl, but it was enough. Coupled with the information he had learned at sea, it took him straight to Crock Street. The captain had spoken with snarling envy of a big house, and he soon located it. He went first to the stables at the rear of the house. The lad who was cleaning the tack recognised the horse at once and was delighted to have the animal restored to his care, but Nicholas did not tell him how the roan had come into his hands. That information was reserved for the mistress of the house. Certain that he was at the correct address, he walked back to the front door to knock. A maidservant took his name then invited him to step inside and wait while she went to see if he would be received.

Nicholas Bracewell stood in a passageway between the shop and the parlour. He could smell leather. A flight of stairs led up to the first floor, and the maidservant had gone up them. He waited patiently until he heard a creak above his head. Looking up the stairs, he expected to see the maidservant return but he was instead confronted by a sight that made his heart thump and his brain mist. Watching him carefully with large, questioning eyes was a young girl in a black dress. Her face was so like her mother's that this had to be her child. Nicholas was transported back twenty years to a time when Mary Parr and he had played together in the streets and chased each other through the churchyard of St

Peter's. He was looking at his childhood sweetheart. Other memories joined the first to turn it sour.

The girl was studying him with intense curiosity. She detected a friend. When Nicholas smiled up at her, she even gave him a small wave of the hand. She was not Mary Parr any longer. She was the deaf-mute daughter of Mary Whetcombe. Though she had something of her mother's beauty, she had hair that was much lighter and a cast of feature that was subtly different. The girl liked him. In that brief moment while he waited at the bottom of the stairs, an affinity existed between them. Nicholas was still wondering what that affinity might be when the maidservant's shoes clattered on the oak treads. The girl vanished and the flat-faced woman returned.

'She will not see you today, sir,' she said.

'Did you give my name?' he asked in hurt tones.

'My mistress is indisposed, sir.'

'She will surely receive me.'

'I have given you her reply.' The maidservant tried to motion him towards the door. 'This is a house of mourning.'

'Tell her I have important news for her.'

'Call again tomorrow.'

'I know what happened to Susan Deakin.'

The maidservant's manner changed at once and she threw up her hands to clutch at her puffy cheeks. Nicholas had rightly guessed that the dead girl belonged to a prosperous household. She had been in the employ of the late Matthew Whetcombe.

'Where is Susan?' said the maidservant anxiously.

'I will tell your mistress.'

'Have you seen her? Is she well?'

'You will hear all in time,' said Nicholas discreetly. 'Susan was servant of the house, I believe.'

'Bless you, sir, yes. Like her mother before her. Susan followed in Joan Deakin's footsteps.'

'Is her mother still alive?'

The maidservant shook her head. 'Dead, sir. Years ago.'

'And was Susan a reliable girl?'

225

'None more so,' she said. 'Susan worked as hard as any-one in the house and took care of Miss Lucy. We were so surprised when she ran away from the house.'

'Ran away?'

But the maidservant had said enough and retreated into a watchful silence. The stranger would not be received. She had given her message and must show him out. Nicholas Bracewell was a name she had heard often but it was ev-idently not welcome there. The arrival of the visitor had had such a powerful effect on Mary Whetcombe that she had needed time to recover, and Barnard Sweete had been equally discomfited. The maidservant judged the newcomer to be the son of Robert Bracewell, and the father was no longer allowed into the house. A man who could cause up-set simply by calling there must be shown the door.

'You must go, sir,' she insisted.

'Commend me to your mistress,' he said. 'Tell her that I will lodge at the Dolphin in the High Street. It is but a small step from here and I can easily be reached.'

'Good day, sir.'

'Remember the name. Nicholas Bracewell.'

The maidservant remembered it only too well as a cause of mild panic in the hall upstairs. She was anxious to hear about Susan Deakin but feared the tidings were not good. Nicholas was ushered to the door and out into the street. As he walked slowly away, he was conscious of being watched, and he turned around to gaze up at the house. Faces moved away from the windows of the hall but one remained at the window in the upper storey. Lucy Whetcombe waved to him again and held something up to him, but he could not see what it was. From that distance, the tiny wooden object was just a vague blob in her little hand. It never even crossed his mind that her doll might be Nicholas Bracewell.

Ellen was propelled by a mixture of envy and daring. Though she had enjoyed all she had seen of the work of Westfield's Men, the role of the apprentices troubled her. Young boys could never be true women. Wigs and dresses

226

only took the impersonation so far. It stopped short of completion. She had watched Lawrence Firethorn play a tender love scene with Richard Honeydew in one play then seduce the lad with equal skill in another, but on neither occasion had they kissed properly. Words took the place of embraces. Passion was distilled into blank verse. If she were on the stage, she believed, the feeling between the lovers would strike a deeper resonance, and it pained her that she would never be given the chance to prove it.

What she could not do in public, however, could perhaps be accomplished in private, and it was here that envy made way for daring. She had simpered and smiled as Judith Grace to lure him to her bedchamber, but a very different net was needed to land her catch this time. Firethorn would be on his guard. If her performance faltered in any degree, he would unmask her. Ellen's daring, however, had another level to it and it was one she kept even from her husband. Firethorn was a dupe, but he was also a handsome, virulent man who gave off a shower of sparks whenever he stepped onstage. She would not have to dissemble on one score. His attraction for her was real. Ellen was confident of her ability to draw him to her bedchamber but she was less certain about what she would do then. Her task was to distract him while her husband was searching Firethorn's room at the Jolly Sailor. There was one sure way to distract any red-blooded man.

There was a respectful tap on the door.

'Are you ready?' asked a voice.

'Come on in and judge for yourself.'

The door opened and a coachman lumbered in. Israel Gunby was transformed by his hat and long coat. He gaped in astonishment when he saw his wife. Ellen had undergone a metamorphosis. The winsome daughter who was such an effective shield behind whom to hide had now become a lady of aristocratic mien. She wore a dress of dark blue satin that was padded and quilted at the shoulders, stiffened with whalebone, lavishly embroidered with a paler blue and slashed to reveal an even richer lining of pure silk. The shoes, which peeped between the low hem, were silvered.

The wig, which swept her whole face upwards, was auburn. Makeup had turned an attractive young woman into a stunning one. Israel Gunby would not have recognized her at first glance.

'He will throw himself at your feet, my love,' he said.

'I will expect no less.'

'This is our greatest triumph, Ellen.'

'Then let it begin.'

They sallied forth and made the short journey to the Jolly Sailor. An assignation had already been set up that afternoon. During the performance of *Love and Fortune*, she had established such a rapport with Lawrence Firethorn from her carefully chosen seat that it needed only a note to fix the time and place. Though they possessed no coach, her coachman nevertheless conducted her into a private room at the Jolly Sailor then bowed his way out. Firethorn was enraptured. For several seconds, he could do nothing more than gaze in wonderment at her and inhale the bewitching fragrance. He wore doublet and breeches of black velvet. Both were embroidered and slashed to show a blood-red satin lining. He removed his hat and gave a low bow then held her hand to bestow the softest kiss on it.

Ellen felt an exhilaration that fuelled her daring.

'You were majestic this afternoon,' she complimented.

'I dedicated my performance to you.'

'It earned my deepest appreciation.'

'My sole aim was to please such a beautiful woman.' He beamed at her. 'Lawrence Firethorn is at your service. May I know the name of the angel who has deigned to visit me?'

'Penelope, sir.'

'Penelope,' he said, caressing the name with his voice. 'Penelope, Penelope, Penelope! It is engraved on my heart hereafter. Sweet Penelope of the Jolly Sailor.'

'This is no fit place for me, sir,' she said with crisp disapproval. 'I agreed to meet but not to sup with you. Westfield's Men are below in the taproom. I would not stay alone with you up here while they joke and snigger. I demand privacy, Master Firethorn. I require discretion.' She gave him a slow smile. 'I am married.'

'Put your trust in me.'

'Consider my reputation, sir.'

'I will.'

She crossed to him and issued her orders in a whisper that stroked his ear with such delicacy that it brought a beatific smile to his face. Ellen savoured each moment.

'Come to the Black Swan in Wine Street an hour from now,' she instructed. 'My husband will not return until late. Use the rear entrance of the inn so that you will not be seen. Wait for my coachman. He will bring you to me.'

'Life can afford no higher state of joy.'

'An hour, Master Firethorn.'

'Lawrence,' he corrected.

'Lawrence,' she repeated dreamily. Then she permitted a light kiss on the cheek and withdrew. 'Farewell, kind sir.'

'The Black Swan.'

'I will be there.'

She opened the door and flitted away like a ghost.

Nicholas Bracewell was shattered by her rejection of him and he could find no explanation of this behaviour that would soothe his hurt feelings. Mary Whetcombe was in serious trouble of some kind and she had sent a message to Nicholas as a last resort. He had responded. Throughout a long and hazardous journey, he was sustained by the idea that she desperately needed him and he put his life at risk to get to Barnstaple. He had assumed from the start that Susan Deakin, as he now knew her to be, was a servant in Mary's household, and the short voyage from Bristol had both reinforced this assumption and given him a valuable insight into her domestic circumstances. If Mary gave a cry for help, why did she refuse to see the man who answered it at such great personal cost? Since she sent Susan Deakin to London, why was she so uninterested in the girl's fate?

The visit to Crock Street had produced one result. Lucy Whetcombe seemed to know him. During a momentary encounter at the house, he felt a bond being forged without quite daring to believe what it might be. Was Lucy part of the reason that her mother refused to admit him? Whose were the other faces at the window? What had the girl been holding when she waved to him? Why did her hair and complexion remind him of someone else? Who *was* she?

There was a possible way to unravel that mystery. Nicholas left his room at the Dolphin Inn and came out into Joy Street. Turning down the first lane, he went through to the open land on which St Peter's Church stood. It had altered since he had last seen it but it still had the same power to wound him. He let himself into the churchyard and went first to his mother's grave, running an affectionate finger over the name that was carved in the moss-covered stone. There was no doubt about the date and cause of his mother's death. His hatred of his father momentarily stirred, but he put the death from his mind. It was a marriage and a birth that had brought him there.

Nicholas went into the church and other memories flew around him like carrion crows. They pecked so greedily at his mind that he lifted an arm to brush them away. A young curate came over with pop-eyed curiosity and welcomed him. Nicholas asked a favour and the curate was happy to oblige. The visitor was soon poring over a ledger that was kept at the rear of the building. The leather-bound volume had its counterpart in every church in England. Henry VIII, father of the present Queen, had decreed that all births, marriages and deaths in a parish had to be scrupulously recorded. Nicholas flicked over the pages with gathering emotion.

He found the date of the wedding first. Mary Parr had married Matthew Whetcombe on a Saturday in June. Nicholas was shocked that it seemed so soon after his flight from the town. He could not blame Mary for marrying someone else when he was gone, but she might have waited a decent interval and she could certainly have chosen someone more worthy of her than Matthew Whetcombe. The merchant was an industrious man with a flair for trade but he was otherwise a highly unattractive character. Mary had sworn she would never wed a man like that, and it bruised Nicholas to see how easily and how soon that vow had been broken.

Nicholas turned to the front of the parish register and read the sonorous words that chimed out like a great bell.

> *Here followeth all the names of such as have been christened within the parish of Bar' from the xth day of October in the year of our Lord God a thousand five hundred xxxviii until the Annunciation of our lady next following according to the king's graces injunction and his viceregent the lord Thomas Cromwell lord privy seal and Knight of the Garter.*

The commandment was dated 1538. Nicholas spared a fleeting thought for Thomas Cromwell whose name enforced the edict. Two years later, he had fallen from favour and was executed with barbarous inefficiency. Somewhere in England was a parish register in which his own death was recorded. But it was the start of a life that fascinated Nicholas Bracewell now and he turned the pages with a trembling hand until he found the correct one. His finger went down the list until he saw her name. Lucy Whetcombe. The girl had been christened barely ten months after the wedding. Matthew Whetcombe was named as the father but her date of birth suggested a startling possibility. Nicholas thought of Lucy's hair and complexion. He thought of those eyes. He recalled the stab of recognition he felt when he first caught sight of her. He remembered something that Mary had been trying to tell him on their last night together. It had all happened so long ago that he could not be certain of dates and times, but an idea now began to gnaw at him. The girl might have just cause to respond to him. Though he was flying in the face of recorded fact, he asked himself if there was a special bond between them.

Could Lucy Whetcombe actually be his daughter?

Gideon Livermore's anger was all violence and bluster but Barnard Sweete did not submit to it this time. He replied with an acid sarcasm that stung the merchant hard.

'Nicholas Bracewell is dead,' mocked the lawyer. 'And even if he lives, there is no way that he will get within ten miles of the town.'

'He will never leave it alive, I know that!'

'Where are your men, Gideon? Still waiting under some tree to jump out on him? Still chasing every shadow?'

'Leave off, Barnard.'

'You stop him by road so he comes by sea.'

'Leave off, I say!'

'Lamparde will kill him. What happened to Lamparde?'

'He failed.'

'There is nothing else but failure here, Gideon!'

They were in the lawyer's chambers and he was not mincing his words. Barnard Sweete had been rocked when the name of Nicholas Bracewell had been brought into the hall. At the very time he was securing Mary Whetcombe's approval of the will, the one man who might repudiate it had come knocking on the door. Partnership with Gideon Livermore was highly productive but it rested on a division of labour. Sweete handled the legal side of things and he left the more disagreeable work to the merchant. The latter had clearly not fulfilled his side of the bargain.

Gideon Livermore tried to reassert his authority.

'My men will take care of him at the Dolphin.'

'Are you insane?' said the other. 'Nicholas Bracewell is no stray poacher you catch on your land and whom you kill to save the law the trouble of prosecuting him. This man is *known* in the town. He has a family here. He has been seen on the quay, at the house, at the church and at the inn. This is not work for another of your Lampardes. We'd have the whole of Barnstaple about our ears. Call off your dogs. It must be handled another way.'

'Teach me how.'

'I'll speak with him.'

'We buy him off?'

'No, Gideon,' said Sweete with exasperation. 'Money will not tempt this man. We first find out how much Bracewell knows. Then I will reason with him.'

'What if he speaks with Mary?'

232

'She turned him away and will do so again.'

'How can you be so sure?'

'I saw her quail when his name was announced.'

'Yet the woman sent for him to come.'

'No,' said the lawyer. 'We were wrong about that. Susan Deakin was not sent. She went to London of her own accord.'

'But *why*?'

'That is what Bracewell has come to find out.'

'Stop him, man. Tie him up in legal knots.'

'I'll do that well enough. But we have another problem which vexes us here. We must keep him away from his father.'

'That is no great matter. He hates Robert Bracewell.'

'We must feed that hate.'

'Why?'

'Because it is to our advantage.'

'Bringing them together might serve us even better,' said Livermore. 'Robert is a testy fellow when roused. If father and son come to blows, it will send Nicholas on his way the sooner and all our cares are gone.'

'You forget something, Gideon.'

'What?'

'Matthew Whetcombe's will.'

'Forget it!' Livermore chuckled. 'Why, man, I damn near invented the thing. You and the others were witnesses. We heard a nuncupative will from a man too ill to speak. You wrote down the terms as I dictated them.'

'I talk of his earlier will.'

'You said you destroyed it.'

'Matthew kept a copy.'

The merchant bristled. 'Where is it?'

'Nobody knows,' said Sweete. 'But if it is found, it could yet bring us down.'

Gideon Livermore now had an excuse to rail once more at Barnard Sweete. It was the latter's job to take care of the legalities and to leave no loopholes. A copy of the earlier will could cause as much damage as the unwanted visitor from London. Both needed to be instantly nullified. Purple with rage, Livermore banged the desk and cursed royally. It was only when his temper finally abated that he thought of a question he had forgotten to ask.

'How is the father involved here?' he said. 'What does *he* have to do with a will made by Matthew Whetcombe?'

'Robert Bracewell was one of the witnesses.'

Lawrence Firethorn was always punctual for an assignation. He arrived at the rear door of the Black Swan at the time set and found the coachman waiting for him. Firethorn still wore the suit of black velvet that he had on earlier, but he had now added a grey velvet cloak fringed with gold braid. Wrapped around him, it gave him a conspiratorial air that helped to heighten his anticipation. Forbidden joys were the sweetest. The betrayal of a husband spiced the occasion. He and Penelope were confederates in sin.

He followed the coachman up the winding backstairs and along a passageway. The man knocked, received a command then opened the door. He held it ajar so that Firethorn could enter then he closed it after the visitor and departed. Penelope was waiting for him. She sat in a high-backed chair beside a table that was laden with wine and fruit. He could see why she had preferred to entertain him there rather than in the more mundane surroundings of the Jolly Sailor. The chamber was large and luxurious with rich hangings on the walls and at the windows. It was divided by a curtain, which she had drawn back at the edge to reveal the four-poster that waited for them. Feather-bedded delight was at hand. They would drink and sup and fall into each other's arms.

'Take off your cloak, sir,' she purred.

'I will so.'

He removed it with a flourish, tossed it onto a chair then gave her the sort of bow he used at the end of a performance on stage. Her hand came forward and he kissed it with gentle ardour. The gloves that she had earlier worn had now been discarded. She felt the firmness of his lips and the heat of his breath. She liked the tickle of his beard against her skin.

234

Ellen was now quivering inwardly with excitement and struggling not to lose control. Fear of discovery had made her precautions thorough. She had placed the candles with judicious precision to throw light away from her. When Firethorn sat opposite her at the table, he could see her through a golden glow that set off her auburn hair while subduing the contours of her face. What she could see was a man in a thousand, an actor whose commanding presence onstage could have an even greater effect in private, a handsome gallant who smiled at her through the gloom. Ellen was safe from discovery but not from herself.

'Will you take wine, sir?' she offered.

'Thank you,' he whispered, picking up the bottle to fill the two goblets. 'To you, my jewel!'

'To us!'

'Amen!'

They clinked their goblets and sipped at the wine. He peered through the gap in the curtains and let out a soft laugh that was as eloquent as his finest soliloquy. Lawrence Firethorn was no slow and ponderous wooer. A glass of wine was all that he needed to smooth his path to the headier intoxication of the bed. Ellen was in a quandary. Schooled simply to divert the actor, she was being pulled towards him. The envy she had felt while watching Richard Honeydew now surfaced again and her daring eased her on to play the kind of love scene that no boy could even imagine. She would never have such an opportunity again. Twenty minutes in the arms of Lawrence Firethorn was a whole career on the stage.

'Wait for me, sir,' she said, rising to her feet.

He was distressed. 'You are leaving me?'

'Only for a few seconds. Be patient.'

Firethorn understood and raised his goblet to her in acknowledgement. She was going to undress behind the curtain and prepare herself for him. His beauteous Penelope blew him a kiss then withdrew into the other part of the room, tugging the curtain after her to close off the gap. He could hear her picking at the fastenings of her attire.

Ellen was removing her lawn ruff when apprehension

came to smother her lust. She was taking too great a risk. If she took him to bed, she surrendered the initiative and removed her disguise. A fiery lover might disturb her wig. Even in the dark, he would recognise her. And if he did not, there was always the danger that her husband would return and catch them there. The loss of a moment of fleeting madness in the arms of Lawrence Firethorn was preferable to the end of her partnership with Israel Gunby. Sanity returned and she put the original plan into action. Gathering up her bag, she stole toward the other door. She would be out of the inn before he even knew that she was gone.

But Lawrence Firethorn had waited long enough. With an impatient hand, he drew back the curtain with a loud swish and stood before her. Ellen spun round in terror. His laugh of triumph filled the room. He drew his sword and advanced.

Israel Gunby walked quickly to the Jolly Sailor, parted with a few coins to learn the whereabouts of Firethorn's chamber then went straight upstairs. There was nobody about in the dark passageway. Standing outside Firethorn's door, he pulled out a small knife but was given no time to pick the lock with it. An ancient chamberlain came trudging downstairs from the upper storey. The light from his candle illumined the bald head and the wisps of white hair. His beard was salted with white and he wore a patch over one eye. The man's whole body had sagged in. Gunby caught the smell of cheese and backed away slightly.

The chamberlain had a Gloucestershire burr.

'Can I help you, sir?' he asked.

'I am coachman to the Lord Mayor,' said Gunby with pride. 'Master Firethorn comes to supper with my master and I am to drive him there. But the gentleman has left a box in his chamber and sent me to fetch it for him.'

'Did he not give you a key?'

'It does not seem to fit.'

'Then let me try this one, sir.'

The chamberlain shuffled to the door and lifted the rings

of keys that hung from his belt. After trying a couple in the lock, he found one that fitted.

'Go on in, sir,' he invited, opening the door. 'Call to me when you leave and I will lock it against thieves once more. We cannot be too careful.'

'Indeed not.'

Israel Gunby went into the room and shut the door behind him. He went straight to the bed and bent down to put a hand beneath it. The heavy capcase came out and he began to undo the straps. Seconds later a heavy purse sat in his palm and he weighed its value with satisfaction. Pushing the capcase away again, he turned to leave but the door was now open again and the doddery chamberlain seemed to have grown in size. A rapier was held menacingly in his hand.

Lawrence Firethorn tore off the wig and flung it on the floor. He had given one private performance that had not been commissioned. Israel Gunby stood there petrified. He had himself escorted Firethorn to a chamber in the Black Swan. How could the actor be in two places at once?

'Sit down and wait, sir,' ordered Firethorn. 'Owen Elias will soon be here with your wife. When you steal money from a man, you only injure his purse. But when you mock his profession, you hurt his pride and that will not be borne.'

Israel Gunby smiled in respect and then began to laugh. A man who had made a career out of duping others had himself been turned into a dupe. He relished the irony.

'You will not laugh on the gallows,' said Firethorn, 'but Westfield's Men will have cause for mirth. We will not only get back the money you stole from us, we will collect a handsome reward for the capture of Israel Gunby.'

'You deserve it, sir,' said the other. 'You deserve it.'

He was still laughing when the others arrived.

Nicholas Bracewell knew that he was being followed. The man had trailed him from the moment he left Crock Street. He was lurking in the churchyard when Nicholas came out. It was not a threatening presence like that of Lamparde but

237

it still irked him. The sky was darkening now and the churchyard was dappled with shadow. Nicholas pretended to make another visit to his mother's grave and knelt in silent prayer. The man crept up behind a yew tree and watched. When Nicholas rose, he slipped his dagger from its scabbard and turned the blade inwards so that the handle showed. He walked past the tree where the man was concealed and went around the angle of a vault. The man waited a few seconds and followed but his was a short journey. As he peered around the edge of the vault, he could not see anyone leaving the churchyard. He moved a pace forward and Nicholas struck hard, bringing the handle of the dagger down on the back of the man's head, knocking him senseless.

When Nicholas reached the gate, he felt another pair of eyes on him and fingered his dagger once more but it was not needed this time. The figure who stepped out from behind the wall was small and friendly. Lucy Whetcombe looked at him with a hesitant excitement then offered her hand. She trusted him. The affinity that he had felt earlier was stronger than ever now. They seemed to know each other. As if understanding his need, she led Nicholas Bracewell back the way that she had come.

Mary Whetcombe sat in the fore-chamber of her house and wept bitterly. It was the room where she had spent most of her marriage. While her husband slept in the Great Chamber next door, she had sought a measure of freedom from him but it was only illusory. His spirit followed her everywhere and there had been many times when he had forced her to join him in the marital bed. Mary had never stayed the night. That was one concession she had refused to make. Matthew Whetcombe had died and released her from all that, but he was now imposing another form of imprisonment from beyond the grave. The terms of his will were punitive. To retain any of the things she valued, she would have to consider the horror of marriage to another rich merchant. Gideon Livermore would be another version of Matthew Whetcombe.

She was completely distraught. At the moment when she was contemplating a hideous future, a name had come out of her past to intensify her distress. After all those long and remorseful years, Nicholas Bracewell had come back. When she had needed him, he had gone away from the town. Why had he returned now and what did he hope to do? Mary could not bear him to see her in this state. She had been young and happy when they were last together. That world had gone.

The tap on the door made her sit up on the bed.

'Go away,' she called. 'I must not be disturbed.'

There was a louder knock and she dabbed at her eyes.

'Leave me alone. I will see no one!'

But the caller was insistent. The tapping got louder and longer and continued until she went across to unlock the door and fling it open with anger. Lucy's whitened knuckles were raised to strike again but Mary did not even see her daughter. It was the tall man who waited quietly behind the girl who seized all her attention. She let out a gasp.

'Nicholas!'

'I must speak with you, Mary.'

'Why are you here? How did you get into the house?'

'Lucy showed me a way in.'

The girl looked up hopefully at her mother who noticed her at last. Since Nicholas had been turned away from the front door, she brought him in through her secret entrance in the granary. Mary was torn between astonishment and alarm. Nicholas was still trying to think calmly. The sheer joy of seeing her again was marred by her patent suffering. Only the girl seemed to be happy that all three of them were together. With a tremor of delight, Lucy held both their hands for a second then ran off quickly downstairs and left them alone together.

'May I come in?' asked Nicholas softly.

'You should not be here.'

'We must talk, Mary.'

She backed into the room and he went after her, closing the door behind him. When he glanced around the room, his eye fell on the bed and he flinched slightly. Their last meeting had also been in a bedchamber though it lacked the elegant furnishings of this one. When Mary sat down, he brought a chair to place opposite her. They stared at each other in hurt silence for some time. Faded memories of what had drawn them together were still there, but they were overlaid with things that would keep them forever apart. Nicholas saw that the gulf that had opened could not be bridged. All that he could hope to do was to call softly across it.

'You sent for me,' he said.

'No.'

'But the messenger came to London.'

'Messenger?'

'Susan Deakin.'

'Dear God!' she said, bringing her hands to her mouth. 'Is that where Susan went? All the way to London?'

'I thought she had come from you, Mary.'

'Is that what she told you?'

'We did not even speak.'

'But you said that Susan came to find you.'

'Someone stopped her reaching me.'

'Then where is she now?'

Nicholas tried to put it gently. 'Susan will not be returning here, I fear,' he said.

'She is surely not dead!'

His expression was answer enough and Mary went off into a paroxysm of weeping. Nicholas put a comforting arm around her but it was minutes before she was able to speak again. Her body still heaved and shook as she looked up at him. A new and deeper level of despair came into her eyes.

'How did it happen?'

'That need not concern you,' he said.

'How did it happen? I must *know*, Nick.'

'She was poisoned.'

'Lord in heaven—no!'

She trembled on the edge of hysteria again and he kept his arm around her, but Mary Whetcombe did not collapse again. Guilt and sadness consumed her. Her voice was a faraway murmur of pain.

'*I* killed that girl,' she said.

'No, Mary.'

'She went to London because of me.'

'You did not send her.'

'Susan wanted to do all that she could. She was a head-strong girl and would not be ruled by anyone.' Mary raised her shoulders in a shrug of remorse. 'I was sorely troubled. I needed help. Susan thought she could find it in London.'

'But why did she come to *me*?' asked Nicholas.

'There was nobody else.'

'The girl did not even know me.'

'Your name was often spoken in this house.'

Mary detached herself from him and walked a few paces away before standing beside a small table. She wrestled with a vestigial fidelity to her husband and then glanced down at the documents that Barnard Sweete had left for her. Matthew Whetcombe had shown her no loyalty and she owed none to him now. He had cut her completely adrift.

'Matthew and I often argued,' she said, tossing a look towards the other bedchamber. 'Your name was much used by him in those arguments. He spoke it with great bitterness and always in a raised voice. You are *known* here, Nick. To every servant in the household, Susan among them.' She turned away from him. 'Then there was your father.'

It brought him to his feet. 'My father?'

'He often came here at one time.'

'Why?'

'Matthew and he did business together.'

'You let my father come *here*, Mary?' he accused.

'Only at my husband's invitation,' she said. 'The name of Bracewell is familiar in this house. Your father never talked about you. He wanted to believe you had died at sea.' She turned to face him. 'He looked so much like you, Nick.'

'How did you know I was in London?'

'From my husband.'

'Matthew?'

'He prospered, Nick. He made a fortune. But the more

241

Matthew had, the more he wanted, and he set up a company in London. He went there last September. They took him to all the theatres.'

'The Queen's Head was amongst them, I'll wager.'

'He saw Westfield's Men three times. The last time . . .'

'He saw me.' She nodded then bit her tongue. 'There is more to come, Mary. Do not spare my feelings. What did your husband say about me?'

'Matthew could be very cruel.' She took a deep breath and blurted it out. 'If I had married you, he said, I would be the wife of a vagabond in a theatre company. He gave me all this—you could offer me nothing!'

'In some sense, that is true,' admitted Nicholas sadly. 'You were better off with Matthew Whetcombe, after all.'

'I was not!' she retorted vehemently. 'I was married to a man I despised instead of to one I loved. Matthew may have given me all this—but he has taken it away again now!'

The force of her outburst had distracted them from the noise of the opening door. Lucy stood there watching them with anxiety. Mary recovered quickly and went across to close the door after drawing the child in. Lucy was carrying her collection of dolls. She set the bundle down in front of Nicholas and unrolled it with great care. One by one, she stood the dolls in a line. When Lucy picked up the last one, she offered it to Nicholas.

'Take it,' said Mary. 'I think it is you.'

'Me?'

'Susan and Lucy made the dolls between them. Matthew would have beaten them again if he had known. That is you.'

Nicholas took the doll and looked at its fair hair.

'But they had no idea what I looked like.'

'They saw your father.'

'This is *me*?' he said with surprise, and Lucy nodded vigorously as she read his lips. He thanked her with a smile then looked at Mary. 'Am I so important in Lucy's life?'

'Yes, Nick.'

The girl was down on her knees, moving the other dolls

about and placing them into little groups. Nicholas looked over her and asked a question with his eyes. The idea had almost become a certainty in his mind, but Mary replied with glistening tears and a shake of the head.

'No,' she said. 'Lucy is not yours.'

'Can you be sure?'

'She was Matthew's child. I should know! He spent most of his time blaming me for her. That is why he's struck back at me now. Because of Lucy and because of . . .' Her voice trailed away.

Nicholas watched Lucy happily at play, at once disappointed and relieved by the news. Mary ran an affectionate hand through the girl's hair, but Lucy did not look up. Her mother turned back to her visitor.

'Susan was Lucy's closest friend,' she said. 'Her only real friend in some ways. I can never tell her that Susan has been . . .' She put a hand to her face. 'Lucy would be heartbroken.'

'Why did Susan Deakin come for me?' he asked.

'She knew that I needed help.'

'How?'

Mary picked up the documents from the table and handed them to Nicholas. He read the first page of the will and understood the nature of the crisis at once.

'Your husband made this will?'

'They say that he did.'

'It cuts you right out of the estate. Apart from a house to live in and a small income, you get nothing. It all goes to Gideon Livermore.' Nicholas knew the name and spoke it with contempt. 'Livermore takes precedence over a man's wife and child. This will is an insult. It is obscene!'

'The lawyer assures me it is legal.'

'He even inherits the *Mary*.'

'That was Matthew's pride and joy.'

'It should be yours now,' said Nicholas. 'You are being abused here, Mary. This will must be contested.'

'I have no means to do that,' she complained. 'They are all against me here. The lawyer, his partner, Gideon

Livermore and even the vicar. Who can hold up against all those?'

'We can,' he said. 'Together.'

'This is not your fight, Nick.'

'It is, Mary. Susan Deakin taught me that.' He held up the document. 'This is a nuncupative will. Did Matthew not write out a will of his own?'

'Yes, but this second one rescinds it.'

'Where is the first?'

'It was lodged with the lawyer but destroyed when this new will was made.' She sighed helplessly. 'Matthew had a copy of the first will but we do not know where he kept it.'

'Who were the witnesses?'

'Why?'

'They will know what was in it.'

'Barnard Sweete was one. He is Matthew's lawyer. He swears the second will is almost a replica of the first.'

'Then why need to make it?' asked Nicholas. 'Can the other witnesses support what this lawyer says?'

'I fear they will, Nick. They are mostly the same men who witnessed the second will. There is but one exception.'

'Is he an honest man?'

'Only you will know that.'

'Tell me who he is and I will go to him at once. This will turns Gideon Livermore into the master here. You would be thrown out of your own house.'

Mary lowered her head. 'He wants me to stay.'

Nicholas understood and his anger soared. The will was not just being used as a way to deprive Mary Whetcombe of her rightful inheritance. It was a crude lever to get her into the bed of an ambitious merchant. Susan Deakin had not understood the details of her employer's plight but she knew enough to summon Nicholas. She had been killed in an attempt to cover deceit and gross malpractice. A legal will did not need a professional killer to enforce its terms. The document was rigged for the benefit of others and it needed to be contested. A huge fortune was at stake. One honest man might guide it into the right hands. If Nicholas could have some indication of the contents of the first will, he could carry the fight forward. But he desperately needed the other witness.

'Who *was* the man, Mary?' he said.

'Your father—Robert Bracewell.'

Chapter Eleven

ALEXANDER MARWOOD HAD SUSPENDED ALL BELIEF in the notion of divine intervention. After a life-long study of the phenomenon, he concluded that there was no such thing as a benevolent deity who watched over the affairs of men with a caring love and plucked those in danger from beneath the wheels of fate. Marwood spent most of his existence beneath those wheels and they had left deep ruts across mind, body and soul. If there really was any pity in heaven, it would surely have been shown to someone in his predicament yet none came to relieve the unrelenting misery of his lot. His plight should make angels weep and archangels wring their hands in sorrow but compassion was always on holiday. He became ungodly.

Work, wife and Westfield's Men. Those were the triple causes of his ruin. A man of his temperament should never have become an innkeeper. He hated beer, he hated people and he hated noise yet he chose a profession which tied him forever to them. His introspective nature was ill-suited to the extrovert banter of the taproom. It was a crime to make him serve out his sentence at the Queen's Head. Marriage had compounded the felony. Sybil Marwood bound him to the inn and fettered him to her purpose. One year of muted happiness in her arms had produced a daughter who was miraculously free from the spectacular ugliness of both parents. It had also turned a tepid marital couch into a cold one and so much ice had now formed around its inner regions that Marwood felt he lay beside a polar bear. Westfield's Men completed his nightmare.

Separately, each of his tribulations was enough to break the heart of man and the back of beast. Together, they were unendurable. The fire at the Queen's Head had somehow welded all three of them together and the combined weight of his afflictions were now pressing the last glimmer of life out of him.

'Have you come to a decision yet, Alexander?'

'Not yet, my love.'

'Move swiftly or we lose the advantage.'

'There is no advantage in a theatre company.'

'Then why does this other innkeeper woo them?'

'Madness.'

'Profit.'

'Suicide.'

'Respect.'

'Ignominy.'

'Fame!' cried Sybil. 'Do not lose *that*, Alexander, or we perish. Be wise, be proud, be famous!'

The polar bear roared at her husband every day now.

Marwood left his wife in the taproom and scurried out to the yard, bracing himself for the sight of devastation and vowing that Westfield's Men would never again be given the chance to set fire to his premises. A surprise greeted him. The restoration work had advanced much faster than expected. Diligent carpenters had now completely removed all the charred timbers and replaced them with sound ones. Behind the wooden scaffolding, the gaping hole was slowly being filled. The galleries no longer sagged in the corner. Fresh supports had lifted them back up to something like their former shape. There was still much to do but the yard of the Queen's Head was recognisably his again.

A less agreeable surprise awaited him. Though busy hammers still banged away and busy ostlers brought horses in and out of the stables, the yard was curiously quiet. There was no crowd of spectators jostling each other, no packed galleries setting up a further buzz, no servingmen calling out for customers as they carried trays of beer amid the throng. Above all there were no players strutting about the stage, flinging their speeches and leaving them embedded like so many spears in the minds of the audience. There was no Lawrence Firethorn to hurl his verbal thunderbolts, no Barnaby Gill to make the boards echo with his jig, no Owen Elias to put the rage of a whole nation into his voice. And there was no applause. Alexander Marwood missed them. It made him feel sick.

'Good morning, sir.'

'You have work to do, Leonard.'

'I'll about it straight when I have done my duty.'

'What duty, man?'

'Give me time, sir, give me time.'

Leonard wiped the back of a massive hand across his mouth then motioned two figures across. Anne Hendrik had been shopping at the market in Gracechurch Street and brought Preben van Loew with her so that they could move on to the cloth market and buy fresh supplies of material. Since they were so close to the Queen's Head, they slipped in to see how the repairs were progressing. Anne had another reason for the visit. Primed by Margery Firethorn, she was ready to lend her weight to the campaign to bring Westfield's Men back to the inn. Though still unsure about one member of the company, she wanted the others to regain a home.

Marwood viewed the pair with cautious respect. Anne was patently a lady but the sober garb and austere manner of Preben van Loew suggested that he had never been inside a taproom. Leonard had no social graces but he managed a few clumsy introductions. As he moved off to work, he threw in a last tactless piece of information.

'Mistress Hendrik is a friend of Master Bracewell.'

Marwood glowered. 'He burned my yard down.'

'That is not what I hear,' said Anne, coming to the de-

248

fense of the book holder. 'Report has it that he saved your inn from total destruction.'

'He starts a fire, he puts it out. That is to say, he gives me a disease then helps to cure it. But I had rather the disease did not come in the first place.'

'The carpenters work well,' noted Preben van Loew.

'When I keep them to their task.'

'Your galleries will be stouter than ever,' said the Dutchman, peering around. 'I was here once before to see a play and I noticed the rot in some of your beams. It was worst in the corner where the fire struck which is why the flames got a hold so quickly. Rotten wood burns best. Had you replaced those old timbers yourself, they might have withstood the blaze much better.'

'Do not lecture me on my inn, sir,' said Marwood.

'I make one simple point. You now have sound timbers where you had rotten. Such neglect was dangerous. Those pillars would have snapped under the weight in time.'

'Preben is right,' said Anne. 'In a strange way, the fire may have done you a favour.'

'It did, Mistress. It showed me my folly.'

'About not replacing bad timber?' said the Dutchman.

'About suffering the deadwood of a theatre company.'

'Westfield's Men gave you a name,' said Anne.

'It is one I disown entirely.'

'That is a poor reward for their patron,' she observed. 'Lord Westfield has brought half the Court to the Queen's Head. Was that not an honour?'

'Indeed, it was.'

'Then why discard it?'

'Wisdom comes with age.'

'Then you must be immensely wise,' said Preben van Loew with a wry grin. 'Please excuse me.'

He went off to view the renovations at close quarters. Anne Hendrik was left with the daunting task of improving the status of Westfield's Men in the eyes of the innkeeper.

'They are feted wherever they go,' she said.

'Who?'

'Westfield's Men.'

249

'God keep them far away!'

'They prosper in the provinces.'

'Let that prosperity hold them there.'

'They will return in triumph to their new home.'

Marwood was interested at last. 'You know where it is?'

'In Southwark or in Shoreditch.'

'Which? The two are separated by the Thames.'

'What does it matter, sir?' she asked. 'You have thrown them out of here. They may go wherever they wish.'

'On what terms, though?' he wondered.

'Better than they enjoyed here.'

'That cannot be.'

'I speak only what I have been told on good authority.' Anne did not mention that the good authority was Margery Firethorn. Having gained his ear, she now pretended to walk away from it. 'I grow tedious, sir. I will go.'

'Wait, wait.'

'Westfield's Men are dead here. This is a tomb now. I will have to send them somewhere else.'

'Send who?'

'I tax your patience here.'

'No, no. You talked of custom.'

'In a small way, Master Marwood,' she said. 'My name is Dutch but I am English, as you see. I speak both languages and that makes me useful in our community.'

'We have a lot of Dutchmen here.'

'And most of them resented like any other foreigner. But a man like you turns nobody away. That is why your inn will always flourish.'

'I do not serve many Hollanders,' he said, glancing across at Preben van Loew. 'They are not ale-drinkers.'

'They are if they are taught to be. And playgoers, too. That is my argument.' She indicated her employee. 'Preben works for me and frowns on all pleasure. Yet when I brought him to a play in this yard, he enjoyed it so much he sent a dozen of his friends back. Each one of that dozen sent a handful more and so on. You stay with me here?'

'Why, yes,' said Marwood thoughtfully.

Anne was into her stride. 'Visitors come from Holland

all the time. When they seek entertainment, I send them here because Westfield's Men never disappoint. All this trade will be lost if the company goes.'

'It *has* to go. They burned my premises down.'

'They are helping to build it up again.'

'How so?'

'Take a closer look at these workmen,' she suggested. 'That man on the ladder is Nathan Curtis, master-carpenter with Westfield's Men. I know him as a neighbour of mine in Bankside. With him is his assistant, David Leeke. When they sent their fellows away on tour, they stayed to rebuild the company's home.'

'At my expense! These repairs are costly!'

'Defray the amount, Master Marwood.'

'If only I knew how!'

'It is not for me to say, sir,' she remarked. 'I am in business myself but employ only a handful of men. Preben there is one. This I do know, however. If I ran this inn, I would seek to spread the cost of restoration.'

'I have tried, I have tried.'

'Everywhere but the easiest place.'

'And where is that?'

'Westfield's Men.'

'They are almost penniless.'

'Not when they fill your yard every afternoon. Think on this. Suppose they agreed to pay half of all the bills that you incur from the fire. Would that not cut your grief in two?'

'How could they afford it?'

'You levy a surcharge on each performance.'

'Explain, I pray.'

Anne was persuasive. 'Westfield's Men pay a rent for the use of your yard, do they not? Add a fire tax to that rent. Some small amount, it may be, and spread over a whole year. At the end of that time, you would have earned back half of all you spent.' She saw a smile almost peeping out at her. 'And that will be on top of all the extra revenue the company will bring in. London has missed them sorely. When they return, this yard will fill in minutes.'

Alexander Marwood could hear the sense in her argument but he still had grave reservations. Anne Hendrik left him with one more idea over which he could mull.

'Their first performance would be the best of all.'

'Why?'

'Because all its proceeds would go to you.'

'They will play for *nothing*!'

'As a gesture of faith,' she said, 'they will donate the takings of an afternoon to the repair fund. If that is not generosity, then I do not know what is.' She waved to Preben van Loew to indicate an imminent departure. 'We must leave you now, sir, but I tell you this in private. I would not have Westfield's Men go to this other inn to play.'

'Why not?'

'It has a most villainous innkeeper. Farewell.'

It was dark when Nicholas Bracewell left the house in Crock Street and there was no question of his riding out to visit his father that night. The confrontation, in any case, needed a degree of forethought. What he had done after his talk with Mary Whetcombe was to walk back to the quay and take a proper look at a place which had meant so much to him at one time. It was empty now but still redolent with activity. He could almost smell the cargoes being unloaded and hear the deals being struck by astute merchants. When his father had first taken him there, Nicholas had loved the cheery commotion of Barnstaple quay. A few small ships floated at their moorings but it was the vessel which lay at anchor in the middle of the river which had captured his interest. The *Mary* was a fine craft, still riding on its reputation as a privateer. Even in the moonlight, he could judge its character. To own such a ship was to own the town. No wonder Gideon Livermore was ready to kill for it.

When the curfew bell sounded, he had gone back in through West Gate and headed for the Dolphin Inn. Sleep came with merciful swiftness. Rain tapped on the window to wake him in the morning but it had cleared by the time he went down to the taproom for his breakfast. Over toast and ale, he read the letter which Barnard Sweete had left for him with the innkeeper. Nicholas was invited to visit the lawyer in his chambers. The subject of discussion was not stated but he could guess at it. Mary had told him enough about Sweete to alert him to the man's cleverness and Nicholas already had a clear impression of the sort of man the lawyer might be. Before taking him on, however, he needed more evidence and that could only come from his father. It was ironic. The man who had torn him away from Mary Parr might now be in a position to offer a kind of restitution.

Nicholas hired a horse and rode northwards out of the town in the direction of Pilton. Two men followed him this time but at a comfortable distance. They were there to watch and not to attack. Nicholas smiled when he came to an old signpost that pointed his way. The village of Marwood was one of three listed and he knew it from his boyhood. Its namesake at the Queen's Head had none of its rural charm and still less of its abiding warmth.

The cottage was not far from Pilton and his first sight of it shocked him. It was a small, low, half-timbered building with a thatched roof. Standing in a couple of acres, it had a neglected and world-weary air. When he got closer, he saw that birds were nesting under the eaves. One of the trees in the garden had been blown over in a gale and was now propped up with a length of timber. Panes of glass were missing from an upper window. The garden gate was broken. A goat chewed unconcernedly outside the front door.

He felt curiously offended. When Nicholas was a boy, his father had been a successful merchant with a wife, two sons and three daughters, all of whom lived in a large town-house in Boutport Street. They had respectability and position. Robert Bracewell had no social standing now. He was a virtual outcast from Barnstaple. A man who had once rubbed shoulders with Matthew Whetcombe and the other leading merchants was now banished to the oblivion of a country cottage. It was a poor reflection on the family name but Robert Bracewell deserved no sympathy. Nicholas reminded himself of that as his knees nudged his horse forward.

Dismounting at the gate, he tethered the animal and went up the path to the front door. The goat did not even look up from its meal of grass and nettles. Nicholas did not need to knock. The door swung open and the suspicious face of an old woman emerged. She was short, stout and wearing a plain dress. Grey hair poked out from beneath her mobcap. Her hands were a network of dark blue veins. After staring at him for a moment, she seemed to half-recognize him and it made her shrink back. She called to someone inside the cottage then disappeared from view. Nicholas waited. A small dog came scampering out and barked amiably at him. The goat aimed a kick at it then resumed its browsing.

The front door opened wider and an old man in a faded suit glared out at him. Nicholas at first took him for a servant, like the woman, but it slowly dawned on him that this was his father. The years had eaten right into the man. The tall figure had shrunk and the powerful frame had gone. Hair and beard were grey and the face was etched with lines. It shook his son. Robert Bracewell was a wreck of the man he had once been. He seemed too small and insignificant to bear the weight of all that hatred of him that his son carried.

A touch of his old belligerence still clung to him.

'What do you want?' he growled.

'I've come to see you.'

'We want no visitors. Who are you?'

'Nicholas.'

'Who?'

'Your son.'

Robert Bracewell glared at him with more intensity then waved his hand. 'I have no son called Nicholas,' he said. 'He sailed with Drake and was lost at sea. Nicholas is dead. Do not mock me, sir. Go your way and leave me alone.'

He stepped back and tried to close the door but his son was too quick for him. Nicholas got a shoulder to the timber and held it open. Their faces were now only inches away. The belligerence turned to an almost childlike curiosity.

'Nicholas? Is it really you?'

'We must speak, father.'

Robert Bracewell became suddenly embarrassed and began to apologise for his humble circumstances. He led Nicholas into the long, dank room which occupied almost the whole of the ground floor of the house. The old woman lurked at the far end. When she saw them coming, she sneaked off into the scullery and shut the door after her. The furniture was better than such a dwelling could have expected and Nicholas recognised several pieces from the old house in Boutport Street. A cane-backed chair kindled special memories. His mother had nursed him in it. Robert Bracewell now dropped into it with the heaviness of a man who did not mean to stir from it for a very long time. Nicholas had already caught the aroma of drink. He now saw that his father's hands had a permanent shake to them.

'Sit down, sit down, Nick,' said his father.

'Thank you,' He found an upright chair.

'Why have you come to Barnstaple?'

'I was sent for, Father.'

'Mary Whetcombe?'

'I called on her yesterday.'

Robert Bracewell nodded and appraised his elder son with mingled pride and fear. They had parted in anger. There was still a sharp enmity hanging between them.

'Where do you live now?'

'London.'

'What do you do?'

'I work for a theatre company.'

'Theatre?' His nose wrinkled in disgust. 'You belong to one of those troupes of strolling players? Like those we used to see in Barnstaple in the summer?'

'Westfield's Men are a licensed company.'

'What does that mean?'

'It would take too long to explain,' said Nicholas.

'Actors? No. That's no fit way for a man to live.'

'Nor is this, father.'

The rejoinder slipped out before Nicholas could stop it and it clearly hurt Robert Bracewell. He drew himself up in his chair and his jaw tightened. He waved a trembling hand.

'This is my home, lad,' he warned. 'Do not insult it.'

'I am sorry.'

'Had you stayed, I might not now be in this state.'

'You drove me away.'

'That's a lie, Nick!'

'You drove Peter away as well.'

'Your brother was different.'

'We were ashamed of you.'

'Stop!'

Robert Bracewell slapped the flat of both hands down on the arms of the chair. Anger brought him to life. His back straightened and his head was held erect. The resemblance to his son was suddenly quite strong and it disturbed Nicholas to be reminded of it. The old man's yell made the door to the scullery open for the woman to peer in before withdrawing again with a hurt expression. His father was shaking with quiet fury now and that would not further Nicholas's purpose. He tried to placate the old man with a softer tone.

'We need your help,' he said.

'*We?*'

'Mary Whetcombe and I.'

A note of disbelief. 'You came back for *her*?'

'A messenger summoned me from London.'

'Mary would never even look at you now.'

'Yes, she would.'

'After the way you let her down . . .'

'We talked for a long while at her house.'

'She despises you!'

Robert Bracewell had always been forthright and it was a habit that made him few real friends. Nicholas and his brother had an abrasive upbringing. Their father loved them after his own fashion, but he was blunt about what he considered to be their faults. Nicholas wondered how his mother had put up with her husband for so long. Rober

Bracewell had not spared his wife. She had suffered the worst of his cruel candour. She had also endured his other vices until their combined weight had crushed the life out of her. Nicholas thought about her lying in the churchyard and resolved to get through the business of his visit before riding away from his father forever.

'What brought you, Nick?'

'Matthew Whetcombe's will.'

'That is no concern of yours.'

'I have made it so.'

'Why?'

'Because the messenger who came to London was murdered before the message was delivered to me. They tried to stop me from getting to Barnstaple. I was attacked by the same man.' Nicholas paused. 'He now lies dead in Bristol.'

'You killed him?' The old man was shocked.

'Defending myself.'

'Who was the rogue?'

'His name was Lamparde.'

'Adam Lamparde?'

'You know the man?'

'I did at one time,' recalled his father. 'Lamparde was a sailor. A Tiverton man by birth. A good seaman, too, who could have looked to have his own vessel one day. But he was too fond of a brawl. A man was killed in a tavern one night. Lamparde disappeared. They say he made for London.'

'Which ship did he sail in?'

'The *Endeavour*. She was only twenty tons, but she flew between Barnstaple and Brittany like a bird on the wing.'

'Who owned the vessel?'

'Two or three. Gideon Livermore among them.'

'His name guided me here.'

The old man snarled. 'Livermore is offal!'

'He stands to inherit the bulk of Whetcombe's estate.'

'Let him. What care I?'

'You were a witness to the man's will.'

'Yes,' said the other with a sigh of regret. 'I could speak

257

to Matthew in those days, visit his house, discuss all manner of business, mix with his friends.'

'You saw that will, Father.'

'I would not have signed it else.'

'What did it say?'

'That is a private matter.'

'You may save Mary, if you can tell us. She is cut out by the new will. Gideon Livermore seizes all. I do not believe that that was Matthew Whetcombe's true wish.'

'He was a deep man, Matthew. A very deep man.'

'What was in the first will?'

'Ask the lawyer.'

'You *read* it, Father!' shouted Nicholas. 'For God's sake, tell us what was in it! Did he leave the ship to Gideon Livermore? Did he leave the house in Crock Street? Did he all but disinherit his wife and child? Tell us.'

Robert Bracewell pulled himself forward in the chair as if to strike his son, but the blow never came. Nicholas was instead hit by a peal of derisive laughter that made his own fists bunch in anger.

'So that's your game, my lad,' said his father with weary cynicism. 'That's why you came back here. For her. You wanted Mary Parr then and you want her even more now that she is Mary Whetcombe and a wealthy widow. That's what my son has turned into, is it? A privateer! Drake has taught you well. Hoist your flag and set sail. Seize the richest prize on the seas. No wonder you want her. Mary Whetcombe is a treasure trove.' The laughter darkened. 'But she'll never want you. She'd sooner look at a rogue like Livermore!'

Nicholas was so incensed that it was an effort to hold himself back from attacking his father and beating him to the ground. The speech had opened up old wounds with the ease of a sharp knife ripping through the soft underbelly of a fish. Nicholas closed his eyes and waited for the pounding in his temples to cease.

Robert Bracewell was typical of the merchant class. He was a practical man, toughened by a harsh upbringing and by the struggle to survive in a competitive world. Marriage

258

was essentially a business proposition to him. Merchants' sons married merchants' daughters. A prudent choice of wife brought in a widening circle of friends and relations who could improve a man's prospects considerably. The dowry, too, was important. It could save many a poor credit balance. That was a factor that weighed heavily with Robert Bracewell, and he had selected a bride for his elder son partly on that basis.

Fathers struck bargains. Katherine Hurrell was selected for Nicholas Bracewell in the same way as Mary Parr was the designated wife of Matthew Whetcombe. Love and happiness were a matter of chance. The commercial implications of the match were far more important. Paternal pressure on all sides was immense, but Nicholas and Mary resisted it. They rejected their chosen partners. They wanted each other, no matter what their fathers decreed. Robert Bracewell had been adamant that his son should marry Katherine Hurrell. His preference for her family had become an obsession.

Nicholas remembered why and his loathing intensified.

'You stopped us!' he accused.

'I had to, Nick. You must see that.'

'You killed our hopes.'

'I had no choice.'

'Mary was waiting for me,' said Nicholas. 'She would have run away with me sooner than marry *him*. She hated Matthew Whetcombe. He had nothing to offer her.'

'Yes, he did,' said his father. 'He offered something that nobody else could match. There was more to Matthew than you might think. A deep man, believe me. Hidden virtues.'

'Mary had no time for him.'

'That is not true.'

'She couldn't bear the fellow near her!'

'Yet she married him.'

If was offered as a simple statement of fact, but it had the impact of a punch. Nicholas recoiled. Matthew Whetcombe had indeed married Mary Parr, but only because Nicholas has deserted her. His one impulsive action all those years ago had committed a woman he wanted to a loveless relationship with a man whose death she could not even mourn. By extension, it had also thrust her into the humiliating situation that now faced her. Guilt pummelled away at Nicholas again but the real culprit was sitting calmly in front of him. His father was enjoying his son's discomfort.

It had been a mistake to come. Robert Bracewell would not help a son who ran away from him or a woman who ruined his marriage plans for that son. The old man would take a perverse delight in obstructing them. Nicholas got up abruptly and moved to the door. His father's voice halted him.

'I witnessed that will,' he said, 'but I am not able to tell you its contents. They are confidential. If you insist on seeing it, apply to Barnard Sweete. He should have a copy of the first will.'

'He has destroyed it.'

'Matthew had a copy drafted.'

'That, too, has disappeared.'

'Find it, Nick.'

'The house has been searched from top to bottom.'

'Search again.'

'Was Livermore the main beneficiary of the first will?'

'Find it and you will know the truth.'

'Will you give us no help at all, Father!'

'What have you done to deserve it?' said the other with scorn. 'Get out of my house! Get out of my life!'

'A crime is being committed here!' urged Nicholas. 'You can prevent it. We need you!'

But Robert Bracewell had said all that he was going to on the subject. The interview, which had been a torment for his son, had been an ordeal for him as well. All the strength had drained out of him and the pouched skin quivered. The woman came in from the scullery to stand behind him in case she was needed. They looked once again like two old servants in a farmer's cottage. Nicholas was saddened.

He went quickly out but paused a few yards down the path, turning to call a question through the open door.

'Why did you go so often to Matthew Whetcombe's house?'

Robert Bracewell got up and lumbered towards him. One hand on the door, he stared at his visitor with a mixture of nostalgia and dismay.

'Why did you go?' repeated Nicholas.

'To see my granddaughter.'

He slammed the door shut with echoing finality.

His mind was an inferno as he rode away from the cottage. Past and present seemed so inextricably linked that they had become one. Mary Whetcombe had reminded him of the young man he once was and Robert Bracewell had warned him of the old man he could become. Both experiences had torn at his very entrails. He rode at a steady canter and vowed never to return to the house. Seeing his father again had laid some ghosts but awakened too many others. The picture of two aged people side by side in a run-down cottage stayed in his mind. Robert Bracewell had once lived with a handsome woman of good family who loved him devotedly and who bore him five children. That wife was sent to an early grave with a broken heart. All that the merchant had left now was a shuffling servant to fetch and carry for him.

So much had happened since he had come back to Barnstaple that he could not absorb it all. Nicholas Bracewell tried to pick out the salient facts. Mary Whetcombe was in serious danger of losing her inheritance through a conspiracy. Gideon Livermore was dispossessing her in order to bring her within his reach. As a rich widow, she would never deign to look at a man like him, but she might change her mind if marriage restored to her all that she had lost. Mary was an essential part of the property, and Livermore would not part with her. She had been forced to marry one man she hated. Why not another?

If she took Gideon Livermore, however, she would be sharing her life with a murderer. Lamparde had killed Susan Deakin and attempted to send Nicholas after her but the orders had come from Livermore. He stood to gain most and had just as much blood on his hands as Lamparde himself. Barnard Sweete was an accomplice. Against two men of such guile, a distraught widow would have little chance. They had even enlisted the aid of the vicar on their side to render Mary Whetcombe completely powerless.

Another consideration scalded its way into Nicholas's brain. Mary was the mother of his child. The feeling that Nicholas had when he first saw Lucy had been strengthened. In spite of her mother's denial, he sensed that the girl was his, and his father had confirmed it. The forlorn creature who was locked away with her dolls in a silent universe was Nicholas's daughter. She deserved special protection.

Robert Bracewell's regular visits to the house were now explained, but questions were raised about Matthew Whetcombe. Did he know that the child was his? Had his revulsion been based on the girl's afflictions or on her true parentage? Nicholas's father had called the merchant a deep man. In what sense? Would such a proud merchant accept a cuckoo in the nest? Was he aware of Mary's pregnancy when he married her? The house in Crock Street was full of phantoms.

Nicholas had gone to such lengths to exorcize the demons from his mind that he could not be certain about dates and times. The specifics of Lucy's birth did not matter. His own instinct was more reliable, especially as it now had his father's endorsement. What hurt him most was that Mary had lied to him about the girl. Their daughter was conceived in love even if she had grown up with very little of it around her. Nicholas was sorrowful as he thought about the thin little body and the pinched face, but he also felt a strange joy. He knew the truth at last.

He passed the signpost to Marwood again and his thoughts turned once more to the company. With all its problems and pressures, life with Westfield's Men was far preferable to this. He had a recognised position there and was able to impose some order. Barnstaple was chaos. Nicholas no longer had a place in the community and his feelings about it were ambivalent. Mary had hardly given him an ecstatic welcome and his own father had treated him like an intruder. Instead of being in control, he was being swept along by events.

Nicholas had to affirm his purpose. Action was needed. His immediate priority was to find the first will. Gideon Livermore was the architect of the villainy but his guilt would still have to be proved. Possession of that first will would be a major piece of evidence against him. If it was not in the house, where else could it possibly be?

He was still asking the question as he rode through a patch of woodland. The horse cantered along and its rider let it find its own way along the trail. It proved fatal. The forelegs of the animal suddenly made contact with the stout cord that had been stretched across its path between two trees. Down went the horse in a writhing heap and Nicholas was thrown clear. He knew at once that it was an ambush. After rolling over on the damp ground, he looked for cover and dived swiftly behind the nearest tree. He was just in time. There was a loud twanging noise and something thudded into the trunk only inches away from his face.

He drew his sword to defend himself and leapt to his feet, but his unseen attacker was already spurring his own horse away. Nicholas examined the short steel arrow which was embedded in the tree. It was the bolt from a crossbow.

They had found a new Lamparde.

Barnard Sweete was livid. As he paced the room, his coolness and poise were cracking audibly around the edges.

'You should have consulted me first, Gideon!'

'And given you the chance to stop me?'

'I warned you not to lay hands upon him.'

'Who are you to give orders?' said Livermore.

'They are not orders!' protested the lawyer. 'I simply want to stay alive. You cannot attack a man like Nicholas Bracewell. It is one thing to kill off a mere servant hundreds of miles from here but we do not want a corpse like this on our doorstep.'

'It is not on our doorstep,' assured the other with a complacent grin. 'My man will have buried it in the woods by now. Nobody will ever find Nicholas Bracewell or know why he came to Barnstaple.'

'Questions will be asked.'

'By whom? Mary? His father?' He shrugged. 'We tell them that he has fled the town. He walked out on both of them before, now and he has done so again. They will never know the truth. Trust me, Barnard. My way is best.'

'It incriminates us.'

'Lamparde has already done that.'

'Faraway in London—not here!'

Gideon Livermore chuckled. 'You are too squeamish, man. Be grateful to me for having rid us of the problem. I was only taking your advice, after all.'

'*My* advice?'

'You said that I could not have him killed off like a poacher who had been found on my land. But that's exactly what I have done. I own this town and Nicholas Bracewell has trespassed on it. I merely enforced the law.'

Barnard Sweete came to rest in front of the table. He sat against it and his foot tapped anxiously as he feared repercussions. If Livermore disposed of his enemies so ruthlessly, what would happen to the lawyer if the two of them ever fell out?

'I still do not like it, Gideon,' he said.

'You will learn to live with it.'

'Think of the risk that you were taking.'

'I am a merchant,' said Livermore. 'Risk is the essence of my business. Every time I send a ship across the sea, I risk its loss. Every time I strike a bargain, I risk a high cost. But these are calculated risks and they have always paid off in the past. Put trust in my merchant's instinct now. This is the most profitable deal I have ever made.'

Barnard Sweete calmed down. Horrified when told about the ambush in the wood, he was now coming to see its positive advantages. Nicholas Bracewell was a threat to the whole enterprise and had to be removed. This way was dramatic and worrying, but it did eliminate the one last obstacle. When he looked down at his hands, they were white

264

and spotless. He might feel the blood on them but there was no visible sign of it.

Gideon Livermore wanted progress. Having disposed—as he thought—of a major problem, he was impatient to take possession of his prize. He had been down to the wharf to see the *Mary* again that morning and had watched her for an hour as she lay at anchor in the middle of the River Taw. She dwarfed all the craft around her. Livermore would soon occupy that position in Barnstaple. In every sense, his tonnage would be the heaviest in north Devon and all would make way for him for fear of being caught in his wash.

He was still preening himself when a knock on the door brought an anxious clerk into the room. When he told them who had arrived at the chambers, both men blanched. Barnard Sweete recovered first. He told his clerk to send in the visitor after two minutes. Alone once more with Gideon Livermore, he treated him to a burst of vituperation. The merchant had boasted of the death of Nicholas Bracewell yet that same man was now calling on the lawyer. Another of the merchant's schemes had miscarried.

After a bitter exchange with his colleague, Sweete showed him into an adjoining room and left the door slightly ajar so that the latter could overhear everything. The lawyer took a deep breath to compose himself before sitting behind his desk. Nicholas Bracewell was conducted in. Brief introductions were made then the clerk withdrew again.

'Pray take a seat, sir,' invited the lawyer.

'I will not be staying,' said Nicholas. 'Why did you wish to see me?'

'On a matter of mutual concern.' He attempted a smile. 'It is a great pleasure to meet another member of the Bracewell family. I acted for your brother, Peter, and I know your father well.'

'I have not long returned from him.'

Nicholas was standing defiantly in front of the table. His jerkin was scuffed and there were traces of mud on his face but he was plainly unhurt. Equally plainly, he was in no

265

mood for polite conversation. The lawyer plunged straight into business.

'I believe that you may have been misled, sir.'

'In what way?'

'Last evening,' said Sweete, 'you were seen leaving the Whetcombe house in Crock Street, though my informant was not quite sure how you gained entry.'

'You need a more vigilant informant. But warn him that he will get more than a crack on the head if I chance to meet up with him again.'

The lawyer swallowed hard. 'Evidently, you spoke with Mistress Whetcombe,' he said. 'She may have raised the question of her husband's will. It may appear uncharitable to her on the surface but there is much comfort for her between the lines.' After pausing for a response that did not come, he went on. 'I am also in a position to offer certain emendations.'

'You are empowered to *change* the will?'

'By no means, sir,' said Sweete fussily. 'It has been signed and witnessed, so its terms must hold. But a number of concessions can still be made.'

'How?'

'By deed of gift.'

'You have lost me, Mr Sweete.'

'I am not quite sure how much you know of the will.'

'Enough to distrust you.'

The lawyer stiffened. 'Do you question my integrity?'

'I do not believe there is any to question.'

'Really, sir!'

'You mention deeds of gift.'

'We are a respected firm of lawyers, Master Bracewell. I will not have you coming here to insult me like this. Do you not understand? I am trying to *help* you here.'

'How do *I* benefit from the will?'

'We may put your mind at rest.'

'About what?'

'Matthew Whetcombe's widow.'

'Nobody could do that,' murmured Nicholas. 'Speak your mind, Mr Sweete. I am needed elsewhere.'

266

The lawyer felt intimidated by the solid presence and the uncompromising manner. He stood up to give himself more authority, but Nicholas was still an imposing visitor.

Sweete became glib. 'The main beneficiary of the will is Gideon Livermore, a name that is not unknown to you. I suspect. He is a generous man and wished to modify the apparent harshness of the will by ceding certain items to the widow by deed of gift. This will be a personal matter between them and separate from the execution of the will itself. The gifts are lavish.'

'Good,' said Nicholas. 'Mary Whetcombe will accept all of her husband's properties, all of his capital and the ship that bears her name.'

'Leave off this folly, sir.'

'Then leave off yours. These are no deeds of gift. They are trifles to soften the blow. They are a device to entrap a helpless woman. Gideon Livermore will give nothing away that he does not expect to reclaim when he forces himself on this lady in marriage.'

Barnard Sweete resorted to a string of protests but Nicholas quelled them with a raised hand. Seeing the strategy that was being used, he cut straight through it.

'There was an earlier will,' he said.

'Now invalid.'

'With the estate honestly distributed.'

'Its terms were that of the later document.'

'Then why draw it up?'

'Because it contained some minor alterations.'

'Yes,' said Nicholas, 'the crossing out of Mary Whetcombe's name and the insertion of that of Gideon Livermore. Because of a minor alteration, a grieving widow faces complete ruin.'

'Only if she remains stubborn.'

'The first will left everything to her.'

'I dispute that and so will the other witnesses. Your father among them.' He saw Nicholas wince and pressed home his advantage. 'I note that Robert Bracewell was unable to help. Your visit to his cottage was a waste of time. Even if he had been ready to lie on behalf of Mary

267

Whetcombe, it would have been no use. What is the word of a drunken and disgraced old man against that of three respectable figures in the community? You have no case, sir.'

'But I do. It is supported by the first will.'

'Show me the document.'

'I do not have it as yet,' said Nicholas, deciding to bluff. 'But I know where to find it.'

Barnard Sweete whitened. When Nicholas headed for the door, the lawyer rushed to intercept him. He gabbled his offer once again and insisted that the deeds of gift would take all the sting out of the nuncupative will.

'Gideon Livermore is a most generous man,' he insisted.

'I know,' said Nicholas, taking out the crossbow bolt from inside his jerkin and thrusting it into the lawyer's hand. 'He sent me this. By deed of gift.'

Lucy Whetcombe did not need to keep her dolls hidden away in Susan Deakin's room anymore. Her mother encouraged her to bring them out and play with them. The girl sat on the floor of the fore-chamber and unwrapped the binding in which they were kept. Her mother watched her with wan affection. Mary Whetcombe had been stunned when Nicholas Bracewell had come into the house unannounced, and she was still dazed by it all, but his visit had one important result. It unlocked her feelings for Lucy. Since her husband's death, she had been unable to give the girl the love and reassurance that she so desperately needed.

The news of Susan Deakin's murder was a devastating blow and Mary did not know how to cope with it. Matthew Whetcombe had died peacefully in his bed with his family close to him, but the servant had been struck down miles away from home while she was doing no more than summoning help for a beleaguered widow. Mary looked down at her daughter and sighed. The girl's handicap kept her in a childlike state. Susan had not been much older, but she was infinitely more worldly and mature. She had been the real mother to Lucy. It was a role that Mary now had to take on again herself.

Lucy found the little replica of her father and tucked it

out of sight beneath the material. He no longer had any place in her game. Mary saw her opportunity. Kneeling beside the child, she picked up the doll that had Susan's plain features dropped onto it by a paintbrush. Lucy tried at first to stop her and clutched at the image of her friend, but Mary was firm. Gently detaching her daughter's hand, she placed the doll beneath the cloth. Lucy gazed up at her and understanding slowly filled her eyes with tears. Her beloved friend would never come back. Mary took the girl in her arms and they wept a long requiem for Susan Deakin. They were still entwined when Nicholas Bracewell was shown in by the maidservant.

Mary got up and the girl rallied slightly. Nicholas soon realised the cause of their distress. He hugged the girl and let her tears soak into his shoulder, then he comforted Mary. For those few minutes, he felt as if he were part of a little family, and it reinforced his conviction that Lucy was his daughter. But he said nothing on the subject. That discussion needed to take place in a very different atmosphere. The rescue of Mary Whetcombe from the designs of Gideon Livermore was the main objective now, and that could only be achieved with a legal document.

'Did you see your father?' she asked.

'Yes, Mary. I fear that it was a mistake.'

'Was he not able to help?'

'Able, perhaps. But very unwilling.'

'Why?'

Even as she asked the question, Mary could supply the answer. The past was too great an encumbrance for father and son. There was so much accumulated bitterness between them that it was impossible for them to communicate with each other. Mary herself was hopelessly bound up in those distant events, and they had left her with her own share of acrimony.

'So you learned nothing from your father?' she said.

'No,' he confessed, 'but the visit yielded further proof of Livermore's villainy.'

'In what way?'

'He set an ambush for me.'

269

Mary gasped in alarm. 'You were attacked?'

'Without success. Some hireling with a crossbow.'

'Nick!'

She put an involuntary hand on his arm and her love was rekindled for an instant. The moment soon passed. He was risking his life to help her and she was eternally grateful, but that did not obliterate the memory of the pain he had once inflicted on her. Nicholas was trying to extricate her from a situation for which he was to some degree indirectly responsible. Mary withdrew her hand but listened attentively as he gave her details of the ambush in the wood.

'I have frightened them, Mary,' he said. 'If Livermore had nothing to hide, he would not need to attack me. They will be even more unsettled now.'

'Why?'

'I told the lawyer that I know where to find the will.'

'And do you?'

'Not yet, but it is vital that they believe me. The more I can draw them into the open, the more chance I have of catching them out.'

'Be careful, Nick. They are dangerous men.'

'Dangerous and corrupt. That is why I must stop them.'

'Not if it costs you your life.'

Her involuntary hand again brushed his arm. Lucy was looking up at him with a hopeful affection. Nicholas could not let the two of them down now. He turned to Mary.

'Where did Matthew deal with his business affairs?'

'In the countinghouse.'

'May I see it?'

'They have already searched the room.'

'A fresh pair of eyes may see something that was missed.'

'Barnard Sweete was most thorough.'

'I have to start somewhere—and immediately.'

Mary was pessimistic. 'Follow me.'

She took him to the countinghouse and showed him the table at which her husband worked. Satchels of documents and trading agreements lay everywhere and more were stuffed away into chests and drawers. It would take an age to sort through them all, and Nicholas did not have unlimited time. He had deliberately offered a lure to Barnard Sweete by telling him that he knew the whereabouts of the first will. That threat would force Livermore's hand. Nicholas had to be ready for him but his position would be immensely strengthened if he really did locate the document.

When Mary left him, he sifted quickly through the papers on the table then opened one of the drawers to take out a sheaf of correspondence. Though he was searching for a will, he paused for a moment to take a look into the life of the man who had taken his appointed place at the altar. Matthew Whetcombe was not just a thriving merchant. He commanded enormous respect. The letters were from local and county dignitaries, all thanking him for benefactions and all praising his character for its goodness. Here was a very different portrait of his rival, and Nicholas was chastened.

He chided himself for prying and stopped at once. He was about to put away the correspondence when he noticed a letter from Gideon Livermore. Brief and explicit, it thanked Matthew Whetcombe for a dinner that he had given at Crock Street. Nicholas was not interested in the contents of the missive. He was intrigued by the hand of the man who wrote it. Inside his jerkin was the letter that he had found on Lamparde in the derelict warehouse. It had shown its value already, for it had convinced the authorities in Bristol that Lamparde was indeed a hired assassin and that Nicholas had killed him in self-defence. The letter had double value. The writing was identical with that in the other missive. The pen that was thanking a friend for a dinner could also set murder in motion. Here was firm evidence of Livermore's guilt.

Putting both letters away, Nicholas sat back and looked around the countinghouse. It was the centre of Matthew Whetcombe's commercial empire. It positively exuded power and significance. If Nicholas had remained a merchant, he would have owned such a place with such a feel to it. This was the world on which he had turned his back, and it caused him a pang of regret. There was safety here

271

and meaning. At the same time, however, there was a narrowing of the mind and the spirit. Nicholas did not want his life to be measured in piles of trading agreements and letters of commendation. To own such a house and to share it with a wife like Mary was a seductive notion, but he decided that he was better off as a mere lodger with Anne Hendrik.

As his eye roved the walls, it fell on a painting that hung in a gilt frame. Every time Matthew Whetcombe looked up from his work, he would have seen and drawn strength from it. The artist had skill. His brush had even caught the shifting colours of the River Taw. A seaman himself, Nicholas admired craft of all sizes, but the sight of the *Mary*, ploughing her way through the water with full sail, was quite inspiring. The merchant's pride was understandable but his priorities shocked Nicholas. The painting of the ship was hung in a far more prominent position than the portrait of the woman after whom it was named.

He continued his search with renewed vigour. An hour or more slipped by before an anxious Mary returned.

'They are still watching the house,' she said. 'I think that they are biding their time until you come out.'

'They will not attack me in the street,' he said. 'I will be safe once I get back to the Dolphin.'

'You would be safer still if you stayed here.'

'Here?'

'Lucy and I would feel safer as well.'

Nicholas was grateful for the offer. He was quietly thrilled at the idea of spending a night under the same roof as a woman who might have been his wife and a girl who might be his child. He was also glad to be able to offer the two of them a more immediate safeguard. Nicholas crossed to the window and looked down at the two men who kept the house under surveillance. She stood beside him.

'The enemies are not only outside the house, Mary.'

'What do you mean?'

'You have one inside as well.'

'Mr Calmady?'

'He is Livermore's creature, certainly, but there is another foe to beware. One of your servants.'

'That is not possible!' she protested.

'Then how did they know that Susan Deakin had taken a horse and ridden to London? Someone has been spying on you. He or she is being paid to tell Livermore and Sweete exactly what is going on inside this house.'

'One of our own servants?' Mary was shaken.

'Who chose them?'

'My husband.'

'Then their first loyalty was to him.'

'But I treated them well and earned their respect.'

'Respect is not enough,' said Nicholas. 'If someone fears that he will lose his place here, he may be only too ready to betray you to a new master.'

'Who could it be?' said Mary, looking around in alarm. 'I have trusted them all. Who could it be?'

'We will find out in time. My guess is that Livermore may have planted someone here a long time ago to keep him abreast of everything that happened. He was able to watch your husband die and choose his moment to move in.' He drew her away from the window. 'Say nothing at this stage and do not show any suspicion. We will use spy against master.'

'How?'

'You will see.'

Mary nodded. 'I will have a bed made up for you.'

'Thank you. I appreciate the invitation.'

'It is only to ensure your safety.'

'I did not think it was for any other reason.'

She gave him a pale smile then went quickly out.

Lawrence Firethorn came out into the yard of the Jolly Sailor and took his horse from the ostler. After a highly productive stay, Westfield's Men would now ride on to Bath, where they were due to give two performances at the home of Sir Roger Hordley, younger brother of their patron. They had not just distinguished themselves on stage. With the assistance of Owen Elias, their leader had brought off the signal feat of capturing Israel Gunby, a highwayman whose reputation stretched from Bristol to London. Money stolen from the company at High Wycombe was now restored. A substantial reward for the arrest of Gunby was also in Firethorn's capcase. What pleased the actor most, however, was not the way that he had outwitted the two confederates, but the fact that it had been immortalised in song. "The Ballad of Israel Gunby" was being hawked all around the city. Firethorn could sing it in his sleep.

The company was happy. Bath was a guaranteed welcome. Harder times might lie on the open road ahead, but they looked no farther than the next couple of days. As they mounted their horses or climbed up onto the waggon, they were brimming with contentment. Even George Dart was smiling. At the performance of *Hector of Troy* on the previous afternoon, the make-shift book holder had survived without any real disasters. Firethorn had actually paid him a compliment. Dart was overjoyed. He was liked.

Last in the saddle were Barnaby Gill and Edmund Hoode. Gill had personal reasons for wanting to quit the city of Bristol, but he had shaken off the effects of the assault by Lamparde, and his old brio had returned on stage. Edmund Hoode was so thoroughly pleased with himself that he made Firethorn stare at him in alarm. The last time the resident playwright had looked that happy was when he was in love.

'Who is she, Edmund?' said Firethorn.

'Clio.'

'A pretty name for a tavern wench. Which one was she? The drab with the filthy hair or that great, fat creature with the cast in her eye?'

'Do not try to drag me down to your level, Lawrence.'

'Ah, I see. You set your sights higher.'

'On the very pinnacle.'

'Then this Clio is some juicy whore in red taffeta.'

'She is the Muse of History,' said Hoode with dignity. 'And she has inspired me in my history of Calais.'

'Your play?'

'Finished at last!'

'God bless you, Edmund!'

'Save your kisses for Clio.'

'Kisses, embraces, pizzle and all, if she wishes,' said the delighted Firethorn. 'This deserves a celebration, man. When may we play the piece?'

'As soon as you have read and approved it. Then it is but a question of hiring some tidy scrivener to copy out the sides and we may put *The Merchant of Calais* into rehearsal.'

'This news gladdens my heart, Edmund.'

'I never thought to complete it.'

'Left to yourself, you'd still be playing with the baubles of your mistress in London. Women are wonderful creatures but the finest plays in creation may be crushed to powder between the millstones of their thighs. Think on that, Edmund. Write first and take your pleasure afterwards.'

'I have learned that lesson,' said Hoode with a laugh. 'I never thought I'd be grateful to a husband who caught me in bed with his wife.'

Firethorn was tactful. 'No, dear heart. I have cause to thank that fine fellow as well. He gave me both playwright and play.'

'Nick Bracewell was my guide.'

'As always, when we need him.'

'*The Merchant of Calais* owes much to Nick.'

'We'll give him a rare welcome when he returns.'

'Where is he now, do you think?'

'Penning a drama of his own, Edmund.'

'Nick, a playwright? What is the piece called?'

'*The Merchant of Barnstaple.*'

After several futile hours in the countinghouse, Nicholas Bracewell widened his search to other parts of the building, but the will could not be found. He was still opening cupboards and peering into nooks and crannies when light faded. With the aid of a candle, he continued to look for secret panels and hidden cavities in every room. It was almost midnight when he finally abandoned his search. The rest of the house had already retired and Nicholas made his way wearily to his own bedchamber. Removing his jerkin, he lay on the bed with his hands behind his head. Convinced that the will was in the house somewhere, he racked his brain to work out where Matthew Whetcombe could possibly have put it.

Fatigue almost claimed him and he struggled to his feet to undress properly. It was then that he heard the banging on the front door below. He ignored it at first but it continued unabated. Nicholas heard someone descend the stair and unbolt the door. The next moment, feet came scampering up towards him and a fist banged on his own door. Nicholas opened it to reveal a panting servant in night attire.

'You have a visitor,' said the man.

'At this hour?'

'He waits below and is in some need.'

'Who is it?'

'Your father.'

Nicholas told him to calm the rest of the household then he went quickly downstairs with a candle to guide him. Robert Bracewell waited in the dark hallway, leaning against a wall for support. As the flame illumined the old man's face, Nicholas saw the blood and the bruises. He reached out to support his father and helped him into the nearest room, closing the door behind them and lowering his visitor into a chair. He held the candle closer to examine the injuries more closely.

'Who did this to you?' he said.

'Who do you think?'

'Gideon Livermore?'

'Two of his men came to see me this evening,' said his father. 'They asked me what I had said to you earlier today. When I told them it was none of their business, they set about me. This was a gentle warning, they said. If I even spoke to you again, they would deal more harshly with me.'

'Stay here,' said Nicholas.

He went to the kitchen to fetch a cloth and water. He

then bathed his father's face, wiping away most of the dried blood and exposing the bruises on temples and jaw. One eye was black and shining. Robert Bracewell's faded apparel had been torn in the scuffle. Nicholas was touched. His father had shown bravery in defying the threat of his assailants. He had ridden through the night to report the attack and to give his son a weapon with which to strike back.

'I was a witness to Matthew Whetcombe's first will,' he said. 'It left everything to his wife.'

'Are you quite sure?'

'I've not made all this effort in order to tell lies.'

'Was Livermore named in the will?'

'Only as a minor beneficiary.'

'The ship was left to Mary?'

'Ship, house and the bulk of his estate.'

'Would you swear to that in court, Father?'

'If they let me live long enough to do so.'

On impulse, Nicholas hugged him with gratitude, but the old man pushed him away. Exhausted as he was, Robert Bracewell still had enough strength to shake with anger.

'Keep away!' he snarled. 'This is all your doing!'

'I am only trying to help.'

'And what has your help brought me? The sight of a son I had hoped was dead and a fearsome beating. I did not want either. Go away and leave me alone.'

'But I can protect you from Livermore.'

Pride flared. 'I can look after myself.'

'Of course, of course. Thank you for coming.'

'I am not here for your benefit, Nick. I came only to help Mary—and to hit back at Gideon Livermore. No man can tell me what I can and cannot say. They may have driven me out of Barnstaple but I am still the master of my house.'

'You must stay the night here,' said Nicholas.

'Never!'

'But you are in no condition to travel.'

'If I can ride all the way here, I can make the return journey just as well.' He got to his feet. 'It is an effort for me to stay under this roof. Matthew Whetcombe once drove

277

me out of this house. Its doors are barred against me. I would sooner sleep in the street than lay my head here.'

'Father—wait!'

'Stand aside.'

'One word before you go. That first will . . .'

'I have vouched for its contents.'

'The document itself would be stronger testimony.'

'Then find it. Matthew surely held on to a copy.'

'I have searched everywhere in vain.'

'You have looked in the wrong places.'

'Which is the right one?'

'The heart of Matthew Whetcombe.'

'I do not follow.'

'He was a merchant,' said the old man. 'He thought and felt like a merchant. Put yourself in his position and ask where you would hide a precious document.' He tried to move to the door. 'Now, out of my way.'

'Let me come with you.'

'No!'

'But there may be danger.'

'It is an old acquaintance and I have learned to face it alone. I would never turn to you. My elder son is no longer alive. He died at sea. You are a poor counterfeit who merely bears his name.' He walked past Nicholas. 'I have done my duty to this house and I am free to go.'

'All that way in the dead of night?'

'I am needed there.'

'That is no way for a man to live.'

'It is my home.'

'You and that old servant—'

'Be silent!'

Robert Bracewell's eyes blazed in the candlelight. Years of hatred and resentment on both sides were suddenly ignited. Father and son faced each other across a chasm of lost kinship and love. There was no hope of reconciliation. They had chosen an appropriate venue for the last time they were ever to see each other. Lying upstairs in the fore-chamber was the woman who had once come between them, and Robert Bracewell could never forgive her for

278

that. But for her, he felt his son would have married Katherine Hurrell and everything would have worked out much more satisfactorily. Nicholas took a different view of the Hurrell family. They had turned a father whom he respected into a man he loathed.

'Let me show you out,' said Nicholas.

'I know my own way!'

'We are very grateful to you for coming.'

The old man looked upwards. 'I did it for others in this house. They deserved help. You do not.'

He opened the door and lurched out into the hallway. Nicholas went after him with the candle, but his father was already lifting the latch on the front door. Without a backward glance, Robert Bracewell let himself out into the street and tottered away. Nicholas had the feeling that something he had said inflicted a more serious wound on the old man than any collected in the attack.

After bolting the front door, Nicholas went up to the counting house. He was fully awake now and ready to resume the search for the will. His father had given him a clue that had to be followed up at once, and it took Nicholas back to the chair in which Matthew Whetcombe had transacted his business. Nicholas gazed around the room once more and wondered where he would hide something of great value. Robert Bracewell told him to look into the heart of the merchant, but the cold and unyielding Matthew Whetcombe had never seemed to possess one. He did not love the wife and child with whom he shared his life. He did not love his family and friends with anything approaching real passion. Could anybody or anything make its way into the heart of such a man?

Nicholas doubted it until his gaze drifted across to the painting. The *Mary* was the merchant's true pride and joy. It was the summit of his achievement, the hallmark of its excellence. The *Mary* was a symbol of all that Matthew Whetcombe valued most in life. Nicholas got to his feet in excitement. His first thought was that the merchant had kept the document hidden away in a cabin aboard the ship, but that would expose it to all kinds of hazards. Even Matthew Whetcombe would not take such a risk as that. The *Mary* would guard his secret but not when she was afloat. He wanted a safer mooring for his will. It hung on the wall.

Lifting the painting off its hook, Nicholas laid it gently on the table with its face downwards. Strips of thin wood had been nailed across the back of the frame to hold the canvas in place. Additional laths had been tacked into position at the bottom of the frame and he soon saw why. Tucked neatly inside the wooden pouch was a parchment. As he began to tease it out with his fingers, Nicholas heard the door behind him open. Mary Whetcombe was standing there in her nightdress with a lighted candle in her hand.

"What are you doing in here, Nick?' she asked.

'Searching for your salvation.'

'I heard noises. Someone banging at the door.'

'All will be explained in a moment.'

Nicholas tugged harder and the document came out of its hiding place. Unfolding it quickly, he held it up to the light before breaking into a quiet laugh of triumph. As his father had told him, the legitimate will of Matthew Whetcombe was a far cry from its putative successor. He passed it to Mary, who put her candle aside so that she could hold the document with both hands. She read it with gathering excitement. When she realised its full import, she let out a cry of utter relief and all but fainted. Nicholas steadied her and helped her into a chair.

'How on earth did you find it?' she asked.

'With great patience.'

'I cannot thank you enough. This changes everything.'

'Not necessarily.'

'But this represents Matthew's true wishes.'

'That may well be, Mary,' he said, 'but we would have to prove that in court. The second will would make this invalid if it were to be upheld. What we have is absolute proof that Gideon Livermore and Barnard Sweete lied to us. This will bears no resemblance at all to the nuncupative version. We must use it wisely to expose them.'

'How do we do that?'

'I will show you.'

Early that morning, Nicholas Bracewell rowed out to the *Mary*. Its cargo had now been unloaded and it was awaiting a refit before embarking on another long voyage. A lone sailor had been left on board to keep watch. He was very suspicious when Nicholas tied up his boat and clambered aboard, but the sailor's manner became deferential when his visitor showed him written proof that he had come on behalf of Matthew Whetcombe. Nicholas had also brought keys to the private cabin, which was reserved for the owner of the vessel.

Envy fluttered as he stood on deck and took a closer look at the *Mary*. It was very like the ship in which he had served his apprenticeship, though that had been smaller and wholly confined to legitimate trade. It also reminded him of the *Golden Hind* on which he had sailed with Drake. That had been somewhat bigger but shared many of the features of the *Mary*. Both had two sheathings on the hull to strengthen it. They were built in the French style, well fitted out and furnished with good masts, tackle and double sails.

Like the *Golden Hind*, this vessel also had top-gallant sails for the main and fore masts, an unusual addition to the standard rig in a middling craft but one that gave them vital extra speed. The *Mary* had eighteen cast pieces, most of them demi-culverins, long-range nine-pound cannon. Nicholas suspected that the crew would also have arquebuses, calivers, pistols and firebombs to support their heavy guns, as well as an array of pikes, swords, bows and arrows. Sir Francis Drake would have been proud to command the *Mary*. She was a floating arsenal and ideal for privateering.

He took direction from the sailor then went below to find the cabin. When he let himself in, he found it small but well appointed. It had a low berth against the wall, a table and chair secured to the floor and some cupboards for storage. A lantern swung gently overhead. Nicholas felt another surge of envy. Like the merchant, he, too, would have kept a private cabin aboard and sailed in the *Mary* whenever he could. A love of the sea infused them both.

A porthole looked out on the river and showed him the looming shadow of the Long Bridge. The plash of oars made him look in the other direction and he saw exactly what he had hoped. Gideon Livermore was being rowed out towards the ship by a brawny figure. He had stayed overnight in the town and been roused early by the servant whom he paid to keep an eye on activities in the Whetcombe household. Nicholas had told Mary to let it be known that they had found out that the document they sought was on board the *Mary*. The news spread quickly through the house and reached its intended destination. Livermore was closing in for the kill.

Nicholas used one of the keys he had brought to unlock a cupboard and take out a sheaf of papers. He waited until he heard the two men come aboard then he pretended to study the papers with great interest. It was not long before the door was flung open. Gideon Livermore regarded him with open hostility. His companion was a thickset man with a broken nose. Nicholas suspected that the latter might well have fired the crossbow bolt at him.

'Where is it?' demanded Livermore.

'What?'

'The will.'

'You have it, sir. It is lodged with the lawyer.'

'I speak of the first will. There in your hand.'

'This is no longer valid.'

'I wish to see it.'

'No,' said Nicholas, thrusting the papers inside his jerkin. 'You merely wish to destroy it.'

Gideon Livermore wasted no more time. He stood aside and his companion came charging in with a raised club in his hand. His brute strength was no match for the other's agility. As the man rushed at him, Nicholas dodged the blow, caught the thick wrist and swung the man against the oak bulwark with a terrifying thud. He collapsed in a heap on the floor and would take no further part in the proceedings.

Nicholas pulled Livermore into the cabin.

'I have the message you sent to Adam Lamparde,' he

282

said. 'Murder a girl, you told him. He obeyed. Now he lies dead himself. Your letter will send you to the gallows.'

Gideon Livermore went puce with fury. He would not let this intruder ruin all his well-laid plans. A knife came out from his belt and he jabbed it at Nicholas. The book holder moved swiftly but the blade sliced open his hand and blood spurted. He closed with Livermore and they grappled in the confined space, banging against the walls and tripping over the inert body on the floor.

Hearing the commotion, the watch on deck came running down to the cabin, but Nicholas ordered him to stand clear. The sailor would be a valuable witness to a fight between a crazed merchant and an unarmed man. Livermore was powerful and the thought of what he stood to lose gave him even greater energy. Nicholas was finding him hard to master. He needed more room to manoeuvre. Twisting Livermore off balance, he released his hold and pushed. The merchant stumbled back and gave Nicholas a precious moment to rush back up on deck.

Gideon Livermore came panting after him. They were in view of the quay now and there were other witnesses on the bridge, but that did not stop the merchant. All his plans could founder on this one man. As long as Nicholas Bracewell was alive, Livermore would never inherit the estate and seize Mary Whetcombe as an agreeable part of the booty. Most of all, he would never take over the *Mary* herself. That was his dream. Gideon Livermore was a pirate trying to lay hold of a pirate ship. It was a fitting place in which to decide his fate.

Open space gave Nicholas more options and his own dagger was now out. The two men circled each other warily. Nicholas was bleeding profusely but he did not dare to look down at the flesh wound on his hand. Livermore could not be underestimated. Though he paid others to kill for him, he was more than capable of doing his own work. The merchant feinted then lunged but Nicholas evaded him. A second attack forced the book holder back and he fell over some coiled rope that lay on the deck. Livermore pounced and his weight took the breath out of his adversary. Nicholas had a grip on the man's wrist but his own weapon had been knocked away.

They grappled, they rolled, they punched and gouged. Livermore even tried to bite him. With sudden power, Nicholas threw him off and got to his feet, but Livermore was after him at once. The advantage had swung back to the merchant now and he was taunting his prey, forcing him back towards the gunwale. Nicholas ran out of space. He was cornered.

'Give me the will,' demanded Livermore.

'The *Mary* will never be yours.'

'Give me the will!'

Nicholas patted his jerkin. 'Come and take it.'

The merchant needed no more invitation. Aiming the point of his blade at Nicholas's face, he charged forward. The book holder was too fast for him. He ducked, grabbed then heaved upwards with all his might, and the body of Gideon Livermore went over the side and into the river. The people on the bridge were so impressed that they gave a cheer. Other boats were now being rowed out from the quay.

Nicholas leaned over the side of the gunwale as the merchant surfaced. The man coughed and spluttered. Though he had learned to swim in the river, he had never done so in heavy clothing when he was exhausted from a fight. Livermore began to flail wildly and call out for help. He was drowning. Nicholas peeled off his jerkin and kicked off his shoes before diving over the side of the ship. He hit the water cleanly and explored its murky depths for a few seconds before coming up again. He was just in time to see Livermore starting to sink. Grabbing the man from behind, he lay on his back and swam towards the ship with Livermore's head supported above the water.

The sailor on watch was waiting to help them aboard, and the other rowing boats were closing in. Spectators on the bridge and quay were applauding Nicholas's heroism in saving the drowning man. But Gideon Livermore himself had second thoughts. He would never inherit the estate and marry the woman he coveted. He would never own the

Mary. All that awaited him was a humiliating trial and a long rope. He would never submit to that.

When Nicholas finally pulled him to the side of the ship, Livermore waited for his moment and then broke clear to plunge headfirst again into the dark water. Nicholas went after him and a few other men from the boats jumped in to assist, but they could not find the merchant anywhere. It was several minutes before the River Taw yielded up its sacrificial victim. When Gideon Livermore bobbed to the surface with his face still submerged, he was way beyond any processes of law.

In one transaction, many debts had been paid off.

It was a windy afternoon, but that did not deter him. He took a long, meandering, valedictory walk through the town to re-acquaint himself with a youth that now seemed a century away. He went down streets where he had once played and across a field where he and his brother had first learned to ride a horse. He left flowers on his mother's grave at the nearby churchyard then walked slowly back towards his old family house in Boutport Street. It looked much as it had done when his parents raised five children in the dwelling. Compared to the cottage where his father now lived, it was a small mansion. A deep sorrow made him turn away.

Nicholas Bracewell went through the gate and left the town, feeling an immediate sense of release. Barnstaple had once been his entire world but it now had the whiff of a prison about it. The pleasure of seeing familiar places was offset by the pain of old memories. He walked briskly on in the stiff breeze until he came to a walled garden. Nicholas halted in alarm. His feet had taken him insensibly to the one house in the area which he had vowed he would never visit again. When he tried to turn back, his legs betrayed him again and impelled him forward to the gate. One look up at the half-timbered dwelling brought it all back.

The home of the Hurrell family had once been filled with noise and laughter, but it now seemed curiously empty. The garden was overgrown and there were no signs of life in the house itself. He pushed the gate back on a grinding hinge and went in. Swept by the wind, the thatched roof was parting with a few of its reeds and somewhere in the property a window was banging. Nicholas followed the sound as it led him to the rear of the house. A rectangular lawn was fringed with flowerbeds that were badly neglected. The grass was ankle high. It was in this same garden that Nicholas had been obliged to court Katherine Hurrell. He shuddered as he recalled how he had allowed himself to become betrothed to her to please their respective families.

The noise took his eye upwards. It was a long, low house with eaves that jutted right down over the top of the walls. The open window was in a bedchamber that he identified at once, and the rhythmical banging was a hammer that nailed a spike into his skull. Nicholas was mesmerised. This house and that window had altered the whole course of his life. Many people had suffered as a result, and there were some things for which he could never forgive himself. Katherine Hurrell had recovered from the shock of his departure to marry another man and to leave the area. Mary Parr had not been so fortunate, nor had her daughter.

Nicholas stared up at the window as it flapped away like the wing of a trapped butterfly. He had no wish to see inside that room again. It was a tomb for so many of his hopes and ambitions. The house was sad and uncared for, but it still held its old menace for him. As Nicholas stood there and looked up, the whole building seemed to tense up in readiness, as if it was about to hurl itself at him. He could bear it no more. The Hurrell house had already struck him down once. Before it could assault him again, he took to his heels and ran all the way back to Crock Street.

It was time to liberate himself from Barnstaple.

'When will you leave?' asked Mary Whetcombe.
  'Tomorrow at dawn.'
  'So soon?'
  'The company is waiting for me to join them.'
  'Can nothing detain you here?'

'No, Mary. I fear not.'

They were in the hall of the house, which she had now rightfully inherited from her husband. Lucy was playing with her dolls at the table. Nicholas had done all that he had come to do. Susan Deakin's death had been avenged and Mary Whetcombe had been rescued from her plight. Gideon Livermore was dead and Barnard Sweete—along with other accomplices—was under lock and key. The spy in the Whetcombe household had been revealed and dismissed. A question still hovered over Arthur Calmady, and his sermons were now tentative and apologetic. His visits to Crock Street had been abruptly terminated. Nicholas wore heavy bandaging on his wounded hand, but it would not prevent him from taking ship to Bristol.

Mary Whetcombe was hampering his departure. Reluctant to see him at first, she now wished to keep him in Barnstaple, and Lucy added a smile to hold him there. When the three of them were alone together, there was happiness in the house for the first time. Nicholas was only briefly tempted. Some memories had been obliterated but others were overpowering. Robert Bracewell still stalked the streets of Barnstaple.

'At least I will know why this time,' said Mary.

'I could not reach you before I left.'

'You did not wish to, Nick.'

'I was too ashamed.'

'But I loved you.'

'It was not enough. I could not saddle you with that burden. It would have been unfair to you. I had to get away from him. You must understand that.'

'What did your father *do*?'

It was a question she had a right to ask and he could not hold out on her any longer. Mary Whetcombe had suffered the consequences of a secret he dared not tell her, and she deserved to know the truth. At the same time, he wanted confirmation that Lucy was his daughter. Mary threw a glance at the girl and looked back at him. In the household of a merchant, his widow was offering a bargain before a mute witness. If Nicholas told her about the last night they had spent together, she would confide in him.

'I wanted you, Mary,' he said. 'I wanted you more than anything in the world, but my father chose Katherine Hurrell for me. It was all arranged with her family. The dowry was large and my father needed a share of it to steady his own business. You were my choice but your dowry was smaller and your father was set on a marriage into the Whetcombe family. It was an impossible situation.'

'There was only one way to break out of it.'

'I tried hard to persuade my father.'

'I know,' she recalled. 'You went home that night to make a final plea to him. If it failed, we were to run away sooner than be parted. But you never came back for me.' Her eyes accused him. 'What happened when you went home?'

'I did not go home, Mary.'

'Then where did you go?'

'To Katherine Hurrell's house.'

'But why?' she said, indignantly. 'You had no cause.'

'We were betrothed. She had a right to be told. I loved you but I could not walk from Katherine without at least a word of explanation.'

'You gave *me* no word of explanation.'

'There was no time.'

'You found time enough for Katherine Hurrell!'

'Mary, please—listen!' Nicholas tried to remain calm. 'This is difficult enough for me. Be patient.'

'All right. So you went to her . . .'

'Yes.'

'And stayed the night there, is that what I am to hear?'

'No.'

'Tell me the truth,' said Mary, trembling with a jealousy that had had many years to build. 'Tell me, Nick!'

'Katherine was not at the house,' he said. 'Nor was her father. The place was almost empty.' Nicholas shivered as he relived the memory. 'I picked my way around to the garden at the rear. The window of Katherine's bedchamber was at the end. I hoped to attract her attention and draw her

288

out so that we could speak in private. There was no answer to my whistle. I did not wish to throw stones up at her window in case the noise woke anyone else who might be in the house.'

'So what did you do?'

'I climbed up the ivy to look into her room.'

'And?'

'She was not there.'

'Well?' pressed Mary. 'What, then?'

'I saw them in bed together.'

'Who?'

'Katherine's mother and . . .'

'Go on.'

'My father,' said Nicholas. 'Robert Bracewell. He was making love to Margaret Hurrell.' Nicholas looked up at her with his bitterness refreshed. 'That was why I was to marry Katherine—to enable my father the more easily to carry on his adultery with her mother. I was not a son being sent off happily to the altar. I was just a factor in a corrupt bargain. It destroyed me.' He winced visibly. 'My mother *knew*, Mary. That's what killed her. She knew all the time but had no power to stop him. My mother knew but said nothing. She simply curled up in horror and died.'

'What did you do when you saw them together?'

'I ran away,' he said, simply. 'All I could think about was getting away from that place and those two people. I looked up to my father. He was a difficult man to love but I had always admired the way he overcame his setbacks. But that night I lost all respect for him and for his values. I wanted nothing to do with Barnstaple and its merchants. My one urge was to take to my heels.'

'Did you not spare a thought for me?'

'Of course, Mary. I did not want to drag you into it. After what I had seen, I felt tainted and did not wish to pass on that taint to you. I believed that if I ran away, I might be able to save you.'

'Save me!' she said with irony. 'From what?'

'From taking on the name of Bracewell. From suffering the same sense of shame. From enduring our disgrace.' He

289

heaved a sigh. 'I was young, Mary. I felt such things deeply. I could not ask you to come into such a family.'

'So what did you think would happen to me?'

'That you would find someone else and forget me.'

'Oh, I found somebody else,' she said. 'And I was lucky to do so in the circumstances. But I did not forget you. How could I? We were lovers.'

Nicholas glanced down at Lucy then back at Mary.

'Is she my daughter?' he asked.

'No, Nick.'

'My father said that she was.'

'He could not have done so.'

'But he did, Mary. In so many words.'

'What exactly did he say?'

'I asked him why he visited your house so often.'

'And he told you it was to visit his granddaughter.'

'Yes—Lucy.'

'No,' said Mary. 'Susan Deakin.'

'The servant girl?'

'She was our daughter, Nick.'

He was completely dumbfounded. The plain girl with the features that enabled her to pass for a boy had been his daughter. He could not believe it at first and yet he now saw, in his heart, that he must have had a faint glimmer of recognition. Susan Deakin had prompted such a compelling sense of revenge in him, a personal commitment such as a man could never feel for a stranger from a distant household. That was what had driven him on. It was not just the desire to get to Barnstaple to help the woman he thought had sent for him. Nicholas had also been seeking atonement for the murder of his own daughter.

He looked across to Mary for enlightenment.

'The last night we met,' she explained, 'I had been carrying your child for some months.'

'Why did you not *tell* me?'

'I tried, Nick, but I could not find the words. I hoped that your father would relent and that we could marry with his blessing. All would be well then. But you left and I was stranded.' She bristled like a hunted animal. 'I had nowhere

290

to go and no chance of hiding my condition for long. What life would I have as an unmarried mother with a bastard child? You had one kind of shame, I would have carried another.' She shook her head in despair. 'I did the only thing that was left to me. I turned to Matthew Whetcombe.'

'You told him the truth?'

'Yes, Nick. Matthew was a hard man but he knew what he wanted. I was to be his wife on any terms. We struck a bargain and I accepted it gratefully. I was confined and everyone was told that I was visiting friends in Crediton.' She shuddered. 'Susan came into the world too soon and almost died. She needed constant attention. Joan Deakin had been my own nurse. She took Susan for her own. That is the name you will find in the church register. Susan Deakin.'

'Then you got married?'

'As soon as I was strong enough.'

'And Lucy?'

'She came along very quickly.' A defensive note came in. 'I had to give Matthew that. He was prepared to let my brat live under his roof but only if he could have children of his own. That was the contract and he enforced it. But Lucy was the first and last.'

'Why?'

'There were complications. I could bear no more. My husband could never forgive me for that. He had accepted Susan and all I could give him in return was this wounded little creature here. Matthew felt cheated. *Your* child was fit and healthy while his was a deaf-mute.'

Nicholas began to comprehend. Lucy had been brought up as the daughter of the house. Susan Deakin—Mary's child by him—had been reared as a servant girl. The strong bond between the two of them was now explained. They were step-sisters. Mary provided further clarification.

'When Joan was dying,' she said, 'she told Susan the truth. The girl knew that you were her father. That's why she came to you in London, Nick. We were in trouble and the one person who could help us was you. Susan idolised you. She stole clothing, took the fastest horse and set out to

291

find you. Can you imagine the risks she must have run? She would only have done such a thing to reach her father.'

Nicholas was sobered. He had fled from Barnstaple but others had stayed to bear the burdens that he had left behind. There was no way that his action could be fully justified, but at least he had been given the opportunity to redeem himself. He did not save Mary from marriage to Matthew Whetcombe, but he had fought off another predatory merchant and rescued her inheritance. To reach Barnstaple, he had put his life at risk: to help Mary, he had even forced himself to confront the father whom he loathed.

He looked down at Lucy as she played with her dolls and he leaned over to place a gentle kiss on her head. But his real sympathy was reserved for Susan Deakin. His daughter had been relegated to an inferior position all her life. When she was told the name of her real father, she was given dignity and status for the first time. Susan showed the bravery of a true Bracewell in trying to contact him, but she had died before they could even speak. He felt her loss like a stone in his heart. The girl had been the hapless child of a doomed love. His only consolation lay in the fact that he had been able to avenge her death.

Nicholas did not wish to spend another night in the house where she had lived. His daughter's spirit hovered there to haunt his conscience. He rose from his seat and began to take his leave, but the others reacted with alarm. Lucy clutched at his arm and Mary made a heartfelt plea.

'Stay here with us, Nick!'

'I may not do that.'

'What is to stop you?'

'There is no place for me in this house.'

'We are making a place for you,' she said, putting an arm around Lucy's shoulders. 'But for you, we would have been driven out of here. But for you, everything that was rightly ours would have been stripped away from us. You gave it all back to us and have a right to share in our good fortune.' Lucy nodded eagerly, as if she had heard every word. 'Make a new life here with us. It is what Susan would have wanted.'

'Is it what *you* want, Mary?'

'I think so.'

'After all that has happened between us?'

'That is dead and buried,' she said. 'Now that you have explained it to me, I can understand why you behaved as you did. And I forgive you. In a way, I am as much to blame. If I had told you that night that I was carrying a child, you would have acted very differently.'

'That is true.'

'Stay here, Nick,' she said, softly. 'We were neither of us able to be real parents to poor Susan. You did not even know that she existed and I had to pretend that I did not care for the child. Let us make amends with Lucy. She can be our daughter now. You will be a real father to her.'

The girl nodded again and held up two dolls. Nicholas recognised himself and Mary, side by side in miniature. It was a powerful image and he was deeply touched. His resolve wavered for a second then he shook his head.

'It is out of the question, Mary,' he said, with a glance around. 'I am not able to support you in this fashion.'

'You would not need to, Nick. We have money enough to keep us in style for the rest of our days.'

'I could never live off Matthew Whetcombe's wealth.'

'Then use it to produce an income of your own. You are from merchant stock. Buy and sell as Matthew did. There is a ship and a crew at your disposal. Would you not like to have control of the *Mary*?'

It was a great temptation and Nicholas wavered again. To own such a ship would be to fulfil a lifelong ambition, and he could use it to restore some respect in trading circles to the name of Bracewell. Mary Whetcombe was showing true forgiveness in making such a generous offer. Yet he could never accept it. To secure the *Mary*, he had to take charge of the woman after whom it was named, and she brought a troublesome cargo in her hold. As long as he remained in the house, he would be locked in with too many ghosts.

'Thank you, Mary,' he said. 'You show a kindness and a forbearance that I do not deserve. I love you for that. But I cannot stay here with you and Lucy. It is impossible for me to make a new life in a place with so many old memories. For my own peace of mind, I must get away from Barnstaple.'

'And from me.'

'From my father, mainly. Everything that occurred in the past stemmed from him. I find it hard to forgive.'

'Do not be too harsh on him.'

'His lust for another woman killed my mother,' he said. 'He drove her into her grave. He was so obsessed with his own needs that he tried to marry his son into the Hurrell family to give him a legitimate excuse to call more often at the house. He would never have consented to our betrothal. My father put his own lascivious urges first.'

'He paid for them in time, Nick.'

'So did we all.'

'Do you know what happened to him?'

'That is evident. He fell from grace.'

'But do you know how—and when?'

'I would rather not dwell on it.'

'But you should,' she insisted. 'You cannot judge him until you know the full picture. I had no idea that his relationship with Margaret Hurrell went back for so many years. It did not come to light until after you had fled from Barnstaple. Your father was very discreet. Nobody suspected for a moment that any impropriety had taken place.'

'Not even Katherine herself?'

'She was a good match and soon married someone else. They live in Exeter with a large family. They were well clear of Barnstaple when the scandal eventually broke.'

'And when was that?'

'Not until a few years ago.'

'They kept it secret for all that while?'

'Your father was a clever man,' she said. 'He knew how to hide things beneath that bluff manner. And he could be charming when he wanted to be. Matthew liked him enough to do business with him and to invite him here as a friend. They did, after all, have something in common.'

'Susan?'

'Nobody told him. Your father guessed for himself. As

294

soon as he saw the girl, he knew that she was yours. He never said anything even when Matthew forbade him to come to the house. He never betrayed us.' She brushed back a lock of hair. 'He was very kind to Susan. He loved her and brought her presents. In his own quiet way, he tried to do right by her. Susan was very hurt when he no longer called here.'

'And when was that?'

'When the truth about him and Margaret Hurrell finally emerged. They were caught together by her husband. You can imagine the way that the scandal spread. Robert Bracewell and the wife of a man with whom he did business. It was the end of your father. Barnstaple turned its back on him. Matthew refused even to speak to him. The whole community treated him like a leper.'

'So he had to leave the town?'

'In complete disgrace.'

Nicholas found a granule of sympathy for his father. He understood what it must have been like to be ostracised by the world in which a man had spent his whole life. Barnstaple was a narrow-minded and inward-looking community. It conferred great respect on its members, but it was merciless with those who forfeited that respect. Robert Bracewell had been hounded out of a town he had honoured. Nicholas's sympathy was soon crushed beneath his hatred. By pursuing one woman so relentlessly, his father had broken the heart of another. Having sacrificed a wife to his lust, he was even ready to sacrifice his eldest son.

'What happened to Margaret Hurrell?' he asked.

'Her husband divorced her.'

'So she was cast out into the wilderness as well.'

'In a sense, Nick.'

'What do you mean?'

'She married your father. They lived together.'

Nicholas was stunned. The old woman at the cottage had not been a servant at all. She had been the wife of a successful merchant and had enjoyed all the trappings of that success. But she had also risked them to be with the man for whom she really cared. Margaret Hurrell had loved

Robert Bracewell so much that she was even prepared to share his disgrace and his straitened circumstances. Nicholas now realised why his father had been so hurt by the reference to his mean cottage and his old servant. It was an insult.

Mary Whetcombe became philosophical.

'We have all been punished,' she said.

'Punished?'

'For illicit love. You and I came together outside marriage and we paid the price for it. What we did was wrong, Nick. We were betrothed to other people.'

'Only in name.'

'God punished us in the same way that he punished your father and Margaret Hurrell.'

'There is no comparison,' he said, hotly.

'But there is, Nick. Their case is not so very different from our own. They loved where they had no right to love. Yes, you may call it lust but it must have been more than that. Lust would have burned itself out long ago. What they have has bonded them together for life.'

It was a chastening thought. The stern father who had tried to bully Nicholas into a marriage for commercial reasons had himself taken a second bride solely in the name of love. It was a crowning paradox. Robert Bracewell had betrayed the values of the mercantile community in which he had made his name. Notwithstanding the enormous cost, he was now ending his days with a woman he had loved for so many years.

Here was a salutary lesson for Nicholas. He had to choose a wife by following his heart and not by seeking any pecuniary advantage. Marriage to Mary Whetcombe would open up a whole new world for him, but it was not one that he had earned. Nor could they ever recapture the infatuation of their youth. He was delighted that they were reconciled and moved by her plea but he could not make a commitment to her.

'Stay with us, Nick,' she said. 'We need you.'

'I have to leave tomorrow.'

'But we can make a fresh start together. You, me, and

Lucy.' He lowered his head in apology and she understood. 'There is someone else.'

'Yes, Mary.'

'Is she waiting for you?'

'I hope so.'

There was no more to be said. Nicholas felt that it would be unwise to spend another night in a house that echoed with so many cruel whispers from the past. He would stay at the Dolphin Inn and sail at dawn on the morrow. Mary Whetcombe threw herself impulsively into his arms and he hugged his farewell. Lucy joined in the embrace and they both kissed her warmly. The girl then broke away and rolled back the piece of material in which she kept her dolls. She sensed that she would never see Nicholas again and she wanted him to have an important souvenir. After stroking one of her dolls with great reverence, she handed it over to him.

Nicholas looked down at the flimsy object on his palm. It was Susan Deakin. His daughter.

Epilogue

MARGERY FIRETHORN WAS NOW A FREQUENT CALLler at the Queen's Head. The gentle pressure which she had at first applied had slowly given way to a more concerted shove. Alexander Marwood's resistance had finally been broken by the joint force of Anne Hendrik, Lord Westfield and that most valuable ally of all, Sybil Marwood, the landlord's wife. Margery had marshalled her troops like a veteran siege-master, and the flint-hard walls of Marwood's resolve had at last been breached. The theatre company would be allowed to return to his innyard. Westfield's Men had a home once more.

'When will they be here?' asked a rubicund Leonard.

'At any hour,' said Margery.

'It seems as if they have hardly been away.'

'A full month, Leonard. And sorely missed.'

'Indeed. But they come back in triumph.'

'Yes,' said Margery. 'They had difficulties on tour at first but they prospered in the end. My husband's letters speak of many glories along the way. They have even written a ballad in his honour. He will no doubt sing it to me.' She gazed around the refurbished yard. 'Is all ready here?'

'The Queen's Head is in fine condition.'

'All the carpentry finished, all the thatching done?'

'We have a new inn, Mistress Firethorn.'

'And a new play to grace it.'

Leonard took her on a brief tour of the yard to point out each improvement. Repairs had been costly, but the workmen had toiled with spirit and finished well ahead of their projected date. Even Marwood was pleased with the results. A decaying part of his property had been destroyed by fire but it had been replaced by sturdier wood, fashioned by excellent craftsmanship. Westfield's Men would be thrilled with their renovated theatre and so would their regular patrons. A month without their favourite troupe had left the play-going public feeling starved and mutinous.

'Will you be here tomorrow?' asked Leonard.

'Nothing would prevent me.'

'I will take my place among the standees.'

'You have earned it, Leonard. You have done your share towards persuading that idiot of a landlord to see sense. Westfield's Men will tread the boards again tomorrow. They left the city as outcasts but they return as conquerors.' A smile flitted across her face. 'I will give my husband the welcome that is due to a victorious general.'

Nicholas Bracewell soon found the spot to which he was directed in the churchyard. A little mound marked the place where his daughter had been buried. In time, when the earth had settled, it would be possible to put a gravestone there to mark the place. He now had a name to carve upon it. A bunch of flowers had been set upon the mound, and he knew that they could only have come from Anne Hendrik. He was profoundly touched. Susan's resting place would not lack flowers from now on. Her father would be there to pay his respects whenever he could. From inside his jerkin, he took out the little doll that Lucy had given him. He scooped a shallow hole in the earth and lay the doll down with the young girl whom it represented. After one last look, he gently covered it up.

Kneeling beside the grave, he offered up a prayer then got to his feet. The rest of the company had gone straight to the Queen's Head, but he had broken away to hasten to

Southwark. Having visited his daughter, he now hurried off to call on Anne Hendrik. Thoughts of her had brightened the journey home. Barnstaple was behind him and she could help to expunge it completely from his mind. When he reached the house, he knocked politely, not sure what sort of a welcome he would get, at once hoping that it would be warm and fearing that it might be frosty.

Anne herself answered the door and smiled in surprise. 'Nick!'

'Good day to you!'

'I heard that the company would return today.'

'We have something to come back to,' he said, searching her eyes. 'At least, that is what we believe.'

'Come on in.'

Nicholas did not get the kiss that he half-expected but at least he was allowed back into the house. Anne walked around him in excitement and asked him a dozen questions that he had no chance to answer. When she gave him a hug, he felt all of the tensions between them ease slightly.

'Margery tells me that you have a new play.'

'*The Merchant of Calais*. First performed in Bath at the home of Sir Roger Hordley. Lord Westfield is very jealous that his brother saw it before he himself.'

'I long to watch it myself at the Queen's Head.'

'Edmund has written a small masterpiece.'

'Will you rehearse it there tomorrow?' she asked.

'No, Anne.'

'But if it is to be staged that afternoon . . .'

'Westfield's Men may rehearse it—but not I.'

'Why not?'

'Because it is time they learned to manage without me,' he said, airily. 'I have given my life blood to the theatre for too many years. Today, I resigned from the company. Let them find a new book holder.'

She was amazed. 'You have fallen out with them, Nick?'

'No,' he said, placing a soft kiss on her cheek. 'I have fallen in with you. Westfield's Men took me away from here. They will not do so again.'

'What are you telling me?'

300

'You asked me to make a choice. I made it.'

'But the choice was between staying and leaving.'

'That is all done now,' he said, briskly. 'I'll never visit Devon again. I have no further cause. That part of my life is closed for good. I want *you*, Anne.'

He slipped an arm around her but she broke away and regarded him with a more critical eye. The euphoria of seeing him again was wearing off and serious doubts were starting to emerge. Barnstaple was not just a town that he could wipe from the map to put it before his commitment to her and she wanted to know exactly why.

"Tell me all, Nick," she said, 'or I'll none of you.'

'Anne . . .'

'I want an honest man under this roof, not one who harbours secrets. Who was that girl and why did you go?"

'To deal with some unfinished business.'

'Of what nature?'

'It pains me even to think of it.'

'No matter for that,' she said, tartly. 'What sort of pain do you think I have suffered here? It was beyond measure. You disappeared into a void. The only information I gleaned about the company was from Margery Firethorn, who showed me her husband's letters. Why did you not write to me?'

'I was not sure how my letters would be received.'

'Better than your silence!'

'It was . . . too complicated to set down on paper.'

'Then explain it to me now.'

'Some things are perhaps best left—"

'*Now!*' she insisted. 'I have waited long enough.'

Anne Hendrik sat on an upright chair with folded arms. Nicholas admired her spirit but he had hoped for less of an interrogation. Information that he had planned to release in small doses was now being demanded in full. He scratched his head and paced the room, not knowing where to begin his tale. Anne prompted him.

'Who was that girl who brought the message here?'

'The servant of a house in Barnstaple.'

'There is more to it than that.'

'Her name was Susan Deakin.'

'You are hiding something from me, Nick.'

'Look, can we not discuss this at a later date?'

'Who *was* she?'

'My daughter.'

Anne took a few moments to absorb the shock before she waved him on. Her expression showed that she feared there was worse to come. Having started, Nicholas plunged on with his story. He told it in a plain and unvarnished way and held nothing back from her. He even recounted the offer that Mary Whetcombe had made to him to share his life with her. Anne Hendrik listened to every word without interruption. Her emotions were deeply stirred and her hands played restlessly. Nicholas was uncertain how she was responding to his confession but he did not spare himself. He talked honestly about the mistakes of the past and how he had done his best to rectify them. When he told her about his visit to the grave where she had left the flowers, Anne was moved. She rose to her feet and allowed him to take her hands. Tears began to course down her cheeks.

Nicholas tried to kiss them away for her.

'We may start a fresh life now, Anne. The two of us.'

'Wait one moment,' she said, drying her eyes with the back of her hand. 'It is not as simple as you imagine.'

'I have had weeks to think of it and I know my mind.'

'Then it is time you knew mine.'

'You were right in your strictures,' he said, quietly. 'I took you for granted. When I lodged here and worked for Westfield's Men, you were a wonderful facet of my life and you enriched it greatly. But I did not pay you the respect you deserved. I did not take you seriously enough.'

'You have realised that too late, Nick.'

'I saw you as a friend who could comfort me in times of need,' he admitted. 'That is all done.' He tried to enfold her in his arms. 'What I want now is a wife who will share my whole life with me.'

She pushed him off. 'Then I hope you find one, sir.'

'Anne, I am offering you my hand!'

'I thank you for that but I have to reject it.'

302

'But I love you.'

'In your own way, I believe that you do.'

'I love you—I *want* you.'

'There is too much between us now,' she said. 'You may be able to forget what happened in Barnstaple but I may not. The sight of that dead girl in my bedchamber will stay with me forever. The fact that she was your daughter makes the memory even harder to erase.' Anne shook her head. 'I am sorry, Nick. While you were away, I thought a great deal about you and longed for your return but my feelings towards you have changed. After what you have told me, you can never be what you once were.'

'You asked for the truth, Anne.'

'And you gave it fairly. I respect that.' She kissed him lightly. 'We will always be friends and I will come often to the Queen's Head but that is the extent of our friendship from now on.'

'But why?' he asked in dismay.

'I have my past and you have yours. I will always be Jacob Hendrik's widow and you will always be the father of Mary Parr's child. There is no altering that, Nick. I will never be the wife that you wanted her to be.'

'I am choosing you on your own merits,' he argued.

'No,' she said, tilting her chin proudly. 'You spurned me when I called to you. London or Barnstaple. That was your choice. You wanted both. It has made me wish for neither.'

Nicholas was wounded. He had told her everything in the hope that it would explain his behaviour but his honesty had been fatal. When he had kept her in ignorance of certain aspects of his life, she had been happy to share a bed with him. Now that he had confided in her—and made the ultimate commitment of a marriage proposal—she was rejecting him. On the long journey home, he had thought the whole matter through and convinced himself that the only way to close a disagreeable chapter in his life was to wed Anne Hendrik. What he had failed to do was to take her feelings properly into account. It was ironic. When he stood in the hall of the house in Crock Street, Mary had begged him to stay. At that point in time, Nicholas felt that he had to choose which of two women he should marry. In opting for Anne, he had now lost both.

'It would not have worked, Nick,' she said, turning to practicalities. 'How would you have looked after your wife?'

'I would have found employment.'

'As a hatmaker? I have workmen enough.'

'Do not mock me, Anne.'

'I merely point to the realities.'

'I would have supported you,' promised Nicholas. 'I can turn my hand to many things. I have talents.'

'Indeed, you do,' she said with admiration. 'And they are seen at their best in the theatre.'

'I was ready to quit that life for you.'

'I believe you, Nick. But how long would it have been before you pined for it again? You ask for too much from me. I could never answer all your needs.' She put her arms around his waist and looked up at him. 'Go back to Westfield's Men. There lies your true family.'

Nicholas gave her a long farewell kiss then left.

Raucous patrons filled the yard at the Queen's Head. The company was back in London with a new play and the crowds thronged to Gracechurch Street. Lord Westfield had offered to underwrite the performance and bestow ten pounds on his company. That made it possible for all the admission money to be given to Alexander Marwood as a first payment towards his fund for fire damage. The innkeeper would never be happy but his trenchant unhappiness was at least partly reduced by the prospect of money. Lord Westfield was there himself with his entourage, seated in his accustomed position and savouring once more the kudos of being the patron of so sterling a troupe of players.

The Merchant of Calais was a new play on old themes. It dealt with love and marriage as financial transactions. A lone English merchant was pitted against the encroaching of wealth and celebrated the ideal of self-sacrifice. At the end, the merchant of Calais gave up everything to be with the woman he loved even though it entailed huge personal losses. A forbidden love achieved a happiness that was impossible in the arranged marriages of the mercantile class.

A sprightly comedy shot through with darker tones, it was played with attack by the company. Lawrence Firethorn boomed as the merchant, Barnaby Gill danced and Owen Elias sang. Edmund Hoode turned in a wry cameo performance as an old French shepherd with an Oxfordshire accent. Richard Honeydew was a winsome heroine. George Dart made four bungled appearances as a foolish constable and was thought by an indulgent audience to be a natural comedian. The afternoon was an unadulterated triumph.

Nicholas Bracewell watched from behind the scenes. The play had a relevance for him that went far beyond its intrinsic worth as a drama. Elements of his own experience were up there on the stage and they caused him to ponder. Lawrence Firethorn might not look like Robert Bracewell but he sounded uncannily like him at times. In the final speech, the merchant renounced wealth and position with fierce sincerity.

> A worthy merchant, I, Adventure's heir,
> Whose hopes hang much upon the wind of chance.
> The sailor's master and the soldier's friend,
> I open up new countries with brave heart.
> Nor Scylla nor Charybdis do I fear,
> Nor any living creature of the sea
> Can sink my bark. It sails eternally
> Beneath the flag of pride, its cannon armed
> With truth, its hold with honesty, its crew
> All loyal lads to high endeavour pledged.
> I plant the earth with foreign fruits galore
> And reap a harvest of degree and wealth
> That makes me honoured throughout the world.
> All this I venture on a single kiss
> From you, my love. Bestow your bliss
> Upon a merchant late of Calais' shore
> Who gives up everything to gain much more!

The ovation was thunderous as the company came out to take its bow. Lawrence Firethorn was at his most flamboyant and drank in the applause as if it were the finest wine. He had just declared his love to Richard Honeydew for the twentieth time in a month but the real and lasting object of his passion was clapping her hands in the upper gallery. Margery Firethorn had laboured hard and shrewdly to bring the travellers home, and she was learning the joys of mending a long absence. Seated beside her was Anne Hendrik, lifted as always by a performance from Westfield's Men and finding deeper meanings in the play than other spectators. She knew how much of Barnstaple had been transposed to Calais. The company's own St Nicholas was indeed the patron saint of merchants.

Nicholas Bracewell himself had seen his hometown set poignantly upon the stage, but he had viewed it from behind. To the audience, it was fresh, immediate and directly in front of them: to him, it was old, detached and receding into the past. He could hear his father without real pain. He could watch events from his own life without undue discomfort. The visit to Barnstaple had helped him to understand and to grow through many of the problems he encountered there.

When he peeped around the edge of the curtain, he saw Anne Hendrik among the sea of faces. She was wearing a distinctive hat that had been made by one of her employees. He felt no bitterness over their parting. Anne had turned down his proposal but her decision had to be respected. He was coming to see that it held advantages for both of them. She regained the independence on which she set such value, and he was joyously reunited with Westfield's Men. Their separate worlds might touch—as they were doing now—but they could never fully coalesce. In marrying Anne Hendrik, he would have been committing bigamy. Nicholas was already wedded to his profession.

As the pandemonium faded, Firethorn brought his company gambolling offstage and the tiring-house became a mass of excited bodies. The players changed quickly out of their costumes and adjourned to the taproom. Good-natured banter enlivened the air for hours and Marwood's ale was consumed in vast quantities. Edmund Hoode was among the last to leave the inn. As he walked away from the Queen's Head, he looped an arm around the shoulders of Nicholas Bracewell.

'We are safely back in port now, Nick.'

'And glad to be so.'

'Those whom we left behind are now back in the company. Westfield's Men are whole again. London has been left in no doubt about that.'

Hoode waited until they were well clear of the inn then he nudged his friend. He wanted a mystery to be at last unravelled.

'What was it really that took you away from us?'

'It is too long and twisting a tale, Edmund.'

'I have all night to listen.' He gave a quiet chuckle. 'Come, Nick, you can tell me. We have no secrets from each other. You talked of your father and he sounded a merchant to his toes. But he was not the reason that you went to Barnstaple, was he?'

'No, he was not. You read the signs aright.'

'I smell romance here.'

'It cannot be denied.'

'You had a silent woman down in Devon.'

'I blush to own it but you speak the truth.'

'Who was she, man? Tell me but her name.'

Nicholas Bracewell smiled wryly. There had been a number of silent women involved. Susan Deakin had been a mute messenger who set him off on his journey. Lucy Whetcombe was speechless by nature. Mary Whetcombe was a silent woman who spoke out of his past, as did Margaret Hurrell. While he was away from her, Anne Hendrik had been a silent woman as well, and he had foolishly taken her silence to be a form of consent. Silence of another kind had helped to still the deafening ambition of Gideon Livermore, who had drowned himself in the River Taw, a name that meant "silent one." Nicholas Bracewell had been surrounded by silence.

There was one more soundless female to add to the list.

'Well, Nick,' said Hoode. 'Give me her name.'

'*Mary.*'

'A pretty name. Where did the lady reside?'

'Upon the river.'

Hoode was puzzled. 'You have a floating mistress?'

'She lies at anchor.'

'Did you board her then?'

'Only to break another long-kept silence.'

'What strange lady is this Mary?'

'A ship,' said Nicholas. '*She* was the real cause of my visit to Barnstaple. A merchant vessel of a hundred tons. I tell you, Edmund, she could drive a man insane with lust. My duty was to protect her honour. The *Mary* was my silent woman.'

Edward Marston

Published by Fawcett Books.
Available in your local bookstore.